"Biddin' starts at two hundred on this 'un!" the auctioneer announced. "It's a bit steep, yeah, but take a good look at her. She ain't only one of the most fetchin' wenches you ever seen, she's edge-acated too. Talks like a bloomin' swell. Say somethin', girl."

I stood perfectly still, my chin held high, staring straight in front of me. Coleman flushed at my disobedience, but he held his whip still, perhaps because Jeff Rawlins was standing there grinning.

"Two hundred!" Rawlins called.

A husky lout with shaggy hair hassled the bid up to three hundred.

There was a moment of silence, and then a cool, bored voice was heard. "One thousand," the man said.

Rawlins turned with a frown, staring at his competitor. "Hawke? Come on, you don't want this wench, I do. A wench like her—the bucks in New Orleans'd go outta of their minds . . ."

But Derek Hawke bought Marietta. As he paid out his twenty-one hundred pounds, Rawlins aimed his parting shot.

"I'll be 'round," he said, "when you begin to regret payin' such a pretty price for something you don't need. I want that girl, and I'll get her."

Books by Jennifer Wilde

Dare to Love
Love's Tender Fury
Love Me, Marietta

Published by
WARNER BOOKS

Love's Tender Fury

By Jennifer Wilde

WARNER BOOKS

A Warner Communications Company

WARNER BOOKS EDITION

Copyright © 1976 by Jennifer Wilde
All rights reserved

Cover illustration by Tom Hall

Warner Books, Inc., 75 Rockefeller Plaza, New York, N.Y. 10019

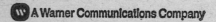 A Warner Communications Company

Printed in the United States of America

First Printing: April, 1976

Reissued: October, 1981

45 44 43

To Rosemary, with all the three A's.

LOVE'S TENDER FURY

PROLOGUE:

London 1770

I

Pale, shaken, the girl descended the stairs clutching her pathetically battered bag and trying not to sob. Her cheeks were stained with tears, her blue eyes filled with a miserable resignation. Jenny was only sixteen years old. She had come to Montagu Square a year ago fresh from the country, a robust, rosy-cheeked lass typical of the thousands of girls who poured into London to go into service. She was thin now, her blond curls wildly disarrayed. The bloom of youth was already gone. Dismissed without references, she had no hope of finding another post.

He stood in the lower hall, vain, lordly, a half-smile playing on his lips as he watched the girl he had used and grown tired of. Jenny moved slowly toward the front door, defiantly, too, for none of the servants ever used the main entrance. Lord Mallory arched one dark brow, amused, but he made no effort to stop her. The girl paused, and for a moment it looked as though she might burst into tears again and plead, begging him to let her keep her job as scullery maid. He frowned, drawing himself up, no longer amused.

Jenny looked at him with sad blue eyes that had long since lost their innocence, but she didn't plead. She simply looked at him, hopelessly, wretchedly, and then she opened the front door and stepped outside. She had no money, no education, no hope of surviving unless she joined that pitiful parade of prostitutes who swarmed over London by the thousands.

As I watched her leave, I shuddered in sympathy. I might be educated, I might have aristrocatic blood in my veins, but my position here was tenuous as hers had been, and I knew that I could easily share her fate.

Lord Mallory sighed and moved over to close the door Jenny had left open. Turning, he looked up and saw me standing halfway up the grand staircase. That half-smile was on his lips again, and his dark eyes gleamed with masculine anticipation I couldn't fail to recognize. I knew full well why he had thrown Jenny out. I knew it was because he intended to have me next. I was his children's governess, true, but I was still a servant. Men like Lord Robert Mallory considered any attractive woman in their employ fair game. He stared at me and then he nodded. I turned on the stairs and hurried up to the nursery.

The children had left to spend three weeks with their grandparents in the country. Tomorrow morning Lord and Lady Mallory would be leaving, too, to be gone a week. I had a week, then, seven days before he would make his first move. Of late his very presence caused a tremulous alarm I found it difficult to conceal. Before, he had been preoccupied with Jenny and paid very little attention to the new governess. But when he began to tire of the girl whose attic room he visited almost every night, he started to stare at me with masculine specula-tion whenever we happened to pass in the hall. He also began to visit the nursery frequently, ignoring the children, asking me far too many questions. His intentions were clear. For the past week we had been playing a subtle cat-and-mouse game, and now that Jenny was gone I knew the subtlety would be replaced by open aggression. He intended to have me. Men like Robert Mallory never hesitated to take what they wanted, would use force if necessary.

Stepping into the nursery, I found that I was trembling

12

inside. Jenny's abrupt dismissal had disturbed me terribly. It clearly indicated his ruthlessness. He could dismiss me just as abruptly, and my plight would be every bit as grave as Jenny's. I knew that I had been exceedingly fortunate to get this post in the first place, and it had come in the nick of time. Only a handful of coins were left in my purse when Lord Mallory interviewed me and told me the job was mine. I had been turned down time after time. I was too young, they told me, too inexperienced, too attractive. If Robbie and Doreen's governess hadn't left when she did, if Lord Mallory hadn't desperately needed someone to replace her . . . I tried not to think of what might have happened when those few coins were gone and I was turned out of the humble, shabby room at the inn.

Distraught, I stepped over the mirror and examined myself with sapphire-blue eyes that reflected my alarm. I wished I were older, wished I were plain and pale and unappealing. I had never been vain, but I knew I was an extremely attractive woman. In the village the men had been after me ever since I was thirteen. The barmaid's daughter, I was their natural prey, but I had ignored their crude invitations, eluded their clumsy caresses. Later on, at that refined, expensive school for young ladies, the other girls had resented me because of my rich auburn hair, my high, sculptured cheekbones, my slender body that was undeniably shapely.

I had my father's cool, patrician good looks, my mother's high color and earthy allure. The combination was as unusual at it was striking. Although I wore my hair in a severe coronet of braid on top of my head, I couldn't conceal its rich luster, neither brown nor red but a vivid combination of the two, gleaming with deep coppery highlights. My plain brown dress was severe, too, long-sleeved, high-necked, but somehow that only emphasized the full breasts, the narrow waist. I might try to minimize my looks, but the fact remained that I was the kind of woman men had always pursued.

"Admiring yourself?" he drawled.

13

I whirled around. Lord Mallory was lounging in the doorway, one shoulder propped against the jamb. He gazed at me with those dark, mocking eyes, and his full, sensual lips still toyed with a smile. Women had spoiled him all his life, and now, at thirty-four, he wore his magnetism with casual disdain, taking it for granted that any woman he encountered would succumb at the snap of his fingers. Most of them did, and he accepted their adulation somewhat wearily, considering it no more than his due.

"You seem upset, Marietta," he remarked.

He had never called me by my first name before. In the past it had always been "Miss Danver." I looked at him, striving to maintain some kind of composure, fighting to conceal my alarm. Lord Mallory was fully aware of my apprehension, and he was enjoying it. He was so utterly relaxed, so confident. Most women would have felt a thrill of anticipation were he to gaze at them as he gazed at me now.

Robert Mallory, I realized, had to have a woman at all times, someone new, someone who would reassure him of his powers over the weaker sex. Lady Mallory didn't count. He treated her with the same indifference he displayed toward his children, humoring her every now and then just to make certain she was still enslaved. There were few secrets among the servants, and I knew that he had never loved her. Not even Lady Mallory had any illusions on that score. He had married her for her money, and she had been thrilled that her merchant father's abundant wealth had enabled her to wed such a splendid creature, a member of the nobility to boot.

"It seems I've been remiss," he said.

"Remiss?"

"I've been neglecting my . . . uh . . . duty," he replied.

"Indeed?"

"You've been here—what? Six weeks? In all that time we haven't had a real conversation. We've discussed the children, of course, but we've not had a real talk. I haven't inquired about your . . . uh . . . comfort." He paused, heavy lids half-veiling those gleaming dark eyes. "Are you happy here, Marietta?"

"I—I find the position quite satisfactory."

"I've been doing some checking up on you," he remarked. He spoke in a lazy drawl. "I've discovered some very interesting things about your background. You had no references when you came for the interview, but you seemed—suitable enough. You did tell me about your education and showed me your diploma from that very fine school"—Lord Mallory hesitated a moment before continuing—"but there was a great deal you forgot to mention."

"I didn't feel it was necessary," I replied.

I was surprised at my own calm, but I refused to be intimidated over something I couldn't help. I wasn't ashamed of either of my parents. He had obviously found out about them, and I wasn't about to apologize.

"Your father was the Duke of Stanton," he remarked.

"That's true."

"A fine old family, one of the finest, a power in Cornwall for generations. Your mother, though—it seems she wasn't from such distinguished stock."

"My mother was a barmaid at the Red Lion in the village where I was born. I was born out of wedlock, yes, but my mother was—"

"A mite too generous with her favors, it would appear. She raised you, and you worked behind the taps yourself on occasion, it seems, never knowing who your father was until after your mother died of pneumonia when you were fourteen. Your father was a widower by that time, and his wife had failed to give him children. He was a lonely old man, and it amused him to take in—"

"My father loved me," I interrupted.

"I've no doubt he did. You were taught how to speak, how to dress, how to conduct yourself like a proper young aristocrat. The barmaid's daughter disappeared, replaced by an elegant young woman of fashion. He sent you away to school to acquire those all-important finishing touches,

15

hoping he might marry you off to some respectable, middle class merchant . . ." Again he hesitated, toying with me, hoping I would break down.

"But it didn't work out that way," I said calmly. "My father died a few weeks after I returned to Stanton Hall from school. His nephew, George Stanton, became the eighth Duke of Stanton, inheriting everything. He found my presence an embarrassment and threw me out. I had very little money, just enough to come to London and take a room at one of the inns while I searched for work."

"And then I hired you," he said.

"And now?"

I waited. Lord Mallory arched a brow, pretending surprise.

"Now?" he repeated.

"Surely you intend to dismiss me."

"Dismiss you?" The brow lifted even higher. "My dear Marietta, I want to *help* you."

"Like you helped Jenny?" I couldn't resist the question.

"Jenny. Ah, that's a different story. The girl was ignorant, a common scullery maid who dropped every 'h,' couldn't even read or write. I took pity on her . . . uh . . . tried to make things a bit more pleasant for her. The girl was most unappreciative. She became quarrelsome and possessive, thought my interest in her gave her certain rights."

"So you threw her out."

"You needn't worry about Jenny. She'll find some man to take care of her—probably a number of them. Her sort always ends up on the streets. It's inevitable."

I was amazed at my own boldness, but I simply couldn't help myself. His arrogant superiority was insufferable. Because he was wealthy, because he was an aristocrat, he thought he could play God with those less fortunate in life, and because he was an attractive male he thought he could automatically enslave any woman he chose to notice. I could feel the color burning in my cheeks. Lord Mallory chuckled.

16

"Spirit," he said. "I like that. A man enjoys a challenge every now and then."

"You think—"

"I think you're quite a challenge, Marietta. I've had my eye on you for some time now."

"I'm . . . not like Jenny. I'm not one of your—"

"Of course not," he interrupted. "You're very, very special. I saw that from the first. I've been—a bit preoccupied with other things up till now, but now I intend to pay more attention to you."

"I'm afraid you'll be wasting your time, Lord Mallory."

"I think not. You see, Marietta, I happen to know you're not the demure, timorous young virgin you pretend to be."

He smiled. He sauntered across the room toward me, stopping directly in front of me. He was so close I could smell his cologne, smell the musky male odor of flesh and perspiration. He was dressed for an evening on the town, and the elegant attire seemed to heighten the aura of animal magnetism that clung to him.

"We're going to be very good friends," he assured me.

"You're mistaken, Lord Mallory."

Once again the smile flashed. His eyes were filled with dark amusement. His face was inches from my own, and I could see the tiny scar at the corner of that full, curving mouth, see the faint smudges under his eyes. My heart was beating rapidly, and I was trembling inside. I detested him and, yes, I was afraid of him, too, but his nearness caused a purely physical response it was impossible to deny.

"Leave me alone," I whispered. "Please—"

"You don't want that, not really. You've got your mother's blood in your veins. The education, the fine manners, the cultured voice—they don't alter that fact. The man I sent to make inquiries was exceedingly thorough. I found out all about her. She was generous to a fault, never could resist a stripping young farmer, a handsome sailor. You might even say it caused her death. If she and her good-looking shepherd hadn't been out on the

17

moors together, hadn't been caught in that rainstorm—"

"How dare you! You've no right to talk about her like—"

"You've got her blood in your veins. You fight it. You're fighting it now, but it's there."

A lock of dark brown hair fell across his brow. He reached up to push it back.

"You're beautiful, Marietta, much too good to be slaving away in a nursery. I have plans for you—splendid plans. I'm going to make you happy. You've no idea how happy . . ."

Slowly, with lazy deliberation, he pulled me into his arms, and when I tried to pull away he laughed softly to himself, tightening his grip. His eyes gleamed, holding mine, and his wide lips parted as he tilted his head and pulled me closer. I opened my mouth to protest, but before I could speak, his mouth fastened over mine. It was a long, practiced kiss, his lips pressing, probing, savoring my own. I was rigid in his arms, but as he continued to kiss me, the weakness came and I melted against him, against my will, and when he finally released me his eyes were dark with triumph.

"You enjoyed that, love. Don't try to pretend you didn't."

"I—"

"You need a man. A woman like you—a woman like you will always need a man. That's the way you're made. Those prim mannerisms, those drab dresses you wear— they can't conceal what you are. You're ripe, ready to be plucked . . . and you're hungry for it."

"I am not! I—"

"You may think not, my dear, but in a short while you're going to be most grateful—"

Lady Mallory cleared her throat. Lord Mallory turned around to see his wife standing in the doorway. I hadn't noticed her before, had no idea how long she might have been there. How much had she heard? How much had she seen? Her thin, pinched face was expressionless, her eyes flat. She wore a white silk dress, and there was a stun-

18

ning emerald necklace around her throat. The jewels seemed to flash with flickering green and blue fires, and their spectacular beauty only made her neck seem scrawnier. her complexion more sallow. Her lusterless blond hair was arranged on top of her head in an elaborate coiffure. Lady Mallory was the epitome of current fashion, but, alas. the fashion did not suit her.

"Here you are, Robert," she said in a dry, colorless voice. "I've been looking all over."

Her husband was not at all ruffled. "I've been conferring with Miss Danver," he replied smoothly. "About the children," he added.

"Of course," she said.

She looked at me with venomous blue eyes. Lady Mallory had disliked me from the first, had raged at her husband for hiring someone so young, so inexperienced, and as she scrutinized me now I could sense that she was going to do everything in her power to get rid of me as soon as possible.

"We'd best hurry, dear," she remarked.

"Uh . . . yes. Wouldn't want to be late."

He turned back to me for a moment, the mocking amusement still in his eyes. His wife's open animosity delighted him, made him feel all the more confident of his male prowess. There was a certain swagger about him as he spoke to me in a low, barely audible voice.

"Alas, love, I have to leave for the country in the morning. Family responsibility, you know, but when I get back——"

He left the sentence dangling, but his eyes were filled with seductive promise. He touched my arm lightly, and then he sauntered across the room to join his wife. She was tapping her foot impatiently on the floor, her eyes flashing, as they moved down the hall her voice was angry and strident. I couldn't help overhearing.

"At it again, I see! The governess this time. Wasn't that pathetic little maid enough? Must you humiliate me under my own roof? The actresses and courtesans are bad enough, but when you——"

19

"I told you I'd get rid of Jenny," he said wearily, "and I promised you I'd spend a week in the country with you. Isn't that enough? Just because I exchange a few words with the governess, you assume—"

"I won't stand for it, Robert! I simply won't tolerate—"

"I'm giving up important business engagements so that I can spend time with you and the children away from London, and still you . . ."

They moved on downstairs, and I could no longer distinguish what they were saying. A minute later I heard the butler opening the front door, and outside the horse hooves pounded on the cobblestones as the coachman brought the carriage around from the mews in back of the house. There was a clatter of reins, the muted sound of wheels spinning as the carriage moved away down the street. I stood there in the nursery for a long time, numb, it seemed, drained of emotion.

I knew how fortunate I was to have this post. I had decent wages, a comfortable room, solid, nourishing food. If I lost it, if he dismissed me . . . *What am I going to do?* I asked myself. *What am I going to do?*

II

The family had been gone for three days, and for three days I had been in a state of suspension, safe, secure, but knowing that would end all too soon. Lord Mallory would soon return and the inevitable would happen, and I had no idea how I would handle things. It was late afternoon now. I was sitting out in the gardens under the shade of a leafy elm. Only residents of the square were allowed inside these lovely, elaborate gardens, each family possessing a key that unlocked the side gate. I had shamelessly appropriated the Mallory key, and as the afternoon sunlight slanted down in thin, fading rays, I thought of all the curious twists of fate that had brought me to this point in my life.

I had been a happy child. I had attended the village school, a bright student, eager to learn, and if the other children shunned me and frequently taunted me, that didn't matter at all. My mother and I lived in a small room upstairs at the Red Lion, and there was always laughter and the sound of hearty voices, the smell of fresh sawdust and ale, a rowdy, festive atmosphere prevailing. My beautiful, vivacious, good-natured mother loved me, and she loved the taproom, loved the men who constantly vied for her attention. She was earthy and generous and utterly natural, and though many called her wicked, I knew that wasn't so. As I grew older

21

I frequently helped her behind the taps. I liked the men, too, with their teasing ways and their compliments, but adroitly managed to fend off any who tried to become too familiar.

I remember my mother coming in that awful night, her auburn hair soaked, her clothing clinging wetly to her voluptuous body. She kissed her handsome young shepherd goodbye and wearily climbed the stairs to our room. She fell ill almost immediately, and soon developed pneumonia. When she knew she was going to die, she sent a message to my father, begging him to come for me and provide for me in the future. He left Stanton Hall and came to the inn as soon as he received her message. She held my hand and looked at him standing there at the foot of the bed, and she smiled, knowing I was going to be cared for. She died only minutes later, and I was desolate. It seemed my whole world had crumbled, but my father took over then and provided another world to replace the one I had lost.

The Duke of Stanton had been a notorious rake at one time, a dashing, devil-may-care buck who had scandalized the countryside with his outrageous conduct, but that was all in the past. When I came to know him, he was in his middle fifties, in poor health, a widower with sad brown eyes and silver hair, delighted to have someone to care for after years of solitude in his splendid, majestic old house. Caring not a fig what society might think, he took me in with open arms and lavished attention on me. The house was filled with tutors and dressmakers, and the barmaid's daughter was transformed into a proper young blueblood. After a year or so, it was difficult to believe I had ever been anything else.

I had the finest education money could buy, and if my blood wasn't one hundred percent blue, I was as refined as demure, as aristocratic as if I had been born to my new surroundings. I soon came to love my father, as he came to love me, and for four and a half years my life was a glorious euphoria. That, too, came to an abrupt end. I returned home from school to find my father gravely ill, his nephew, George Stanton, in attendance. George, who was overweight, sullen, and mean in spirit, found my presence at Stanton Hall an embarrassment. Because of the law of primogeniture, he would inherit Stanton Hall and everything that went with it; still, he bitterly resented me. When my father had a sudden stroke and died a few weeks later, George wasted no time in throwing me out. I was not even permitted to attend the funeral.

I had no choice but to try and find some kind of employment. Thanks to my education, I had every qualification to become a governess, and I arrived in London with only a few pounds to spare and two bags full of fine, expensive dresses totally unsuitable for a would-be governess. I managed to sell a few of them, replacing them with more sober garments, and the rest now hung uselessly in the wardrobe in my room. I had applied for various positions, in vain. My money was running out and I had almost given up hope when Lord Mallory took me on as governess to his young son and daughter. Now . . . now I was in danger of losing this post unless I let him have his way with me.

Was I going to succumb to him? I still didn't know the answer to that question.

The sun had almost disappeared as I stepped out of the gardens and locked the gate behind me, walking across the street to number 10. As I stepped into the front hall and closed the door, Millie came up from the shabby but comfortable sitting room the servants shared below stairs. A friendly lass with a wide, amiable mouth, freckled cheeks, and wide blue eyes, she had tarnished gold curls and a stout, sturdy build.

" 'Ere you are, luv," she said. "I was beginnin' to worry 'bout you, 'deed I was. 'Ave a nice sit in them gardens?"

"It was lovely," I replied.

"I wager you're enjoyin' yourself this week without them kids. It's a relief, I'm sure. That Doreen—some kiddies shoulda been put down at birth, an' that brat's one of 'em. Now Master Reggie, 'e's a regular luv, 'e is, gentle as a lamb. Can't imagine who 'e *takes* after."

23

Millie shook her head, sighing heavily. "Will you be wantin' a tray sent up?" she asked.

"I think not, Millie. I'm not really hungry. I think I'll just go up to my room and read a while."

"All that readin'—can't be good for you. Don't know that I'd care to know how. You go up now, luv. If you need anything, just let me know, you 'ear?"

I smiled at the girl and moved on down the hall. Although technically I was "above" the servants in station, I had always considered myself one of them and had never given myself airs. As a result, I was very popular with all of them. Jeffers, the butler, considered me his equal. Mrs. Branderson, "Brandy," the housekeeper, loved to chat with me, and Cook always sent special trays up. Without their friendship, life at number 10 would have been uncomfortable indeed.

My room was just off the nursery, completely isolated from the other rooms. Jeffers, Brandy, and Cook had quarters in the basement. Millie and the other maids slept in narrow little cubicles up in the attics, and the two footmen had rooms over the carriage house with the groom and coachman. I enjoyed the isolation, for it gave me a sense of privacy. The room was large, with windows looking out over the mews in back of the house. If the furniture was second best, everything a bit shabby and worn, it was still comfortable and snug.

The light was almost gone now, its thin rays fading on the old blue and gray carpet with its pattern of pink roses. I lighted the lamp and took off my dress, hanging it up in the enormous mahogany wardrobe with its heavy door that never shut properly. I removed shoes and stockings and, wearing only a white muslin petticoat, took down my coronet of braids and shook them loose. Hair fell to my shoulders in abundant red-brown waves, coppery highlights gleaming. Sitting in front of the mirror, I brushed it until it gleamed even more, and then I put the brush down and stared at the woman in the mirror.

The petticoat was exceedingly low-cut, my breasts more than half revealed. The bodice was form-fitting, the full,

24

flaring skirt adorned with row upon row of white ruffles. In this elegant garment, and with my hair falling about my shoulders in such rich profusion, I looked totally unlike the demure Miss Danver with her severe hair style and drab brown dress. Lord Mallory desired me. He would desire me even more if he could see me like this, I thought, and then I frowned, my blue eyes once again dark with concern. I left the dressing table and moved over to sit in the large, comfortable pink chair in front of the windows.

The sky was ashy gray now, and the world below was etched in gray and black and dim whites. The lamp was low, and shadows spread inside the room multiplying beyond its softly diffused pool of light. I thought about Lord Mallory, and there was a strange ambivalence that hadn't been there before. I detested him, I told myself, yet I was undeniably attracted to him. I remembered that kiss. I remembered his tall, strong body, his arms crushing me against him, and I remembered the sensations that had exploded inside me like tiny buds blossoming.

Recalling what he had said about my mother, I wondered, did I indeed take after her? I was a virgin, and I had never even contemplated sleeping with a man before. I was respectable and decent, yet, even though I hated him and everything he stood for, I couldn't deny that I found Robert Mallory physically attractive. I knew that I would never willingly submit to him, but if he took me by force would I really be as distraught as I told myself I would be? Was I a shameless creature for desiring him as I did? Surely women, decent women at least, weren't supposed to be attracted to rakes like Robert Mallory. Perhaps there was more of my mother in me than I realized.

Night had fallen now, and now the black and gray and white was gilded with silver on the rooftops, spilling down over the sides of houses. A cool breeze caused the curtains to stir. They billowed into the room like waving white sails, billowing, falling limp, billowing again. The breeze felt wonderful on my bare arms and shoulders, for it had been a sultry day. The lamp flickered and went out, the blossom of golden light vanishing abruptly. I didn't get up to light it again. Weary, worried, I sat in the comfortable chair, drowsy already. I closed my eyes, and in a few minutes I was fast asleep.

The sound of footsteps awakened me. I had no idea how long I had been asleep, no idea what time it might be. I sat up, startled, and then I felt panic grip me. I recognized the footsteps. He had a long, lazy stride, and those tall black knee boots he wore made a certain ring. I jumped to my feet. My heart was pounding. Lord Mallory was in the country with his wife and children. It couldn't be him, I told myself, but as the footsteps drew nearer, I knew I wasn't mistaken.

Moonlight spilled through the windows, and the room was filled with a hazy silver light, every detail clear. The footsteps stopped outside the door of my room. Had I locked it? No, no, of course I hadn't. I never locked it, for one of the children might want something during the night. The children were gone now, but their father was here, and he wanted something I was not prepared to give. Paralyzed with fear, I stared at the door, saw the knob slowly turning, and then the door opened and he stepped inside.

"Hello, Marietta," he said, in a lazy drawl.

"You—" I whispered.

"Surely you were expecting me?"

"You're supposed to be in the country. You took your wife and—"

"I took her, yes, and I spent three dreary days with her, and then I suddenly remembered a . . . uh . . . very important appointment. I took my leave of her with proper reluctance. She and the children will stay on for several more days, but I have other plans—" He glanced around the room. "Snug and cozy, isn't it? Would you believe I've never been inside this room before? There was never any reason. Nice furniture, I see, a nice, large bed."

"Lord Mallory—"

He closed the door behind him, and locked it.

"Nicely located, too," he continued. "None of the servants could possibly hear us. We can make as much noise as we please. We're going to have a grand time, Marietta."

His manner was exceedingly casual. He seemed almost bored. He wore the tall black boots, snug black trousers and a loose-fitting white silk shirt open at the throat, the sleeves very full and gathered at the wrists. In the moonlight I could see his face: the familiar half-smile on his lips, lids drooping heavily over glowing dark eyes. His thick brown hair was disarrayed, a fringe falling across his brow. He looked like a handsome, ruthless buccaneer come to plunder and despoil. My knees felt weak, and for a moment I thought I might actually crumple at his feet.

"You're trembling," he remarked. "Surely you aren't frightened?"

"Please go away."

"You don't want me to go away, Marietta."

"I've never—"

He arched an eyebrow. "No?"

"I—I'm a decent woman. Please—please don't do this. I've never had . . . relations with a man. I—"

"You don't really expect me to believe that?"

"It's true!"

Lord Mallory laughed softly. "A man can sense things. I sensed what you were immediately. The prim manner, the drab clothes never fooled me for a minute. If I hadn't been . . . uh . . . preoccupied with Jenny, this visit would have come about much sooner. Relax, Marietta—"

He moved slowly toward me with panther-like grace, his dark eyes glittering. My pulse leaped, and my heart was palpitating rapidly, so rapidly it seemed it must burst at any moment. He stopped, standing very close to me, his hands resting lightly on his thighs. I tried to speak, but my throat was dry and no words would come. Lord Mallory studied me, savoring what he saw, those dark eyes taking in every detail: the hair cascading about my

27

shoulders, the low-cut petticoat with the clinging bodice that left shoulders and most of my bosom bare.

"Your hair—your body. It's a crime to hide a body like that," he said. There was a husky catch in his voice. "I've known a lot of women, but never one so utterly superb—"

"Don't touch me—"

"I'm going to touch you all over, and you're going to love it."

Panic overwhelmed me then. I tried to move past him toward the door. He seized my arm and jerked me toward him. I struggled. He laughed huskily as he wrapped his arms around me, holding me in front of him, my back against his chest. One arm curled tightly around my waist, he lifted my hair and planted his lips against the side of my neck. My flesh seemed to burn.

"Agatha and the children will be in the country for another week," he murmured. "We have seven full days, and I'm going to teach you things, Marietta, wonderful things. You're going to be a most appreciative student—"

He turned me around in his arms and then kissed me with that lazy deliberation that seemed to cause liquid fire to spread through my veins. He cupped one large hand around my breast, his strong fingers squeezing, kneading. I refused to acknowledge the sensations sweeping over me. I had to stop him. That was all I could think about. I had to stop him.

Certain of victory, he released me. His lips were parted. Heavy lids almost concealed his eyes. In the hazy silver light his face was all planes and angles, deeply shadowed, evil, but also very handsome. Catching his thumbs in the straps of my petticoat, he began to pull them down, ever so slowly, revealing more and more firm, rounded flesh. He was in no hurry, no hurry at all. He wanted to savor each second. He was like a man transported. Nothing existed for him now but his throbbing manhood and the warm female flesh that would gratify its quickening demands.

As he stroked my breasts, pressing, probing, they

seemed to have a life of their own, swelling under his touch, flesh hardening. I gasped, and a weakness seemed to sweep over me as he bent down to kiss each nipple. Now, now, I cried out silently, I must stop it now . . . before it's too late. Lord Mallory straightened up and made a soft, growling noise in his throat, clutching both my breasts in his hands.

I pulled back. I slapped his face with all the force I could muster. The sound it made was like an explosion. Lord Mallory cried out, startled. My palm stung viciously. I darted toward the door, fumbling with the key. I didn't know where I would go, what I would do, but I knew I had to get out of this room as quickly as possible.

He grabbed my arm. He swung me violently across the room. I screamed, and he clamped a hand over my mouth, chuckling to himself, not at all angry, delighted that I intended to put up a fight. That would make it all the more interesting.

"So that's the way you want to play?" he said. "All right, wench, that's the way we'll play it!"

He forced me over to the bed, shoving me down onto the soft mattress. I tried to get up, and he shoved me back down again, eyes gleaming, lips spreading into a rakish smile. I kicked his shin, and he shook his head as though I were a naughty child. He slapped me across the face, his slap even more forceful than my own had been. My ears rang; lights seemed to burst inside my head. I fell back, sobbing, and Lord Mallory looked down at me with one brow arched high.

"Such games we're going to play, wench. Such lovely games—"

"No!" I cried. "No!"

"Scream all you like. No one will hear."

And then he was on top of me, crushing me, the weight of his body pinioning me. I struggled, still I struggled, and he enjoyed that, smothering my protests with his mouth, kissing me with a wild abandon that caused every fiber of my being to quicken. He was on his knees now, one leg on either side of my thighs, and he was still smiling. He pulled at my skirt, lifted it, exposing my legs. Sobbing wretchedly, I tried to throw him off, but it was futile. He fumbled with his trousers, and then he caught my wrists in his hands and held me spread-eagled beneath him.

"No!" I cried again.

He laughed. He loomed over me, a dark demon bent on my destruction. I shook my head back and forth, silently pleading. I tried to free my hands. He held them in a brutal grip. Waves of panic rose and crashed over me, and I was trembling all over.

"All right, wench," he said amiably. "The lesson is about to begin."

He lowered his body over mine, and I cried out as he entered me. He covered my mouth with his hand. Tears spilled over my lashes as he drove deeper and deeper with steady deliberation. I was screaming inside, and still I fought, struggling beneath him, and then it seemed the whole world exploded and I went hurtling into oblivion, falling, falling, and I clung to him as senses shattered and nerve ends snapped and life itself seemed to hang suspended in midair.

III

Clothed in a light-blue dressing gown, I stood at the window, peering out at the fleeting night shadows, not really seeing them at all. Lord Mallory was stretched out on the bed, and I could feel him watching me. Neither of us had slept. I hated him. I had never hated anyone so much in my life, and I doubted that I ever should again. He had used me viciously, repeatedly, like a whore. He had forced me to respond, and I hated him for that most of all.

I thought about Jenny. I wondered where she was at this moment. Jenny had been his victim, too, but I wasn't going to share her fate. Something inside of me had hardened, and I discovered a tight core of strength and determination that I hadn't been aware of before. I promised myself that I would never again be weak and vulnerable. Every illusion had been shattered. I had no one to turn to. I had only myself, and I decided I would do whatever was necessary in order to survive.

"It's almost dawn," he remarked.

I didn't reply. I didn't even turn to look at him.

"That needn't bother us, though," he continued. "We have days and days to play our little games."

"And then?" I said.

"And then you'll go on acting as governess to my children, and whenever I feel the urge, I'll visit your room.

Agatha will find out about it, of course—she probably suspects already—but that won't make any difference."

"I'm to go on teaching your children? After . . . after this?"

"Naturally."

"You're wrong."

"Oh?"

"I've no intention of staying on under those circumstances."

"You'll do as I say," he informed me.

I heard the bed springs creak as he got up. I turned to see him yawn and stretch, a sleek, splendid male animal, entirely naked, but that splendid male beauty left me utterly cold. I felt chilled through and through, felt I would never be warm again. Shoving the fringe of hair from his brow, he smiled lazily and padded across the room to stand in front of me.

"God, you're a magnificent creature," he said. "You were beautiful before, of course, but there's something new—an unmistakable glow. I knew you were a sensual creature, Marietta. Tonight proved it."

"You think so?"

"Don't pretend you didn't enjoy it. After that first time, you took to it readily enough. You were made for love."

"And you're going to have your fill in days to come?"

"You can count on it."

"I'm afraid you can't," I told him.

"What are you talking about?"

"I told you—I've no intention of staying on here—in this house, in this room. I've no intention of continuing as governess to your children, not after this. If you intend to use me as your mistress, I want—"

One dark brow lifted. "*You* want?" he interrupted.

"I want lodgings of my own—fine lodgings—and a generous monthly allowance."

"Could you possibly be making demands?"

"I suppose you could phrase it that way. I'm not some illiterate little scullery maid like Jenny. I'm an educated woman. If you're going to use me like a whore, I intend to be paid like one."

Lord Mallory's eyes were dark with amusement, he shook his head in mock dismay.

"My, my," he said, "you're certainly learning quickly. Where is that demure Miss Danver with meek expression and lowered eyes?"

"I'm afraid she vanished—along with her maidenhead."

My voice was hard. I gazed at him with cool, level eyes, making no effort to conceal my loathing. This seemed to amuse him all the more. Again he shook his head, dark eyes gleaming.

"You're being very unwise, love," he drawled.

"Am I?"

"With no job, no references, you'd be in rather unfortunate straits."

"I'm at your mercy—is that what you're trying to say?"

"You're at my mercy, love, and you'd better not forget it. You'll do as I say, when I say, on any terms I decide to set. This is beginning to bore me, Marietta. You'd better watch yourself. You could find yourself out on the streets"—he snapped his fingers—"like that!"

"I really don't think it would be necessary for me to walk the streets, Lord Mallory. I'm a 'magnificent creature,' as you put it, and I'm also intelligent. I feel quite certain there are dozens of fine, wealthy gentlemen in London who'd be delighted to provide lodgings and an allowance. I imagine I could do quite well for myself in that particular market."

"I don't like this, Marietta. No woman is going to dictate terms to me. It's never happened before. It's not about to happen now."

"I don't intend to be your victim, Lord Mallory. I don't intend to let you use me and then toss me out like you did Jenny. If you want me, you're going to pay, and you're going to pay dearly."

"If I don't set you up in lodgings and give you money, you'll find someone else who will. Is that it?"

"That's it," I replied calmly.

33

"That sounds suspiciously like blackmail."

"Call it what you like."

Lord Mallory sighed. When he spoke, his voice was smooth and silken, almost gentle.

"You're going to regret this, love."

"Am I? There's nothing you can do but turn me out. That doesn't worry me in the least. It shouldn't take me long to find a protector."

Before Lord Mallory could reply, there came the sound of a carriage clattering down the alley, wheels rumbling, horse hooves pounding. Leaning out of the window, he peered down. The carriage came to a halt directly below the window. He drew back quickly.

"Damn!" he exclaimed. "Agatha's back!"

"That worries you?" I asked idly. "I thought you controlled your wife with an iron fist. I thought she wouldn't dare interfere with one of your affairs—"

"Christ! What a bloody nuisance! I'll have to get to the bedroom and climb in bed before she comes up. Where are my boots?"

He scowled as a querulous feminine voices rose from the mews below, followed by the husky voices of coachman and groom. Lord Mallory hastily gathered up his clothes. There was a bumping noise as luggage was unstrapped and taken down from the top of the coach. Clutching breeches, shirt, and boots, Lord Mallory scowled.

"She suspected all along, damn her soul! She could at least have had the decency to wait till morning!"

"Life is filled with these little tragedies," I remarked.

Lord Mallory looked at me, extremely displeased. For a moment those dark eyes held my own, and then, hearing more noises below, he said "I've got to leave now, but I'll be in the nursery at eleven o'clock to talk to you." His voice was smooth and silken, yet there was an undeniable menace as he continued. "I suggest you think things over, Marietta. I suggest you forget your little blackmail scheme—for your own good."

He left the room then, quickly, and as I heard his bare

34

feet padding down the hall I remembered that subtle menace in his voice. I wasn't afraid of him, I told myself. I tried hard to convince myself of that.

Sunlight streamed through the windows and as I sat in front of the dressing table I could hear the grooms talking in husky voices in the mews below. A bird was warbling throatily. It was a gorgeous day, a day for strolls in the park, for buying flowers from the carts, for flying kites and sailing boats on the pond, a day for lovers. It might as well have been bleak and gray as far as I was concerned, for I knew he would soon come up to the nursery.

He couldn't possibly do anything worse than what he's already done, I assured myself. I brushed my hair briskly, and then, putting the brush down, I gazed at the woman in the glass. There was a new hardness that hadn't been there before, in the set of the chin, in the curve of the mouth. The deep-blue eyes were filled with a steely determination. The nervous, vulnerable nineteen-year-old girl had vanished completely, and the woman who looked back at me was much more interesting. There was a patina of sensuality that had been latent before, a new maturity that sharply defined the classic, patrician features. Marietta Danver had become a woman, and with the new knowledge had come a sense of power that was immediately evident.

Leaving my hair spilling about my shoulders, I stepped over to the wardrobe to select a dress. I ignored the drab browns, the plain grays, and finally chose a sumptuous bronze taffeta with long tight sleeves, a low, form-fitting bodice, and a full skirt that stood out over the bouffant petticoats. The prim, self-effacing governess was gone forever. No longer would I try to hide my beauty with plain dresses and severe hair styles. That beauty was my only commodity now—that and the lessons I had learned so well the night before.

I had meant every word I said to him. If he wouldn't find me other lodgings, I would find someone else who would be only too happy to keep me in style. A month ago such an idea would have appalled me, but I had grown up since then. I knew now who I was: I was the bastard daughter of an illiterate barmaid and a peer of the realm. I belonged to neither her world nor his. I had been thrown out of my father's house, abruptly banished from the way of life I had known there, and the training I had received had made it impossible for me to return to my mother's way of life. I had come to London naively believing I could put my education to good use. My education didn't matter. My wits did. In order to survive I would have to use them at every turn, for it was a hard, cruel, unfeeling world for a woman alone.

I hated Lord Mallory for what he had done to me, but the day might come when I would actually be grateful to him, for in one act of relentless violence he had shown me exactly where I stood in the world. He had shattered my every illusion, but, unknowingly, he had given me the determination I needed to forge ahead. Poor Jenny would probably be dead from starvation or venereal disease before the year was out, but that wasn't going to happen to me. I would never again be penniless, and never again be dependent solely on what others were willing to allow me.

Lord Mallory strolled into the nursery shortly after eleven, looking unusually handsome in a dark-blue suit and a stunning white satin waistcoat embroidered with silver thread. A sky-blue stock was carefully folded under his chin. Lids dropped heavily over his eyes, and a lazy smile was on his lips as he looked at me.

"Superb," he said. "There's not a woman in London who could come anywhere near you—and to think you're all mine."

"You've decided to provide lodgings and an allowance?"

Lord Mallory lifted a brow, surprised. "I told you last night, I don't like to be blackmailed. I assumed you'd come to your senses."

"I'd best start packing," I replied. "I have very little money, but there's enough to pay for a room for two

36

or three nights. I don't imagine I'll need much longer to find a . . . suitable protector."

"You intend to go through with it, then?"

"I intend to go through with it," I said calmly.

"I do wish you'd change your mind, love."

"My mind is made up."

"Women don't leave me," he said. "I leave them—usually leave them in tears, begging me to stay. I don't intend to take this gracefully, love. You'll regret it, I promise you."

"You don't intimidate me, Lord Mallory."

"I could beat you, of course, but that would only provide a momentary satisfaction. No, I . . uh . . . don't think I shall use my fists. I'll have to think of something a bit more refined."

"You can't do a thing to me."

He smiled wryly. "No? We shall see, love."

He sauntered out of the room then, and after a moment I returned to my bedroom. Taking down my two bags, I opened them on the bed and began to pack. I did it neatly, methodically, folding the clothes carefully and smoothing them down. I was perfectly calm, not at all frightened by the step I was taking. I had little money, true, but I doubted I would need much. London was full of wealthy rakes on the look-out for someone new, someone to tantalize their jaded appetites. I would take a room at one of the finest inns, and tonight I would visit one of the notorious gambling halls where elegant courtesans plied their trade. I had no doubt the venture would be eminently successful.

It was almost one o'clock before I finally finished packing. I had just closed the bags and fastened them when there came a timid knock on the door. Millie stepped inside, her face pale, her blue eyes wide with apprehension. Her cap was askew atop her tarnished gold curls, and the apron she wore over her black dress was twisted and crumpled, as though she had been wringing it in her hands.

"Mi—milady wants to see you downstairs in th' parlor,"

she said. Her voice trembled. "She—she wants to see *all* of us. Somethin's *afoot*, Miss Danver. Somethin' awful 'as 'appened, I just know it! Cook's in tears, she is, threatening to quit, an' even Jeffers is upset—'e's to come to th' parlor, too. *All* of us are."

"What's wrong, Millie?"

"I—I don't *know*, Miss. Th' master an' th' mistress 'ad 'em a long talk in th' sittin' room, talkin' for over a hour, like they was plannin' somethin', an' then th' master comes out wearing' a grin an' e' fetches Alfie an' sends 'im off to Bow Street to deliver a message to mi-lady's uncle. You know who 'e is, don't-ja?"

"I believe he's a magistrate."

"That 'e is! 'E's got twenty thief-takers workin' for 'im, scoundrels who round up wrong-doers 'n bring 'em in to 'im. 'E sits there behind 'is desk 'n sentences 'em. 'E sends 'em to *New*gate, Miss Danver, 'n if 'e don't like their looks 'e sends 'em to th' gallows!"

"Relax, Millie," I said gently. "You've done nothing wrong, have you?"

"No, Miss, but—"

"Then you've nothing to worry about."

"Alfie came back in a big black coach. Two of them thief-takers were with 'im, rough, churlish-lookin' blokes with mean eyes. They're in th' parlor now, talkin' with Lord Mallory—"

Millie shuddered. Like most of the lower class, she had a terrible fear of the thief takers, a rough, vicious crew who were frequently much more corrupt than the criminals they pursued. They were paid a small sum for every culprit they brought in. Some of the "culprits" were children, street urchins who, on the point of starvation, might have snatched a loaf of bread. The real criminals, the rich and powerful hooligans who reigned with terror, were rarely brought in, for the thief-takers could be bought off easily enough for a share of the spoils, as, indeed, could the magistrates themselves. A newspaper had recently stated that there was very little difference between those who enforced the law and those who broke it, and reforms were already underway to remove corrupt officials who used their position for gain, thriving on blackmail and bribery and actually encouraging crime. The present system of law enforcement was a net that pulled in all the little fish while allowing the big fish to swim in smooth waters. Although there were, of course, scrupulously honest magistrates with complete integrity, most of them were thoroughly venal.

"We—we're to join 'em down there," Millie stammered.

"Very well, Millie. I'm sure there's just been some kind of misunderstanding. It'll be all right. You'll see."

"Oh, Miss Danver, I'm *scared* . . ."

I patted the girl's hand and left the room with her. I was not at all worried, nor in the least suspicious, not even when Lord Mallory passed us on the staircase. He nodded and stood aside to let us pass, a sly smile on his lips, and then he went on up as we continued to descend. I wondered what it was all about. Whatever it was, it was highly inconvenient, and I wouldn't have bothered to come downstairs at all had I not felt Millie needed my support. As soon as this meeting in the parlor was over, I would ask Alfie to bring my bags down and fetch a cab for me, and then I would leave number 10 Montagu Square forever.

The parlor was a large, spacious room on the ground floor with ivory walls and a gilt ceiling from which hung a superb chandelier dripping with glittering crystal pendants. A rich blue carpet covered the floor, and the draperies were a darker blue damask. The white-and-gold furniture was exquisite, each piece imported from France. I wondered why Lady Mallory should be holding this meeting in such elegant surroundings, but as we entered I realized it was the only room in the house sizable enough to hold all the servants without crowding. The others had already arrived, and they stood in a nervous cluster: Cook belligerent, Jeffers pale and alarmed, Mrs. Branderson tearful. The maids were all as jittery and upset as Millie, the footmen apprehensive, the grooms and coachman surly.

Two strangers stood apart, observing them all.

One of the strangers, a tall, skinny man dressed all in black, had a face like a death mask, with gaunt, deep hollows beneath his cheekbones, gray smudges beneath eyes as black as coals. His lips were thin, his nose a sharp beak, his hair a blazing red. The other was a husky, burly fellow with enormous shoulders and a coarse, brutal face. His mouth was too large. His nose was humped, obviously broken in some brawl and never properly mended. Heavy lids drooped like hoods over fierce brown eyes. He wore muddy brown boots, a dark tan suit and a waistcoat of brown broadcloth, a burnt-orange stock untidily puffed under his chin. The pair of them looked like denizens of some dark, foul back alley, capable of the vilest crimes, and I tried to suppress a shudder as the burly one looked at me with unmitigated lust.

"These th' last of th' lot?" the redhead asked.

"These are the last," Lady Mallory said.

She had been standing behind a small white table, casually turning the pages of a book. Now she set the book down and came toward us. She was wearing a lovely pearl-gray gown adorned with pink velvet bows, and although it was exceedingly elegant, it did nothing for her thin, scrawny body. Her faded blond hair was fashionably arranged in a style that merely emphasized her sour, pinched features. As Millie and I went to stand with the other servants, Lady Mallory glanced at me. A thin smile flickered on her lips, and there was a malicious glitter in her eyes.

"Now that you're all here, allow me to introduce these gentlemen," she said. She indicated the redhead. "This is Mr. Clancy. His colleague is Mr. Higgins. They are law enforcers, commonly referred to as 'thief-takers,' and they are employed by my uncle, Roderick Mann. As you may know, he's a magistrate on Bow Street."

"What's that got to do with *us*!" Cook exclaimed, her huge body quivering with indignation. "We ain't done nothin'! Not a one of us! Been workin' here nigh on ten years, I 'ave, and never once 'ave I been so . . . so 'umiliated! I'm not gonna stand 'ere and—"

"Shut your mouth!" Higgins growled.

He glared at her with vicious brown eyes, looking as though he'd like nothing better than to knock her down. Cook went pale, clasping her hand over her heart and backing away. One of the maids began to sob. The grooms grumbled—one of them clenched his fists—but all the servants were much too intimidated to say or do anything that might agitate the thief-takers. These men were clearly ruthless, and they represented a cruel and merciless authority that brooked no insubordination.

Lord Mallory strolled casually into the room, a pleased look on his face. His wife looked at him. Lord Mallory gave her a nod. That thin smile flickered on her lips again, and then she continued in a pleasant, almost chatty tone of voice.

"Last night, when I returned from the country, I brought my emerald necklace with me. It was in a long white leather case. I set the case on the dressing table in my bedroom. This morning it was gone."

Millie began to tremble. I squeezed her hand. The other maids began to babble, but one sharp look from Higgins shut them up. Lady Mallory patted a faded blond curl, quite pleased with herself. She looked straight at me. There was triumph in her eyes. I knew then. My heart began to palpitate. My whole body seemed to grow cold. Lord Mallory leaned against the wall, his arms folded across his chest, watching me with that dark, mocking amusement. I knew why he had been going upstairs and why he had nodded to his wife when he came back into the parlor.

"There was no sign of forced entry," Lady Mallory continued. "Jeffers swears that all the doors and windows were securely locked when he made his rounds this morning. That leaves us with only one conclusion—one of you slipped into my bedroom and took the necklace. As none of you have left the house today, we'll undoubtedly find it hidden in one of your rooms."

These last words created a sensation. Cook began to shriek. Brandy began to bawl. The maids and the grooms and foot men vehemently protested their innocence. I was silent. I seemed to be paralyzed. I stared across the room at the man leaning so nonchalantly against the wall, unable to believe he had done what I knew he had done. He and his wife had planned it together, and Lady Mallory was savoring my plight as much as her husband was, perhaps even more. When the furor finally subsided, Lady Mallory exchanged looks with her husband. Both were enjoying themselves immensely.

"Your rooms will be searched one by one," she said. "We wouldn't want to give the thief an opportunity to slip up to his or her room and remove the necklace, so Clancy and Higgins will take you to your rooms one at a time, search it, then bring you back down here where the others will be waiting. No one will leave the room until they leave with these two gentlemen from Bow Street. We'll begin with the maids. I think—yes—Millie will be first. Millie, you'll take Mr. Clancy and Mr. Higgins up to your room and stand aside while they search it."

"I 'aven't stolen anything!" Millie cried. "I 'aven't! I'm *scared* to go up there alone with 'em! I know what they do to poor workin' girls. I've 'eard tales. Please, milady, don't make me—"

Higgins stepped over to the girl and slapped her across the mouth with such brutal force that she stumbled back against the other servants, almost falling. She began to cry hysterically, the imprint of his hand burning a bright pink on her face. Brown eyes smouldering, Higgins seized her arm and jerked her forward. Millie struggled, and he gave her arm a savage twist, thrusting it behind her and up between her shoulder blades.

"I reckon she's th' guilty one, milady," he said. "They don't carry on like this 'less they've got somethin' to hide. You're gonna be sorry you opened your mouth, wench. Clancy and I know how to handle the likes of you—"

"No!" Millie cried. "Milady, please—"

Higgins held her arm in a brutal grip, and when she continued to struggle he gave it a sharp upward thrust. Millie screamed, bending forward. With his free hand Higgins seized her hair, gripping the tarnished gold curls in his fingers and jerking her head back against his shoulders, putting even more pressure on her arm. The girl almost passed out from the pain. The other servants watched in horror, much too terrified to go to her aid.

I stepped toward them. "Let go of her!" I ordered.

Higgins was so startled that he actually obeyed me. Millie stumbled forward, and Brandy hurried over to her, wrapping her arms around the girl and murmuring words of comfort. Everyone else stared at me, and then Higgins turned to Lady Mallory as though for direction.

"What's this?" he asked huskily.

"Yes," Lord Mallory drawled, "what *is* this?"

"There's no need carrying on this elaborate charade," I said in a flat voice. "The necklace is in my room. You know it is. You put it there just a few minutes ago."

"*Did* I?" Lord Mallory looked amazed. "Really, Miss Danver, you have quite an imagination."

"There's no need to subject the other servants to any further humiliation. I'll take these two—two creatures up to my room. I'm quite sure they'll find the necklace. It would save time, of course, if you'd simply tell them where you planted it."

Lord Mallory shook his head, looking at the thief-takers with a perplexed expression. "The lass is out of her mind," he said, "but if she wants to be first, let her be first, by all means. My wife and I will keep an eye on the others while you accompany her to her room, gentlemen."

Summoning all the dignity I could muster, I walked out of the parlor, my chin held high. Higgins and Clancy sauntered along behind me, talking in low voices as we moved up the staircase. My bronze taffeta skirt made a crisp, crackling sound. I was perfectly calm because this wasn't real. It was happening to someone else. As I opened the door to my room and stood aside to let

43

them enter, I felt as if I were far away, watching with cool objectivity some drama on a stage that didn't concern me at all.

"Cool one, 'er," Clancy remarked.

"Cool as can be," Higgins agreed. "A bit too high and mighty to suit me, I don't mind tellin' you. I see she has her bags all packed, ready to make a quick getaway. Reckon we might find the gems in one of 'em."

"Reckon so," Clancy said.

They opened the bags, pulling garments out and tossing them aside. In a matter of moments my clothes were strewn all over the room, on the floor, across chairs, over the bed. Higgins examined my undergarments, chuckling to himself. I stood against the wall, watching, feeling nothing but the curious numbness that made it impossible for me to believe this could really be happening.

"Ah," Clancy exclaimed. "'Ere's th' white leather box, just like milady described it, and—why, look 'ere, 'iggins, 'ave you ever seen such pretty baubles?"

He held the emeralds up for his colleague to admire. They sparkled and flashed with shimmering green and blue fires, just as they had when I had seen them resting against Lady Mallory's bosom. Clancy dangled them between his fingers, shaking his head as though unable to believe he was beholding such splendor. Higgins looked thoroughly disgruntled.

"Reckon we 'ave our thief," Clancy said.

"Reckon we do," Higgins grumbled. "I was hopin' to get that maid up to her room and teach her to show a little respect for the law. I was lookin' forward to a spot of fun."

Clancy glanced at me, his gaunt face expressionless. "I 'magine we'll both 'ave a spot uv that 'fore this is all over with."

Higgins's wide lips curled into a grin, and his brown eyes gleamed with anticipation. "Yeah," he said. "We'd better go down now 'n' turn the jewels over. Later, in the coach—"

He left the sentence dangling and took hold of my

44

wrist, clamping his fingers tightly around it. I made no effort to pull free as he led me out of the room and down the stairs. Clancy moved ahead of us, slinging the necklace around and around as though it were a watch chain. Lord Mallory was standing in front of the door to the parlor, waiting for us.

"I see you found the necklace," he remarked.

Clancy handed him the string of glittering emeralds. "We found it, all right. Wench 'ad it 'idden in 'er bag. If we 'adn't got here when we did, she'd 'ave made a clean getaway."

"I suppose you'll be taking her down to Bow Street now."

"Aye, them's our orders," Clancy replied, nodding gravely. "She'll spend th' night in th' cell there. I 'magine 'is lordship will pass sentence tomorrow. 'E don't waste no time."

"I want to thank you gentlemen," Lord Mallory said, his voice ever so smooth. He reached into his pocket and took out two gold coins, handing one to each man. They were amazed—and delighted. "And . . . uh . . . you'll be gentle with her, won't you?"

Higgins caught his meaning immediately. He grinned again, nodding slowly. "Gentle as can be," he said. His hand tightened on my wrist.

"I thought I could count on you," Lord Mallory replied. "She's a bit uppity, gives herself airs. I imagine a couple of chaps like you might be able to teach her some humility."

"We'll do that very thing," Higgins promised.

Lord Mallory stepped over to the front door and held it open for us. My numbness had worn off now, and fear possessed me, fear such as I had never felt before, but I refused to show it and give him that satisfaction. Lord Mallory smiled, savoring his triumph, and as Higgins led me past he made a courtly bow, mocking me. I pretended not to see. The sunshine was dazzling as we stepped outside. Higgins jerked my arm viciously, causing me to stumble down the steps.

45

A large black closed carriage stood in front of the house. Two powerful horses stood in the shafts, stamping impatiently. The driver perched high on his seat in front, smoking a cheroot. Clancy opened the carriage door, and Higgins thrust me inside. There were two seats facing each other, upholstered in split brown leather. The interior reeked of tobacco and sweat and gin. The curtains at the windows were brown velvet, ragged, the nap worn. Higgins squeezed in beside me and wrapped a muscular arm around my shoulder, pulling me against him. When I tried to pull away he tightened his grip, crushing me to him.

"You wanna be friendly, wench. Me 'n' Clancy, we don't like to be snubbed."

Still standing on the pavement and holding the carriage door open, Clancy yelled at the driver, telling him to take his time getting back to the station, and then he climbed inside. Sitting down on the seat opposite us, he slammed the door shut. As the carriage began to move down the street, he pulled the shabby curtains over the windows, shutting out the sunlight. It was dim and dusty inside, but I could see Clancy's bony face and that mop of blazing red hair. His black eyes were burning with anticipation, and a wide grin split his mouth.

"Well-well-well," he said, " 'ere we are, all snug 'n'-cozy."

"Lass don't wanna be friendly, Clancy," Higgins told him. "I believe she thinks she's too good for us."

Clancy stared at his colleague in mock dismay. "You don't mean it? 'N' 'er a common thief. Stealin's a 'angin' offense."

"Like as not she'll swing," Higgins agreed.

"Seems a waste, don't it?"

"Terrible waste, but we got plenty a time. It's gonna take Jenkins 'alf an hour to reach th' station. You ever done it in a carriage?"

"Can't say as I 'ave," Clancy replied.

"Reckon I'd better go first then, show you how it's done."

46

I struggled violently, trying to pull away from him. Higgins shoved me against the side of the carriage and slapped me across the face, again, again, until my cheeks seemed to be on fire. He jerked me toward him, then planted his mouth over mine. He wrapped his arms around me, crushing me to him. I thought my bones were going to snap. He finally pulled his head back, savoring my panic.

"She don't *like* us," Clancy exclaimed.

"Reckon we're gonna have to show her what a couple uv dandy sparks we are," Higgins said. "Fight all you want to, wench. Truth to tell, I like it that way—makes it more excitin'."

The carriage bounced and jostled, swaying from side to side as it passed over the rough cobblestones. Higgins pushed me down flat on the seat, pulling up my skirts. I fought, scratching at his face. He clutched my throat and squeezed viciously until I could fight no more, and then he fell on me, the weight of his body knocking the breath out of me. He began his assault, and Clancy applauded, urging him on. During the night that Lord Mallory had used me repeatedly, I had thought I knew what it was to be degraded. I hadn't. Until now I hadn't even known the meaning of the word.

IV

There were three cells in back of the building on Bow Street. Although I knew the other two were occupied, as well, I could neither see nor communicate with the other prisoners, as thick stone walls separated us. Not more than ten feet square, my cell was like a small stone box with a heavy iron door. The rough stone floor was littered with damp straw, and there was one narrow cot with no mattress cover and, in the corner, a cracked chamber pot. The air was fetid, reeking with the odors of sweat and excrement and fear. The one tiny window in the back wall, barred, let in very little fresh air. It looked out over a filthy alley lined with squalid hovels.

As soon as I had arrived, the gruff, strapping locksmith had put two tight iron bracelets on my wrists, a heavy chain suspended between them. My ankles had been shackled, too, the chain just long enough to allow me to pace the floor in short, cautious steps. Twice each day the bailiff unlocked the door and set down a tray holding a bowl of thin gruel, a hunk of stale bread, and a small earthen jug of water. I had been here for two days now, and he had not seen fit to empty the chamber pot, but then prisoners were not to be pampered.

At least it wasn't Newgate. I could be thankful for that. Squalid and uncomfortable as it was, the cell was luxurious compared to that dreaded prison whose inhabitants lived no better than the rats that infested it. I had read about the horrors of Newgate, reports that chilled the blood, and I knew that death was preferrable to internment in that monstrous hell hole. Would I eventually be sent there? The mere thought of it caused me to grow weak with terror.

I had already given up any idea of a fair trial. Lady Mallory's uncle, the magistrate, was undoubtedly in league with his niece and her husband. He had the power to sentence me, and I was at his mercy. By rights I should be taken to Justice Hall Court in the Old Bailey and there tried before the six judges in scarlet robes and long, woolly white wigs who sat in their tall wooden chairs. By rights I should be given an opportunity to defend myself, but I knew it wasn't going to be that way. Roderick Mann could do with me as he wished, the finer points of the law be damned. Justice, real justice, was for the rich and powerful.

Still, I wouldn't give way to fear. It would be all too easy to succumb to the panic inside, to scream and cry and become a helpless wreck, but that would accomplish nothing. If I gave way now, I would be utterly defeated. I had to summon all the strength inside and cling to it. I had to endure the filth, the cruelty, the hunger, the humiliation with a stoic calm. The nightmare would soon be over. I had to keep telling myself that, over and over again. If I could endure that horrible carriage ride, I could endure anything else.

I had actually wished for death. Higgins had taken me, using me with brutal force, deliberately hurting me, while Clancy watched—a pitiful voyeur. When the coach finally stopped in front of this large, formidable brown building on Bow Street, they had had to drag me down the dark, narrow corridors, for I had been unable to walk. Now, forty-eight hours later, my body was still bruised and sore. My bronze taffeta dress was torn and soiled, my petticoats filthy. Auburn hair was damp and tangled, and there was a cut on my cheek. I knew I must look like some battered harlot from the foulest back street, but that hardly mattered.

There was a distant rumble of thunder. Cautiously, my chains clanking as I moved, I stepped over to the window and, holding onto the cold iron bars, peered out. The sky was a dark slate gray filled with ponderous black clouds that seemed to drip a sinister purple light. The alley below was littered with fruit rinds and paper and rotting debris, and the row of flimsy brown wooden hovels seemed to be clinging together to keep from collapsing. Something long and furry scurried among the debris. A cat perched on one of the narrow window sills let out a long howl and pounced, catching the rat between its jaws and dashing down the alley with it. I shuddered.

As I clung to the bars, an aged, grotesque obese old woman in a filthy blue dress and tattered black shawl staggered into view, clutching an almost empty bottle of gin. Glancing up as she passed, she grinned a toothless grin and waved at me. I could hear her cackling with delight that someone else was behind bars and she was still free to shuffle through the squalid alleys with a few drops of gin left in the begrimed bottle.

Turning away from the window, I moved across the cell and sat down on the cot with its filth-crusted paper-thin mattress. The faint sunlight slanting through the bars had awakened me hours ago. It must be almost noon by this time. Would the mighty Roderick Mann send for me today? Probably not, I told myself. They would . . . they would keep me here for a week, perhaps a little longer, and then I would be released. Of course I would be released. He wanted to punish me, to crush my pride, to put me in my place, that's all. He wouldn't let me be sent to Newgate. He wouldn't let me hang . . .

Half an hour passed, and then I heard a key turning in the lock. It must be time for lunch, I thought, nauseated at the prospect of more of the thin, oily gruel and mouldy bread. The heavy door swung open, and the bailiff entered, but he brought no tray. He was a short, stocky, affable fellow in scuffed boots, soiled tan breeches, dingy

50

white shirt, and leather jerkin. His chatty, pleasant manner didn't deceive me at all. I knew that he could become brutal at a moment's notice. One of the other prisoners had displeased him yesterday. Even though the stone walls were thick, I had heard him using his fists, heard the prisoner's screams. He stepped into the cell now with an amiable grin. The locksmith was right behind him, a ring of heavy keys hanging from his belt.

"Afternoon, luv," the bailiff said. "Time to visit 'is lordship. 'E's waitin' for you in th' courtroom. Burt 'ere's gonna take th' shackles off your ankles, though we'll just leave th' others in place for th' time bein'."

I was still sitting on the cot. The locksmith squatted down in front of me and flipped my skirts up over my legs. He gripped one of my calves and began to rattle the keys. The bailiff stood there watching, the grin still in place as he eyed my legs. When the shackles were finally off, the locksmith ran his hands over my legs. I knew better than to protest. He gave my knee a tight squeeze and then stood up, his face expressionless. The bailiff pulled me to my feet.

"We're goin' for a little walk now, luv. You be'ave, 'ear? If you was to try anything foolish, I'd 'ave to 'urt you. Wouldn't wanna do that, you bein' such a lady 'n' all."

Gripping one of my elbows, he led me out of the cell and down a long, dim corridor. The chain suspended between my wrists clanked loudly. We turned a corner and moved down a much wider corridor with candles burning in brass wall sconces. Finally, we entered an extremely narrow hallway and stopped in front of the door at its end.

"You go on in, luv," the bailiff said. " 'E'll be waitin. I'll stay out 'ere standin' guard, so don't try nothin' clever now—"

He opened the door for me. I stepped forward to find myself on an elevated platform at the side of the courtroom, waist-high wooden banisters on three sides, the door behind me. The platform was perhaps four feet

51

up from the floor. The courtroom was dark and gloomy, paneled with varnished brown wood. There were several rows of benches in front of another, much wider, platform with three carpeted steps leading up. Here the magistrate sat behind an enormous fumed oak desk, a clerk sitting in a chair to his right. Both were immersed in paperwork, and neither looked up as they heard me enter. There was no one else in the room.

I studied the man in whose hands my fate rested. He was extremely thin, his shoulders wide and bony. His lips were like two sharp slits, his nose a crooked beak, his hard gray eyes half-concealed by lowered lids. He had the same sour, pinched look as Lady Mallory, the same icy manner. The powdery white wig on his head was slightly askew. The clerk asked a question, pointing to one of the papers. Roderick Mann snapped a reply that caused the clerk to flush uncomfortably.

I gripped the banister in front of me. My chain rattled noisily. The magistrate looked up with venomous eyes.

"Marietta Danver?" he said harshly.

"That is my name, sir."

"Lately of number 10 Montague Square?"

I nodded. I could feel the hope draining away. This man was cold and hard, a man who thrived on hatred and had no knowledge of compassion or mercy. He gathered up a sheaf of papers and waved them at me.

"Marietta Danver, I have here evidence that you are guilty of a most grave offense." His voice was like ice splintering. "These are sworn statements—from Lord Robert Mallory and his wife, Lady Agatha, from Patrick Clancy and Bernard Higgins, two men in my employ. They testify that you—"

The room seemed to spin, and I gripped the railing tightly, losing track of his words. All at once I knew that the hope I had been nourishing had been sheer folly. The three of them had probably taken tea together, discussed my fate, and decided upon it. There would be no trial; I would have no chance to defend myself. This parody of justice was a mere formality. I was doomed,

52

had been doomed since the moment I first defied Lord Mallory. He and his wife and her uncle were merely using the law as an instrument of vengeance. The magistrate's voice went on and on, hard, unyielding, and I shook my head, knowing I had no way to protect myself.

"—my duty to pass sentence upon you," he concluded, "but before I do, is there anything you wish to say for yourself?"

"I'm innocent," I whispered.

"Speak up!"

"I'm innocent! I—the jewelry was not stolen. You know that. This—this is a mockery! I want a trial! I—"

"Enough!"

"You—you're part of it. She's your niece. You can't—"

"Silence!"

I continued to shake my head, and tears spilled down my cheeks despite my efforts to check them. I felt faint, and had I not been gripping the railing I would probably have crumpled to the floor. The room seemed to be filled with a fine mist now, a mist that thickened, gradually enveloping me. It stung my cheeks, stung my eyes, and I lowered my lids, moving my lips in a silent prayer. His voice seemed to come from a great distance.

"It is my duty . . . Newgate Prison, to be confined until . . . public execution on the gallows at Tyburn Fields . . . to swing from your neck until dead . . ."

A cloud of black wings rushed over me, closing everything else out, and I heard him shout for the bailiff. The door behind me flew open, and strong arms seized me before I could fall. The bailiff held me tightly, and gradually the wings vanished. I was in a state of shock, and through the mist I could see the man who had just condemned me. He tapped his long fingers impatiently on the desktop, eager to be done with it.

"Is she all right now?" he asked querulously.

"I think so, your lordship," the bailiff replied. "I'd best 'old to 'er, though, just in case she 'as another spell."

"It is my *duty* to send you to Newgate and thence to the gallows," the magistrate continued in a bored voice, "but as you have no previous criminal record and as your employers asked the court to show mercy, that sentence shall not be passed. Instead of hanging, you shall be transported to His Majesty's colonies in North America. An article of indenture shall be issued, and you shall be sold at public auction to the highest bidder, to serve no less than seven years . . ."

The rest of his words seemed to fade away, and the next thing I knew, the bailiff was leading me back down the corridors to my cell.

"You're lucky," he told me. "Most thieves'd 'ang. Not you, luv. 'Is lordship gave you a break. You oughta be thankful. You oughta get down on your knees 'n' thank th' Lord that Roderick Mann 'as such a kind, merciful 'eart—"

PART ONE:

Carolina

I

I'll never forget my first sight of the new land, America, the wild and tumultuous country where fate had brought me. I was standing on the ship's deck, surrounded by coils of rope and wooden lifeboats, the clutter concealing me. I spent much of my time there—anything to escape the foul atmosphere below with its filth, congestion, and horrible odors. I wasn't supposed to be on deck, of course. It was forbidden. We were given our "exercise" once a day, closely supervised, and the rest of the time we were to remain below. This secret place was my haven, shown to me by the strapping blond sailor who had befriended me only a few days after the ship left Liverpool.

He was a rugged, roughhewn lad with a merry smile and flashing blue eyes. Brawny, illiterate, he had spotted me the first time I slipped up the stairs to catch a breath of fresh air. He didn't turn me in. Instead, he led me past barrels of tar and showed me this small area where I could take fresh air without being discovered. I was exceedingly grateful. One of the other women had come up on deck only the day before. She had been caught, had been tied to a mast and brutally whipped as an "example." I had been willing to risk that, and young Jack had admired my courage.

Naturally he expected to be paid. I paid. His lovemaking was rough and energetic, yet there was a surprising tenderness, as well. Afterwards he would hold me in his arms, stroking my breasts, stroking my hair, as though I were some precious object he had miraculously been given to relieve the tedium and rigorous hardships of the voyage. I gave willingly, and I was not ashamed of it. This crude, muscular sailor with his gruff voice and amiable grin showed me that lovemaking could be wildly elating, could be satisfying to a woman as well as a man. I enjoyed it, and I was grateful as well. After the treatment I had received from Lord Mallory and the two thief-takers, I might well have nourished some terrible fear about the act of love, might have connected it in my mind with disgust and loathing, had it not been for Jack and his healthy, robust attitude. He taught me a great deal. He also enabled me to survive the voyage.

Not all of us did. One of the women went insane and ran screaming up the stairs to hurl herself over the railing. Almost everyone was sick from scurvy. Two of the women died from it, teeth and hair falling out. The brawling, bickering group of female prisoners who boarded the ship at Liverpool were soon turned into a lethargic, dispirited lot who huddled on their narrow bunks like zombies, patiently enduring the filth, the abuse of our "keepers," the wretched, skimpily doled-out food and the horribly fetid air. The male prisoners who were kept down in the hull on the other side of the ship fared no better. There were beatings every day with the cat-o'-nine-tails, horror and humiliation a way of life for all prisoners.

Jack saved me from that. Not only did he provide me with a haven on deck, he also had a "talk" with the three brutal guards whose duty it was to watch over the female prisoners. Hands on hips, a lopsided grin on his face, he casually informed them that he had a "special interest in th' redhead" and added that any man who touched me he'd choke to death with his bare hands and then toss overboard without a second thought. Since he was well over six feet tall, with a bronzed, muscular body, he was formidable indeed. The guards left me alone. Surly, sadistic, they took great delight in abusing others, but I never tasted the lash, never had to endure the rutting, grunting sexual assaults that were nightly occurrences for the other women.

Jack also brought me food—beef, ale, decent bread, cheese, lemons and limes to prevent the dreadful scurvy. I knew he was running a great risk, but he seemed to enjoy defying his superiors and putting something over on "th' bloody sods." Jack was a dandy fellow, popular with all his fellow sailors. They knew about me, of course. There was no way they could help knowing, but while they might envy Jack and make coarse jokes about his "private piece of tail," they helped him keep it from the ship's officers. Had any of the officers discovered his little escapade, Jack could have received fifty lashes, could even have been hanged for associating with one of the prisoners. This danger merely added another fillip of excitement as far as Jack was concerned. He considered it all a jolly lark.

The stars were fading and dawn was about to break that last time we were together. He had made a nest of blankets under one of the lifeboats, and he held me loosely in his arms, idly caressing my breasts. I felt warm and secure, loving his salty, sweaty smell, his large, muscular body. I had grown quite fond of him, and I hated to think that I would soon lose my protector. Jack sighed, wrapping his strong arms around me, pulling me closer against his sturdy frame.

"We'll be landin' today," he said. "I reckon it'll be sometime this afternoon—early on, I figure. Should be able to see th' shore soon as it gets light enough."

"I—I hate to think about it," I confessed.

"You've grown kinda fond-a Jack, ain't-ja?"

"Of course I have."

"Makes me feel right proud. I've 'ad my share of women, but I ain't never 'ad one like you, wench. Strange, ain't it, us meetin' like this? I reckon you wouldn't give me a second look under normal circumstances. No, you'd be a 'igh 'n' mighty lady, much too good to even speak to th' likes-a me."

"That—that isn't so," I lied.

"Aw, no sense pretendin'. I've been bloody lucky an' I know it. Crude chap like me—gettin' to 'ave a wench like you. It's a bloody miracle. All my mates're green with envy. Ol' Jack really landed in a pot o' jam this time, they say. Not one of 'em wouldn't give everythin' they 'ave to be in my boots right now."

"They never betrayed us."

"Naw, they wouldn't. Wouldn't dare. Know I'd 'ave their 'ide if they so much as 'inted to any of th' officers what was goin' on. I could beat any man jack of 'em to a pulp an' they know it. They're good chaps, though, my mates. They wouldn't-a told even if they wasn't afraid o' my fists."

"The stars are almost gone," I said quietly.

"Yeah, in just a few minutes th' sky's gonna turn all pink an' gold an' orange. I'll 'ave to be gettin' about my duties. I reckon we won't 'ave a chance to see each other again."

"I suppose we won't, "I said in a sad voice.

"No use bein' grim about it," he replied. "We still 'ave time for one more round. Come on, lass, let's say goodbye to each other in th' best possible way."

Later, Jack rolled off me and climbed to his feet, buttoning his breeches and fastening his belt. Reaching for his jersey, he pulled it over his head. The cloth strained and stretched across his powerful shoulders and chest. Shoving the damp blond locks from his brow, he stared out across the railing. The stars were gone. The sky was a faint, misty gray with a barely perceptible touch of pink. The ship rocked. I could hear waves sloshing against the hull, hear the creak and groan of wood. I sat up and adjusted the bodice of my dress, feeling sleepy and satisfied and extremely sad. This man had come to mean a lot to me. I might very well owe him my life.

Jack turned to look at me. His expression was grim.

"Don't you fret none, lass. I know what you're thinkin'

—you're thinkin' of what's to come. It's gonna be rough, no doubt about that, but you're gonna make it. You're gonna come through it all with flyin' colors. You got strength an' you got character, an' nothin' is gonna hold you back for long."

"I—I wish I weren't so frightened. They're going to auction us off like—like African slaves. We're going to be sold to the highest bidders. I—I've tried not to think about it, but—"

"I know, lass. I ain't never 'ad much ambition, ain't never 'ad any desire to be a rich man, but this is one time I wish I 'ad me a whole stack of gold. If I 'ad, I'd jump ship soon as we land. I'd go to that auction an' buy you myself. We'd set out across America together, regular pioneers we'd be. We'd love and we'd fight an' even though I'd set yuh free, you wouldn't want your freedom. You wouldn't want nothin' but Jack Reed—night 'n' day."

"If only it could be that way."

"Take 'eart, lass. A wench looks like you, 'as such a fine education an' all, she's gonna fetch th' 'ighest price goin'. Anyone who 'as enough gold to pay for you is bloody well gonna 'ave enough sense to take good care of 'is investment."

Catching hold of the lifeboat, I pulled myself to my feet. The ship rocked precariously, and I stumbled. Jack caught me, holding me against his chest. I wrapped my arms around his neck and tilted my head back to look up into his eyes. He smelled of sweat and salt and tar, and he was not at all good-looking with his too-wide mouth and sharp nose, but he was the kindest man I had ever known. My heart was actually aching, and I could no longer hold back the tears. They spilled over my lashes and made tiny wet trails down my cheeks.

" 'Ere," he said in a scolding voice, "that ain't no way to carry on. Tears're for them weak, whinin' women who ain't got no backbone. You're strong, Marietta. You got determination an' a will of iron."

"I don't feel very strong at the moment."

Jack wiped the tears from my cheek. "You're gonna

make it, lass, just like I said. No more cryin', you 'ear? Come on now, let's see a smile."

I smiled feebly, but my heart wasn't in it. Jack held me tightly as the gray disappeared from the sky and the clouds were tinged with gold. We could hear the crew moving busily about their duties now, calling to one another in rough, coarse voices. It was time for him to go. Both of us realized that.

"We'll never see each other again," I said.

"Aw, I don't know about that. Life's a crazy thing. Who knows? I ain't aimin' to be a sailor th' rest of my life. I have a hankerin' to see somethin' of this vast new country we're comin' to. In two or three years I just might give up th' seafarin' life an' give the colonies th' once-over. Maybe we'll run into each other."

"Maybe so," I replied, without conviction.

The sky was a blaze of pink and orange now, and for one brief moment the sea was a-spangle with flecks of gold that danced and shimmered as the waves moved. I looked up at the man who had been my salvation these long, misery-laden weeks, and then, standing on tiptoes, I kissed that wide, amiable mouth, brushing my lips tenderly against his. Jack gave me one last squeeze, an exuberant hug that almost cracked my ribs. Making a fist with his right hand, he tapped me gently on the chin, grinned his rakish grin, and sauntered around the lifeboats and out of sight.

I stood at the railing, gripping it tightly in an attempt to control my emotions. I tried to believe what he had told me. I tried to believe that I would come through it all with flying colors, that I was as strong as he said I was. I was afraid of the future, now more so than ever, for with Jack I had had a respite from the horror and humiliation. He had protected me, and now he was gone and I had no one to turn to. I was desolate and feeling utterly vulnerable.

Heavy gray clouds obscured the sun. The flecks of gold vanished from the water, the waves a lead gray now, the air thick with mist. I could smell salt, and I could smell land, too. In the distance there was the shrill, squawking cry of a gull. I knew that I should go back down to the hull and gather my few things up, but I lingered there at the railing to stare down at the swirling water that slapped so viciously against the ship, causing it to crack and groan like some ponderous brown wooden animal with canvas wings. The warm, wondrous glow that was the aftermath of our lovemaking had gone now, and I felt cold, chilled to the bone.

A long time passed. The heavy gray clouds began to thin and separate, evaporating, and I saw patches of steel-blue sky through the rift. Sunlight spilled down in bright silvery rays that reflected in the water, and as the gloom left the sea, so did it leave me. That hard core was still inside me, still sustaining me, and the determination to survive was stronger than ever. I had survived the sea voyage, and that in itself was something. Three women had died, and the others were pitiful shells of humanity, dull, dispirited. If anything, thanks to Jack's care, I was healthier than I had been at the beginning of the voyage.

I thought about Jack, objectively now. I was fond of him, and I would miss him, miss his robust male body and the sensations it summoned, but, in truth, I had merely used him. Like a prostitute I had traded my beauty, my body, for the comfort and protection he could give me. I wasn't proud of that, but neither was I sorry. I was a woman alone. I had youth and beauty and intelligence, and I knew full well that I was going to have to use them again and again in time to come. They were the only weapons I had, and I fully recognized the power they gave me. There would be other men like Jack Reed, and each would be a stepping stone to . . . what? I was down now, I would be literally a slave to anyone who bought me, but I had a curious feeling that I wouldn't be down for long.

I heard one of the sailors high up on the mast give a loud, joyous cry—"Land! Land ahoy!"—and I leaned against the railing, peering at the shimmering violet-gray

63

mists in the distance. For a moment or so I could see nothing, and then the mists seemed to part and I saw a mound of brown and green, barely visible, and I knew that it was America, the land of my future. My earlier apprehension vanished completely. I felt excitement stir within. It was a new land. I would have a new life there on that vast continent. There would be hardships, and I was already handicapped, but as the mists parted even more and the land loomed up out of the water like a huge, slumbering sea monster, I felt a distinct challenge.

Life had dealt me many hard blows. I had been thrown out of my father's home. I had been brutally raped by a dissolute aristocrat and framed for a crime I hadn't committed. I had been subjected to incredible humilation that would have broken a weaker person . . . but that was all in the past. I had learned several valuable lessons about life, and I was eager to put them into practice. I might be coming to this country as a prisoner, a slave, the lowest of the low, yet it still seemed to beckon to me now, seemed to hold a promise of fulfillment and success.

Always interested in the new world, I had read everything I could find about it over the years. I knew its size was staggering, the English colonies stretching up and down the seaboard and separated by huge areas of untamed wilderness filled with savage Indians and wild beasts. The French were there, as well, and the Spanish, and there were hundreds of thousands of miles to the west still unexplored. Of course, the Americans were little better than hooligans, rough, illiterate, crude despite the scattering of elegant cities they had hewn out of the wilderness. They were a wild, defiant breed, but they were ambitious, always striving, always reaching out. A young, determined woman would have great opportunities in a country like that, even if she did arrive as a common criminal.

Hearing footsteps behind me, I turned, thinking perhaps Jack had returned. It wasn't Jack. It was Angus Blackstone, one of the guards, a huge, hulking brute with short-clipped black hair and savage brown eyes. He wore sea boots, soiled tan breeches, and a rough leather jerkin over a coarse white cotton shirt with the sleeves rolled up over his forearms. He gripped a worn leather riding crop in his right hand. I had seen him use it on several of the women, beating them into submission, but I had also seen him cringe with fear and cowardice when Jack spoke to him. I stared at him defiantly.

"Figured I'd find you 'ere," he said. His voice was thick, guttural. "Thought maybe your fine sailor boy'd be with you, 'avin' a last go-round 'fore we land."

"Jack has duties to attend to."

"So 'ave I, wench, so 'ave I. I gotta get you sluts ready to land. You come on with me an' get your things together before we put th' shackles back on ya. Don't give me no argument, now. I ain't laid a 'and on you, but I 'ave to confess I'm spoilin' to. It'd do my 'eart good to give you a taste of my lash—"

I moved past him with dignity, my chin held high. Blackstone made a grimace, but restrained himself, his fear of reprisal being greater than his desire to put me in my place. I went on down the dark, narrow stairway to the congested area lined with wooden bunks. The other women were stirring about, lethargically gathering up their belongings like lost souls preparing for hell. When we had first boarded the ship so many weeks ago, they had fought and scratched at each other like vicious caged animals. The contrast now was extraordinary.

Angie was the exception. Like me, she had found a way to better conditions for herself during the journey, and she too looked healthier than she had at the beginning. Angie had the bunk next to mine, and she kept an eye on my things while I was with Jack, else they would have been stolen immediately.

" 'Ave a nice time, luv?" she inquired.

I nodded. Angie made a face as Blackstone approached us.

" 'Urry it up, sluts," he growled. "They'll be comin' to put th' shackles back on any minute now."

"Piss off!" Angie hissed.

" 'Ere, you lookin' for trouble?"

"Don't touch me, you bloody sod!"

She glared at him fiercely, and although he made threatening noises, Blackstone backed away. Angie sighed as though he were merely a bothersome insect she had brushed away, then turned her attention back to me. Barely seventeen years old, Angie was small and thin with long, silky blond hair and enormous brown eyes. Pale golden-brown freckles were scattered lightly across her cheeks, and her full pink mouth curled down at the corners with disgust and resignation. Although she looked like a fragile, vulnerable child, that impression was highly misleading.

Angie had been a prostitute since the age of twelve, living like an alley cat in squalid back streets of London, selling herself for pennies, stealing food in order to survive. Angie had been convicted of thievery just as I had, her crime snatching a handful of coins from a shopkeeper's till. On our very first day on board she had picked out one of the three guards and played up to him shamelessly, and although she had had to service him regularly, patiently indulging his somewhat unusual whims, she had never been assaulted, nor had she ever been beaten. The guard had watched after her just as Jack watched after me. Tough, scrappy, Angie was a natural survivor.

"Well, I guess it's almost over," she said. "God knows what's gonna 'appen to us now. We'll probably end up in some 'ore'ouse. There're men who pick out women at th' auctions, you know. They buy 'em, fatten 'em up, an' then sell 'em to 'ouses. 'Appens all th' time."

"It may not be that way, Angie. We—we both might be lucky."

"I ain't countin' on it," she said grimly.

"As soon as you're put on the block you'll probably be snatched up by some sturdy young farmer who's been

66

looking for a girl like you. You'll have him wrapped around your little finger before a week goes by."

"Like 'ell—knowin' my luck, I'll be stuck out in th' fields to pick cotton alongside th' blacks. You, though, I ain't worried about *you*. In a few years you'll probably end up ownin' 'alf th' bloody country. If you ain't scalped, that is."

"Scalped?"

"Them Injuns—that's what really worries me. Cliff Barnes 'as been tellin' me all about 'em. They're roamin' all over th' place, just pantin' to get 'old of white women, an' do you know what they *do* when they get one? Cliff told me all about it. 'E said—"

"No doubt he was merely trying to frighten you."

"Bleedin' sod—'im an' 'is back-door 'abits. I'll be glad to see th' last of '*im*, I can tell you for sure! Still, I guess 'e served 'is purpose."

"We've both been lucky," I said.

"We damned sure 'ave—just look at th' rest of these cows. It's been nice 'avin' at least one friend on this stinkin' tub. Christ! 'Ere comes Barnes, an' 'e 'as that look in 'is eye. 'Ere's your things, Marietta, safe an' secure—"

She cut herself short as Cliff Barnes joined us. Barnes had flat gray eyes and tawny gold hair that fell about his head in lank strands; he was a large, brutal man built along the same lines as Blackstone. Wrapping one huge hand around Angie's arm, he pulled her to him. She sighed, wearing a bored, resigned expression.

"We 'ave time for one more trick, luv," he said, leering.

"Yeah, sure." She sighed again and let him lead her away.

I began to rearrange my things in the shabby valise Angie had been guarding. We had been permitted to bring a few personal belongings with us, and before we departed, Millie, the maid, had risked the wrath of Lord Mallory to bring me some of the clothes I had left behind at the house. The girl had picked out the most elaborate, expensive gowns I had, garments that would be of little or no use to me in America. Once on board, I had traded them for more suitable things, exchanging one of them for a sewing kit, as well. Thanks to Jack, I had been able to have the new things laundered, and I had spent hours altering them to fit me. They were a motley collection, true, but they would serve me much better than silks or bronze taffeta.

I had just closed the valise when the locksmith came down to put the shackles on us. The guards shouted commands, and I lined up with the other women to have the iron bracelets with chain suspended between them put on my wrists. Angie was the last in line, an aggravated expression on her face as she rubbed her backside. When my turn came, I patiently submitted to the locksmith. These shackles weren't nearly so heavy nor so tight as those I had worn in the cell on Bow Street, and I was relieved to find our ankles weren't to be shackled as well. All the same, it was humiliating, a pointed reminder that we were criminals, the lowest scum in the eyes of society.

Properly shackled, we waited. Two hours passed, three, and we sat in silence in our bunks, even Angie's ordinarily high spirits dampened. The air was fetid, the floors covered with filth. It was a wonder any of us had come through it all alive. Several of the women were deathly ill. All, with the exception of Angie and me, were pale, drawn, battered, hair hanging over faces in limp locks. Who would want to buy any of them? Two or three of them would certainly not recover from their illness, and none of the others looked capable of even the lightest work—much less like candidates for a brothel.

I could tell from the motion of the ship that we were coming into the harbor. Sounds of great activity could be heard above. Finally there was a loud, scraping noise of wood against wood. The great ship rocked mightily, seemed to shudder all over, then grew still. Blackstone had gone up on deck to await orders, and the other two guards prowled about with menacing expressions, whips in hand. Two or three women were weeping silently. The others sat on their bunks sunk in lethargy. A huge brown rat scurried across the floor, but no one paid any attention to it. We had all grown accustomed to the rodents that thrived below deck. Angie gave an impatient sigh and reached up to run a hand through her blond hair. The chain suspended between her wrists clanked loudly.

"You'd think th' bleedin' sods'd 'urry up an' let us outta this 'ell 'ole! It's 'ot as blue blazes down 'ere. 'Ey, Barnes," she called, "When're we gettin' outta 'ere?"

"Pipe down, slut!" he bellowed.

"That's gratitude for you," she told me. "For weeks 'e's been stickin' it in me. Now that we've landed, I guess th' romance is over. Oh, well," she added, "what can a girl expect?"

It was almost an hour before Blackstone returned. We were lined up and marched up the stairs and onto deck. After the dimness below, the sunlight seemed blinding. Across the railing I could see stacks of boxes and cargo piled up on the dock and, beyond that, a row of grayish-pink brick buildings with slate roofs. There was much activity on shore. The whole town, it seemed, had come to watch the felons disembark. Jack Reed was nowhere in sight. I was glad. We had said our goodbyes, and I didn't want him to see me shackled like this.

Angie was in line behind me. "I wonder where we *are*," she said.

"Jack said we'd be landing in Carolina," I replied, "but I have no idea what the town is called."

"Oh gawd," she whispered. "Look at them poor men—"

I looked up to see six wagons with wooden cages built over them, the sort of vehicles used to transport wild animals in traveling circuses. Three of the wagons were already filled with the male prisoners. Stunned, apathetic, the men clung to the bars, oblivious to the catcalls from the crowd. A band of rowdy little boys poked at the men with sticks and hurled rocks at the cages. The crowd seemed to find this highly amusing, but the caged men had grown so accustomed to such abuse that they

69

seemed hardly to notice. The other three wagons stood empty, waiting for us.

Five men were standing at the foot of the gangplank. Four of them were husky chaps in sturdy boots, black breeches, and green and black jerseys, a sullen lot with stern features and belligerent eyes. Each of the four held a whip coiled in his hand and looked all too eager to put it to use. They were obviously our new guards. The fifth man was burly and broad-shouldered, roughly dressed in tan breeches, coarse white linen shirt, and leather jerkin. His eyes were flat and cold. Dirty brown hair fell across his tanned brow. His name, I was to learn, was Bradford Coleman, and he was to be in charge of us.

Coleman scowled, watching us descend the gangplank.

"Hurry it up, you lot!" he bellowed. "I ain't got all day. Christ! Look at 'em! It'll take me two weeks to get 'em in shape for the auction. All right, men, get 'em into the wagons! Any of 'em give you any trouble, you know what to do!"

II

I had no idea where we were. The settlement, for it couldn't possibly be called a town, was a full day's journey from the port where we had landed. We had been kept in a large stockade for two weeks, well fed and tended like cattle. A doctor had examined us, had prescribed medicine for those women still sickly, and now that the day of the auction had finally arrived, all of us looked considerably better than we had upon arrival. Early in the morning we had been given bars of soap and were led down to the river to bathe, then, back at the stockade, instructed to don our very best clothes and groom ourselves for the sale.

A carnival atmosphere prevailed at the settlement. People had been arriving in wagons for the past three days, some of them coming hundreds of miles, and booths and striped tents had been set up. A noisy, festive crowd spilled over the area. Women in bonnets and calico dresses gossiped and sampled the food sold at the booths. Children ran wild, darting from booth to booth, shouting, fighting, unrestrained. Strapping men in rough clothes drank huge mugs of ale, argued with each other, examined the poultry and livestock, frequently engaged in rowdy bouts or fisticuffs. Angie was terrified when she saw the Indians wandering over the grounds, tall, sickly-looking creatures adorned with beads and feathers, but one of

71

the guards assured her that these were "tame redskins."

The men had been auctioned off the day before. We were taken from the stockade and herded to a small, roped-off area behind the auction block. A number of people came to peer at us, but they didn't jeer. They examined us with the same thoughtful, serious expressions they employed when looking over the cattle penned across the way and the horses that were for sale. Most of the women had regained their high spirits. Two weeks of hearty food and fresh air had worked wonders. Our shackles had long since been removed, but two guards with coiled whips hovered over us, as did Bradford Coleman, the stocky, leathery-faced former slave-runner who had been in charge of us since our arrival.

Angie gave me a sharp nudge in the ribs, pointing to a husky lad with tousled brown hair who stood just beyond the rope. He wore brown boots, black breeches, and a coarse blue cotton shirt with full-gathered sleeves. With his merry brown eyes, broad, pleasant features, and wide grin he looked like an amiable young farmer, surely not more than twenty. I felt certain he smelled of the barnyard.

"Look at 'im," Angie whispered. "Ain't 'e a dandy specimen? I do declare, I think 'e's givin' me th' eye. 'E is! I wouldn't mind bein' bought by that 'un, I tell ya for sure. 'Ello, darlin'," she called. "I 'ope you 'ave somethin' else in your pocket 'sides that pistol."

The farmer grinned, delighted with her bawdy comment. Reaching into his pocket, he pulled out several gold coins, showing them to us.

"Land sakes, Marietta, 'e's rich, too! I 'ope you're in a buyin' mood, sweet'eart. I'm th' best bargain you're ever gonna find—"

"Shut up, wench!" one of the guards warned.

"Go snatch yourself," Angie told him.

The young farmer bellowed with laughter and sauntered off into the crowd. Angie looked elated, certain he was going to buy her. A large tent had been pitched at the end of the enclosure for us to use, and she hurried inside to take out her mirror and brush to do some last minute primping before the auction began. Their initial curiosity satisfied, several of the other women wandered inside, too, wanting to get out of the blazing sun. Only a few of us remained outside, including young Martha Roberts, a fifteen-year-old girl convicted of thievery.

Pale and pretty with light-brown hair and haunted blue eyes, Martha had been ill throughout the sea voyage, a wraithlike creature who rarely spoke. The doctor who had examined us upon our arrival at the stockade had pronounced her pregnant, and the girl had dissolved into tears, confessing later on that she had shared a filthy room back in London with her older brother, that he had been having his way with her since she was twelve years old. The child would be his, and she would rather die than bear it. Coleman had had to keep her confined in a tiny log hut, heavily shackled, to prevent her from taking her own life.

Unfettered now, standing in the blazing sunlight in front of the tent, Martha looked dazed, as though she had no idea where she was. Someone in the crowd fired a pistol. The girl jumped, terrified, and then she began to scream hysterically. Coleman and one of the guards rushed over to her and tried to quieten her. Martha struggled violently, still screaming, and finally Coleman drew back his fist and slammed it against her jaw. The girl stumbled backwards, almost falling. Coleman started to hit her again.

"No!" I cried.

I rushed over to her, gathering her into my arms. Martha stared up at me dumbly, unable to comprehend what had happened. I knew the poor child was demented, her mind finally pushed over the edge by all the horror she had had to endure.

"Get away from her, Danver!" Coleman roared.

"She—she's ill. You had no right to hit her like that—"

"I said get away from her!"

He seized my arm, pulling me away from the girl. I glared at him defiantly, my eyes blazing. Angie rushed over to Martha, took her hand, and led her into the tent. Coleman stared at me with flat gray eyes, his face a hard, brutal mask.

"You've been asking for it for a long time, Danver. Seems to me you need to be taught a lesson."

"Go to hell!"

Coleman flushed, unable to believe his ears. He was accustomed to total obedience, a brutal tyrant who relished his power and the fear he inspired. He slapped me across the face so hard that I lost my balance and toppled to the ground. When I looked up, he was uncoiling the whip he wore fastened to the side of his belt. It was like a long brown snake slithering on the ground beside me. He cracked it in the air, smiling when I flinched. I saw him draw his arm back and heard a loud hissing noise. I closed my eyes bracing myself for the slashing pain.

"I wouldn't, Coleman." The voice was soft and pleasant.

I opened my eyes to see a tall blond man in buckskins standing beside Coleman, holding his arm in a tight restraining grip. Coleman looked startled, then furious. He tried to pull his arm free. The man in buckskins smiled an amiable smile and tightened his grip, applying so much pressure that Coleman let out a curse and dropped the whip.

"That's mighty wise of you," the stranger said. "I'd 've hated to 'av to break your arm."

"This is none of your affair, Rawlins!"

"Ain't it? I'm thinking of bidding for this one, and I wouldn't want to be buying damaged goods. A whip can do a lot of damage, man. Run on about your business, now. Leave the wench alone."

"Now, just a minute, Rawlins! You got no right to—"

"Easy, fellow," Rawlins said. "I don't like your tone. You do what I say now—run along. Oh . . . one other thing. If you so much as lay a finger on the wench before the auction, I'll kill you. Do you understand? You know I don't make idle threats."

Coleman muttered something unintelligible and stalked into the tent. The tall blond looked down at me and grinned, and then, reaching down for my hand, he pulled me to my feet.

"Jeff Rawlins, ma'am," he said. "Pleased to make your acquaintance."

His voice had that soft, slightly slurred accent I was to learn was typical of people who lived in the southern part of the country. It was a lovely, melodious sound, extremely pleasing. Jeff Rawlins grinned, as though the two of us had just shared a delicious joke.

"I suppose I should thank you," I told him.

"Not particularly. I'm afraid I acted from purely selfish motives. A bullwhip can leave pretty bad scars, and like I told Coleman—I wouldn't wanna be buying damaged goods. I reckon you're gonna cost a pretty penny. A woman like you'll have every man in sight losin' their senses and biddin' like crazy."

"Indeed?"

"You're a magnificent wench. Don't know as I've ever seen another one as appetizin' as you on the block, not in all the years I've been comin' to these here auctions."

I stared at him, any gratitude I might have felt quickly destroyed by his casual, matter-of-fact manner. Jeff Rawlins was superbly built, lean and muscular. Though not really handsome, he had pleasant features. His dark-brown eyes were warm and amiable, his wide, full mouth made for merry smiles. His sandy hair was decidedly unruly, spilling over his brow in a heavy fringe. He was undeniably virile, yet there was a curious boyish charm that seemed entirely out of keeping. Coleman had been frightened, and I had the feeling that this tall, friendly fellow in his fringed buckskins was quite capable of carrying out the threat he had made so nonchalantly.

"Like what you see, wench?" he inquired.

"I—I see a backwoods savage."

"Oh? Probably smell one, too. Afraid we ain't got the

75

refinement a lady like you 's accustomed to. Satin breeches, lace shirtfronts, perfumed handkerchiefs—we haven't the time for such folderol. We're a crude rough lot over here."

"I've noticed," I told him.

"You'll soon get used to it," he said. He grinned. "Matter of fact, you'll soon get to liking it. I'll see to that."

Those warm brown eyes held mine, and all the while that boyish grin played on his wide mouth. Jeff Rawlins exuded an aura of sexuality no woman could help noticing. His raffish, amiable manner, his little-boy charm merely emphasized it. One automatically thought about bodies and bedrooms. Against my will, I acknowledged the attraction. Rawlins seemed to be reading my mind, and the grin spread, his full lips turning up at the corners.

"I always did have a fancy for red-haired women," he remarked. "I've got a feelin' you're gonna bankrupt me, wench, but I reckon it'll be worth it. Auction's about to begin. See you later."

He gave me a friendly nod and then sauntered away, nimbly stepping over the rope surrounding the area. Angie hurried over to me, her mouth wide open as she watched him disappear into the crowd.

"Gawd," she exclaimed, "who was 'e?"

"His name is Jeff Rawlins."

"I've never seen anyone like 'im! Lord, just lookin' at 'im made me melt all over. Any women able to curl up in bed with th' likes of 'im should thank 'er lucky stars. Them eyes—" She shook her head. "Is 'e gonna bid for you?"

"I imagine so, Angie."

"Keep your fingers crossed, luv. Let's 'ope 'e 'as a pile of gold."

"You two," Coleman said harshly, "into the tent! The auction's gonna begin in a minute, and I don't want the crowd gapin' at you two while I'm gettin' rid of them dogs. You two are the prize goods, and I'm savin' you for last."

76

"I think 'e's payin' us a compliment, Marietta. Fancy that. 'Ey, Coleman, just who *is* this Jeff Rawlins?"

"He's a bloody whoremonger," Coleman retorted, "th' blackest villain in all of Carolina. Murderin' rogue like that oughta be strung up. He probably will be one day. I hope he buys you, Danver. I really hope he does."

Angie and I stepped inside the tent, and a few minutes later the others were ordered to gather up their belongings. Most of them were excited, making the best impression possible in hopes of attracting the men. As they were led outside, Martha Roberts moved as though in a trance, gripping her pitiful bundle of clothes, clearly unaware of what was happening to her. I prayed she would find a kind, sympathetic master.

Alone in the tent now, Angie and I could hear the auction beginning. There were loud, excited voices and raucous laughter. Coleman's voice was robust and encouraging as he presented first one woman, then another, lauding her virtues, calling for higher bids. Angie and I exchanged looks. She shook her head, and I could tell that she was apprehensive and depressed, but she refused to give in to it. She made a face, pushing a strand of silky blond hair from her temple.

"It's in'uman, a-course, but—'ell, I reckon I'll be better off than I was back in London, screwin' for pennies, diggin' in th' garbage bins for a scrap o' mouldy bread. I'm 'opin' that 'usky farmer'll buy me. I'll 'ave 'im eatin' outta my 'and—"

"It's going to be all right, Angie."

"I ain't nothin' if not optimistic. I just 'ave to serve seven years. When that's over I'll still be in my twenties. Both of us are goin' to do just fine, Marietta. I can feel it in my bones."

Stepping over to the large, broken mirror propped up against one of the tent poles, I examined myself critically. My coppery-red hair fell in lustrous waves, and my sapphire eyes were hard. Despite the patrician features, I looked exactly like Meg Danver's daughter now, a wench

77

created to serve ale in a barroom and tumble in the hay with lusty males. My white blouse was the type Italian peasant women wore, the short sleeves puffed, the neckline low, revealing half of my bosom. My leaf-brown skirt was of coarse, heavy cotton, tightly belted at the waist and cascading over several petticoats. I thought about my father, glad he couldn't see me like this, knowing it would have been far better for me had those years at Stanton Hall never occurred.

"Thinkin' about that Rawlins fellow?" Angie asked.

"I—no, I wasn't."

"For a minute there you looked so—well, 'ard, like you was mad at th' world. Ain't no use grievin' about th' past, Marietta. It's over an' done with. It's th' future what counts."

"You're right, Angie." My voice was cold.

"Bearin' a grudge against th' world—'ell, that don't do no good. Me, I learned that years ago. It's just a waste-a time. I'm too busy lookin' out for Angie to look back on what might uv been. You'd best devote all your energies to lookin' out for Marietta, luv."

"I intend to," I replied.

"Us, we don't 'ave nothin' but our brains an' our bodies, 'an we 'ave to use both. Think I liked sleepin' with that bleedin' sod on board ship? 'Ell no, but I knew it was something I 'ad to do. Like you an' that 'andsome sailor. Men are damned fools, Marietta, an' they're th' ones with all th' power. A woman 'as to know 'ow to manipulate 'em."

Both of us looked up as one of the guards stepped into the tent.

"You," he said, pointing at Angie. "He's ready for you. The others've already been sold."

"I guess this is it," Angie said. "You remember everythin' I said, luv. Gawd, I hate partin'—"

Her enormous brown eyes were suddenly filled with tears, and she grimaced, angry with herself for displaying such weakness.

78

"Hurry it up!" the guard called.

She threw her arms around me and gave me a tight hug, and I clung to her, as moved as she. She sobbed just once, and then she drew back, a wry resigned look on her face. She stepped over to the corner of the tent to pick up the bulky blue bundle that contained her personal belongings, and then she shook her head, her lips turning up in a brave little smile.

"Well, 'ere goes, luv. Keep your fingers crossed for me. I'm gonna go out there an' dazzle that bleedin' farmer till 'e's ready to spend 'is last penny on me. I— I ain't gonna say goodbye. I 'ave a feelin' you an' I'll see each other again someday—"

Angie left with the guard, and I had never felt lonelier in my life. I had grown very close to the scrappy, amoral little ragamuffin with her stoic outlook and wicked tongue. I could hear them bidding for her, hear Coleman shouting encouragement. I heard Angie, too. "Come on, luv, you can do better'n *that*!" she shouted, and the crowd roared with laughter. There was more bidding, more laughter, and then the guard came for me and I picked up my bag and followed him out into the brilliant sunlight.

I climbed the steps up to the wooden platform and stood beside Coleman, setting my bag down. An excited murmur ran through the crowd. "Marietta!" Angie called. She was leaving with the husky young farmer, and she waved, wreathed in smiles. I waved back, and then she and her new master disappeared around the side of a tent. I was happy for her. Angie would get along nicely. The young farmer would be putty in her hands.

"Biddin' starts at two hundred on this 'un," Coleman announced. "It's a bit steep, yeah, but take a good look at her. She ain't only one of th' most fetchin' wenches you've ever seen, she's edge-acated as well. Speaks like a bloomin' swell. Say somethin', Danver."

I stood perfectly still, my chin held high, staring straight in front of me. Coleman flushed, frustrated, but he was afraid to do anything about my disobedience, perhaps because Jeff Rawlins was standing a few yards away. Rawlins grinned.

"Two hundred!" he called.

"Two twenty," shouted a husky lout with shaggy black hair.

"Two fifty," Rawlins said.

"Three hundred," the shaggy-haired man called eagerly.

There was a moment of silence, and then a cool, bored voice was heard. "One thousand," the new bidder said.

"One thousand!" Coleman was beside himself with glee. He received a hefty percentage of every sale made. "One thousand pounds! That's more like it."

"Too steep for me," the husky man grumbled, stepping away from the platform.

"One thousand—" Coleman said. "Going, going . . ."

"Eleven hundred!" Rawlins called.

"Fifteen hundred," the cool voice said.

Rawlins turned with a frown, staring at his competitor. "Hawke, is it? Thought I recognized that voice. What's got into you, fellow? You ain't got that kind of money to toss around."

"Fifteen hundred," the man repeated.

"Sixteen!" Rawlins said quickly. "Come on, Derek, you don't really want the wench. You got all kinda niggers on your place. What you need a gal like this for?"

"Seventeen," Derek Hawke said calmly.

He stepped forward, and people moved aside to make room for him as he approached the front of the platform. As the two men confronted each other, people moved back, clearing a space around them, and a hush fell over the crowd. The air seemed to crackle with tension.

Derek Hawke was even taller than Rawlins, long and lean and muscular. He was one of the handsomest men I had ever seen, his features perfectly chiseled, with strong and broad cheekbones. His windblown hair was black, his eyes gray, grim. Dressed in high black knee boots, clinging black breeches, and a white linen shirt with full sleeves gathered at the wrist, he looked like an aristocrat pirate, icy, remote. Men would be instinctively wary of such a man, women automatically fascinated. He gave Rawlins a curt nod. Rawlins responded with an amiable grin.

"I aim to have the wench, Hawke," Rawlins said.

"So do I," Hawke replied.

"Seventeen!" Coleman cried. "Come on, gentlemen. Eighteen? Who's gonna make it eighteen?"

"Eighteen!" Rawlins called.

"Two thousand," Hawke said.

"Two thousand!" Rawlins protested. "That's all the money I have with me. Come on, Hawke, be a sport. I have a terrible hankerin' for the girl. You don't need her. You—"

"Twenty-one hundred," Derek Hawke said coldly.

"You son of a bitch," Rawlins muttered, though without malice.

"Twenty-one hundred! Twenty-two? Anyone gonna go for twenty-two? Anyone? Rawlins? No? All right, then. Going. going . . . *gone*! Sold to Mr. Derek Hawke for twenty-one hundred pounds!"

Coleman slammed his gravel. The crowd applauded. I picked up my bag and moved down the steps to stand beside the man who had purchased me. Coleman joined us a moment later, waiting patiently while Hawke counted out the money. Coleman pocketed it, then gave Hawke the Articles of Indenture that officially made me his property. Hawke folded it up and thrust it into his pocket without so much as glancing at it. Jeff Rawlins lingered nearby, looking disappointed but, ultimately, good-natured about his defeat. He extended his hand, and Hawke shook it somewhat reluctantly.

"No hard feelins, Derek," Rawlins said. "You got yourself a prize there."

"Indeed," Hawke replied. His voice was cold.

"You ever wanna get rid of her, you just let me know, mate. A wench like her—th' bucks in New Orleans'd go outta their minds. If I'd had more money with me—"

81

He shook his head regretfully. "Oh, well, you can't win 'em all. You takin' her back to Shadow Oaks?"

Hawke nodded crisply. Rawlins muttered something unintelligible, shook his head again, and strolled away. Hawke curled the fingers of his right hand around my elbow, clasping me lightly but firmly.

"It's a long drive back," he told me. "We'd better start at once. Come along."

He led me through the crowd toward the wagons at the end of the clearing. A straw-haired lad with freckled cheeks was watching the horses. Hawke gave him a coin, then helped me up onto the front seat of a rough wooden wagon with muddy farm tools and bags of grain piled in back. Swinging up beside me with lithe grace, he took the reins and clicked them. The two sturdy chestnuts began to move away from the clearing. As we left, I saw a plump pleasant-looking woman in a pink calico dress leading young Martha Roberts away from the clearing. Martha moved as a blind person might, frequently stumbling, and the woman wrapped an arm around the girl's waist, speaking to her in a gentle voice. I was relieved to see that her new mistress would obviously care for the girl.

The wagon creaked and groaned, wobbling from side to side as the wheels passed over deep ruts in the road. We soon left the settlement behind and seemed to be heading directly into the wilderness. The trees grew thick on either side of the road, tangles of heavy underbrush twisted about their trunks. Birds cried out shrilly. I had never seen such woods, wild, tangled, formidable. I kept remembering what Angie had said about Indians, and, instinctively, I moved closer to Hawke, unnerved by the gathering shadows. I imagined redskinned savages lurking behind every trunk.

At least an hour passed. It was growing darker. Derek Hawke had not said a single word to me since we had climbed in the wagon. He might have been alone. I glanced up at that handsome profile, wondering what made him so cold and aloof. He couldn't be more than thirty, yet he had the demeanor of a much older man.

"You don't talk much, do you?" I remarked.

"Only when I have something to say."

"I'm not a criminal, Mr. Hawke. I was working as governess for an English lord. He—he wanted me to perform other services as well, and when I refused he planted an emerald necklace in my room—"

Even as I spoke I realized it sounded like the wildest fabrication. I could tell that he didn't believe me. There was no earthly reason why he should. Hawke made no comment, and a long time passed before I summoned enough courage to speak again.

"Are—are there Indians in these woods?"

"Might be a few," he replied. "They shouldn't bother us."

"How far are we going?"

"Quite a ways. We should reach Shadow Oaks tomorrow afternoon."

"You mean—we're going to spend the night in the woods?"

Hawke nodded. I shivered, trying to control my apprehension.

"You've nothing to fear, wench. I didn't buy you to warm my bed."

"No?"

"I was looking for a housekeeper, a stout, sturdy woman capable of splitting logs, scrubbing floors, helping the blacks out in the fields. You're hardly what I had in mind, but I suppose you'll have to do."

"If that's what you wanted, then why *did* you buy me?"

"To keep Rawlins from having you," he replied.

"You and he are . . . rivals of some sort?"

"Hardly. I simply didn't fancy seeing you end up in some whorehouse in New Orleans. Rawlins comes to all the auctions and buys cheap, resells the women in New Orleans at a steep profit. It's a filthy business, one I don't approve of."

83

"You've bid against him before?"

"As a matter of fact, I haven't. I don't rightly know why I started bidding against him this time. Damned foolish of me—" Hawke frowned, clicking the reins.

"I—I suppose I should be grateful to you."

"You're going to work, wench. You're going to work damned hard. I paid too much for you, far more than I could afford, and I intend to get good value for my investment."

"I see."

"I treat my slaves well, I take good care of 'em, but I don't tolerate laziness. I won't tolerate it from you, either. You'll find me a stern master, stern but fair."

I did not reply. Hawke turned his head, looking at me for the first time since we had left the settlement.

"One other thing—and we'd better get this straight from the beginning. My slaves know their place. They stay there. I don't like gabby servants. I don't like familiarity. Do you understand?"

"Thoroughly, Mr. Hawke."

Neither of us said anything else. We rode in silence for what seemed hours, and finally Hawke turned the wagon off the road and stopped in a small clearing. Trees were close all around, long shadows spreading across the grass as darkness fell. I could hear water running nearby. Hawke unharnessed the horses and led them down to the river, tethering them to a tree when he returned. He handed me a canteen, then took a long rifle from the back of the wagon and disappeared into the woods again. A short while later I heard a shot, then another, and Hawke returned carrying two dead rabbits. Squatting on the ground, he took out a hunting knife, cut off the heads and began to skin the animals. Appalled, I watched, and, sensing my revulsion, Hawke looked up with a grim expression.

"Don't just stand there," he said sharply. "Gather firewood!"

I obeyed. The sun had gone down now. A deep purple

84

haze settled over the woods as shadows thickened. Hawke built a primitive spit with two Y-shaped branches, driving them into the ground on either side of the stack of firewood, skewering the rabbits on another branch and placing it across the standing branches. He took flint from his pocket and soon had the fire going. By the time the flames danced like greedy orange tongues, the woods were entirely shrouded in darkness, and the flickering light was reassuring. Grease dripped from the rabbits, popping and crackling loudly. It was a pleasant sound. I was reminded of a gypsy encampment back in England. With his untidy raven hair and stern, handsome face, Derek Hawke might well have been some savage gypsy king.

As I leaned against the wagon, waiting for the rabbits to cook, I realized that I was famished. Behind me, leaves rustled noisily. Branches creaked. I thought I could hear stealthy footsteps in the woods, and I fancied I could feel hostile eyes watching us. Hawke seemed utterly unperturbed, although I noticed that he kept his rifle within easy reach. Removing the rabbits from the fire, he let them cool and then pulled one off the stick and handed it to me. He returned to the other side of the fire, sat down, and began to eat, tearing hunks of meat off with his hands. After a moment I did the same, much too hungry to be concerned with niceties.

The fire had died down by the time we finished eating. It had grown much colder. I shivered in my thin blouse, folding my arms around my waist. Noticing this, Hawke strolled over to the wagon and pulled out two rather moth-eaten blankets and tossed them to me.

"You sleep under the wagon. It'll be warmer there. Drier, too, in case it rains."

"You don't intend to tie me up?" I asked. There was sarcasm in my voice.

"I don't imagine it'll be necessary. You won't try to run away. If you did, you wouldn't get far. If you're harboring any such foolish notions, wench, forget 'em.

You wouldn't care for the consequences, I can assure you."

Crawling under the wagon, I spread one of the blankets out on the ground, lay down on it and pulled the other blanket over me. Hawke scooped sand over the glowing coals and then went to see about the horses. I could hear him speaking to them in a soft, gentle voice. I wondered how long it would be before he joined me under the wagon.

I waited. Time passed. The darkness was blue-black, pale silvery moonlight streaming across the clearing. Insects buzzed. Leaves crackled. The wind through the trees made a steady, monotonous noise like hoarse whispers. It had grown much colder. I wrapped the top blanket closer about me, shifting my body, trying to find a comfortable position on the hard, stony ground. I could hear him moving around, and I felt something akin to anticipation. I wouldn't welcome his advances, but I would welcome his nearness, because I was afraid of Indians, and I would welcome his warmth, because I was shivering cold. I waited . . . and eventually I slept.

I woke up with a start, terrified. There had been a noise, some dreadful cry . . . It came again, and I realized that it was merely an owl hooting. Several hours must have passed, for the first layers of darkness were beginning to evaporate, black gradually melting into deep gray. In the thin, misty moonlight I could see Derek Hawke stretched out on the ground several yards away, on his back, one arm curled under his head, the other at his side. He was fast asleep, the rifle beside him. He had no blanket, and I realized that he had given both to me, a curious bit of gallantry that seemed out of character.

I wondered why he hadn't come to me. I was his property, his slave. He moaned in his sleep, changing positions and I gazed at him, studying the long, lean body, the incredibly handsome face. He didn't seem nearly so severe now. In fact, in his sleep he seemed curiously vulnerable. Derek Hawke was an enigma, a man of many depths. Any other man would have pleasured himself, yet he had refrained from taking what was rightfully his. I tried to tell myself that I wasn't disappointed.

III

I was already in the kitchen preparing the master's breakfast when Cassie appeared, much later than usual. Seventeen years old, she was a superbly beautiful girl with luminous brown eyes and high, broad cheekbones. Her stiff black hair was clipped short, fitting her skull like a cap, and her skin was a creamy brown. Tall and slender, she wore a pink calico dress that clung to her generous curves. She looked exhausted this morning, and I detected a faint grayish pallor about her cheeks.

"Sorry I'm late, Miz Marietta," she said quietly. "I'm feelin' bone-weary, an' my stomach's actin' up somethin' awful. I—I thinks I'm breedin'. I ain't bled for th' longest time."

"Sit down, Cassie. Here, let me pour you a cup of coffee. Did you have breakfast with the others?"

Cassie shook her head. "Mattie's already done fed th' others an' they're already goin' about their work. I . . . I just couldn't seem to pull my bones outta bed this mornin'. Adam scolded me somethin' awful, told me to git myself over to th' big house 'fore th' master come and whup me."

"He wouldn't do that," I remarked, reaching for a fork to turn the ham sizzling in the skillet.

"He would so, Miz Marietta. Th' master treats us fair, treats us much better'n most of th' planters treat

88

their slaves, but he don't tol'rate no slackness. He don't whup any of us very often, but when he takes a notion to do it, he whups so's you ain't likely to forget."

"He . . . he hasn't beat any of the slaves since I've been here."

"No 'um, there ain't been no need. None of th' niggers uv given him a reason to whup 'em. He ain't never used that ridin' crop on me, ain't never used it on any of us wimmin that I know of, but me, I ain't lookin' to be th' first."

Derek Hawke had only thirty slaves, far fewer than most of the other planters in the area, and the majority of them were field hands. Since Mattie had been banished to the cabins, Cassie was the only 'house nigger,' assigned to help me with my chores. They all lived in the row of cabins behind the barn, Cassie sharing a room with her husband, Adam, Hawke's chief hand, a powerful black who acted as overseer to the other slaves. Adam's father had been a king in Africa, Cassie informed me, and there was an undeniable majesty about Adam himself. Captured by slavers when he was ten years old, Adam was magnificiently built, his skin like polished ebony. Other planters had offered Hawke a small fortune for the buck, but Hawke adamantly refused to sell.

"I . . . I'd better help you," Cassie said. "It's gettin' late. Th' master'll be expectin' his tray."

"You sit still, Cassie. Finish your coffee. I'll prepare his tray."

The girl looked relieved, slumping lethargically in the wooden chair. I took the skillet off the stove and placed the fried ham on a plate, then opened the oven door to check on the biscuits. During the two months I had been at Shadow Oaks I had become a pretty fair cook, an accomplishment of which I was exceedingly proud. Mattie had taught me everything she knew. Weighing well over two hundred pounds, slow-moving, amiable, Mattie had served as Hawke's cook-housekeeper ever since he had purchased Shadow Oaks twelve years ago. She was well over sixty now and delighted to be relieved of her heavy responsibilities. When she wasn't supervising the slaves' meals out in the cookhouse, she spent most of her time rocking on the porch of her cabin and dipping the snuff Hawke so generously supplied.

"There," I said, "the tray's ready. Don't stir yourself, Cassie. I'll take it to him."

"You . . . you ain't never done it before. He might not like it, might think I'm shirkin'—"

"Nonsense."

"I cain't just sit here, Miz Marietta. I has to be doin' somethin'."

"You can start peeling those peaches in the bucket over there. I'm planning to bake a peach pie for his supper this evening."

"You's always doin' somethin' special like that," Cassie remarked. "You caters to him like he wuz a spoilt little boy, havin' everything just so for 'im. His things ain't never been kept so fine, the house ain't never been kept so clean an' proper. He ain't never been fed so well, either. Mattie never baked him no peach pies."

"It's my job to see that he's pleased, Cassie."

"An' he treats you just like one of us niggers. When he brung you to Shadow Oaks and gave you his wife's old room, we all reckoned you was goin' to be his woman as well as takin' over Mattie's chores. He ain't never even tried you."

"That's none of your concern, Cassie," I retorted, my voice much sharper than I had intended. "It's not your place to gossip about the master's—the master's business."

"I'm sorry, Miz Marietta. I wuzn't meanin' to be uppity, but . . . well, it's just that you's a white lady and beautiful as sin and it don't seem natural-like, him havin' you in th' house an' not wantin' you. 'Ticularly when you're hankerin' for it."

"That's enough, Cassie! Get started on those peaches!"

Taking up the tray, I left the kitchen abruptly, my cheeks burning. The girl had meant no harm, I knew, but her remarks had been much too close to the bone. Derek Hawke had not touched me, not once during the two months I had been here, nor had he shown the least inclination. His manner had been cool and stern and remote. Although I knew he was pleased with my work, he never commented on it, and he rarely spoke unless it was to issue an order. I told myself that I was fortunate that he didn't expect me to perform those more intimate services, but deep down I had to admit that I would have performed them almost willingly.

The wide main hall that intersected the house was still dim, the walls washed with soft blue gray shadows, although rays of early morning sunlight slanted through the glass panes above the front door. Shadow Oaks was much smaller than those houses we had passed on our way back from the auction. Its one-story white frame structure had a wide verandah on three sides and a bricked-in kitchen in back. Shabby, run down, sadly in need of a new coat of paint, it had no impressive columns, no elegant trimmings, and the furnishings could hardly be called splendid. The giant oaks that surrounded the house added a touch of regal beauty, but the "plantation" was actually little more than a farm.

I tapped softly on the door of the master bedroom, then pushed it open. The faded gold brocade draperies had already been parted, sunlight spilling through the windows to make bright patterns on the threadbare rose-and-gray carpet. The huge mahogany four-poster was empty, pillows dented, sheets and gold brocade counterpane pushed back in a tangle. Hawke stood at the mirror, shaving, his back to me.

"You're late, Cassie!" he said sharply. "You should have been here a good half-hour ago. I should already be out in the fields. Set the tray on the bedside table and then get out of here. I'm in a foul mood!"

"So I see," I remarked.

Hawke had put his razor down and was wiping his face with a wet cloth. He turned around, startled by my voice.

"Where's Cassie?" he demanded.

91

"She's in the kitchen. She's not feeling well this morning."

"Oh?"

"I think she's pregnant."

"Pregnant?" Hawke looked pleased. "She and Adam are both splendid creatures. Their child—a son, I hope—is bound to be superb, worth a good deal of money."

"Undoubtedly."

I set the tray down and turned to leave.

"You think me callous?" he inquired.

"It's not my place to judge you one way or another, Mr. Hawke."

"That's quite true. You do, though. I can see it in your eyes. You think me a callous, mercenary brute. Slaves are like cattle, extremely valuable livestock. Mine receive much better treatment than most."

"I don't doubt that."

"I feed 'em, I cloth 'em, I see that they have a warm, dry place to sleep, fetch a doctor for 'em when they're sick. I work 'em hard, yes, but that's what they're for."

"Indeed."

"I don't breed 'em for a profit—a number of planters I could name run regular breeding farms, even hire out their bucks for stud service. I don't do that, though I've been offered a pretty penny for Adam's services. When my fellow planters couldn't buy him from me, they wanted to rent him to service their wenches. I—hell, why should I be justifying myself to you!'

"Why indeed," I replied.

Hawke stared at me, not certain whether or not a rebuke was called for. Had I been impertinent? He had already pulled on his tall boots and gray breeches, but his chest was bare. His torso was lean and smoothly muscled. The sight was mildly disturbing, and I lowered my eyes, wishing he weren't so young and strong and handsome, wishing I could hate him as he deserved to be hated.

"If there's nothing else—" I began.

"We'll want to lighten Cassie's duties somewhat," he

92

informed me. "I wouldn't want to risk anything happening to the child. She's not to take on any of the heavy work, no lifting, no straining. I suppose I could bring one of the other wenches in to help out—" He hesitated, clearly not taken with the idea.

"That won't be necessary," I replied. "I can manage nicely with Cassie handling the lighter tasks."

"Fine," he said curtly.

I left the room and returned to the kitchen. Later, when I was certain he had left the house, I went back up to his room and made the bed, smoothing back the sheets that still smelled of his body, pulling the counterpane back over the pillows. As I ran my hands over the silky gold fabric, I wondered about this strange, enigmatic man who owned me, who was apparently unaware of me as a female. I wondered, too, about his wife, Alice, who had slept in a smaller room down the hall, the room he had assigned to me. What had happened to her, and why had it been necessary for them to have separate bedrooms?

Hawke had never once referred to her in my presence, and when I had questioned Cassie and Mattie about her, both women had looked frightened. Mattie finally confessed that the master had forbidden any of them to so much as mention her name.

"She wuz a bad un, Mis Marietta,' Mattie told me. "Lawd, what she done to th' master—it ain't fittin' to speak about."

She had refused to say more, and I had not pressured her. I wondered if Alice was responsible for that icy, impenetrable shell he had built around himself. It seemed likely, I thought, longing to know more about the woman who had once lived at Shadow Oaks, whose name Hawke forbade any of the servants to speak.

Cassie ordinarily carried Hawke's lunch out to him where he was working in the fields. I didn't know whether this qualified as "heavy work" or not, but after I had finished packing the basket and folding a clean cloth over it, I told the girl that I would take the master his lunch myself. Cassie looked relieved, for it was an extremely warm day, the sun blazing fiercely. The heat and the long walk to the north field wouldn't have been good for her.

Leaving by the kitchen door, I stepped outside, passed under the giant oaks that veiled the yard with hazy violet-gray shadows, and moved past the weathered old barn with hay spilling out of the loft, past the stables and the row of cabins. Half-naked black children were playing noisily in the sun. Two strapping wenches in cotton dresses and bandanas were stringing laundry up to dry. Mattie was sitting in a rocker in front of her cabin, heavy, lethargic, contentedly dipping her snuff. I smiled, waving, and the old slave acknowledged my wave with a nod. Her grandson, Caleb, was halfheartedly repairing a wheel on the old wooden wagon I had slept under so many weeks ago.

"Mawnin', Miz Marietta," the boy said pleasantly.

A tall, stringy youth of fourteen, Caleb had creamy, coffee-colored skin, enormous eyes, a slack mouth. Mattie called him "a no-'count nigger" and accused him of being shiftless and "totin' things that don't belong to him," but I found the boy warm and friendly, a dreamy lad who was undeniably slow-moving but always eager to do errands for me. Too thin and sickly to work in the fields, Caleb did odd jobs around the place, like repairing the wheel, although Mattie claimed he spent most of his time down by the creek fishing with a bamboo pole.

"You goin' to need me for somethin' this aft'noon, Miz Marietta?" he asked in his softly slurred voice.

"Not this afternoon, Caleb."

"You goin' to make some of them molasses cookies an' slip me some liken you did last week?"

"I'm afraid not, Caleb. I'm baking a peach pie for the master."

"Peach pie," he said dreamily. "Ol' Mattie don't never make us niggers somethin' like that."

"You ask real nicely, Caleb, and perhaps she will."

The boy sighed and went back to his work. I strolled under the oaks that bordered the grounds and started across the field of cotton that seemed to stretch to infinity. The sky was a hard steel-blue, the sunlight blinding, and heat waves rose from the ground and shimmered in the air above the rows of sturdy green plants. I was soon perspiring and the bodice of my blue cotton dress clung damply to my breasts. A white apron was belted tightly around my waist. I lifted a corner of it to wipe my face. My hair fell in deep waves that seemed heavy and damp. I wondered how men could possibly work hour after hour in such intense heat.

I could see Hawke and Adam in the distance. Both men had hoes, and they were clearing weeds from around a row of plants. Adam wore no shirt. His back and shoulders gleamed like varnished ebony. The sleeves of Hawke's white cotton shirt were rolled up over his forearms. The garment was plastered to his chest in wet patches. As I drew nearer, he put down his hoe and came toward me, removing his broad-brimmed straw hat and shoving a wet black lock from his forehead. Adam continued to work.

"You've brought my lunch," Hawke said.

"I didn't think Cassie should be out in this heat."

"Nor should you," he replied, taking the basket from me. "You could easily get sunstroke, not being used to it."

"Then you'd have to buy another housekeeper."

Hawke let the comment pass. He lifted the cloth and examined the food with considerable interest.

"Fried chicken, potato salad, cold biscuits with butter, even a jar of iced tea—you take good care of me, Marietta."

I was startled. It was the first compliment he had ever paid me.

"That's why I'm not going to do anything about that sarcastic remark," he continued. "I suggest you guard your tongue in the future, though. I'm not likely to overlook another such barb."

"Yes, sir," I said, elaborately meek.

"What are you serving for dinner tonight?"

"Ham hocks, beans, cornbread. I thought I'd bake a peach pie this afternoon."

"You spoil me, Marietta."

He gazed at me, and for a moment there was something like admiration in his eyes. Flushed, sweaty, a streak of dirt across his cheek, he didn't seem nearly as remote as he ordinarily was. That icy barrier was gone, and I sensed a warmth that had never been there before. He seemed about to say something more, and then he scowled, the steely reserve returning.

"Next time you come out in the sun, you wear a bonnet, you hear? I don't want you getting sick on me. And if you're going to bring my lunch to me, bring it on time! The niggers have already eaten their meal and come back to work. I should have had this basket an hour ago."

"You'll have it on time in the future."

"See that I do," he said curtly.

I turned and started back across the field, my cheeks burning. He was a monster, I told myself, without feeling. I had imagined that moment of warmth. I must have. Derek Hawke was incapable of warmth. incapable of any genuine human emotion. As I hurried back down the rows of cotton, I was horrified to feel my eyes stinging and trails of salty tears running down my cheeks. I brushed the tears away savagely, irate that I should have shed them. I was his servant, his slave, nothing more, and that's the way it would always be. I hated him, I told myself. I hated him with all my heart, and I was glad he never noticed me, glad he never come down the hall at night and into my bedroom. He was cold and ruthless and hard and . . . and I was *glad* he didn't want me in bed.

Passing under the oaks again, I moved more slowly across the yard, past the cabins, past stables and barn, trying to control the conflicting emotions inside. During those interminable weeks aboard ship, Jack had shown me the true meaning of passion, and he had proved beyond a doubt that I was my mother's daughter. Her blood was in my veins, but I would overcome it. I felt a hollow feeling in the pit of my stomach and an undeniable aching sensation inside every time I was near the man who owned me. I desired him, yes, but it was a purely physical sensation. I would thrust it aside. I would forbid myself ever to think of him in that way again. I would bank those fires in my blood, smother them, and I would be as icy and frigid as Derek Hawke was himself.

I worked furiously that afternoon, scrubbing the kitchen floor, cleaning woodwork, polishing the furniture in the front parlor. Later on, while Cassie sat at the kitchen table cleaning the silverware, I made the peach pie, sorry that I had mentioned it to him and was therefore obliged to make it. There would be no more special dishes in the future. I promised myself that. I would do the work he had brought me here to do, and I would cook his meals, but I would never again go out of my way to please him. He could take his peach pie and . . . and choke on it!

The kitchen window was open and after I took the pie out of the oven, I set it on the window sill to cool. As I did so, I heard a wagon coming around the side of the house. Hawke and his men were still out in the fields, and I wondered who could be calling at this time of afternoon. Wiping my hands on my apron, I stepped out the back door to see. The old farm wagon was pulled by a plump gray horse, and the woman holding the reins was almost as plump as her horse. Eccentrically dressed in scuffed black kid boots and a shabby emerald-green riding habit that was deplorably soiled, she had a lined, leathery face and wildly untidy steel-gray hair piled on top of her head in what resembled a bird's nest. Stopping the wagon under one of the oaks, she alighted with surprising agility for one her size.

"You must be Hawke's new housekeeper," she said warmly. "I'm Widow Simmons, gal. I own Magnolia Grove, the plantation to the east o' here. You can call me Maud. Everyone else does."

"I'm Marietta Danver."

"Lands sake, honey—I hope you don't mind my being

97

frank, but you don't look like no convict gal *I* ever saw, and you sure as hell didn't pick up that accent in the slums o' London. I mean no offense, honey."

"None taken, Mrs. Simmons."

"Maud, honey, call me Maud. I've been dyin' to meet you so's I could spread the word to all the other planters. We're a gossipy bunch, like to keep close tabs on each other. Hawke's a loner, keeps to himself, and that makes him all the more intriguing."

"What can I do for you?" I inquired.

"Actually, one of my horses pulled a muscle and I'm fresh outta liniment. Hawke generally keeps a bottle in the stables, and I thought I might borrow some."

"I'm sure he wouldn't mind. I'll go see if there is some."

"I'll tag along with you, honey. I rarely get a chance to chat with anyone. Runnin' a big plantation like Magnolia Grove ain't no job for a woman alone. I've been runnin' myself ragged ever since my Bill died goin' on twelve years ago."

As we strolled toward the stables, I noticed Caleb lingering under one of the oaks, watching us closely. Maud Simmons moved along beside me in brisk strides, chattering merrily. She seemed an amiable soul, frank and earthy, starved for a chance to talk. A pungent odor clung to the skirt of her emerald riding habit, and I noticed that her boots were caked with mud. I hoped it was mud. We found a bottle of liniment on a shelf in the stables, and after we stepped back outside she seemed reluctant to leave.

"I'm glad Hawke's got someone like you to take care of him," she confided. "I've been worried about him for some time, I don't mind tellin' you. Ever since that awful woman did him the way she did, he's been . . . well, antisocial ain't the word for it."

"Oh?"

"He never has anything to do with the rest of us, never comes visitin', never invites anyone to Shadow Oaks.

Ever since she ran out on him, he's kept to himself, brooding, nursing his bitterness."

I could see that she was eager to gossip, and although I knew it was wrong to encourage her, I couldn't resist the opportunity.

"I . . . I suppose you're referring to . . . Mrs. Hawke," I said. "I'm afraid I don't know anything about her. He's never mentioned her name."

"I ain't surprised," Maud replied. "It's been four years now since she ran off with that actor fellow, three years years since she died uv the fever in a squalid room in Charleston."

"She . . . she was unfaithful?"

"Unfaithful? Honey, that ain't the word for it. Even when they was first married and had just moved to Shadow Oaks, she had her eye on the other men. She was a pretty thing, one of them delicate blonds with sultry blue eyes and finicky ways. She wasn't finicky about men, though. She came from one of the best families in Carolina, but she had the morals of a trollop."

"Did he—love her?"

"He thought she hung the moon. In the beginning, that is. Later on, he stopped caring. He *forced* himself to stop caring. Her conduct was an open scandal, and she couldn't have cared less. Then this group of actors came to the neighborhood and pitched their tent and put on shows. Alice couldn't take her eyes off the leading man. When she ran off with him, I think Hawke was relieved. He refused to take her back. The actor dumped her after a few months, and she was stranded in Charleston without funds. She wrote to Hawke, begging him to come fetch her, but he wouldn't even answer the letter—" Maud paused, shaking her head.

"What happened?" I prompted.

"She found herself another man. Her kind always does. We finally heard that she had the fever—some say it was the fever, some say it was something else, something polite folks don't mention. A month later she was dead. Hawke sent money for her burial, but he refused to go

99

to Charleston for the funeral. He's been a different man ever since."

"I'm glad you told me all this," I said. "It helps me understand a lot of things."

Maud examined me closely, her head tilted to one side. "You in love with him, girl?"

The question took me by complete surprise. I flushed, unable to reply.

"You are," she remarked. "It's plain as day."

"I'm an indentured servant, a slave, and he—"

"That don't matter in the least, not when it comes to affairs of the heart." Maud took my hand and squeezed it tightly. "I don't know anything about you, girl, don't know how you happened to run afoul of the law, but I know character and breeding when I see it. Derek Hawke needs a woman like you, and I'm glad he's got you."

"I'm not his woman," I said stiffly. "I'm his house-keeper, nothing more."

Maud's leathery old face registered complete surprise. "You mean he hasn't—" She shook her head, the crazy gray bird's nest threatening to topple. "I find that hard to believe—a gal who looks like you, a man as healthy as Hawke—"

"Mrs. Simmons," I interrupted. "I really don't think it's any of—"

"Don't you fret, gal. He'll come round. He's bound to. That woman hurt him, hurt him bad, and no doubt he bears a grudge against all women for what she done to him, but he's a *man* and with a gal like you under the same roof—" She clicked her tongue. "It's just a matter of time, honey. Just a matter of time."

I made no reply, knowing anything I might say would be misinterpreted by this good-natured busybody. Maud said she'd best be getting back to Magnolia Grove, and I walked over to the wagon with her. Clutching the bottle of liniment, she swung nimbly up onto the seat, her swaying skirts exuding a pungent odor. She thanked me for the liniment, told me she'd had a delightful visit and, clicking the reins, bade me goodbye. I stood there under

100

the shade of the oak, watching her turn the wagon around in the back yard and circle around to the front of the house.

I lingered under the tree for a long time, thinking of all she had told me. Then, realizing that it was getting late and knowing I should already have started dinner, I went back into the house. Cassie had finished cleaning the silver and was getting ready to mix up the cornbread batter. I had put the beans on much earlier, and they were bubbling on top of the stove with scraps of ham for flavor. Cassie seemed apprehensive, her lovely brown eyes full of alarm.

"I'll do that," I said, taking the wooden spoon from her hand. "Dinner should be ready on time. I had no idea Mrs. Simmons was going to stay so long."

I cracked eggs on the side of the heavy blue bowl and began to beat them into the meal. At first I thought that Cassie was alarmed because she feared dinner would be late, but I could see that that wasn't what was bothering her. I asked her what was wrong, and the girl seemed reluctant to answer. She frowned, gently gnawing her lower lip.

"It—it's that pie, Miz Marietta. The one you done baked for th' master."

"What about it?"

"It's gone," she said. "One minute it was restin' there on th' window sill, coolin' off, and th' next minute it was gone. Someone took it, Miz Marietta. It wuzn't me, I swears it."

"Caleb," I said to myself.

"He was hangin' around in th' back yard. I wuzn't gonna say anything 'bout it—me, I don't wanna get no one in trouble—but it must-a been him, Miz Marietta. He's always takin' things, sneakin' into th' kitchen to see what he can tote off. Mattie used to get after him somethin' awful, but she never told on him—"

"I shan't tell on him, either, Cassie. I'll reprimand the boy myself. There's no reason why the master should find out about it."

"Th' master, he knows Caleb's totin' ways. Mattie never told on him, but th' master knowed anyway. He called Caleb in an' told him if he ever caught him stealin' food again, he'd peel his hide. He will, too. Th' master don't make idle threats."

"Don't worry, Cassie. I'll cover for him."

Through the open window I could hear the slaves returning to their cabins. Mattie and her girls were busy in the cookhouse, preparing the evening meal. I saw Caleb sauntering across the back yard, a satisfied expression on his face, and a few minutes later I heard Hawke come in. By the time he had washed and changed clothes, I had the table set in the dining room and was ready to serve his meal. He entered just as I was bringing the food in from the kitchen. As I placed it on the table, I told him that Mrs. Simmons had come by and that I had loaned her a bottle of liniment. Hawke grimaced, clearly disliking the woman, but he made no comment.

Returning to the kitchen, I found Adam and Cassie already sitting at the battered old wooden table. As Cassie took her meals here with me, I had requested that Adam be permitted to join us for dinner each evening. Hawke had shrugged his shoulders, saying that if I wanted the buck to eat in the kitchen with me it didn't matter to him. Cassie had set a place for me, and she was buttering the cornbread as I sat down. Both of them looked grim. I could tell that Cassie had already told her husband about the missing pie.

"That boy goin' to get his butt skinned yet," Adam said. His voice was deep and throaty, somewhere between a purr and a growl. "I told him, I says, 'Caleb, you better watch yore step, boy.' I told him th' master wuz just spoilin' for a chance to take th' whip to him, but he didn't pay me no mind. Effin th' master finds out—"

"He won't, Adam. Caleb's just a boy. I'll speak to him, and I'm sure he won't do anything like this again."

"That boy don't have no sense. He don't have no real job, jest gets to idle about while we's workin' in th' fields.

He have it easier'n anyone, and he pulls somethin' like this. I'd like to whup him myself."

"Eat your beans before they get cold, Adam," I said, more sharply than I had intended.

Adam scowled, his expression quite fierce. With his great size and immense strength he easily dominated the table. Despite his patched tan breeches and faded blue workshirt, I could easily imagine him as chief of some proud, savage African tribe. I thought it a shame that such a splendid man should be little more than a beast of burden. Slavery had existed ever since the Greeks, of course, but that made it none the less unsavory. For all practical purposes, I was a slave myself.

When Adam finished his plate of beans, Cassie lovingly spooned out more for him, then got up to fetch more cornbread. As she put it on the table, she rested her hands on his shoulder, rubbing it gently, her eyes glowing with a love poignant to behold. Cassie found it hard to believe she had such a man, and she found it difficult to keep from touching him at every opportunity, as though to reassure herself that he was real. Adam accepted her worship as his just due, and though he frequently scowled and pushed her away, pretending indifference, I knew that he was equally proud of her. On occasion, when he thought no one was observing, he let his guard down, and I had seen that same love burning in his eyes as he watched Cassie going about her duties.

Cassie rested her palm against the side of his thick neck, leaning over so that her right breast touched his arm. Adam shoved her away from him, his expression sullen, but as she took her seat again, his dark eyes took in her voluptuous curves and his face muscles tightened. There could be no mistaking what was on his mind. Both of them were eager to get back to their cabin. Sometimes, when I thought of the passionate bouts of love they shared each night, I felt an emptiness inside. Their love and the pleasure each gave the other in such full measure made my loneliness seem all the harder to bear.

I had just finished my meal when I heard the bell ring

103

in the dining room. I went to see what Hawke wanted, surprised that he was still at the table. Ordinarily he retired to the library-study for a glass of port as soon as he finished eating.

"You wanted something?" I inquired.

"I'm waiting for the pie," he said.

"It—" I hesitated, nervous. "I—I'm afraid there isn't any."

"No? I thought you told me you were going to bake a peach pie."

"Did I? I—there was so much to do, you see, and then Mrs. Simmons came and—"

"Why are you so nervous?" Hawke scrutinized me with those dark gray eyes. "You're hiding something, Marietta."

"That's absurd. I just—"

"Did you or did you not bake a pie this afternoon?" His voice was stern, and there was a deep crease between his brows.

"No, I didn't," I replied, trying to keep my voice from trembling.

Hawke got up from the table and moved briskly across the room, throwing open the door to the kitchen. I followed him, my heart beating rapidly. Cassie and Adam leaped to their feet, looking at him with guilty expressons.

"You, Cassie," Hawke said brusquely, "did Miss Marietta bake a pie this afternoon?"

Cassie glanced at me, her eyes full of misery. I shook my head quickly, praying the girl would give the right answer.

"Answer me!" Hawke thundered.

"Ye—yessir," Cassie stammered. "She baked one."

"What happened to it?"

"It done disappeared."

"Disappeared?"

"Miz Marietta set it over there on th' window sill to cool an' then that lady in th' wagon come an'—an' I wuz cleanin' th' silver and that pie just vanished."

"Was Caleb anywhere around?"

"Well sir, I—"

"I *gave* the pie to him," I said quickly. "He was hungry, and—"

Hawke whirled around, his eyes flashing. "You shut up! Adam, go and fetch Caleb. Take him out to the barn and tie him up. I warned him about stealing food. It's time he had a lesson!"

Adam hurried out the back door. Cassie began to cry. I gathered her in my arms, staring at Derek Hawke with fear and loathing. He stood with his hands on his thighs, legs spread apart, his face a mask of rage. I had never seen him like this, and it was frightening. I wanted to plead with him for the boy's sake, but I was afraid to open my mouth. He glared at me for a moment, and then left the room. I could hear him going upstairs to fetch his riding crop.

"I—I wuz afraid to lie, Miz Marietta," Cassie sobbed. "I was afraid he'd blame *me*."

"That's all right, Cassie," I said, releasing her. "Stop crying now. There's nothing either of us can do."

I heard loud, frantic wails in the back yard and, stepping over to the window, saw Adam holding Caleb by the wrist, pulling him toward the barn. The boy struggled violently, wailing all the while, and Adam finally wrenched his arm up between his shoulder blades and clamped a hand over his mouth. Caleb squirmed, looking like a tiny, helpless doll in the clutches of the powerful black man. They disappeared into the barn, and a moment later I saw Hawke strolling under the oaks, riding crop in hand. I could feel the color leave my cheeks when he stepped into the barn. I turned to Cassie, my throat so tight I could hardly speak.

"You—you'd best go start clearing the dining room table," I told her. "We have a lot of work to do."

I began to stack up the dishes and cooking utensils. There was an ominous silence in the barn. Cassie came back in with more dishes. As she set them down, a plate slipped and fell to the floor with a loud crash. Both of us jumped. Cassie began to sob again. I spoke to her sharply, ordering her to sweep up the pieces and dispose

105

of them in the dustbin. I was tense, listening, waiting, and finally there came a sharp, hissing sound immediately followed by a bloodcurdling scream. It seemed to go through me like an arrow. My knees buckled. I gripped the drainboard tightly to keep from falling.

The sounds came again, and again, and I knew I couldn't stand it any longer. Without stopping to think, I flew out the back door and hurried across the yard. I stumbled over the root of an oak tree and fell to the ground, my breath knocked out of me. As I climbed to my feet there was another sharp hiss, another shrill scream. I rushed to the barn, catching hold of the door to steady myself. Fading gold rays of sunlight streamed into the interior, illuminating the nightmare scene.

Caleb was naked, his wrists strapped together, the rope pulled taut over one of the rafters, forcing the boy to stand on his tiptoes. His back was to me, so I couldn't see his face, but I saw the bare buttocks, the smooth brown skin already streaked with tiny red threads. Adam stood in the shadows beside the ladder leading up to the loft, holding the boy's clothes, his face expressionless. Hawke stood behind the boy, and as I watched, he flexed his wrist and drew his arm back again. The riding crop sliced through the air with a savage hiss, and the thin leather thongs made contact. Caleb's body jerked convulsively, and his scream was deafening, one long, shrill note of agony.

Hawke drew his arm back to strike again.

"No!" I cried.

I rushed over to him and seized his arm. He was startled, that for a moment he stood immobile, staring at me with cold fury. Then he caught me by the shoulders and thrust me away from him with such force that I crashed against the wall several feet away. I crumpled to the ground against some sacks of grain, so stunned that it took me a moment to focus properly. Hawke spread his legs, took careful aim and slashed again, and again, and again. When he finally stopped, his white shirt

106

was drenched with perspiration, plastered wetly against his back and shoulders.

He put the riding crop down. Caleb hung limply, almost unconscious. Hawke shoved his hair back from his forehead and turned to Adam. He looked weary now, all anger spent.

"Cut him down," he ordered. "Take him to his grandmother and see that she tends to him properly." He prodded Caleb's calf with the toe of his boot. "You, boy—I hope you learned your lesson. You got off lightly this time, just ten lashes. If there's a next time, it'll be fifty."

Caleb sobbed something unintelligible. Hawke turned to look down at me. I was still on the ground, clinging to one of the bulging sacks as though for support.

"Don't you *ever* try to interfere like that again, do you understand?" His voice was chilling. "You may be white, you may speak with a fine accent, but you're my property, same as they are. You try something like this again and you'll pay for it. You'll pay dearly."

Then he turned around and walked out of the barn. The orange light was fading rapidly, deep blue-black shadows gathering. Adam took a knife and cut the rope. Caleb collapsed on the ground in a heap, sobbing. Adam scowled and pulled him to his feet.

"You goin' live, boy. Stop that blubberin'. You done brought it all on yoreself." He thrusts the boy's clothes at him and wrapped a powerful arm around his shoulders to keep him from falling. "Stop that blubberin', I says. Th' master only give you what you deserved."

Holding the boy firmly against him, Adam turned to look at me.

"You all right, Miz Marietta?"

I nodded, not trusting myself to speak.

"Want I should send Cassie out to you?"

I shook my head, and Adam looked hesitant, not certain whether he should leave me alone or not. Caleb whimpered quietly. After a moment Adam frowned and tightened his grip around the boy's shoulder, leading him out of the barn. I sat huddled there against the sack of grain and watched the orange light glow paler and paler as the shadows multiplied. A few chickens wandered into the barn, clucking noisily and scratching the dirt. A long time passed, and still I sat there, nourishing a terrible pain that had nothing to do with my fall. When I finally forced myself to get up and leave the barn, the first stars had already begun to twinkle frostily against the cold night sky.

IV

Caleb waved and came running as I started across the back yard carrying the lunch basket. It had been two weeks since he had been whipped, and I hadn't seen him since then. He showed no effects of the beating now, I noticed, pausing under one of the oaks to talk to him.

"What you got in that there basket?" the lad inquired. "Somethin' good to eat?"

I nodded. Caleb wore an expectant look. "I'm afraid it's not for you, Caleb. I'm taking it to the master out in the fields."

"When you goin' to bake some more of them cookies?"

"I—one of these days, Caleb. Doesn't Mattie feed you?"

"I reckon," he drawled, "but she don't make good things like you does, Miz Marietta. That peach pie—I reckon it wuz worth th' whuppin' th' master give me."

"How are you, Caleb? I haven't seen you around."

"Mattie, she done forbid me to hang around th' back yard. She says I gotta stay back behind th' cabins mendin' things lessen you sends me for somethin'. I been bein' busy, fixin' things an' helpin' Mattie. My backside wuz sure sore, but Mattie done put some stuff on it for a couple-a-days an it's healed up now. Th' master, when he whups, he whups good. There ain't nothin' in that basket he wouldn't miss?"

He looked for all the world like a great, gawking

puppy dog, his wide brown eyes full of entreaty. Unable to resist, I reached into the basket, took out a crisp brown drumstick and handed it to the boy. Caleb's eyes lit up with pleasure and, taking the drumstick eagerly, he bounded away just as Mattie stuck her head out of the door of the cookhouse and yelled for him to get back to work 'fore she kicked him good. Caleb disappeared behind the cabins, Mattie shook her head in despair, and I waved, calling good day to her.

It was an extremely warm day, the sun pouring down in furious rays, but this time I wore an old wide-brimmed yellow straw hat with brown ribbons that tied under my chin. The hat protected my face, but my dress was soon damp with prespiration. Light beige cotton sprigged with tiny brown and blue flowers, it was faded and patched, the puffed sleeves dropping off the shoulders, the bodice low-cut and clinging tightly. Shabby as it was, it was the most fetching garment I owned, and I wondered if Derek Hawke would notice the way it accentuated my bosom and slender waist. Probably not, I told myself, moving along the rows of cotton.

I had hardly exchanged a dozen words with him since the incident in the barn. He had not referred to it, nor had I, but since then his manner had been even colder and more remote. When it was necessary for him to give me an order, his voice was like chipped ice, his expression always harsh. After what his wife did to him, I supposed he was not anxious to get entangled again. Of course, I was his chattel, his property, and, as a woman, beneath his notice. I accepted that, and I fought the feelings he was able to arouse simply by being in the same room with me. I tried to hate him, tried desperately, yet I couldn't help feeling that behind that icy barricade dwelt an extremely vulnerable man greatly in need of warmth and understanding.

Mattie sounded the gong in the cookhouse. The blacks working in the fields put down their tools and started toward the line of oak trees where, under the shade of the boughs, they would have their lunch. I saw Adam in

110

the distance, moving toward the trees with the others, towering over them. Hawke never lunched with the slaves. Although he permitted them half an hour's break for their meal, he stayed out in the fields himself, pausing just long enough to eat the basket lunch brought to him, then going right on with his work.

I wondered why he drove himself so hard. The other planters didn't. When she had come back to Shadow Oaks to return the liniment, Maud Simmons had told me quite a lot about life among the gentlemen planters. Most of them, I learned, had hired men to manage their plantations for them, leaving them free to live a clubbish sort of life with cool drinks on the verandah and hunting parties and constant socializing at their various plantation houses. Hawke had never participated in any of these leisurely pastimes, had always taken the full responsibility of Shadow Oaks on his own shoulders. He had done extremely well, too, Maud confided. The annual yield at Shadow Oaks had been more than satisfactory, and by rights Hawke should have a tidy sum stashed away in the bank at Charleston. He didn't. There was only a few hundred dollars in his account there. Maud had discovered this the last time she had made a deposit and had talked with that charming bank manager. What on earth, she wondered, had happened to all of Hawke's money? It was a question I was unable to answer.

He certainly hadn't poured it back into Shadow Oaks. True, I had cost a great deal—more than he could afford, he had told me—but I knew that he had bought no other slaves during the past four years, nor had he spent money refurbishing the house. Everything was shabby and run-down, and to all outward appearances Shadow Oaks was little more than a farm. Yet his crops had consistently brought him a great deal of money, as much as many of the larger plantations. It was a bloomin' mystery, Maud told me, adding that she had heard rumors that he had been sending vast sums to a lawyer back in London for a period of years. Hawke had come from England originally, though no one knew anything about his background there. He'd simply appeared in Carolina, married Alice Cavenaugh and promptly purchased Shadow Oaks "for a song," turning a broken-down, second-rate plantation into one that yielded a generous profit each year. He'd been here for ten years, ever since he was twenty-three years old, and for ten years he had lived like a poor man.

I had thought about all Maud had told me as I strolled across the fields, basket in hand. I had always assumed that Shadow Oaks was poor, that Hawke had to struggle to make ends meet, yet as I gazed at the acres and acres of vivid green plants—and this was only one section of fields—I could easily see how the harvested crop would bring in a large sum. I couldn't help wondering what had happened to the money. Was he indeed sending it back to a lawyer in England? If so, why? The more I learned about Derek Hawke, the more enigmatic he became.

I could see him up ahead now, working with a hoe. His boots were covered with dust. His dark tan breeches were old, almost threadbare. His thin white cotton shirt was damp with sweat, open at the throat, sleeves rolled up over his forearms. Although he was superbly built and wonderfully handsome, he nevertheless looked like a poor dirt farmer. Why? He could be sitting on the verandah in glossy boots and an elegant suit, taking his ease. Why did he live in a poorly furnished, tumbledown house when he could transform it into a fine mansion? Hearing me approach, he turned around, leaning on his hoe. As those cool gray eyes rested on me, I felt that familiar response inside, wanting him, hating myself for it.

"Cassie ill?" he inquired. This was the first time I had brought him his lunch since the day I had baked the peach pie.

"She's busy at the house, polishing the parlor furniture. I didn't want to interrupt her. so I decided to bring you your lunch myself."

"You're not working her too hard?"

"Indeed I'm not," I said coldly.

112

Hawke didn't like my tone, but he made no comment, taking the basket from me. He smelled of sweat and soil. His wide. beautifully shaped mouth was set in a stern line. Why did I have to visualize those generously curved lips parting, spreading to cover my own? Why should the very sight of him cause my pulse to race when I had every reason to loathe him? Hawke leaned on his hoe, idly gazing at me, and I had the feeling he knew full well the effect he had on me, no matter how I tried to conceal it.

"I see you wore a hat this time," he remarked.

"As ordered."

"You've never worn that dress before."

"You disapprove of it?"

"I couldn't care less what you wear as long as you do your work. You look like a waterfront whore, but that hardly matters—" He shrugged his shoulders to indicate his indifference.

"That's what you think I am," I said acidly. "You never believed what I told you about my background. You've always thought I was a common criminal, a—"

"It matters to you what I think?" he asked.

"Not in the least, Mr. Hawke."

He arched one eyebrow, his lips curling at the corners in faint amusement. "Perhaps you wish I'd gone ahead and let Jeff Rawlins have you. That kind of life might have suited you much better."

"I'm sure you think so," I replied.

"I think you'd be a superb whore," he said idly. "You'd make a grand mistress, too, no doubt, a beautiful plaything for some man with more money than sense. Is that what you expected me to do with you—make you my mistress? You're a fetching wench—you're well aware of that, of course. Mirrors don't lie—but I paid good money for a housekeeper and cook, not some red-haired hussy to wrestle with in bed."

I could feel my cheeks burning. I longed to fly at him with claws unsheathed. Hawke seemed to read my mind, and he was clearly amused, had been deliberately baiting

113

me. The anger seethed through me, and when I spoke my voice trembled.

"I consider myself fortunate that you haven't—haven't made demands on me. Not many men would have such scruples."

"Scruples? I've very few of those, I assure you. I do have good sense, though—sense enough not to bed some wench just because she's got a body designed by the devil and eyes like blue fire, a wench who's plainly all to amenable to a nice, long—"

I swung my hand back and slapped him across the face with all the strength I could muster. I hit out instinctively, without thinking, and was almost as startled as he was. Hawke let out a shocked cry, dropping the hoe. The side of his face turned a bright, burning pink. My hand stung painfully, and I gasped, horrified at what I had done. He stared at me, stunned, and then his eyes burned with anger and his mouth became a hard, tight line as he balled his fist and delivered a powerful blow that sent me reeling back against the plants. I fell to the ground, green stalks crushing under me, and the sky seemed to turn from blue to black as pain exploded inside my head.

Half-conscious, I stared up at him. He loomed over me, his legs wide apart, both hands balled into fists now, and I knew he would probably kill me. My head seemed to spin; my jaw was on fire, and I was seeing him through a wet, misty veil that wavered and blurred outlines and caused everything to tilt and topple: the tall green plants standing tall all around me, the man, tilting crazily, the sky above him blue now, spinning like my head. I sobbed, forcing myself to rise up on one elbow, and it was then that I heard the hiss and saw the rope uncoiling and saw it fly through the air and attach itself to Hawke's thigh.

Derek Hawke screamed. Then he took the rope in his hand and hurled it to the ground where it writhed and spat and coiled itself to strike again. I realized with horror that it was not a rope, but a snake, one of the deadly copperheads Mattie had warned me about. Hawke seized the hoe and struck at the snake and its tail seemed to fly straight up in the air, its head still rooted to the ground by the hoe. It thrashed and flailed and Hawke jammed the heel of his boot on the hoe, crushing the metal into the ground, and the horrible flailing finally stopped as the snake's head was severed from its body.

Hawke dropped the hoe, gripping his thigh. I climbed quickly to my feet, my own pain forgotten as I saw the look on his face. My heart was beating rapidly and my head was still reeling. Hawke sobbed. His cheekbones were the color of chalk. He seemed about to fall face down. I stumbled forward, seizing his arm.

"What can I do? Derek! What can I—"

"God! Oh. God! The knife! Quick, the knife—"

"I—I don't—"

"It's folded up in my pocket. The left pocket. Get it! For God's sake, Marietta, get it quickly!"

I jammed my hand into his pocket and pulled out the long bone-handled knife with its blade folded up. Hawke gasped and almost fell on top of me, throwing his arms around me for support. I staggered under his weight, holding him, more frightened than I had ever been in my life. He clung to me, his eyes half-crazed with fear and shock and pain. I think he passed out for a moment, his head falling on my shoulders, his body limp, and then he raised his head and looked into my eyes and tried to speak coherently.

"You—you'll have to cut—to cut my leg where it bit. —Do you understand? You'll have to cut and then—the venom—you'll have to suck the venom out of—"

I nodded, and he let go of me and tried to stand up straight, weaving to and fro. He finally steadied himself, and I dropped to my knees and opened the knife, the blade glittering in the sunlight. Gripping the back of his leg with one hand, I cut away the threadbare tan cloth and exposed the already-swelling flesh of his thigh with the fang marks two tiny dots, the skin around them

115

puffed up, turning yellow and brown and violet. Hawke staggered and almost fell.

"Do it! Quickly!"

"I couldn't. I knew I couldn't. I stared at the discolored flesh and shook my head and knew I could never drive the knife into it! Never! But then he let out such an agonized groan that I bit my lower lip and sliced the swelling flesh and blood spurted, flowing down his leg. He staggered again and grabbed hold of my shoulders to brace himself, and I put my mouth to the wound and sucked and spit out the blood and sucked again and again, knowing his life depended on it. His hands gripped my shoulders tightly, violently, bruising the flesh, and I was showered with the sweat that poured from his body. When finally I was through, he sighed and loosened his grip and I stood up and he wrapped his arms around my neck, holding on to me like an impassioned lover, dazed, almost unconscious.

"You—you're still bleeding. I should tie up the—"

"Let it bleed. The house. You must get—Mattie has herbs—a poultice. She'll know what—"

I managed to turn him around so that he was at my side, one arm still crooked around my neck, the forearm pressed against my throat; I held on to his forearm and wrapped my other arm around his waist and we started forward, both of us stumbling. I could never make it. He was much too heavy, and I was supporting almost his full weight. I tripped and fell on one knee, bringing him down with me, and his arm gripped my throat, half-strangling me. I managed to get back up, and somehow we moved down the rows of tall green plants, both of us prespiring heavily, clothing drenched, skin gleaming wetly. He was in a delirium now, had no idea where he was or what had happened. I called upon all my strength and forced myself to move and forced him to move along with me. Blood still streamed from his leg, but that was good, I knew, for it probably contained the deadly venom, but he was growing weaker and weaker by the minute, and if he bled too much he might . . . I stumbled forward, holding him tightly, dragging him with me, and then we were in sight of the oak trees and I called out.

Adam came rushing along the rows of cotton, several other slaves behind him. "Snake," I whispered hoarsely. "Copperhead." That was all I needed to say. Adam snapped orders, commanding one of the slaves to fetch Mattie, commanding another to rush to the cookhouse and start water boiling immediately Then he gathered Hawke up in his arms, cradling him against his massive chest, and hurried toward the line of oak trees I staggered along behind him, under the trees, across the yard, through the back door and into the kitchen.

"Upstairs, Adam," I said. "In his bedroom. Cassie, is—"

"Mattie done got the news. She's gatherin' her herbs already, fixin' to make that poultice. You better sit down, Miz Marietta. You look awful, face all white like a ghost. I'll—"

"I've got to go upstairs with Adam. I have to stay with him. He might die, and—"

"Don't you worry now," Cassie said gently. "Mattie knows what to do. Them snakes has bit lotsa folks, an' Mattie's herbs always works. She'll have that poultice ready in no time. Th' master ain't gonna die."

I hurried out of the kitchen and down the hall after Adam, following him up the stairs and into the bedroom. I yanked the counterpane and top sheet down to the foot of the bed, and Adam tenderly placed his master on the bed. Hawke groaned, unconscious now. I told Adam to go fetch some cloths and a bowl of water, and as he left the room I sat down on the side of the bed, took hold of Hawke's shoulders and lifting him up into a sitting position, pulled his shirt off him and tossed it on the floor. He gave a loud groan as I eased him back against the pillows and smoothed the damp hair away from his forehead.

He opened his eyes and looked up at me, and I knew he didn't know who I was, knew that he wasn't seeing me at all. I stroked his forehead and rested my hand

117

against that lean, smooth cheek I had slapped so viciously such a short time ago. He tried to say something, but no words would come and his eyes filled with panic.

"It's going to be all right," I said softly. "Everything is going to be all right—"

Adam returned with the water and cloths, Cassie entering the room behind him, and I told Adam he'd have to help me remove Hawke's boots and breeches. Adam nodded. Hawke cried out as the tall black man started pulling off his boots. He flung his arm out, hitting me across the side of my neck, almost knocking me off the bed.

"I reckon you'd better hold him down, Miz Marietta," Adam told me in his husky growl. "It's gonna hurt him, gettin' this boot off, and he ain't gonna like it a bit."

I leaned over Hawke and placed my hands on his shoulders as Adam tugged at the boot. Hawke fought viciously, trying to throw me off, but he was too weak to do so now, and he finally passed out as first one boot, then the other dropped to the floor. Removing his breeches was much easier. When he was naked, I dipped a cloth into the water and began to bathe his face. His leg was still swollen and discolored, but not nearly so much as it had been before. Blood seeped out of the wound in tiny trickles. He was still now, unconscious, breathing heavily. I bathed his shoulders and chest, and when I dipped a fresh cloth into the cool water and applied it to his wound, he showed no reaction at all. Adam and Cassie stood silently on the other side of the bed, both looking grave and worried. Cassie rested against her husband, and Adam curled his arm around her shoulders, holding her close.

I had just finished bathing him when Mattie came bustling into the room, moving quite briskly for a woman her size. She carried a platter covered with what looked like mud, still steaming with heat, filling the air with a pungent odor. I moved away from the bed and watched her cake the mixture over his wound. I was in a daze myself now, and I seemed to be seeing everything through

118

a shimmering haze. My body ached painfully. My jaw was sore. I was praying, praying that he would be all right, and I was crying, too, hardly aware of the tears slipping down my cheeks.

"There," Mattie said, applying a final pat of the muddy goo. "I'll just bind it up with a clean rag an' he'll be right as rain in no time. Lucky you wuz there tuh suck th' venom out, Miz Marietta. If you hadn't of, he'd-a died for sure."

"Is—is he going to be all right?"

"Oh, he'll have a fever for a day or so. He'll toss an' turn and carry on, an' he'll sweat like a pig, but when that fever breaks, he'll be mendin' licketysplit, be back out workin' hisself to death in three or four days. You don't worry none now, yuh hear?"

"I was so—so frightened."

"Reckon you wuz, gal, reckon you wuz. You lookin' plumb sickly yoreself. I want you to go wash yourself an' change them clothes and take a nap 'fore you fall in your tracks."

"I—I'll have to stay with him. He might—"

"Me an' Cassie'll watch after him for a while an' you can spell us after you've waked up." She turned to Adam, her expression suddenly fierce. "You, boy!" she snapped. "Get back out in them fields and get them niggers back to work! I reckon that's what th' master's gonna be most concerned with when he comes 'round, and I reckon you're th' one who's gotta take charge-a th' works while he's in bed."

Adam scowled, resenting her tone. "Yes, *ma'am*," he retorted.

"Don't you get uppity with *me*, boy! You may be a hulkin' brute of a buck, but I figures I could still take you over my knee if I wuz a mind to! Get on outta here now!"

Adam grinned in spite of himself, and when he was gone, the enormous black woman shook her head and clicked her tongue and told Cassie she was one lucky wench, havin' a buck like that in her bed every night.

Cassie was still too alarmed to respond, and Mattie told her to switch her tail out to her cabin and fetch the tin of snuff she'd left on the porch. Cassie left, but I still stood at the front of the bed, wringing my hands. The old woman pulled a chair over to the side of the bed and settled her great body into it, sighing wearily.

"You go on an' mind me, Miz Marietta," she said gently. "Your man's goin' be jest fine. Them herbs is already pullin' th' rest of th' poison outta his system. Aint no need sendin' for a white doctor, either, 'cause it'd take two days to get one here an' by that time th' master'd be outta bed an' mean as ever. Go on, git! I'm tired-a lookin' at you!"

I went to my room and undressed and washed and changed into a clean petticoat. Even though I knew it would be impossible to sleep, I stretched out on the bed and watched the rays of hot afternoon sun stealing into the room through the open windows. I closed my eyes, frightened, worried, sore all over, my jaw throbbing painfully, and I seemed to sink into a nest of darkness, floating through the shadows. When I opened my eyes, the room was filled with a heavy violet-gray mist. The curtains billowed softly as cool breezes drifted in from outside. Alarmed, I sat up, realizing that I must have slept for hours. The sun had already set, the last vestiges of twilight turning into night. I lit an oil lamp and brushed my hair. Then I slipped on a clean blue cotton dress and, barefooted, hurried down the hall to the master bedroom.

"Here you is," Mattie said warmly, shifting in her chair, "an' you look all rested up, too. I goin' get on back to my cabin now, I reckon. He goin' sleep th' rest of th' night."

"Is—is he all right?"

"Oh, he's been tossin' 'bout some, mumblin' in his sleep. Sweated somethin' terrible, too, an' me an' Cassie done changed th' sheets, rollin' him over to get 'em on. Th' master didn't like that none, but it wuz somethin' had to be done. I fed him some broth a while back— don't want him starvin' on us."

"Thank you for all you've done, Mattie. I'll take over now."

"Nursin's 'bout all I'm good for now, that an' bossin' them wenches in th' cookhouse. That Cassie's still hangin' around in th' kitchen, didn't wanna go join her man till you wuz up. On my way out I'm goin' have her fix a bowl of that broth an' bring it up to you. You eat it, hear?"

I nodded, distracted, looking at Hawke. Mattie heaved a sigh, put the tin of snuff in the pocket of her apron and climbed heavily to her feet. She shuffled over to give me a hug, and I found myself dangerously near to tears for the second time that day. Mattie looked into my eyes, her own full of sympathy and understanding, for Mattie had known all along what I was just now beginning to realize.

"It's goin' work out, Miz Marietta," she told me. "He went an' builded a fence around hisself after that woman done him th' way she did. He won't let hisself feel like other men, 'fraid he'll get hurt again, but one-a these days he's goin' open his eyes an' see what's right here in front of 'em, an' that's th' day you goin' be th' happiest woman alive."

Mattie hugged me again and left the room. I could hear her moving ponderously down the stairs, heaving and puffing as she went. She knew I was in love with Derek Hawke, and I hadn't even suspected it, not until this afternoon when he had nearly died. I was attracted to him, strongly attracted from the very first, and I had told myself that was all it was: physical attraction. When had it turned into love, I wondered, for love him I did, deeply, with every fiber of my being. His very presence caused a joyous glow inside, a heady sensation as though I were inebriated from the finest of wine. The physical attraction remained, an aching torment, but it was only part of something even stronger, something that filled me like sweet, silent music.

Hawke moaned in his sleep, flinging out an arm, kicking at the sheet pulled up over his chest. The room was stuffy, and I stepped over to the windows to let in the cool night air. The oak boughs outside the window groaned, leaves rustling crisply, and I could see fireflies in the distance, soft golden lights glowing on and off in the dense shadows around the shrubbery. The long gold brocade draperies swelled in the breeze, flapping gently. I turned as Cassie entered the room with the bowl of soup. I told her to set it down by the bed and then turned back to gaze out of the window, not wanting to talk just now. The girl tiptoed out of the room, and I gazed up at the velvety-black sky frosted with stars like chipped diamonds glittering.

"Marietta," he said.

I turned. He was looking at me, weak, his beautiful face as pale as ivory, dark gray eyes surrounded by shadow. I stepped over to the bed and sat down beside him and took his hand, and he looked up at me silently. The cold, ruthless Hawke I knew had been replaced by a man who needed my warmth, my love.

"Doan—don't go," he pleaded. His voice was a hoarse croak.

"I'll be here, Derek."

"You . . . called . . . called me . . . Derek."

"Yes, love," I whispered.

"Dis-- disrespec—ful wench."

I placed my fingers over his mouth, gently touching the firm pink flesh. "Hush now," I said. "Don't try to talk. I'm going to give you some more of Mattie's broth."

"Doan—don't want it."

"You're going to eat it. You've lost a lot of blood. You need to get your strength back."

I eased him into a sitting position and propped the pillows behind him, and then I fed him the soup Cassie had brought for me. He made a face, trying to look threatening, but he obediently opened his mouth each time I carried the spoon to his lips. Only one lamp burned in the corner of the room, creating a softly diffused yellow glow, and the rest of the room was dim and hazy, blue-gray shadows spreading over the walls. The draperies

122

stirred as the cool breezes drifted in and out. Derek finished the broth and closed his eyes, and he was fast asleep even before I pulled the pillows away from his back. I sat there beside him, gazing down at his face, a luxury I had never been able to indulge in before.

Hours passed, and he slept peacefully, and then, around two in the morning, he began to mumble, frowning in his sleep. He began to sweat profusely, and I took a cloth and wiped his brow. He tossed and turned, grimacing, and I stroked his cheek, murmuring endearments, hoping to calm him. After fifteen minutes or so, he grew still. I sighed with relief and started to get up off the bed. He sat up abruptly, his eyes wide open, crazed. He seized my wrist, clamping his fingers around it so tightly that I winced at the pain.

"Don't go!" he thundered angrily.

"I—I was just—"

"They all go! All of them! *She* did—my mother. She left me in that horrible damp brown school and went away and I never saw her again—"

His eyes were full of venomous hatred, and he twisted my wrist viciously, pulling me across his chest. He was in a delirium, had no idea what he was saying or whom he was saying it to. I realized that, but I was frightened nevertheless. If he had been weak before, he now seemed changed with super-human strength. He caught both my wrists and pinioned them to the bed.

"And Alice—that bitch! I loved her—" His voice broke in something like a sob. "One day I could have given her everything she ever wanted, but she couldn't wait! It might take years to get it settled, I told her, but it'll be settled, I said, it'll be settled and we'll win and Hawkehouse will be ours and you'll have a title and riches and—but she left! She left me, just like my mother did, just like they all do!"

"Derek! You're hurting me—"

"They go! Can't trust 'em! Can't trust any of 'em—"

He let go of my wrists and seized my throat, his fingers tightening furiously. I cried out, and he choked off the cry, laughing demoniacally, and I thought I was going to die as the blood rushed to my head and my vision began to blur. He squeezed, his fingers digging into the soft flesh of my throat, and then, abruptly, he released me, and when I opened my eyes I saw him gazing down at me in total bewilderment. A deep crease cut between his brows as he frowned.

"Marietta? What did I—"

"You were delirious—" I whispered hoarsely, barely able to speak.

"I hurt you? I hurt you, yes, because you were created by the devil, you see—" His voice was tender, caressing, and I realized that he still had no idea what he was saying, was still delirious even though the mood was entirely different.

"I saw you, and I knew Rawlins couldn't have you, knew I had to have you myself—" and he pulled me toward him gently.

"Yes—" I whispered. "Yes—let me take off my dress—"

"Yes," he moaned. "Marietta, sweet, sweet—"

And then the energy seemed to go out of him and he went limp. I sat on the side of the bed and pulled him toward me. His head rested on my shoulder, his lips touching my right breast, and he slept, the delirium over. I stroked the back of his head, his shoulders, running my hands over the muscles of his back. A gust of strong wind swept into the room and blew out the lamp. The room was plunged into darkness dense and black, soon softened by moonlight. I held him against me, savoring each moment, knowing I might never again feel his warmth, his weight, might never be able to touch and explore the texture of his skin, his hair.

He slept deeply, shifting position only occasionally. Moonlight faded and darkness lifted slowly, ever so slowly, and it was as the first pinkish rays of dawn seeped into the room that he gave a mighty yawn and rolled off away from me, clutching one of the pillows with both his arms and cradling it against the side of his face. I slipped carefully off the bed and adjusted the bodice of my dress. On his stomach now, stark naked, he slept, the strengthening sunlight streaming through the windows and across his legs and buttocks.

Leaving the room, I went down to the kitchen, where Cassie was already preparing a pot of strong coffee. I sat down at the battered wooden table and accepted a cup of coffee, shaken by what had happened, what had almost happened, wondering how much of it he would recall.

Derek slept most of the day, waking only twice, and then only long enough to eat. While he was asleep Mattie removed the bandage and took off the poultice. She stared at the wound and nodded her head in satisfaction, and then she washed it and applied some medicine and put on a new bandage, but Derek didn't wake up. I sat in the chair beside his bed throughout the night. He woke once and asked for water. I held the glass for him, and he cupped his hands around mine and drank, falling back to sleep immediately. When morning came I went back to my room and changed and then joined Cassie in the kitchen.

When I came into his room with the breakfast tray, he was sitting up in bed wearing a shabby navy blue velvet dressing robe with black velvet lapels. His hair was brushed, and he was freshly shaved, smelling of talcum powder. Although most of his pallor was gone, there were still faint shadows under his eyes, and he looked drawn. I paused, startled, and he arched one eyebrow, looking at me as though I were an irritating, dim-witted child.

"Are you going to give me my breakfast, or are you going to stand there all morning?"

"You—you got out of bed."

"Of course I did," he said patiently.

"But—your leg—"

"I had to hobble a bit, but I could stand on it long enough to shave. It's healing fast. If you're finished gawking, Marietta, I'd appreciate my breakfast. I'm ravenous."

I set the tray on the bedside table and stepped back. "I—I'm glad to see you feeling so much better. You were in a bad way there for a while."

"It seems I'm going to recover. I assume Mattie put one of her famous poultices on my leg?"

I nodded, nervous, at a loss for words. Hawke looked up at me with an irritable expression. He was clearly not at all pleased at being confined to the bed, his position of authority diminished. He reached over to the tray and poured a cup of coffee.

"You saved my life, Marietta. I'm grateful." His voice was brusque. "I remember the copperhead, remember killing it, and everything after that is foggy. You took my knife, didn't you? You cut my leg and then sucked the venom out. Right?"

Again I nodded. Hawke sipped his coffee, found it too hot, and scowled, setting the cup back down.

"I'm surprised you didn't let me die," he remarked. "If I remember correctly, I'd just clipped you across the jaw rather forcefully. Yes, I see you have a slight bruise. Lucky for you the snake struck when it did. I had every intention of giving you a very sound beating."

"You—you were delirious afterwards," I said. "You don't remember anything about the past two days?"

"Not a bloody thing," he admitted.

"And—the other night?"

"Is there something I should remember?"

"You—you were rather violent, right before your fever broke. After that you—slept soundly."

"Violent? Did I hurt you?" His voice was dry, indifferent.

"You tried to strangle me."

"Indeed? Well, I see you survived the attack. I intend to give Mattie a large supply of snuff as a reward for what she did. What would you like?"

I gazed at him, a hollow feeling in the pit of my stomach. It was a moment before I could reply.

126

"Nothing," I said.

Hawke arched his brow again, surprised. "No?"

"Nothing at all," I whispered.

And then I turned and left the room, quickly, before the emotions welling up inside could give me away.

V

I fetched a bar of soap and a huge towel and left the house, starting toward the creek on the other side of the west fields. July was gone, and it was late August now, six weeks since Hawke had been bitten by the copperhead. Although it was already after seven o'clock, the sun was still a blazing yellow ball, and the heat was as intense as ever. As I strolled through the fields the cotton was like snow, popping out of the pods, almost ready to be picked.

It was a long walk to the creek, almost a mile and a half, for after leaving the fields I had to pass through the thinly wooded area beyond, but I didn't mind the walk, tired as I was. I felt hot and sticky, coated all over with grime after a day of heavy housecleaning. I had taken all of the rugs out back and beaten them with a long paddle. Then, I had scrubbed all the floors before bringing the rugs back in. I wanted a thorough bath, the kind I couldn't get in the tin tub I had to haul into the kitchen and fill with water. Hawke had retired to his study immediately after dinner, and there was little chance he would miss me.

Leaving the fields, I started through the woods. A squirrel scurried up a tree, chattering at me, and a scarlet cardinal left its perch and soared away. Bluejays scolded, and all around were the heady smells of earth and moss and lichen. I took my time, enjoying the sense of freedom, anticipating the bath. I shouldn't be doing this, I knew, for I was no longer on Hawke's property and hadn't asked his permission to leave. He would be extremely displeased if he found out, but I didn't care. The thought of the long, luxurious bath ahead of me made the possibility of incurring his wrath well worth the risk.

Athough he was as remote, as indifferent, as he had ever been, his manner as cool, he seemed to treat me with a bit more courtesy than he had before the snakebite. He had displayed no warmth, yet he had not spoken to me sharply even one time. Because I had saved his life? After brusquely expressing his gratitude the morning I had carried breakfast in to him, he had not referred to the incident again, nor had I. I tried to avoid him whenever possible, afraid I might somehow betray myself. As Cassie's morning sickness was behind her and she was blooming with health, I let her carry his lunch out to him, and although I still served his evening meal, I did so unobtrusively, never speaking unless spoken to.

I had baked no more pies for him. I served him efficiently, as silently as possible. If I could help it, Derek Hawke would never know what I felt for him. I firmly repressed the emotions inside, refusing to allow them to blossom freely. Hard work provided an outlet, and I had thrown myself into it with a vengeance, deliberately pushing myself, working as I had never worked before. Things had gone smoothly these past six weeks. I just hoped they would continue to do so.

I could see the river through the trees ahead. There was a wide, sandy bank, and the water was still a large blue-green pool shimmering with reflected sunlight. I slipped off my shoes, digging my bare toes into the damp, squishy sand, savoring the sensation. Removing my dress and petticoat, I draped them over an old fallen log along with the towel. Completely naked, I stepped into the water with the bar of soap in my hand, moving out until it was up to my waist. The water was deliciously cool and invigorating, and I abandoned myself to its joys, splashing myself, feeling almost like a child again. The soap Mattie had made was soft and creamy and scented with lilac. I reveled in the rich lather, smearing it over my arms and breasts, giving my hair a thorough washing as well. I spent almost half an hour bathing, swimming about, and it was with great reluctance that I finally climbed out of the water and toweled myself dry.

My hair was still damp, and I decided to let the sun finish drying it before putting my clothes back on. I spied a large, flat gray rock near the water. Spreading the towel over it, I stretched out on my back, propping one knee up. Surrounded by trees and water, I felt like a wood nymph and I smiled to myself at the thought. It was extremely unlikely that anyone would chance to see me and I was perfectly content to let the sun stream warmly over my body. The water lapped gently against the banks. A frog croaked. Birds warbled. Rustling leaves made a dry, crisp sound like whispers. I had rarely felt so relaxed and content, finding the solitude a great luxury after a busy, noisy day.

The sun was fading, but since I had at least an hour before it would begin to grow dark, I closed my eyes and let my mind wander. I thought about Angie, wondering what had become of her. I hoped her situation was better than my own. The husky young farmer who had bought her was probably waiting on *her* by this time. I wondered if I would ever see that tough, scrappy little English sparrow again. Our days together on board ship seemed years and years ago. And the experiences I had had at number 10 Montagu Square might have happened in another century. I could think of all that now without either anger or bitterness. The past was over and done with, far behind me, and the future loomed ahead like a vague, unsettling question.

I must have drifted off to sleep, for when I opened my eyes my hair was dry, curling in feathery waves about my head. Something had awakened me, some unusual noise. I sat up, suddenly uneasy, experiencing the distinct sensation of being watched. A horse neighed, startling me, and I turned to see Derek Hawke sitting astride one of the chestnuts several yards away. His face was expressionless. I had no way of knowing how long he might have been there. I stood up, momentarily forgetting that I was naked, and he continued to look at me without any reaction. The horse grazed on the short grass at the edge of the woods. Hawke sat casually in the saddle, the reins held idly in one hand.

"I thought I might find you here," he remarked.

I scooped up the towel and quickly wrapped it around me.

"I looked all over for you," he continued in a calm, level voice, "in the house, in the yard, in the barn. Cassie finally told me she'd seen you leave with a towel and a bar of Mattie's lilac soap. I figured you'd come to bathe in the river."

"Your assumption was correct."

"Your hair's like fire in the sunlight—soft clouds of fire. You know you should never have left the property without my permission. Marietta. If one of the blacks did it, I'd have to use my whip."

"And do you intend to use it on me?"

"I think not," he said idly. "Not this time, at any rate. You took a mighty risk, coming here like this. There are a number of rowdy young men in the area—Higman's son, a hellion if ever there was one, and Jason Barnett, a young rascal with a total lack of morals. What if one of them had come upon you stretched out like that, looking like some flesh-and-blood statue of Venus?"

"Neither of them did," I replied. "How—how long have you been sitting there?"

"That needn't concern you," he replied.

So he *had* been there for some time, long enough to note that I looked like a living Venus, long enough to observe that my hair was like soft fire in the sunlight. He must have approached quietly, walking the horse slowly through the woods. He had made no attempt to awaken me. The horse's neighing had done that.

"Your eyes are full of challenge," he said. "You com-

131

mit a serious offense, and then you stare at me with those blue eyes as though daring me to do something about it. Where is the submissive wench who served my dinner with lowered eyes an hour or two ago?"

"I'm sorry if you're displeased, Mr. Hawke," I said coolly.

"Ah, that cool, aristocratic accent. You read books, too. I noticed the volume of John Donne missing from the shelf in my study. I assume it's in your room?"

"I'll return it as soon as I get back to the house."

"There's no hurry. You're free to read any book in the house, so long as it doesn't interfere with your work. It seems I've got myself quite an accomplished servant."

"Slave," I corrected, "bought on the auction block. Your property for the next fourteen years."

"I suppose I should consider myself a lucky man. You know, for a while I thought you might have run off, tried to escape. When I couldn't find you anywhere, I felt something—akin to panic. Then Cassie told me about the towel and bar of soap. I was mightily relieved."

I did not reply. Holding the towel in front of me, I gazed at him calmly, my composure belieing the nervous tremors within. We had not exchanged this many words since before the snakebite, and I found his manner strangely disconcerting. Despite those impassive eyes, he seemed more relaxed than I had ever seen him. He had never been so personal, so familiar, and there was a faint teasing quality in his voice that had never been there before. Was he finally beginning to see me as something other than a chattel, a piece of valuable property? Had the sight of my body stirred something inside of him he had refused to acknowledge before?

"I suggest you put your clothes on, Marietta. We should get back to the house. It'll soon be getting dark."

"I'll walk back," I informed him.

"You'll ride on the back of the horse," he corrected. "I don't want Jason Barnett stumbling across you in the woods—even fully dressed. Hurry up. Get your things on."

132

He obviously had no intention of turning away while I dressed. I hesitated only a moment, and then I stepped over to the log and calmly draped the towel across it, picking up my petticoat. Although I didn't look up, I could tell that he was watching me, and I deliberately took my time, taking a perverse satisfaction in doing so. I slipped the petticoat over my head, smoothed the bodice down and adjusted it at the waist, then donned the faded beige and brown striped cotton frock with its carefully patched skirt. I ran my fingers through my hair and shook my head so that it would fall properly, then casually slipped into my shoes. The whole performance took a good five minutes, and I hoped that he had enjoyed it.

"Ready?" he asked idly.

I picked up the towel and nodded. He walked the horse over to where I was standing and held his hand down for me. I gripped it and put my foot in the stirrup, swinging myself up behind him, and then I wrapped my arms around his waist. Hawke flicked the reins and gave them a gentle tug, and the horse started slowly through the woods. Neither of us spoke. I noticed the way his thick dark hair curled at the back of his head, noticed the way the white cloth of his shirt stretched across those broad shoulders. My legs touched his on either side, and I could feel the power in his thighs. When the horse moved over rough ground, I leaned against him, resting my cheek on his back. I thought how glorious it would be to be able to love openly, to express that love freely, in words, in action. I had successfully suppressed it for weeks now, but at the moment it was like a pain inside, hurting . . . hurting so much.

The sun was going down at last, and as we started across the fields I saw the blaze of scarlet and gold on the horizon, fiery colors that melted and blended together, tinting the air a hazy orange. The cotton, so white before, was stained soft pink now, and shadows spread thickly over the ground. It was beautiful and touching, and I wanted to cry because of the beauty and because of what I held inside and couldn't express. Hawke sat very straight in front of me, his back ramrod stiff. I wondered what he was feeling, what he was thinking. Was he thinking of me? Was he remembering the way I had looked stretched out on the rock, or was he thinking of something else, the price of cotton, the chores to be done tomorrow?

The sun had already vanished and it was twilight by the time we reached the yard. The oak trees cast long purple shadows, and the air was a misty blue as the sky darkened. Hawke stopped in front of the stables and called the boy who was waiting for him to return. The slave stepped out to take the reins, and Hawke dismounted. Then, placing a hand on either side of my waist, he swung me down beside him. Crickets chirped as we started toward the house. The fireflies were already swarming around the fig trees beside the back porch. The old house loomed up ahead, a ghostly white spread with moving shadows from the oak boughs. I felt pensive, sad.

"You were looking for me, you said," I remarked quietly. "Was there something you wanted?"

We stopped in front of the back steps. A light burned in the kitchen, streaming out on the porch, and I could see his face. It was still expressionless . . . guarded, as though it required a concentrated effort to conceal any emotion.

"I'm going to Charles Town tomorrow, Marietta. I thought you might like to come with me."

I was surprised, too surprised to reply, and Hawke waited a moment before continuing. His voice was flat as he did. "You refused any kind of reward for what you did when the copperhead bit me. I thought a trip to Charles Town might suffice. I'm sure there are things you need to buy for the kitchen—sugar, coffee, surely we're running low of something."

"I thought you bought all the supplies."

"Ordinarily I do."

"I—I don't know why you'd want to take me. I don't expect any kind of reward for what I did. I did it because—"

134

"Look," he interrupted, and his voice was edged with irritation now, "I'm going, and you can go with me or stay here. It doesn't matter to me! I simply thought the trip might please you. I'll be leaving at six o'clock in the morning—I'll expect breakfast on the table at five-thirty. If you plan to go with me, be ready!"

He marched up the steps, strode across the porch, and opened the back door, letting it slam behind him as he disappeared into the house. I could hear angry footsteps moving through the kitchen and down the hall, and then there was only the sound of the crickets under the steps. That sudden outburst of temperament surprised me, and it pleased me as well. I wondered if that icy wall he had built around him was finally beginning to crack.

VI

The sky was still a murky blue-black when we departed the next morning in the wagon Hawke had used to bring me to Shadow Oaks. He owned no elegant carriage, no jaunty rig, this creaking old farm wagon sufficed for all his needs. After breakfast, he had given orders to Adam and Mattie regarding everything he expected to be done while he was gone. Adam had been concerned about the cotton, venturing the opinion that it should be picked immediately. Hawke told him it could wait until he returned. The weather was hot and dry. There was little chance of rain. A rainstorm, I knew, could destroy the crop, but we would only be gone for three days, arriving back home on the afternoon of the third. He wasn't really running a risk by putting off the picking for such a short time.

Hawke had not commented when he saw me dressed and ready to accompany him. I wore the best dress I owned, a rusty brown cotton striped with thin gold stripes, but even so, it had been laundered too often and was patched in a number of places. My silk stockings were a pair I had saved from more affluent days, and the brown high-heeled slippers showed signs of age. Hawke wore his work clothes, although I knew he carried finer things in the bag in the back of the wagon.

The sun began to come up as we rode down the rough

136

dirt road, and by the time we passed Magnolia Grove, Maud Simmons's place, the pink blush of dawn had given way to bright sunlight. Slaves were working in the fields, picking the cotton and dropping it in huge cloth bags they dragged along behind them. In the distance I saw the plantation house, small but lovely with tall white columns supporting a double verandah. On either side grew the tall waxy green trees that gave the place its name, the limbs studded with huge white blossoms that looked even more like wax. Magnolia Grove made Shadow Oaks seem even shabbier in comparison, as did the other plantation houses we passed during the next few hours. In almost every field the slaves were busily picking the cotton, and I was beginning to wonder whether Hawke had been wise to leave at this particular time, weather or no.

The road didn't get any better. It was uneven, filled with holes, and I was frequently thrown against him. Once I had to grab his arm to keep from tumbling off the seat. There were stretches of road where tall trees grew on either side, their limbs interlocking overhead to form a living green tunnel. The oaks were dripping with the same grayish-green moss that hung from those back at the plantation. Mattie had identified it as Spaniard's Beard. It was lovely, trailing down over the road in lacy shreds, unlike anything I had ever seen in England.

Derek Hawke was in an uncommunicative mood. He had not spoken to me since we left the house. I wondered if he was still angry with me because I hadn't burst into paeans of joy when he told me about the trip. On three occasions he had to steer the wagon over to the side of the road so that the carriages coming from the opposite direction could pass. Each time the occupants stared openly, and I knew that it wouldn't take long for word to get around that Hawke was on his way to Charles Town with his indentured wench at his side. I felt sure that all his neighbors already believed I was his bedmate, and I felt just as sure that Hawke couldn't have cared less what they thought. I knew from what Maud had

137

told me that he was adamantly independent, a man unconcerned with the opinions of others.

Around one o'clock, when the sun was high, he pulled the wagon off onto a grassy slope beneath some oak trees. We got out of the wagon, and I took down the basket of food I had prepared before we left. While I spread a cloth and took out the food, Hawke stretched out on the grass, on his back, his hands behind his head. He still hadn't spoken to me, and I was determined not to be the first to break the silence. Lolling there on the grass like that, he looked like some indolent pasha, lids drooping heavily, wide lips slightly parted. I longed to throw the iced tea in his face. Instead, I poured it into the glasses I had brought along.

"It's ready?" he asked idly.

"It's ready." My voice was crisp.

"Hand me a drumstick."

"You're just going to lie there and let me—"

"Right," he drawled.

He rolled over on his side and propped himself up on one elbow, taking the drumstick in his other hand. I waited on him like an Oriental handmaiden, doing everything short of dropping grapes in his opened mouth, and Hawke enjoyed every moment of it. Although I was fuming inside, I had to admit that I preferred this lazy, languorous Hawke to the tight-lipped, stony-faced man who had been sitting beside me all morning. I realized anew that I didn't really know him at all. Behind that icy wall he ordinarily kept around him dwelled a creature of mercurial temperament, capable of many moods. The Hawke stretched out beside me now was a superb sensual animal. He gazed at me with slumbrous eyes, as though he were contemplating long hours of unhurried lovemaking here on the grass, beneath the boughs of the oaks.

"Are you finished?" I asked.

Hawke nodded, his dark gray eyes continuing in that disturbing fashion.

"Then I suppose we'd better be going," I remarked.

"There's no hurry. Charles Town's only three or four hours away. We have plenty of time."

The sun slanted through the boughs overhead in wavering yellow rays swirling with dust motes, and the long grayish moss trailing down swayed slowly to and fro. I packed the things away, nervous, my hands trembling, and his eyes never left me. I knew full well what he was contemplating. It was there in his eyes. Derek Hawke wanted me. I was no longer merely his chattel. I was a woman, warm flesh, capable of satisfying the craving that plainly throbbed within him.

"You're a beautiful woman," he said.

I folded the cloth and placed it on top of the basket, not looking at him.

"A woman like you could drive a man to distraction— if he let her, if he was fool enough."

I turned then and looked him full in the face, sitting there with my legs folded under me, my hands in my lap. I sat very still, waiting, my pulses racing, the back of my throat tight and dry. I longed for him to reach out to me, and yet I was frightened, too, frightened by the sheer intensity of feeling.

Both of us heard the horse hooves and rumbling wheels at the same time. Hawke scowled, and the heady aura of sensuality vanished abruptly. He climbed to his feet in one quick movement, shoving his hand against the front of his breeches at the same time. He stepped over to the horses and began to fiddle angrily with the harness, and I stood up and carried the basket over to the wagon, placing it inside just as the carriage drove past. The man driving it waved. Hawke nodded curtly.

"Get in the wagon!" he said sharply. "We've wasted enough time."

He was seething with anger, his face stern and stormy, lips set in a tight line. He was angry with himself because he had almost been a "fool," angry with me because I was the temptress who had almost made him abandon his good judgment. He blamed me, I knew, even though I had done nothing to stir that urgent lust that had swelled

139

within him. It was unfair, terribly unfair, and I resented his anger, though I dared not say or do anything that might make it worse. I climbed into the wagon with as much dignity as possible, and Hawke swung himself up beside me and took the reins in his hands.

We rode mile after mile in silence. An hour passed, and then another, and though the seething anger had vanished, he had never been more remote. Back there on the side of the road I had seen a relaxed, lazy male animal, and once or twice before I had sensed a curious vulnerability about this steely, unapproachable man who sat beside me on the wagon seat. I wondered what he had been like before he had thrown up his protective shell. Had there been openness and warmth and charm? Would I ever know the real Derek Hawke?

I loved him, and he knew that now. When I had turned to him there on the grass, waiting, waiting for that awesome moment to pass, for him to reach out to me, I had been unable to conceal the emotions inside. I knew that my love had shone clearly in my eyes, and I knew that he had seen it and recognized it for what it was. I had vowed he would never know, yet I hadn't been able to help myself. In that instant before the sound of the approaching carriage shattered the mood completely, my eyes had been filled with longing for him, with love, and though he had given no sign, Hawke had seen.

For better or worse, he knew, and while the knowledge was a weapon he could use against me to inflict deep hurt, I didn't care. I had fallen in love with Derek Hawke against my will, against all reason, and I knew in my heart that I would never love another man. A strange destiny had brought us together, and though destiny might separate us, there would never again be this beautiful and tormenting emotion that was now as much a part of me as the blood coursing through my veins. He was the one fate had decreed I love, the only one who would ever be able to stir this feeling that quickened and glowed like some radiance caught inside of me.

Another hour passed. I began to smell the salty tang

140

in the air and knew we were nearing the coast. The road was wider, less rough than before, and the wagon moved at a leisurely pace. There were many more carriages and wagons and, as we drew nearer the city, fine houses and tall tropical trees I couldn't identify. We arrived in Charles Town around six o'clock in the afternoon. It was much larger than the port that had been my first sight of America. America might be a vast wilderness, but Charles Town had an air of Old World charm and a curious sophistication that was immediately apparent. The cobbled streets were lined with shops displaying fine wares. In the distance I could see the masts of the ships docked along the waterfront.

Hawke left the wagon at the stables and led me down the street to the inn, one of a row of beautifully constructed buildings already showing signs of age and the damp sea air. A raggedly dressed black boy followed with our bags, setting them down when we entered the inn and grinning broadly when Hawke handed him a coin. The proprietor bustled forward to greet us. A plump, jovial soul, he seemed surprised when Hawke asked for separate rooms. Scooping up our bags, he led us up the narrow staircase to the second floor and down the hall, chatting exuberantly about the various cargoes currently being unloaded on the docks.

My room was small, with a low, beamed ceiling and creamy plaster walls. The double bed was covered with a patchwork quilt, and there was also a wing-backed chair and a dressing table with murky silver-blue mirror hanging on the wall above it. The single window looked out over the harbor, and a door connected the room with the one adjoining it. I could hear Hawke moving about, putting his things away. Although the proprietor had observed his request for separate rooms, he had seen fit to make any kind of dalliance easily and tactfully accomplished were Hawke to feel so inclined.

I was standing at the window, immersed in thought, when the door between the two rooms opened and Hawke stepped inside.

141

"You haven't unpacked," he remarked.

"Not yet. It'll only take a minute or so. I . . . didn't bring much."

"You look tired," he said. His voice was without emotion. He might have been speaking to a total stranger.

"It was a long trip. I suppose I am a bit weary."

"I suggest you rest for a while, and then I'll take you to dinner. There's a particularly nice restaurant down by the wharf. You'll need to change into something a bit less tattered."

"I haven't anything else," I replied. "This is my best dress. The other one I brought is even—" I hesitated, feeling miserable.

"I hadn't thought about that," he said.

"It doesn't matter. I'm . . . really not hungry."

"Nonsense. We'll eat in the taproom downstairs. It's noisy and rowdy, but the clothes you're wearing will do. I won't change, either. You get some rest. We'll go down around eight."

He left the room, closing the door behind him. I unpacked my bag and, as there was no wardrobe, placed my things in the drawer of the dressing table. Taking off my dress, I gave it a thorough brushing, discovering a new tear in the skirt as I did so. I took out my sewing kit and mended the tear as well as I could. Then I sat down at the dressing table and washed my face with water from the pitcher. This accomplished, I brushed my hair until it gleamed with rich coppery highlights, all the while studying my reflection with blue eyes dark with speculation.

His manner had been cool and curt, yes, but there had been no sign of the anger that had been there earlier. He had even been . . . considerate, decreeing that we would eat in the taproom because I didn't have anything suitable to wear to a decent restaurant. He had noticed that I was tired, had told me to rest. Was I reading too much into it? Was I being wildly foolish to hope that he still might drop that icy reserve and let himself be "fool enough" to do what he had been ready to do this afternoon? This trip to Charles Town was my "reward" for saving his life, he claimed, but Derek Hawke never did anything on impulse. He had wanted me with him, had wanted my company. That was a very good sign indeed.

True to his word, he hadn't changed clothes when he came to take me down to the tap room, although he had cleaned his brown knee boots. He looked exceedingly rugged and strong in the clinging tan breeches and somewhat tattered white shirt with its wide, full sleeves gathered at the wrist. I noticed the barmaid looking at him with frank appraisal as she led us to a table in the corner of the room. Although she was an attractive wench with sultry brown eyes and dark golden hair that fell to her shoulders in a cascade of curly locks, Hawke hardly noticed her. He seemed preoccupied, ordering our meal tersely and then settling back in his chair, immersed in thought and ignoring me completely.

The taproom smelled of beer and sweaty bodies and cigar smoke. Sawdust was scattered over the rough wooden floor and the rumble of hearty male voices, loud and exuberant, was frequently augmented by bursts of raucous laughter. I glanced around curiously. Even though it was in the basement of the inn, and though there was no dart board, the place was not too unlike the Red Lion back in Cornwall where I had sometimes helped my mother serve the customers so many years ago. A number of brawny sailors crowded around the tables, exchanging tales with drunken glee, and several elegantly dressed young blades lounged about looking lordly and ready for mischief. I saw one of them seize the barmaid and give her an ardent, clumsy kiss, plunging his hand into the top of her low-cut white blouse. The girl pulled away from him and slapped his hand, then moved away from the table with hips swaying provocatively. The young man grinned appreciatively, banging his pewter mug on top of the table.

Several minutes passed, and I was beginning to feel uncomfortable. Hawke was still immersed in thought, apparently unaware that I was sitting across the table from him, and I had the distinct impression that someone was staring at me. I could actually feel a pair of eyes directed at me with such intensity that it was almost like physical contact, most unsettling. I turned to see a young man sitting at a table across the room. He didn't bother to look away when our eyes met. He kept right on staring with eyes that boldly challenged, their message unmistakable. Surely not more than twenty, he had a lean, wolfish face with a sharp, jutting nose and wide lips that were frankly sensual. His dark brows were peaked, his dark-gold hair clipped in short, uneven locks. Those gleaming green-brown eyes were hypnotic, holding my own, making it impossible for me to turn away.

"You're staring," Hawke said sharply. "Stop it at once!"

"I—I didn't mean—"

"He's trouble, bad trouble."

"You know him?"

"All too well. Jason Barnett. I believe I mentioned his name yesterday. The boy's a notorious womanizer. What he can't get with his wily ways or his father's money, he takes by force. No woman's safe around him."

I turned to look at the youth again.

"I told you not to stare!"

"I—I'm sorry. I was just—"

"Damn! He's coming over here. If there's anything I don't need, it's a run-in with a surly young devil like Barnett. I shouldn't have brought you down here! I should have known you couldn't keep your eyes off the men."

"That's not fair," I protested. "I felt him staring at me, and I merely—"

"Shut up!" Hawke ordered.

Barnett stopped in front of the table. He was long and lean, dressed in a dark-gray suit and emerald-green waistcoat. A pearl stickpin held his white silk stock in place. Although the youth was not at all good-looking, he exuded an aura of sexuality that many women would find attractive. I was frightened, sitting in my chair with

144

lowered eyes, praying the boy would go away before Hawke grew even angrier.

"Well, well, well," Barnett said. "What have we here? You've been holding out on us, Hawke. Heard you got an indentured wench this spring, but I never figured she'd be anything like this. Didn't know you could buy this kind or I'd uv been going to them auctions myself a long time ago."

"Shove off, Barnett."

"Hey, that ain't no way to treat a neighbor. Isn't friendly at all. Ain't you gonna introduce me to your friend?"

"I suggest you leave, Barnett. Promptly."

Ignoring Hawke, the youth turned to me, his wide lips parted in a smile that could only be called hungry. Those bold, gleaming eyes seemed to remove every stitch of my clothing.

"I'm Jason Barnett, ma'am, known far and wide for my way with a wench. I didn't know Hawke here was keepin' something like you on the place, or I'd uv come callin' weeks ago."

Derek Hawke was outwardly calm, but his face was nevertheless frightening to behold. His facial muscles were taut, his mouth set in a tight line. His dark-gray eyes were murderously cool.

"I'm warning you, Barnett, you'd better shove off."

"I been lookin' for me a piece of tail ever since I got here," the boy continued, oblivious to the lethal tone in Hawke's voice. "Haven't had a speck-a luck, and then I saw this 'un here and I thought maybe you'd like to be real neighborly and share your good fortune. make yourself a bit o' quick cash. I got plenty o' money on me, and the wench sure looks like she's willing enough—"

Derek Hawke climbed slowly to his feet. "I'll give you ten seconds to leave," he said.

The air cracked with tension as the two men looked at each other. Hawke was icy cold, in complete control of himself, but I saw a muscle in his cheek tighten almost imperceptibly. Barnett's eyes were sullen, his mouth curled

145

in a surly pout, the lower lip thrust out. He stared at the tall, menacing figure who looked as though he could kill without blinking an eyelash, and then he muttered something under his breath and turned away. Hawke stood there until the youth had made his way across the room and moved up the stairs to the door, then he sat down again, calmly, apparently unruffled by the incident.

The barmaid came over to our table and set the food down, once again looking at Hawke with that frank appraisal. Once again he ignored her. He might have been carved of stone. The girl pouted and tossed her hair, moving away from the table. Hawke began to eat.

I was so shaken by the incident with Barnett that I just stared at the food. I had never seen such cold deadly fury. I had no doubt that Hawke would have beaten the boy to a pulp had Barnett not turned away when he did. I picked up my fork and promptly dropped it. It hit the edge of my plate with a loud clatter that caused me to start. Hawke didn't even bother to look up. Raucous voices filled the air around us. One of the sailors had taken out an accordion and was playing a lively jig. I toyed with my food, unable to eat. When he finished eating, Hawke observed my plate, slowly arching one dark brow.

"You're not going to eat?"

"I can't. I'm—too upset."

"Pity to waste that food."

"You—you think I encouraged him, don't you?"

"I don't care to discuss it, Marietta."

"You blame me. I can tell. I was looking at him, I admit that, but—"

"I told you I don't care to discuss it. If you're not going to eat, then I suggest we leave."

We got up, and Hawke summoned the barmaid over to pay her. As he handed her the coins, his eyes narrowed slightly, and I knew he was taking in that ripe, voluptuous body, those sultry eyes that so frankly advertised her availability. He curled his fingers around my elbow and led me out of the smoke-filled room, up the stairs

146

and into the now-deserted lobby. Only one lamp burned, casting a pale light over the battered mahogany counter, the dusty furniture, and the potted green plants. Hawke paused at the foot of the narrow staircase leading up to the second floor.

"I suppose I can trust you to go up to your room alone," he said.

"I suppose so," I replied coldly.

"Go to your room. Go to bed. Don't forget to lock the outside door."

"I won't."

"I'll awaken you in the morning."

I went on up the stairs, and when I reached the top and looked back down, Hawke had already vanished. Disappointed and at the same time, furious, I went on to my own room, knowing full well where he had gone, knowing full well how he intended to spend the rest of the evening, and with whom. I wanted to cry, and I wanted to rage. Instead, I blew out the lamp and took off my dress and stood at the window in my petticoat, peering out into the night.

It was a long, long time before I finally went to bed, an ever longer time before I slept. I kept thinking of him with the barmaid. She was probably in his arms at that very moment, his mouth covering hers, his long, powerful body sprawling over hers. Later, as the moonlight streamed through the window in thin, milky rays, I waited for the sound of his footsteps coming down the hall. I couldn't sleep as long as I knew he was with her. I couldn't think about anything else but the two of them together and the anguish and loss that kept me company in this dark, lonely room. I waited, and still he didn't come, and finally sheer exhaustion induced me to sleep.

VII

The sun was flooding hotly into the room when I finally woke up. It took me a moment to remember where I was. I sat up groggily, pushing my hair from my face. I wore only a thin white petticoat, the bodice leaving half my bosom exposed, the full, ruffled skirt deplorably wrinkled and twisted about my legs. Sometime during the night I had kicked the bedcovers to the foot of the bed, and the untidy top sheet and dented pillows bespoke a night of restless tossing and turning.

In the mirror across the room I caught a glimpse of myself: hair all atumble, face drawn. My eyes filled with desolation as I remembered what had happened the night before. How many hours had I stayed awake, waiting for him to return? At what time during the night had I finally slept, the adjoining room still empty? Pain and anger and frustration swept over me, but the edge was taken off by a much more tangible sensation—hunger. I was ravenously hungry. I had eaten very little at lunch yesterday, had eaten nothing since.

I could hear Derek Hawke moving about in the next room. I wondered what time it was. The sunlight pouring into the room was a radiant silver, making dazzling pools on the hardwood floor. If the sun was that bright, that forceful, it must be late indeed, I thought, climbing out of bed. The floor was warm to my bare feet. I stepped over to the window to see a sky like white silk faintly stained with blue, the sun a silver ball in its center. Surely it was almost noon. I turned as the connecting door opened and Hawke entered.

"What— what time is it?" I asked.

"It'll soon be one o'clock," he replied. "You slept quite late."

"I didn't mean to."

"I saw no reason to awaken you," Hawke said dryly. "Yesterday was an exhausting day. You needed the rest. I've ordered a tray of food for you. It should be brought up shortly."

I had never seen him so elegantly attired. The dusty boots and shabby work clothes had been replaced by a superbly tailored navy blue suit and a pale blue satin waistcoat embroidered with black silk patterns. His white silk stock was expertly arranged under his chin, his high black boots shined to a glossy sheen. The rough, sweaty farmer who toiled in the fields with his slaves had been transformed into an aristocratic dandy who might frequent the finest drawing rooms in London. His magnificent attire made him seem even more remote. He looked cool and arrogant and superior, his dark-gray eyes revealing nothing as they took in my disheveled hair and rumpled, low-cut petticoat.

"You're going out?" I asked.

"I have business to attend to." Hawke reached into his pocket and took out several folded bills, placing them on the dressing table. "I won't be back until almost six," he continued. "I trust you can keep yourself occupied with shopping."

"But I checked all the supplies. We don't really need—"

"You mentioned last night that you didn't have a decent dress to wear. Buy yourself one, and whatever else you need to go with it. You'll find a number of shops nearby that cater to the ladies. Don't go too far afield. Stay in this immediate area."

"You intend to just turn me loose?"

"I hadn't contemplated locking you in your room, if that's what you mean."

"I—I could run away so easily."

"I doubt that you will," Hawke replied in that same dry voice. "First of all, you know I'd come after you—and I'd find you. You wouldn't like the consequences, I assure you. Secondly—"

He hesitated, giving me a long, lingering look.

"Secondly?" I prompted.

"You don't want to run away from me," he said.

"No?"

Hawke did not reply. It was not necessary. I had been wildly foolish to let him see how I felt about him, but it had been unavoidable. He knew, had just acknowledged it in his own enigmatic way. How I wished I could demolish this icy, arrogant male with some scathing comment that would convince him he was mistaken, but no words would come.

"We'll dine out tonight," he informed me. "I expect to find you ready and waiting in your new clothes when I return at six. I've left plenty of money. I expect you to spend it all."

"You're very kind," I said quietly.

"No, Marietta, I'm not kind at all. Never delude yourself into believing that. I'm quite ruthless."

"And proud of it?"

"In this world, it's the only way a man can survive. Men who are kind, men who're compassionate—" He cut himself short, grimacing. "Get dressed!" he said sharply. "You look like a trollop in that petticoat. The man will be up with your tray in a minute or so, and I don't want anyone seeing you like this!"

He turned and left the room abruptly, pulling the door shut behind him. That sudden outburst of anger told me a great deal. He might have shown no reaction, but Derek Hawke had noticed the way the thin white bodice clung to my body, had noticed the swelling mounds of my breast straining against the low neckline. Had he wanted to set them free and fondle them?

150

Had he wanted to tumble me on the already rumpled bed and make ardent, savage love? Was that why he had spoken so sharply, left so abruptly?

As I dressed, I heard him leave his room. A few minutes later there was a knock on the door, and I opened it to find a grinning male servant with a heavily laden breakfast tray. I thanked him, took the tray, and set it on the bedside table. Hawke had been generous indeed in ordering the food. There was enough to feed two people. How considerate of him to think of it. How thoughtful of him to leave me money for a new dress. He might see himself as ruthless, but I knew that wasn't the case, even though he tried his best to act the part. He might think himself indifferent to me, too, might tell himself that he was immune, but that wasn't the case, either. Little by little, Derek Hawke was breaking down, revealing more and more of his true nature.

I was in an unusually good mood when I finally left the inn, experiencing a sense of well-being and optimism I hadn't felt in many a day. The sun was dazzling and the salty air was invigorating. I had all afternoon long at my disposal, and it was glorious to feel so lighthearted, so carefree, particularly after those solemn, sleepless hours of misery in my bed in the darkened room. He *did* care. He tried to conceal it, but he couldn't, not quite. In no hurry to buy my dress, I wandered down to the docks and watched the men unloading the cargo ships, and then I simply strolled about the streets, soaking up the atmosphere of the fascinating city.

I was young, I was beautiful, and I was very much in love. I smiled at passers-by. I paused to admire a cart full of flowers—orange, gold, red, vivid blue—and I marveled at the tall, exotic trees and the many shops and realized, suddenly, that I was happy. This exhilarating sensation that seemed to bubble up inside was one I hadn't experienced since before my father's death, before my whole world was turned upside-down. As carts and carriages rumbled down the narrow street, as the cries of hawkers filled the air and people moved busily up and

151

down the walks, I paused, reflecting. I had been so miserable last night, and today . . . today I felt as though I were filled with lonely, lilting music, and the reason was obvious. It wasn't merely because I loved Derek Hawke. It was because I was sure now that he loved me, too.

He had been fighting himself for some time now, but . . . the battle was about to be lost. The feelings that stirred inside of him might be easy enough to repress, might be concealed by a stern, rigid manner, but there was another, stronger, emotion not so easily denied. He could combat the love, but the lust—the purely physical craving that rose in his blood—was too potent to be dismissed with a scowl and a show of indifference. He didn't want to love me, but he wanted me physically, and he wasn't going to be able to hold out much longer. Yesterday, by the side of the road, he had almost given way to that urgent, pulsing need, and last night, had the barmaid not been so brazenly available . . . I moved on down the street, knowing that I was going to win him before much more time passed.

Madame Clara's was on a side street, not too far from the inn, a small shop with an unusually attractive display of bonnets in the window. A bell tinkled overhead as I opened the door. The woman behind the counter put down her fashion pamphlet and looked at me with one brow arched inquisitively. Wearing a lovely violet silk dress, she was slightly plump, in her late thirties, I judged, with hair too blond to be natural. Her shrewd, attractive face was made more so by a subtle and skillful use of makeup. Jet earrings dangled from her ears, and she smelled of some exquisite perfume. There was no one else in the shop.

"Hello, honey," she said, "I'm Clara. You must be new in town. All the girls come here, but I haven't seen you before." She examined me closely with dark, worldly blue eyes, taking in my run-down shoes, my patched and faded dress. "I think you'd better come back later on, honey, after you've gotten yourself established. My shop is the best in Charles Town, true, but I'm frightfully expensive."

"I have quite a lot of money with me," I informed her.

Clara arched her brow again. "That accent! Lord, honey, I thought you were—"

"I know what you thought."

"No offense, dear. I used to be one of the girls myself—in New Orleans. I was one of the best, too, one of the most expensive, and a helluva lot smarter than most. I actually saved my money. When the face and figure began to go, when the men started looking for someone younger, I had enough money to leave the city of my sins and open a dress shop here in Charles Town. I'm afraid my reputation followed me, but my dresses are so elegant even the grand ladies started coming in. I prefer the girls, if you want to know the truth. At least they pay their bills on time!"

I was rather startled by the woman's frankness and effusive manner, but I couldn't help warming to her. World-weary, disenchanted, she nevertheless had a friendly air that was immediately engaging. I suspected that Clara saw the world around her with a wry, humorous outlook that promptly dismissed any kind of sham or pretention.

"How much money *do* you have, honey?" she inquired.

I told her, and that eyebrow shot up once again.

"He must be generous indeed. I mean—no offense, honey, but when a girl who looks like you waves a roll of bills like that, there *has* to be a he! What on earth are you doing wearing those *rags*?"

"We—we've been in the country."

"Well, honey, all I can say is he's been *wise* to keep you out in the backwoods, dressed like that. When the men in Charles Town get a good look at you in the gown I'm going to provide, your man's going to have some very stiff competition." Clara paused, a deliciously wicked twinkle in her eyes. "I mean that literally," she added.

I smiled in spite of myself. Clara stepped from behind the counter, her violet silk skirts rustling crisply.

"Lord, if you knew how *bored* I've been today. One single sale this morning—to a rich matron who looks like she should be out milking cows in some muddy pasture. What fun it's going to be to outfit someone who'll do justice to my clothes! There's enough money there for everything, honey, shoes, stockings, gown, all the trimmings. We're going to have a marvelous time getting you all done up."

Clara flitted through the shop, examining dresses, taking down boxes, tossing tissue paper about, chattering all the while with considerable vivacity. Later on, after we had selected the gown and were searching for accessories to match, I found myself telling her all about my relationship with Derek Hawke. Clara showed no surprise when I said that I was an indentured servant. It was a joy to be able to talk to someone who was sympathetic. When I finally concluded my story with a description of my lonely vigil in the bedroom the night before, Clara sighed heavily and patted her sleek blond hair.

"Men, they're impossible! Yours seems a particularly tough specimen, but don't despair, honey. After he sees you all decked out tonight, he's going to forget all about his noble resolutions."

"I—I don't know why I told you all that. I'm not usually so—"

"Everyone needs to talk now and then, honey. It's done you a world of good, and I do adore a good story. Yours is absolutely fascinating! Tell you what, I'm going to throw in a few extras, just for the hell of it. Do you have any makeup?"

I shook my head, and Clara promptly went behind the counter to fetch a small case covered in pearl-gray leather.

"Everything you need's in here," she informed me. "Lip rouge, powder, eye shadow—even a tiny bottle of my own perfume. It's guaranteed to make any man lose his senses in ten seconds flat. This kit comes all the way from Paris, incidentally. The very best coquettes wouldn't be caught without one well in reach."

"You must let me pay for it," I protested.

"You couldn't afford it, honey. The perfume alone costs a small fortune. I want you to have it—but don't worry, I'll make it up. Next time one of those grand matrons comes sashaying in for a new bonnet, I'll add the cost of the kit to the price of the bonnet. They'll love it. The more they pay, the happier they are."

"You've been so kind—"

"Nonsense. I've rarely enjoyed myself so much. What time is it? Four? When's your man coming back?"

"Around six."

"Well, honey, you rush back to the inn and order a bath. They'll bring a tub and kettles of hot water up to your room. I'll send Clarice over with your packages, and she'll stay to do your hair. She's my maid, a Creole, been with me ever since New Orleans. Clarice is a wizard when it comes to styling hair, and she'll have a fit when she sees yours—that color, that texture—" Clara shook her head, a wistful look in her eyes. "Honey, if I were ten years younger, I'd hate your guts."

I was moved by the woman's kindness and generosity. But when I tried to express my gratitude, Clara waved her hand airily, smiling a rueful smile.

"Ordinarily I'm a raging bitch, but I happened to be in a good mood today. My heart's not golden, honey, it's hard as stone. Your man gave you quite a lot of money, remember? You're leaving the shop flat broke. Do run along now, and good luck."

I gave her a sudden hug, unable to resist the impulse. Clara looked surprised, then pleased. Her lusty laughter followed me as I hurried out of the shop.

Half an hour later I was soaking in a tub of hot water in my room, my hair tied up on top of my head. I had scrubbed myself thoroughly and was luxuriating in the water and suds. Just as I stepped out of the tub to dry off, I heard a timid knock on the door. I wrapped the towel around me and opened the door to see a pair of black slippers, a full maroon silk skirt, and two arms

155

holding a stack of packages that completely concealed the rest of her body.

"You must be Clarice," I said. "Just drop the packages on the bed."

The girl obeyed and then turned to give me a dazzling smile. Perhaps two or three years older than I, she had dark, luminous black eyes, smooth golden skin and beautifully arranged hair the color of polished teak. Predominately French, the strain of Negro blood gave her a rich, exotic beauty that was most unusual.

"Madame says tonight is a very special night and that I'm to help you do your hair. It will be a treat for me—such lovely hair." The girl spoke in a lilting voice with a distinct French accent. "You get into your new petticoat while I go fetch someone to take out this tub."

When I opened the first box it was to find an entirely different petticoat from the one I had purchased. I had picked out a simple white shift. This one was beige silk, with half a dozen full skirts festooned with exquisite lace. The message on the card I picked up was simple and direct: "It goes with the dress, honey. I'll up the price on another bonnet." When I slipped the sumptuous garment on, it made me feel like a queen.

After the two servants who returned with Clarice had carried out the tub, water, and kettles, the girl sat down in front of the dressing table and began to comb out my hair. When she left half an hour later, I gazed at myself in the mirror, amazed at the marvels she had wrought. She had pulled my hair back sleekly, shaping it to my skull, and a dozen long, perfectly curled ringlets dangled down in back. I carefully applied dark cinnamon mascara on lashes and brows, tannish-mauve shadow on my lids. I used the rouge sparingly, heightening the color on my high cheekbones, and applied the coral lip rouge just as lightly. We had secretly practiced using makeup when I was in school, and I knew the idea was to subtly emphasize one's natural coloring.

Derek Hawke might not notice the makeup, but he was definitely going to notice the perfume, I vowed, using it most generously. After slipping on the new stockings and high-heeled leather shoes, I took out the gown Clara and I had selected. It was topaz-colored silk, with long sleeves and a low-scooped bodice that fitted snugly. The skirt swirled out in glistening folds over the petticoat, pointing up my slender waist. Simple, unadorned with ribbons or ruffles, it was wonderfully elegant, and I knew that we had made a wise choice.

I felt like a different person as I went down to the lobby to wait for Derek's return. The happiness I had felt earlier on had been magnified by Madame Clara's warmth and generosity. I had gone through some bad times, had encountered some terrible people, but it was reassuring to know people like Clara existed in the same world.

The lobby was deserted, as dusty and depressing as ever, but I didn't notice its shabbiness now. I was filled with a glow of anticipation, eager for Derek to see me, eager to see the reaction he had when he saw the splendid transformation Clara and Clarice had made possible.

As I waited, I wondered about the "business" he was attending to today. I doubted seriously that it had anything to do with Shadow Oaks, else he wouldn't have been dressed so grandly. Did it have something to do with the lawyer back in England? As I had done many times before, I thought about those revealing phrases he had sobbed out in his delirium: "It'll be settled, I told her . . . Hawkehouse will be yours and you'll have a title and riches . . ." I knew so little about him, nothing about his past. Why had he left England? Why had he bought a run-down plantation in Carolina and then worked like a slave himself to make it successful? Maud claimed he had very little money in the bank, and he must have made thousands. Was he sending it to England, hoping to gain something in return? Had Hawke been cheated out of an inheritance? That would explain his bitterness, his grim determination to succeed.

Lost in thought, I hadn't heard anyone enter the lobby, but I suddenly felt a pair of eyes staring at me, just as I

157

had felt them last night down in the taproom. I turned around, uneasy, and the uneasiness increased when I saw Jason Barnett leaning against the counter, arms folded across his chest, his brown-flecked green eyes full of devilment. A ray of sunlight burnished his short-clipped gold hair, making it gleam darkly, and his face took on an even more wolfish look as his lips spread in a wide grin.

"Seems like this is my lucky day," he remarked. "Yes, indeed. Who'd a-thought it after I lost a pile in that card game earlier this afternoon? You waitin' for me, wench?"

"I'm waiting for Mr. Hawke," I said coldly.

" 'Mr. Hawke,' is it? Aren't we grand and formal. Me, though, I like a wench with class. You got that, gal. Don't know how Hawke ever lucked across you. Shame I wuzn't at that auction."

I turned away haughtily, refusing to reply. Jason Barnett moved over to me with a lithe, stealthy grace. He stood in front of me, grinning, and though he wasn't at all good-looking, not with those sharp features, that too-wide mouth, there was something about him that was intriguing. I gazed at him with cool, level eyes, praying he'd leave before Derek arrived.

"Feel like havin' a little fun, wench?" he inquired.

"Go away, Mr. Barnett."

"Hey, that ain't no way to be. Me, I can show you a real good time. Dozens-a women'll testify to that. I got stamina, real lastin' power. They all squirm and squeal with delight. You look like you could use a treat—"

"I think you're disgusting!"

"Do you now? That's interesting. Reckon I'm gonna have to take you up to my room and show you what a nice chap I can be. Hawke may not like it, but I couldn't care less about him. You're somethin', wench—"

He took hold of my wrist and began to lead me toward the stairs. When I tried to pull free, Barnett chuckled, jerked my arm and pulled me against him, wrapping his free arm tightly around my waist. Panic welled up inside of me. My heart began to pound. The more I

158

struggled, the tighter he held me, grinning all the while. "Let go of me!"

"Frisky, ain't you? I like a woman with spirit, makes it more excitin'. You hold yourself pretty high, don't you? Carry yourself like a regular lady. Hell, you're a convict, an indentured servant. Why, you ain't one bit better'n a nigger gal, even if your skin is white."

The arm wrapped around my waist forced me up against him. His face was inches from my own, and his mouth seemed wider than ever as he parted his lips and leaned down to kiss me. I tried to pull away, but he gripped my chin in a tight clamp and forced me to meet his lips with my own. The boy kissed me ardently, thoroughly, bending me at the waist and forcing me to lean back as his mouth worked greedily. When he finally raised his head, the grin still played on his lips.

"Still wanna argue? You liked that, wench. You liked it a lot, and that's just a small sample. I'm gonna show you what it's all about, and when we're through, know what you're gonna do? You're gonna beg Hawke to sell you to me—"

"You're vile!"

"Don't get too frisky," he warned. "I like a little spirit, but there's a limit. I can get mighty ugly if I want to, and you wouldn't like that."

I lifted my foot and kicked his shin with all the force I could muster. Barnett cried out. His eyes widened in shock. His mouth fell open. He released me abruptly, so abruptly that I fell back against the wall at the foot of the stairs. When he reached down to rub his shin, I tried to slip past him, but he seized my wrist again, clamping his fingers around it in a tight, wiry grip I found impossible to break.

"No you don't, wench," he said, pulling me toward him. "Come along now 'fore I have to get rough."

What happened then happened so quickly that it was difficult to follow. Barnett pulled me toward the steps, a wide grin of anticipation on his lips, his eyes alight with excitement, and then he gave a startled cry and I saw a

159

large hand gripping his hair, the fingers tugging at the dark gold locks and pulling him away from the stairs. Barnett let go of me, his arms waving in the air as he stumbled backwards. It was Derek, of course. Neither of us had heard him enter the lobby. He whirled the boy around and delivered a blow across his jaw that sent Barnett reeling across the room. He crashed against the counter with a loud bang and sank to his knees, completely stunned. Derek stood over him, legs wide apart, fists clenched at his side, ready to strike again if necessary.

"If you so much as touch her again, I'll kill you," he said, and his voice was calm, frighteningly calm. "If you so much as look like you want to, I'll kill you. Do you understand, boy?"

Still on his knees, Barnett shook his head to clear it and groaned, rubbing his jaw, wincing at the pain. He staggered to his feet, leaning back against the counter and looking up at Hawke with the eyes of a petulant little boy who has been unjustly punished.

"I just wanted a bit-a fun," he whined, all his bravado gone now. "I don't know why ya had to hit me! Hell, she ain't nothin' but an indentured wench—"

Derek's hands unclenched and flew to the boy's throat, gripping it with a brutal force that caused his shoulder muscles to bunch up beneath the navy blue jacket. Barnett gasped and made gurgling noises, eyes wide with fright. Although I couldn't see Derek's face, I knew it must be as cold and expressionless as his voice.

"I said I'd kill you, boy, and I meant it—"

His fingers tightened even more, and he shook the boy as a terrier might shake a mouse. Barnett's face turned a bright pink, his eyes beginning to protrude. Derek shoved him back until he was leaning over the counter, his feet barely touching the floor, his body like that of a limp rag doll. Horrified, I leaned against the wall, my throat dry, my pulses racing. I was afraid he was actually going to choke the boy to death then and there. I tried

160

to call out, to plead with him to let go, but no sound would come.

"All I'd have to do would be squeeze just a tiny bit more," Hawke informed Barnett, ever so calmly. "That's all it would take. Do you understand? Nod if you do."

Barnett was panic-stricken. His face was a deep plum color now, his eyes about to pop out of his head, yet he managed to nod. Derek released him. Barnett slid to the floor, coughing and gasping. Unruffled, looking as though he might have just exchanged a few friendly words, Hawke turned and strolled toward the stairs.

"Come along, Marietta," he said.

He started up the narrow wooden staircase, and I followed, turning once to look back at Barnett, who was on his hands and knees, still making spluttering noises. Hawke strolled down the hall, moved past the door of his room, and opened the door to mine. I was trembling inside, still badly shaken by what had happened. The expression on his face as he held the door open for me was not at all reassuring. Although his features were composed, his gray eyes flat, I could sense the anger that possessed him.

My topaz silk skirts rustled with the sound of dry leaves as I stepped into the room. I stood by the bed, clasping my hands together, desperately trying to still the trembling. Hawke closed the door and stood looking at me, silent, and although a flood of words rushed up in my throat, I couldn't speak, either. That glorious exhilaration I had felt throughout the afternoon had vanished completely. I felt helpless, guilty of some dreadful crime even though I had done nothing to encourage Barnett. I knew full well what Hawke was thinking. I knew it would be futile to try to convince him of my innocence.

"I see you got your new dress," he remarked.

"Yes. I bought it from the most unusual woman. She—"

"You bought make-up, too, I see, and perfume. You did your hair. I'm wondering why you didn't have a sign

161

made up while you were at it—Tail For Sale in bold block letters."

"That's not fair—"

"Barnett's not to blame, of course. He only did what any red-blooded youth would have done. When it's there and all too obviously available, a man reaches for it."

"I came down to the lobby to wait for you. I wanted to surprise you. I thought you'd be—"

"It's a lovely dress, Marietta. Take it off."

I stared at him in dismay, startled by his words. His mouth was set in a grim line, and those dark gray eyes were filled now with a brutal determination that filled me with apprehension.

"What—what do you intend to do?" I whispered.

"What you've wanted me to do all along. Take off the dress!"

"Derek. I—not like this. Please. Not like—"

"Do you want me to remove it for you? I'll probably tear it to shreds in the process."

Reaching around in back, I unfastened the dress and slipped the bodice down. He stood a few feet away, watching, eyes growing darker, one corner of his mouth turning up. My hands trembled. The topaz silk crackled as I pushed the gown over my legs and stepped out of it. The curtains had been drawn over the window. The room was dim, a shadowy blue-gray. I folded the dress carefully and put it away in the drawer of the dressing table, and then I sat down on the edge of the bed to remove my shoes and stockings.

Derek took off his stock and tossed it on the chair, pulled off his jacket and waistcoat and dropped them on top of the stock. The full sleeves of his white silk shirt billowed. He watched me slip off my shoes and peel off the stockings, his eyes half concealed by heavily drooping lids. I let the stockings flutter to the floor like silken shadows and stood up, my bosom heaving, breasts straining against the thin cloth that imprisoned them. I could feel his anger, seething still, not the least diminished by the sheer lust building steadily. Tears spilled down my cheeks because it shouldn't be this way, so deliberate, so unfeeling, his anger driving him to do what passion should have prompted.

"Come here," he said. His voice was deep, husky.

"Derek—"

"I said come here!"

I shook my head, backing away from him until my legs touched the side of the bed. Hawke moved over to me in three brisk strides and caught hold of my shoulders, his fingers gripping tightly, hurting me, and when I refused to look up at him he seized my curls with his left hand and tugged at them, forcing my head to tilt back, forcing me to look up at that handsome face now stamped strongly with desire. Then he kissed me, a hard unyielding kiss, as he would kiss a whore. I was rigid in his arms, unable to respond, and after a while he drew back, looking into my eyes with fierce intensity.

"You wanted this," he said, his voice a throaty growl.

"Not—like—this—"

"You want romance? You want compliments and gallantry? You want me to say I love you? What kind of fool do you take me for? You're no fine lady. You're a wench from the prison ship, bought and paid for at a public auction!"

"I'm a human being! I—I have feelings—"

"You've wanted me to do this from the first—teasing me, tormenting me, trying to make me forget my—trying to—" He cut himself short, a savage frown creasing his brow. "Look at you! Painted up like a whore, smelling like a whore, hoping you could trap me!"

He kissed me again, ardently, his lips firm, moist, warm, forcing my own to open so that his tongue could plunge and probe. One arm curled around my shoulders, the other wrapped tightly around my waist, he held me against him, his thighs molded against mine, my breasts crushed against his chest. I trembled all over, trying not to feel, willing myself to keep those buds of sensation tightly furled, but it was futile; flesh and blood responded while my mind cried out that it was wrong, that it must not happen this way, in anger, without tenderness. He moved his mouth away from mine and buried his lips in the hollow of my throat.

"No," I whispered. "Derek, please, you must—"

"You've been waiting for this and, by God, so have I!"

He caught hold of the straps of my petticoat and jerked them down, causing my breasts to pop out of their silken prison. They were swollen, the nipples pulsating pink buds that grew larger, tighter, as his hands closed over them, squeezing so fiercely that I gasped. He shoved me back onto the bed. The springs creaked violently. Caught up in the frenzy of his lust, he made a deep, growling noise and then he whipped up the skirts of my petticoat, jerked down the top of his breeches and fell upon me.

I was an object, a receptacle for his lust. He hadn't even bothered to undress. I fought. I tried to throw him off. I fought Derek Hawke, and then I fought myself, fought the sensations exploding inside me with unbelievable ecstasy. Though he thrust inside me, brutally, as if inflicting a harsh punishment, I flung my arms around him and held him even closer and clutched at the white silk covering his back. Then, there was nothing but need and he cried my name and kissed me once more, holding me tightly, shuddering, and I knew that the conquest, however made, was not his but mine.

VIII

I had drawn back the curtains and opened the windows earlier, and the room was deliciously cool with night air and filled with moonlight that streamed in in wavering rays, intensifying the blue-black shadows that coated the walls. I could see the murky-silver blue of the mirror, and Derek's white silk shirt rested on top of the chair like a weary ghost, his tall black boots standing on the floor and drooping limply. He was naked beside me, fast asleep, his chest rising and falling. I had removed my petticoat, another ghost spilling out of the half-opened drawer.

The moonlight seemed thinner, silver gradually fading to a pale milky white, and it seemed the shadows stirred, black velvet melting into a softer, lighter shade, more blue now than black. Had we been in the country, the first cock would begin to crow shortly, and in the east faint golden stains would begin to touch the ashy gray horizon as the moon retired and stars twinkled off one by one. I had awakened a few minutes earlier, filled with a marvelous languor that glowed inside and warmed my whole body. Naked, I welcomed the cool breeze that chilled my skin. All the bedcovers had been kicked to the foot of the bed. Afraid I might wake him up, I made no effort to pull them back up over us. It would be time to get up soon enough.

Derek moaned in his sleep, an irritated frown creasing

165

his brow. He turned on his side, facing me, throwing his left leg over both mine and wrapping his arm around my waist. His skin was satin smooth, warm, and he smelled of sweat. I stroked his arm, moving my palm up his hard muscles, sliding it over the curve of his shoulder. He moaned again and pulled me closer, shifting position, resting his head heavily on my shoulder and breast, his half-open mouth moist against my skin. I lifted my right hand and stroked his hair, thick, soft, like coarse silk. He stirred again, neither asleep nor awake, and I could feel him growing taut, pulsating with warmth.

Sleepily, he opened his eyes. I touched his mouth with my fingertips. He caught hold of my shoulders and pulled me over to him. Still half-asleep, he kissed me, a long, lingering kiss wonderfully tender, so unlike that ardent plunder a few hours ago. I smoothed my palms over the curve of his shoulders and down his back, resting them on his flat buttocks as they lifted and he reached down to catch hold of mine.

He had had me before. Brutally, with no thought for my comfort or pleasure, he had taken me and given nothing. He made love to me now. He might never say the words, might, with morning, be as cool and remote as ever he had been, but words were not necessary. His body, his being expressed everything with painstaking tenderness. He gave of himself and sensations swirled and skin seemed to shred slowly like silken webs tearing and his mouth covered mine as the cry rose up in my throat, trapping the cry inside me as love rushed up to meet the outpouring of our passion. I shuddered, as did he, and he fell limp on top of me, asleep soon, eventually rolling over to sprawl beside me in heavy, blissful slumber.

I had washed and dressed in my old clothes by the time the first yellow rays of morning sunlight floated through the window. Derek was still sprawled out on the bed, fast asleep. I left the room quietly and went downstairs to find the lobby deserted. After a brief search, I finally found the kitchen in back of the inn. The cook had just gotten out of bed and shuffled about sleepily, mumbling to herself as she lighted the stove and put a pot of coffee on to brew. Fat and grumpy, her black skin glistening, she grumbled irritably when I told her I needed breakfast for two, looked incredulous and overcome when I said I would help her prepare it.

"Land sakes, chile, ain't you an angel. Jest let me have my coffee an' we'll whip up th' best breakfast you ever seen."

She was as good as her word. The breakfast that I carried up on an enormous wooden tray twenty minutes later looked and smelled incredibly delicious. I smiled to myself, filled with a shimmering happiness that seemed to sing inside me. Balancing the tray carefully, I opened the door to find the room ablaze with sunlight. The bed was empty. Derek was gone, as were his clothes he had discarded during the night. I set the tray down on the dressing table just as the connecting door opened. He had already washed and shaved and was dressed in his old clothes.

"Efficient as ever, I see," he remarked.

"I thought we'd want to get an early start back."

"Right. I'm starved. I imagine you are, too. We never got around to having dinner last night."

That was the only reference he made to what had happened. It was something both of us accepted, and we were not going to discuss it. His manner was rather brusque and matter-of-fact. The coldness was gone, but there would be no warmth, no intimacy. Things would be as before. He was not going to allow any sort of familiarity, was not going to admit to himself that our relationship had altered in any significant way. I knew that I would have to settle for that until he was ready to face the truth about his feeling for me.

After breakfast, after both of us had packed, I returned to the kitchen and arranged to have a lunch made up for us. An hour later we were traveling back to Shadow Oaks, Charles Town well behind us. Derek was immersed in thought, but the silence between us was a comfortable one. I felt I could have spoken to him without the least hesitation. I was content to sit close beside him, lost in a daydream. The horses clopped along at a steady, unhurried pace, the wagon creaking and joggling.

"Was your business successful?" I inquired, much later.

"Satisfactory," he replied.

"It had nothing to do with Shadow Oaks, did it?"

"No, Marietta, it didn't. I went to see a lawyer."

"I didn't mean to pry. It's just that I know so little about you."

"The lawyer in Charles Town corresponds with another lawyer, in London. The man in Charles Town keeps me informed on the progress the man in London is making."

"A London lawyer? You're involved in a court battle?"

"Very much so. By rights I should be Lord Derek Hawke. I should possess an Elizabethan manor house, several thousand acres in Nottinghamshire and three dozen tenant farms. I was cheated out of it by an uncle who, with his sons, is currently living in the house, drawing all the revenues."

"I see."

"Hawkehouse belonged to my father, my grandfather, my great-grandfather, and so on back to the days of Good Queen Bess. Lord Robert Hawke was one of her favorite courtiers. She gave him the house and lands as a token of her esteem. By the law of primogeniture, it should belong to me, the only son of Lord Stephen Hawke."

"I know all about the law of primogeniture," I said, remembering my cousin, remembering the way he had turned me out of Stanton Hall. "Do you want to tell me your story, Derek?"

"I see no reason why you shouldn't know. My father was an avid traveler in his youth and early middle age. He was something of a rakehell, a devil with the ladies. There were a great many ladies and quite a number of illegitimate children but, until he met my mother, no wife. He met her in a small town in Germany. It was famous for its mineral wells. He was into his forties then and already suffering from gout. She was there with a

Prussian officer. She was English, blond, bewitching and quite notorious in certain circles. My father was enchanted with her and, shrewdly, she refused to sleep with him unless he married her. He wasn't at all taken with the idea, but he finally gave in—"

Derek paused, tightening his hold on the reins. When he continued, I detected a certain harsh undercurrent in his voice.

"They were married there in Germany, with only an eccentric and rheumatic old English duchess as witness. My mother returned to Hawkehouse with him, his legal wife, but relatives, neighbors, and friends of my father weren't prepared to accept her as such. They treated her as if she were a flashy mistress he had installed. She was not accepted. She couldn't have cared less. She had all the luxuries she had always dreamed of, a husband who doted on her. That was enough, at least for a while. I was born a year or so later. For some inexplicable reason, I was never christened, although my birth was duly recorded in the registry office."

"You grew up in Hawkehouse?" I inquired.

"I lived there until I was seven years old. Then one night my mother came into my room and told me to dress while she packed a few things for me. We stole out of the house in the middle of the night. A carriage was waiting for us at the end of the lane. A very handsome young man was inside. He and my mother laughed as the carriage drove away. We went to France and then to Italy, and the young man deserted her and she found another man in Rome, a bit older, a bit more dissolute. Two years passed, and I had several more 'stepfathers' before we finally returned to England. My mother took me to a bleak brown school and left me there. I never saw her again. She drowned in a yacht that overturned during a storm in the Mediterranean a few months later."

"How dreadful for you. What happened then?"

"I stayed in the school. She had been kind enough to inform my father of my whereabouts. He sent funds, but he never came to visit me. When I left school, he arranged further education at Oxford, where I did quite well. When I left Oxford, he arranged a commission for me in the army. I was sent to the East. Near the end of my term of service, I learned of his death. But when I was finally able to return to England, I found that I had been declared illegitimate. My uncle and his family were firmly entrenched in Nottinghamshire. He claimed he was the rightful heir, and, as no record could be found of my father's marriage, the court agreed."

"You must have been very bitter."

"Not bitter. Determined. I contacted a very famous lawyer who had once given a speech at Oxford. He was interested in my case and agreed to take it, although he warned me it would be very expensive and might well take years. I had very little money, and I knew I could hope to earn very little in England, being legally declared a bastard. I went to London and visited a few of the gambling halls. I won quite a lot of money, enough to pay my fare to America where, I had heard, a man could make his fortune in cotton. I had enough left over to buy Shadow Oaks. I was foolish enough to marry, but we won't go into that."

The wagon bounced as one of the wheels passed over a rock and I caught hold of his arm to steady myself. Trees cast long shadows across the road. The sunlight was even thinner, the sky a darker gray.

"My lawyer finally found proof of the marriage," Derek continued, "but the documents were declared a forgery. My uncle has a very shrewd set of men working for him. They've had the case thrown out of court repeatedly, but my lawyer hasn't given up, nor have I. I'll win. It may take another ten years and all I can earn during those years, but I'll win."

"It means so much?"

The question was a foolish one. I had been unwise to ask it. Derek fell silent, his mouth tightened, and I could see that he regretted having revealed as much as he had. We continued on down the road, rarely encountering another vehicle either coming or going. Hours had passed

170

since we'd left Charles Town. I was beginning to grow hungry, but I wasn't going to be the one to suggest we stop for lunch. I sat silently, swaying with the wagon, savoring his nearness, staring at the long brown road that stretched ahead. The road was lined with beautiful oaks dripping with moss. There was a light breeze, and the moss swayed back and forth like shreds of ancient lace.

I understood now where all the money had gone, why Shadow Oaks was so shabby, and why he had so few slaves. The case had been a steady drain on his income, but he was convinced that the eventual rewards would compensate for all that. He was a man with a purpose, and I understood what drove him to work so strenuously alongside his slaves, what had shaped him into the grim, sober, embittered man he was today. His uncle's treachery and the disastrous marriage that had followed soon after had left deep wounds. I longed to tend them, but the balm I could offer was the very thing Derek feared most. He had been vulnerable once before. He did not intend to let his guard down again. I hoped that with my new knowledge I might eventually sway his resolution, and, for now, that hope would have to sustain me.

Derek eventually pulled the wagon over to the side of the road, and we ate the lunch the cook and I had packed. He was still moody and uncommunicative. After we finished eating, I packed away the things and got up to put the basket back in the wagon. Derek was sitting with his back against the trunk of a tree, his long legs stretched out in front of him, his arms folded across his chest. I could feel him watching me as I moved toward the wagon. A gust of wind caused my skirts to billow. Tree limbs swayed with a groaning noise. Leaves rustled crisply. It was much cooler than usual; the sultry heat and humidity had lifted.

Derek climbed slowly to his feet and brushed bits of twig from the seat of his breeches. After the meal and short rest, he seemed more relaxed, the tension gone.

"I think I struck a good bargain," he remarked.

"In Charles Town?"

"At the settlement—several months ago. I damn near bankrupted myself in order to buy you, but—I'm beginning to think it was money well invested."

"Indeed?" My voice was light.

"I felt guilty for a long time, wiping my bank account out like that for a red-haired wench who'd never be able to split wood or work out in the fields. It was an insane thing to do. I regretted it."

"And now?"

"And now I think maybe I got a good buy."

He sauntered over to me and rested his forearms on my shoulders, looking into my eyes with a thoughtful expression. I had to tilt my head back to meet his gaze.

"I've needed a woman," he said. "I was a fool to wait so long. A man has needs."

"I know."

He looked into my eyes, and his lips parted. He ran the tip of his tongue around them, and then he kissed me, casually, without passion or any real tenderness. He was merely savoring his property, appreciating me as he might appreciate a fine Havana cigar he was rolling between his fingers. He wrapped an arm around my waist and, holding me in a loose grip, glanced over my shoulder at the wagon, as though debating whether or not there was time to savor me more fully.

"We got a late start," he remarked. "We'd better be on our way."

"I suppose so."

"There'll be plenty of time later."

We both knew what he meant. I belonged to him, and in the future I would perform more intimate services, whenever he was so inclined. I would cook and mend his clothes and clean his house and, when he was swollen with need, assuage that need, without question, without discussion. He would welcome no show of affection, would harshly rebuff it. I was his wench, to be used at his convenience. Derek Hawke would not admit to himself that I was anything more.

He let go of me and moved toward the wagon, throwing his shoulders back and stretching his arms out, a satisfied man, muscles relaxed after the gratifying release of months of sexual tension. He climbed up on the seat and gathered the reins in his hand. I climbed up beside him, trying to resign myself to his attitude, telling myself I could only wait and hope he would eventually recognize the feelings he had expressed this morning with such tenderness.

The horses swung back onto the road. The wagon rocked. We were soon moving down the road at a steady pace. Derek was still relaxed, very much at ease with himself and the world.

"Yeah," he said lazily, "I think maybe I got a bargain."

"Did you really almost bankrupt yourself?"

"Almost. I never intended to spend that much. I'd just transferred a large sum to my lawyer's account in London. There wasn't much left over. No worry, though. The crop will replenish the coffers. If it weren't for that, I'd be in pretty bad shape."

I glanced at the sky apprehensively. It was solid gray and there was an ominous stillness. What if it rained? What if something happened to the crop? I couldn't help feeling a certain apprehension, but Derek knew far more about Carolina weather than I did, and he didn't seem in the least concerned. Still, I found myself wishing the cotton had already been picked. Adam had been concerned about it, I recalled, and the other planters had already picked theirs. The fields we passed were stripped of the plump white balls, only the stalks remaining.

"Tell me about yourself," he said.

"What would you have me tell you?"

"Everything. How you came to speak with that educated accent, how you came to end up in shackles on a prison ship."

"I told you once," I reminded him. "We were on our way to Shadow Oaks after you'd bought me, and—"

"Tell me again. Start at the beginning."

So I told him about my life, about my mother, her

173

death, my father and the education he had given me. I told him about being thrown out of Stanton Hall after my father's death, realizing that my story was quite similar to his own, although in my case there could be no question of my illegitimacy. As the horses cantered along, chestnut coats gleaming, as the wagon rocked and creaked, I told him about my job at Montagu Square, about Lord Mallory and the emeralds he had planted and everything that followed until my arrival in America, omitting nothing from the narrative except the relationship I had had with Jack Reed on board ship. I had enough sense to leave that out.

"An interesting tale," Derek said when I had finished.

"You don't believe me, do you?"

"I'm sure much of it is true."

"You think I—"

"Does it matter what I think, Marietta?"

"Not at all," I said crisply.

"The only thing that matters is that you're my property now. You'll be provided for, protected, fed, clothed—"

"And you think that should satisfy me? You think I should be—"

"I think you should be grateful," he interrupted. "You could have been dealt a much worse fate, I assure you. Rawlins could have bought you. You've had it easy these past months."

"I've been a slave."

"And I've been a damn good master. I could have beaten you, abused you. I could have raped you that first night."

"You could have, yes."

"You've very little to complain about, Marietta."

"I'm a human being. Human beings have—"

"This conversation is beginning to bore me," he said, cutting me short. There was an edge of irritation in his voice. "I don't have to justify myself to you. I paid good money for you, a hell of a lot more than I could afford, and you're damned lucky it was me instead of Rawlins."

"You want me to thank you?"

"I want you to shut up!" he said tersely.

I bit back the sharp retort that sprang to mind and lapsed into silence, humiliated and seething with anger. Derek's irritation soon vanished and he seemed as relaxed as ever, but my own anger didn't abate one jot. At that moment, I wished Jeff Rawlins *had* bought me. I wished I had never heard of Derek Hawke of Shadow Oaks. For a short time I actively hated him, and then, when that passed, I thought how much easier it would be if I *could* hate him. I . . . I could escape, I told myself. I could run away to a big city like Charles Town. I would be free to manage my own life, decide my own fate.

As the wagon bumped down the road, I was lost in revery, stepping into a fantasy world where I was free and affluent, dressed in beautiful gowns, surrounded by handsome men who vied for my attention. Derek would see me and want me, and I would smile at him and then go off on the arm of his rival, disdaining him, leaving him angry and frustrated, sorry he never appreciated me when he had the chance. He would come back again and again, and each time I would reject him. When he was utterly miserable, I would finally condescend to spend an evening with him, and he would . . .

The loud rumble startled me, causing my dream world to shatter abruptly. I looked up in alarm. Derek was tense, his facial muscles tight.

"What—what was that?" I stammered.

"Thunder."

"Thunder? You mean it's going to—"

"It's going to rain!"

He clicked the reins, urging the horses to go faster. The sky was an even darker gray now, tinged with a deep purple. Ponderous black clouds moved across the sky. There was another rumble of thunder. Derek flicked the reins again, spurring the horses on, and soon they were rushing down the road at a mad gallop, hooves pounding, tails and manes flying like skeins of silk. The wagon bounced and swayed, swerving from side to side as our speed increased. I clutched the edge of the seat, afraid

I would be thrown off. Derek leaned forward, half standing, clutching the reins tightly. His whole body was tense, and he was perspiring freely even though it was almost cold now.

Trees seemed to fly past us, dancing dark green forms that blurred together, the road a rapidly unwinding brown ribbon that seemed to propell us forward. A strong wind blew up, tearing at my hair and causing my skirts to flutter up wildly. There was a sudden silver flash as a streak of lightning ripped across the sky. I was terrified, but the terror was minor compared to the wrenching realization of what the storm would mean to Derek. The crop would be destroyed. He would be in desperate financial straits. As tree limbs waved like agitated demons and the horses flew down the road and the wagon bounced savagely, I prayed the rain wouldn't come.

The wheels whirled over a particularly deep rut in the road. The wagon seemed to jump in the air. Losing my grip on the seat, I cried out as I was thrown forward. Derek slung an arm around my shoulder and pulled me back, holding me in a tight grip. The muscles in his arm tightened brutally, but I was hardly aware of the pain. There was another streak of lightning and a distant explosion, and then it began to rain, furiously. Both of us were drenched immediately. Derek shouted to the horses, urging them to go even faster. Through the swirling gray sheets of rain I could see Maud Simmons's fields, stripped of cotton. We were almost home, but it was too late, too late. The brown ribbon of road was already a gleaming brown-black, turning to mud, mud and water splashing as horses and wagon hurtled forward.

It seemed an eternity before we finally reached Shadow Oaks. Derek halted the horses under one of the oaks in back and leaped from the seat, racing towards the fields. I sat there for a moment, stunned, and then I climbed down and, somehow, managed to unharness the horses and lead them through the driving rain to the stables. Where were the slaves? Why wasn't there someone to help? As I turned to leave the stables I saw Cassie dash down the back steps and rush through the rain toward me. By the time she reached the stables her pink dress was plastered against her thickening body, her hair a sleek wet cap. The girl was terrified, trembling as I led her away from the door.

"It's goin' all be lost!" she cried. "Adam hustled everyone out to th' fields soon as th' sky started turnin' dark—everyone, th' wenches an' th' chillen an' even fat Mattie—I wanted to help, too, but he wouldn't let me—"

"Have they—"

"They ain't been able to pick hardly nuthin', Miz Marietta! It'd take three days o' hard work to pick it all, an' they've just been out there since lunch time—"

The girl was crying, her voice a hoarse rasp. She was shivering violently. I reached for an old horse blanket and wrapped it around her, brushing the wet black tendrils of hair away from her face. Lightning streaked, exploded in bursts of silver-gold-blue, and the rain was worse than ever, driven into the stable in sheets by the raging wind. There came a sudden loud pelting on the roof as though the place were being beseiged by artillery fire, and as Cassie and I watched, the rain turned to hail and the hail hurled down like millions of glittering pellets. It lasted for perhaps five minutes, and then it ceased abruptly. There was silence, a terrible silence all the more intense after the barrage of noise.

"It's over," Cassie whispered. "Th' crop is done ruined for sure."

We stood there for several minutes, silent. Cassie was crying. I felt a terrible despair, knowing what this meant, knowing what Derek must be feeling. Rain dripped slowly from the eaves. The yard was littered with hail that glittered and gleamed like crystal. In the distance I saw the Negroes returning from the fields, wet, dejected, dragging limp cloth bags. Adam saw us standing in the doorway of the stables and joined us. There was no need for words. He gathered Cassie in his arms and held her tightly, folding the blanket more closely around her.

"Is—is he still out there?" I asked.

177

Adam nodded gravely. "He jest stands there, lookin' at th' fields."

I left the two of them and moved quickly across the yard, hail crunching beneath my feet. I passed through the oaks and entered the fields. The ground was muddy, the plants all beaten down and broken, the cotton like soggy snow. The purple sky had faded to a pale violet, and thin silvery rays of sunlight streamed down, weak, wavering. I saw Derek up ahead. He stood with his hands thrust into his pockets, and he stared at the desolation as though unable to comprehend it, as though it were a mirage. His hair was plastered against his head. As I drew nearer, I saw his expression, and it gave my heart a wrench. His eyes were filled with anguish. His mouth drooped. He looked lost, defenseless.

I hurried toward him. He looked at me and shook his head, and then a strange, pathetic smile played on his lips. I reached up to smooth the wet locks from his brow. Derek wrapped his arms around me, holding me against him, holding me tightly, tightly, as though he feared he might lose me, too. Neither of us spoke. I had never loved him so strongly, my whole being filled with tremulous emotion. He looked at the fields and shook his head again, and then he looked down into my eyes.

"I still have you," he said. "Thank God for that."

IX

Derek returned to Charles Town two weeks later, traveling on horseback, leaving long before dawn and arriving back at Shadow Oaks late at night. Although he didn't discuss the trip with me, I knew that he had gone to see about getting a loan, and I could tell by his manner the next morning that the trip had been unsuccessful. Later, after breakfast, I was in the kitchen, working at the drainboard, when he entered with a parcel clumsily done up in brown paper and string. He set it on the battered wooden table and tersely informed me that it was for me.

"A present?" I asked, surprised.

"We're going to the county fair two weeks from now. You'll need something to wear. The gown you bought in Charles Town is hardly suitable."

"Fair? You haven't mentioned—"

"Open the package, Marietta," he interrupted. His voice was edged with irritation.

I cut the string and removed the paper and held up the generous length of cloth. It was cotton, a deep, rich red printed with tiny black flowers, more than enough to make a dress. I was moved, not just because the cloth was exceedingly beautiful but because he had thought to buy it for me. He watched me examine it, his eyes guarded, his lips curling in a surly line. I wanted to thank him, but I could tell that it would be unwise.

179

"You'll have plenty of time to make a dress," he said. "I assume you know how?"

"Of course. Thank you, Derek."

"I want you to look presentable when we go to the fair."

He left the kitchen then, abruptly, going out the back door. Through the window I could see him striding briskly across the lawn. The cotton crop had been destroyed, he was near bankruptcy, and he was driving the slaves and driving himself harder than ever, coming in each afternoon just as the sun was beginning to set, worn, exhausted, so weary it took an effort for him to even eat the meals I prepared. Now he was planning to go to the county fair. Why? It was so unlike him. Derek Hawke avoided his neighbors whenever possible. Ordinarily he would have welcomed an event like the fair as he would welcome the plague. I felt sure something was afoot.

I was still mystified when, two weeks later, we were on our way to the fair, the horses moving down the road at a brisk, energetic pace, the wagon rocking and creaking. This road was unfamiliar to me, more narrow than the one we had taken to Charles Town. Lined on either side by tall, leafy trees that kept out most of the sunlight, the road was cool and shady. It was late in the morning, for Derek didn't care to arrive until noon, and it was only an hour's drive from Shadow Oaks.

I was wearing the new dress I had made from the material he purchased in Charles Town. It had puffed sleeves, a modest neckline, and a snugly fitting bodice, the skirt full-gathered and rustling in rich red folds over my petticoats. Cassie had exclaimed over the dress, declaring that it made me look like a queen, but Derek had made no comment. Silent and withdrawn, a worried, preoccupied look in his eyes, he gave no indication that he even noticed. I was too sensible to be hurt, but it would have been nice had he mentioned the dress.

Derek wore polished brown knee boots that had seen better days, as had his brown broadcloth suit. His vest was a dull gold satin striped with thin bronze stripes, his neckcloth of mustard-colored silk. The clothes weren't nearly as elegant as those he had worn in Charles Town, were, in fact, just short of seedy. He had lost weight during the past four weeks and looked drawn and tense, with fatigue shadows beneath his eyes, slight hollows beneath his cheekbones. He had suffered a great set-back, and I wondered if I even had an inkling how enormous it was.

When he purchased me, Derek had intended to rely upon the money the crop would bring in to restore his finances. But the crop had been totally destroyed. I knew that he kept a supply of ready cash in a cigar box in the bottom drawer of his desk in the study. I had seen him take money from it this very morning. Was that all he had? If so, his situation was desperate. I longed to ask him about it, but I knew that would be a mistake. Derek was not one to share his problems.

"Is it much farther?" I asked quietly.

"We're almost there," he replied.

"I—I'm rather nervous."

"There's no need to be."

"Facing all those people—it won't be particularly pleasant. From the first they've assumed that—"

"What they think doesn't matter in the least," he said sternly.

"I still don't know why you decided to go. It—it's not like you."

"I have business to conduct. You'll be on your own part of the time. I'm sure you'll be able to amuse yourself."

"You're going to leave me on my own? After what happened in Charles Town? What if I run into Jason Barnett? What if—"

"That doesn't worry me, Marietta. Not now," he told me.

I was strangely affected by his words, for they proved that he trusted me. Although he would never acknowledge it to me, I felt sure he believed all I had told him about my past, believed I had been framed for a crime I hadn't committed. During the past four weeks there had been a subtle alteration in his manner toward me. I was still his

181

housekeeper, still waited on him, serving him as before, serving him in a new capacity at night. Although he certainly didn't treat me as an equal, there was a new courtesy and consideration that hadn't been there before, so subtle it wouldn't even be apparent to anyone else.

A short while later Derek turned off the road. I could hear loud, brassy music in the distance, and as we rounded a bend I could see tents and booths set up in a clearing surrounded by oaks. Derek pulled the wagon under the shade of a large tree, near where dozens of others were lined up. Two small boys rushed over, and Derek gave each a coin. They assured him they would look after the horses. He helped me down from the wagon, and we strolled toward the tents and booths.

"It's really not unlike the county fairs back in England," I remarked. "Back home there would be gypsy dancers and fortune tellers, but this is much the same."

"Really merely an excuse for the smaller farmers to sell their goods," Derek told me. "There are pigs and chickens and cattle for sale, and pies, cakes, preserves. There'll be a shooting gallery and probably a boxing match, and stands where you can buy beer and refreshments—as you say, much like the fairs in England. A lot of bartering is done, a lot of trading, buying, selling. Mostly it's an opportunity for people to get out and get together and raise a little hell."

There were dozens of gaily striped tents, dozens of wooden booths. A raucous, festive atmosphere prevailed. The noise was incredible. Children raced about, shouting, laughing, scuffling. Dogs barked. Chickens clucked noisily. Pigs squealed. Rifles blasted at the shooting gallery. A carousel of brightly painted horses went round and round, a calliope playing as the horses dipped up and down. A wooden dance floor had been constructed near the edge of the clearing, and a decidedly amateur band played with considerable brio as young people stomped lustily about the floor, faces flushed with excitement. On every side there was color and movement, with almost two hundred people thronging the small area.

Tables and benches had been set up near the refreshment stands under a huge canvas canopy that provided shade. Derek bought two plates of beans and ham hocks, bought buttered cornbread and two glasses of cold apple cider, then led me over to one of the tables. People stared openly. Everyone knew I was Derek Hawke's wench, an indentured servant, and everyone assumed, rightly now, that I was his mistress as well. Several of the women looked offended. Three of them at a table nearby moved to one farther away, muttering shrill complaints at his audacity in bringing "that hussy in red" around decent women. It didn't bother me in the least. I was proud to be with him, proud to be his woman. Derek paid no attention to the stares, the hostility. He gave no sign that he even noticed it.

"It's all rather exciting," I said. "It's so—merry."

"That won't last," Derek replied. "As the afternoon progresses, the merriment will vanish. People will be tired, and most of the men will be drunk by the time the sun goes down. Tonight there'll be colored lanterns. Youngsters will steal off in pairs for quick romance in the shrubbery, and there'll be fist fights and arguments. We'll be gone by then."

"How long are we going to stay?"

"As long as it takes me to get my business accomplished," he replied, deliberately cryptic.

Derek had no intention of telling me why we were here. My curiosity was strongly aroused, but I had better sense than to ask him straight out what his business was. He would undoubtedly tell me to remember my place. If he wanted me to know, I would know in time. I had a strange feeling that whatever he was planning was something I wasn't going to be at all happy about.

As we ate, I noticed a man sitting across the way who seemed to be even more of a pariah than we were. He sat at a table, alone, all the tables around him empty. People stepping under the canopy with plates of food refused to sit near him, frequently sharing tables with other people rather than take one close to the man. Middle-aged, robust, he had moody blue eyes and blazing red hair and beard. He wore a severe black suit shiny with age, the cloth seeming to strain across his enormous shoulders. A battered-looking Bible was on the table in front of him, and he turned its pages as he ate his beans and cornbread.

"Elijah Jones," Derek remarked, noticing my interest. "He's from New England, an unsuccessful preacher who sometimes holds revival meetings. A lot of people go in order to boo and hiss. He has a small farm on the other side of Maud Simmons's place, barely scratches out enough to live on."

"Why is everyone avoiding him?"

"He claims slavery is a vile evil, preaches about it, goes around trying to get the planters to release their slaves. If that was his only offense, they'd consider him a harmless eccentric, but unfortunately he gives aide to runaway slaves and helps 'em escape."

"Isn't that against the law?"

Derek nodded, his expression grim. "Elijah's very crafty at it. No one has ever been able to *prove* anything against him, but it's more or less an open secret that he's an important link in a network of fanatics who help runaway slaves get up North."

"There are others?"

"A small organization," Derek replied. "They work under the cover of night, on the sly. A couple of slaves will appear on Elijah's doorstep in the dead of night, say, and he'll hide them until he can transport them to the next safe haven—another farm perhaps fifty miles from here. They'll hide out there until the farmer can smuggle them on to yet another place, even farther away. They pass from place to place until they eventually reach safety."

"It sounds terribly complex, and dangerous, too."

"It is, but it frequently works. These men are very sly, very slippery. They're dedicated to a 'cause' and are willing to risk anything in order to help those 'poor, lost souls,' as they call 'em."

"And this Mr. Jones is part of that?"

184

"As I say, no one's been able to prove anything against him, and naturally he denies it, but everyone in these parts is convinced he's guilty. None of the planters'll have anything to do with him. If they had their way, he'd be tarred and feathered and run out of the country on a rail, but you can't treat a 'Man of God' that way without proof."

I studied Elijah Jones, secretly admiring him. Although Derek's voice was harsh and bitter when he spoke of the man, I couldn't help thinking him unusually brave. With his blazing red beard and long red locks, his sullen blue eyes and ravaged face, he did indeed look like a zealot. I could see him behind a pulpit in that same shiny black suit, shaking his fist, lambasting his audience with thunderous denunciation for their part in a grievous wrong. Derek and the other planters considered their slaves mere property, like cattle, but Elijah Jones considered them men and women with souls and a right to freedom. If he was indeed a part of the underground network, I wished him well.

"Lot of folks down here don't believe in keeping slaves," Derek continued. "I'll tell you one thing, though: My slaves are a helluva lot better off than most black men who try to find work on their own. At least they get plenty to eat, decent living accommodations—"

He cut himself short, scowling angrily. I knew that he was exceedingly sensitive about the subject of slavery, and I had no desire to discuss it with him, feeling as I did. I was relieved when he pushed his empty plate away and asked me if I was finished. I nodded, and we left the table, moving slowly back down the row of booths. A towheaded lad rushed past, two others in hot pursuit, a yapping brown and white spotted dog following close on their heels.

Derek paused in front of one of the stands and, reaching into his pocket, pulled out some coins.

"Here," he said, handing me the money. "I want you to amuse yourself for a couple of hours. Buy yourself some ribbons or something. I'll meet you by the carousel around . . . say, around four. I should be finished by that time."

"I wish you wouldn't leave me alone, Derek."

"You worried about running into Barnett again?"

"No, but—"

"Run along, Marietta. You can take care of yourself."

Derek didn't give me a chance to argue. He turned and strolled away briskly. I saw a group of planters up ahead, all of them elegantly dressed, all of them drinking port they purchased from one of the booths. As I watched, Derek joined them, and soon the whole group of them wandered away to inspect the livestock. Nervous, disoriented, I clutched the coins in my hand and stood in front of the stand like a lost child. People moved past, talking loudly, laughing, and the shrill, discordant music was a constant background.

"Lands sake, honey! I never expected to see *you* here."

Maud Simmons stopped, hands on hips, a warm smile on her lips.

"Mrs. Simmons, how nice to see you."

"Maud, honey. My, you look lovely! Is that a new dress?"

I nodded. "Der—Mr. Hawke bought the cloth in Charles Town. I made the dress myself."

"Damned fine job you did, too. You're a regular seamstress. I could use a few new clothes myself—never have time to fuss with 'em, though."

Maud was wearing the same emerald-green riding habit she had worn when she came to borrow the liniment. It was as deplorably soiled as before, although she had pinned a gaudy coral brooch to the lapel. Coral earrings dangled from her ears. Her hair looked as if it had not been touched by comb or brush since the last time I saw her. The smile still spread on her lips, and she looked genuinely pleased to see me.

"Enjoyin' yourself, honey? You looked rather forlorn, standin' there all by yourself. Your man leave you to your own devices for a while? They do that, no consideration whatsoever! Tell you what, why don't you come with me? I'm going to have a look at the quilts, see if there's any of 'em I'd care to buy."

"I'd enjoy that."

"These affairs bore the bloody hell out of me. So noisy. So many people, but sometimes you can pick up some real bargains. All the farmers bring their wares— you name it, honey, they bring it. Never seen so much junk. Last time one of th' farm women was sellin' her china. She and her husband'd had a spell of bad luck and needed some quick money. Would you believe it was genuine Sèvres? Came all the way from France. I bought the whole lot for next to nothing."

Maud chattered volubly as we strolled past tents and booths, and I was grateful for her company. Each time we passed someone she knew, Maud insisted on stopping and introducing me, taking a perverse pleasure in the stiff expressions and tight smiles of the women she forced to acknowledge my presence. "Pack-a bloody hypocrites," she called them, bursting into gales of raucous laughter when one of the prim ladies drew herself up and marched on past us without so much as a nod.

"Ain't any of them none too respectable themselves," she declared. "Me, I know where the bodies are buried! 'Course they got a right to resent you—most of 'em have been pantin' over Derek Hawke ever since he moved into Shadow Oaks. One nod from him and half th' married ladies in th' county'd come a-runnin'. If I was a few years younger I'd give him a merry chase myself! Ah, here are the quilts. Hmmm, shabby lookin' lot, wouldn't you say? That blue and brown and yellow one—now, I might be able to live with it if it don't cost an arm and a leg."

While Maud examined the quilts, I looked at some beautiful samplers, all of them made by the worn-looking farm woman who stood behind the booth. At the shooting gallery nearby, guns were going off in a chain of deafening explosions and men shouted lustily as ringing pings indicated a hit. Three young men staggered past, arms locked together, stumbling tipsily and bellowing a bawdy song. Maud bought her quilt, exclaiming over the quality of the workmanship and the bargain price. We moved along down the rows of booths, stopping every now and then so that she could examine the merchandise.

"What beautiful neckcloths," I remarked, pausing before yet another booth. "This pearl-gray silk—I wonder if I could afford it? I'd love to buy something for—"

"How much have you got, honey? Oh sure, that's enough. Bessie here'll be glad to sell it to you for that, won't you, Bessie? This here's my neighbor Marietta, and she wants to surprise her man. Come on now, Bessie—it didn't cost you nothing to run up that neckcloth."

Bessie was plump and belligerent and reluctant to part with the cloth for the sum I had, but Maud persisted. I was shamelessly eager to buy it, for the stock was beautiful and would be perfect with Derek's navy blue suit, but I let Maud do the bargaining. Bessie finally heaved a sigh, took my coins, and wrapped the cloth up in brown paper, tying it with string. I thanked her and smiled, anticipating Derek's surprise when I presented it to him.

A few minutes later Maud stopped in front of a booth where a man was selling beer, declaring she could use a mug and asking me if I would join her. Maud looked disappointed when I refused.

"You sure? All right, Jim, give me a mug. This your special home brew? Hope it tastes better'n it did last year. Thanks." She gripped the pewter mug, blew the foam off the top and downed the beer thirstily. "Hmmm, I think you're gettin' better, Jim. Give me another."

"I saw one of your neighbors a little while ago," I remarked.

"Oh? Who'd that be?"

"Elijah Jones. Derek said he had a small farm on the other side of your place."

"If you want to *call* it a farm. Just a run-down house, really, and a vegetable garden—a couple of acres of cotton. Works it himself. Won't have any slaves on his place, not that he could afford 'em."

"Is what they say about him true?"

188

"You mean about him helpin' runaway niggers?" Maud glanced over her shoulder and, seeing that Jim was eavesdropping, took my elbow and led me around to the side of the booth.

"Me, honey, I *like* Elijah," she began. "He's never done *me* no harm. One time when I had a bad case o' th' grippe, he came over to look after me, just upped an' came without anyone askin', had my cook make hot soup, fed it to me himself, brought some medicine over, too. He bored th' *hell* outta me, prayin' over me, askin' th' Lord to spare my soul an' all that, but he nursed me till I was up an' able to get about."

"Derek said he—might be part of an anti-slavery group."

"Everyone says that, honey, but no one's ever been able to prove anything. A few months back—" Maud hesitated, as though debating whether or not to confide in me. "A few months back two of Ben Randolph's bucks ran away. That night I was takin' a stroll and I *might* have seen Elijah takin' two niggers down to his storm cellar—it has an outside door on th' side of his house facin' my place. I reckon he must have some kind of secret room down there, behind all those shelves."

"You didn't tell anyone?"

Maud shook her head. "If you treat your niggers right, they ain't got no cause to be runnin' away. Randolph, now —he treats 'em mean, real mean. He loves usin' his whip and don't like to put himself out seein' they have decent food and sleepin' quarters. They're gonna up and turn on him one of these days, you mark my word. I never said a word about what I mighta seen, kept my mouth firmly shut. You're the first person I ever mentioned it to, and I know you ain't *about* to spill the beans."

"Of course not."

"I don't *approve* of what Elijah's doin', make no mistake about that, but neither do I approve of Ben Randolph and men like him. My niggers are loyal. I spend a fortune every year seein' they get proper treatment. They eat damn near as well as I do, and each cabin has a wood stove. I never work 'em too hard, and any time one of 'em gets sick I fetch a doctor and look after 'em like I would a child. What Elijah's doing is wrong, but I figure if a slave runs away it's because he ain't been treated right. I keep rememberin' that damned hot soup and those bloody prayers—I guess I may be some kinda traitor to my class, but I've no intention of givin' Elijah away. I shouldn'ta even told you, honey."

"I can assure you it won't go any further."

"Oh, I know that or I wouldn'ta opened my mouth in the first place. You know something? I never *did* replace that liniment I used, been weeks and weeks since I brought the bottle back. I'm going to buy a new bottle right now. They're sellin' it at one of the booths. I'll just give Jim his mug back—"

Maud purchased the bottle of liniment and gave it to me, and then she sighed and said she'd enjoyed my company mightily but she'd best be getting back to Magnolia Grove. She gave me a hug and, clutching her new quilt under one arm, tottered away, her soiled emerald riding skirt trailing in the dirt, her wild gray bird's nest bouncing. As it was still some time before I was to meet Derek, I decided to stroll back to the wagon and store the neck-cloth and liniment in back, under the empty seed bags. I would surprise Derek with the present tonight after we returned to Shadow Oaks.

It was cool and shady under the trees where the wagons stood. Heavy boughs kept out the sun and cast thick violet-blue shadows over the ground. There was no one else around, not even the little boys who were supposed to be watching the horses, and I lingered there beside the wagon for a while, stroking one of the chestnuts. Lost in thought, I didn't hear the man and his two pack mules approaching until they were almost even with the wagon. He was whistling a jaunty tune, as merry and unconcerned as a boy. One of the mules balked. He stopped and turned around to scold the animal.

"Come on, love," he said pleasantly, tugging at the reins, "that's no way to be. You're carrying a load of nice trinkets in those packs and I aim to sell the lot of 'em. We're late as it is. No nonsense now——"

I recognized him immediately. I remembered the soft, pleasingly slurred voice, the amiable brown eyes, and the shaggy sandy locks that fell across his brow in a heavy fringe. He was wearing the same brown boots and buckskins he had worn before, the jacket adorned with long, leathery fringe. When the mule refused to move, Jeff Rawlins shook his head and gave an exasperated sigh, and then he caught hold of one of the mule's ears, took it between his teeth and bit down forcefully. The mule brayed angrily.

"Serves you right, actin' like a bloody prima donna. Why can't you behave yourself like your brother here? *He* never balks. You ready to move along now?"

The mule actually nodded. Jeff Rawlins gave it an affectionate pat on the nose, and then he turned and saw me standing beside the wagon. He looked dismayed, then delighted. A wide grin played on his lips.

"If this don't beat *all*," he exclaimed. "I was thinking about you just a little while ago——God's truth I was. I thought seein' as how I'll be in the neighborhood for a while I oughta stop by Hawke's place, see if he needs any thimbles or thread or knives or things like I'm sellin', see if he still has that magnificent wench he beat me out of."

"Hello, Mr. Rawlins," I said coldly.

"You remember me? 'Course you do. Once they encounter Jeff Rawlins, the ladies can't get him outta their minds——it's these cursed good looks and my carefree charm. There's been many a time I've wished a few of 'em *had* forgot, I don't mind tellin' you."

"I remember you well."

"I'll bet you were disappointed when I lost out to Hawke, weren't you? Come on, wench, confess it."

"Actually I was——at first. Then I learned about your affiliations in New Orleans."

Rawlins looked hurt. "I say, has Hawke been bad-mouthin' me? That ain't no way to do. I'm just an honest

191

peddler travelin' around with my pack mules, trying to make an honest living. Anyone can see that."

He spoke in a light, jesting tone, grinning all the while. Rawlins had charm, all right. I had never encountered such charm. Breezy, engaging, he had the manner of a raffish little boy. He wasn't really handsome, the mouth too wide, the nose slightly humped, but there was a magnetism far more potent than good looks could have been. Those eyes and that grinning, sensual mouth would have stirred the coldest breast. I knew what he was and I detested him for it, yet I felt an attraction in spite of myself.

"Surprised to see me?" he inquired.

"A little," I admitted.

"I finished my business in New Orleans and came back along the Trace to do a bit of tradin' till the next auction. Me and the mules've been going around the county, visiting various plantations to sell my goods. I 'spect I'll sell the rest this afternoon."

"I wish you luck."

"Really? That's mighty nice, knowin' you care."

Rawlins strolled over and stood before me with his hands resting on his thighs, his head cocked slightly to one side. He was so close I could feel the heat of his body, smell his musky male odor. I should have been uneasy. I wasn't. Sure of myself, sure of my feelings for Derek, I felt immune to Rawlins's seductive charm.

"I must say, wench, you look even more appetizing than I remembered. I *do* adore redheads. I fear I've a weakness for 'em."

"That's too bad, Mr. Rawlins."

"Hey now, you ain't going to be unfriendly, are you? And me such an engaging chap." He shook his head in mock sadness. "That's no way to act."

"I couldn't help but smile. It was impossible not to like him, impossible not to respond to that affable manner. I found it hard to believe he was as vile as he was painted. Too, it was flattering to be found attractive and

192

appealing. Jeff Rawlins made me feel exceedingly feminine.

"That's more like it," he told me. "I say, what're you doin' all by yourself out here?"

"I'm waiting for Hawke," I lied. "He should be joining me any minute now."

"Damn, just my luck. I was hopin' we could have a quick tumble under the wagon—or somethin'. Today just isn't my day."

"I'm certain you'll find several amenable women at the fair, Mr. Rawlins."

"Probably so," he teased. "I usually do. Gets to be a bit tiresome after a while—all this charm, all those women. None of 'em will be anything like you, though. Hawke happy with you?"

"Very."

"Don't reckon he'd be interested in sellin'?"

"I doubt it, Mr. Rawlins."

"Be a fool if he *was*. I'm headin' up to the auction in a couple days. On the way back I might just stop by Shadow Oaks on the off chance I can persuade him to change his mind. Be wastin' my time, probably, but I got plenty of time to waste."

"Another prison ship has arrived?"

Rawlins nodded. "I don't expect to find any prizes, I might as well confess it. Truth to tell, I'm beginning to lose interest in that particular little enterprise. It's a helluva lot of trouble for damned little profit."

He glanced around. There was still no one in sight. We were alone, surrounded by empty wagons and carriages. Tree limbs swayed gently in the breeze. The deep shadows danced over the ground. His wide pink mouth spread in another grin.

"I say, Hawke's certainly takin' his time—"

"He's bound to be here in just a minute."

"Even so, I reckon there's time for a quick kiss—"

He pulled me into his arms in one quick movement, clasping me in a light firm grip. I opened my mouth to protest, but before I could even shape the words, his

193

mouth fastened over mine and he was kissing me quite thoroughly. I struggled, trying to break free, and Rawlins's arms tightened around me. He was strong, much too strong. There was nothing I could do but give in to the dizziness . . . and the delight.

Rawlins drew his head back and, still holding me, looked at me with mischievous brown eyes.

"That wasn't so bad, now, was it?"

"You—you're a rogue, Mr. Rawlins!"

"Always was," he confessed. "Bad blood, I reckon."

"And you need a bath! You smell of sweat and the woods and—"

"Don't pretend to be nothing 'cept what I am, wench. A backwoods savage. You called me that once, remember? I'll tell you something, though. I could have you lovin' it in no time at all."

"Let go of me."

Rawlins released me, grinning again. I wanted to slap that grin off his face, but, in truth, I wasn't nearly as angry as I should have been. Those sensations were still swirling inside. I felt weak and vulnerable and curiously elated, as though I'd had too much wine much too quickly. Rawlins was fully aware of the effect he had on me.

"Reckon I'll be moseying along now," he said. "Got a lotta goods to sell and not too much time left to sell 'em. You take good care of yourself now, wench. I'll be seein' you again 'fore too much longer."

"Hawke will run you off the place!"

"A friendly chap like me, trying to make an honest livin'? Why should he? You're not going to tell him about our little kiss. It was a harmless peck—and you enjoyed every second of it."

He made an elaborate bow then and tipped an imaginary hat. Then he strolled back to his mules, caught up the reins, and led them on towards the fairgrounds, their heavy packs wobbling as they moved. I was filled with a variety of emotions, most of them disturbingly pleasant. I loved Derek Hawke with all my heart and soul, yet I

194

had been strongly attracted to Jeff Rawlins. It was purely physical, yet it worried me nonetheless. I felt that I had somehow betrayed myself.

I did not mention my encounter with Rawlins when I met Derek by the carousel, nor did I mention him during the journey back to Shadow Oaks. Derek was moody and withdrawn, and I felt no inclination to talk myself. I wondered if he had accomplished his purpose at the fair. It was impossible to tell from his manner. It was growing late by the time we reached the plantation, and I was pleased to see that Cassie had already started the evening meal. I took over, grateful to have something to do.

Hawke retired to his study after dinner, and I helped Cassie clear up and wash the dishes. Her morning sickness had long since passed, and she was all aglow, radiantly beautiful as she moved about the kitchen under the gaze of Adam, who sat at the table with a cup of hot coffee. Although it had already been let out once, Cassie's pink dress was again too tight, her swollen breasts and stomach straining against the cloth. When our work was finished, she leaned against her husband's chair, resting her hand on his shoulder. Adam looked up at her, his dark eyes full of pride and love. The two of them together like that were an incredibly lovely sight, so touching that it almost brought tears to my eyes.

"This man," Cassie said, touching the side of his face. "I'm a lucky wench, Miz Marietta, and I knows it."

Adam scowled fiercely, pretending to be displeased. "Git on about yore business," he growled. "Stop pawin' over me."

"Ain't he a man? Ain't he beautiful?"

"He's goin' whup yore hide effin you don't stop moonin'."

Cassie smiled, knowing the threat was hollow, knowing he loved her as deeply and passionately as she loved him. It was already dark outside, a thick, velvety summer darkness, and the lamps burned warmly in the kitchen, creating a soft, intimate atmosphere that was a perfect setting for their love. Cassie poured another cup of coffee

195

for him and brought him some of the molasses cookies I had baked the day before. The three of us visited for a while, weary, relaxed, talking lazily about nothing in particular, and it was after nine before they finally went out to their cabin.

I had gone up to my bedroom and was just starting to get undressed when Derek stepped into the room. He had removed jacket and waistcoat. His shirt was slightly rumpled, tucked loosely into the waistband of his breeches. I was pleased, for he hadn't come to my bedroom the past two nights. Derek never talked when he visited me. He came, he slept with me, and then he returned to his own bedroom. He never fully undressed, either. It was almost as though taking off all his clothes and climbing under the covers with me would indicate a commitment he wasn't prepared to make. He used me as many of the planters used their Negro wenches, but I wasn't at all perturbed. In the act itself Derek expressed all those feelings he refused to acknowledge openly, and one day, one day soon, I hoped, he would express those feelings openly, without fear.

"I have something for you," I told him.

"Oh?"

"It's here, in the drawer—" I took out the small parcel Bessie had wrapped for me and handed it to him. Derek wasn't at all pleased, frowning as he tore away paper and string.

"I thought it would go nicely with your navy-blue suit."

"You bought it at the fair?"

I nodded. Derek examined the neckcloth, still frowning, then placed it on the dressing table.

"I intended you to buy something for yourself," he said.

"I wanted you to have it, Derek. I—I hoped you'd be pleased."

Derek did not reply, but stepped over to me and, reaching around, began to unfasten my dress in back. He looked bored and indifferent, even as he pulled the bodice down and slipped the dress below my waist. It fell to the floor, a rustling circle of red sprigged with tiny black

196

flowers. I held my breath as he caught the straps of my petticoat and tugged at them, exposing my breasts. Catching hold of my arms, he backed me up against the bed, shoved me gently onto the mattress.

An hour later he stood at the side of the bed, tucking the tail of his shirt back into the waistband of his breeches. He had made love to me twice, powerfully, with an almost frantic zest, yet he still seemed worried and preoccupied now. Languorous, replete, filled with a sweet ache that seemed to glow inside, I pulled my bodice back up and smoothed my skirts and watched him step across the room to the mirror. Although his back was to me, I could see his face in the glass. He brushed the sweat-damp hair from his brow and stared at his reflection as though to find an answer to some grave question. The hollows beneath his cheekbones and the shadows about his eyes seemed even more pronounced than they had been earlier. It wasn't like him to linger like this. He usually returned to his own room as soon as he adjusted his clothing.

"Something's bothering you," I said quietly. "There—there's something you want to tell me."

Derek turned and nodded, frighteningly grim. "You'll have to know sooner or later—Randolph will be here early next week."

"Randolph? I don't understand."

"Ben Randolph. He'll be coming to pick up his property."

"You—" I hesitated. A hand seemed to clutch my heart.

"I'm selling Adam," he told me.

"Derek! You can't do that!"

"I have no choice," he said. His voice was cold, hard. "Randolph'll give me two thousand pounds for the buck. He's been after me to sell him for the past two years."

I was standing now, trembling. My knees felt weak, and it seemed the floor was about to drop from under me. I caught hold of the bedpost for support, gripping it tightly.

"Cassie's expecting a baby! You can't separate them! They—they love each other. It's inhuman. It's—"

"God knows I don't want to sell him. I have no choice. I tried to get a loan in Charles Town. I couldn't. I tried to get a mortgage on Shadow Oaks. That fell through, too. I have to have money, Marietta, and I have to have it now, or we'll all starve."

"You can't do it—not Adam. Derek, you simply can't—"

"I told Randolph about Cassie, told him she was expecting, offered to sell her, too, so they wouldn't be separated, but he wasn't interested. It's something I have to do, Marietta."

"You can't! Ben Randolph—Maud told me about him, told me how he mistreats his slaves. The man's a sadist, a—"

"He isn't going to mistreat Adam. He's investing two thousand pounds."

"I won't let you do it!"

"Goddamit!" he exploded. "Do you think I *want* to sell him? Do you think I haven't gone through all the agonies of hell? It's the toughest decision I've ever had to make in my life, but I had to make it! I could sell Adam, or I could sell you! Randolph'd buy you in a minute, or Jason Barnett, or a dozen other men I could name! I prefer to sell Adam."

"He—he's a human being. He's a husband, and—and soon he'll be a father. There must be something else you can do. It's—"

"It's done," he said crisply.

He turned then and left the room abruptly. I heard him striding briskly down the hall, heard him enter his room and slam the door shut behind him. I stood there clutching the bedpost, tears streaming down my cheeks, so distraught I could hardly think coherently. I cried, and then I wiped my cheeks and turned out the lamp and went to sit in front of the window. I stared out at the night, and I was a part of the darkness, filled with an anguish almost impossible to bear. Hours passed, and dawn came. Reason

198

returned. It would kill Cassie if she lost her man. It would destroy Adam, too. That majestic splendor would vanish and he would be a mere shell. I couldn't let it happen. I couldn't.

I thought of Elijah Jones then, and I knew what I had to do.

X

"Stop crying, Cassie," I said sharply. "That isn't going to help matters at all, and—and it's beginning to irritate me!"

"You don't *care*," she wailed. "Th' master done put Adam in chains an' locked him up out in th' shed, and dat man's goin' be here tomorrow to take him away."

"I'm fully aware of that, Cassie."

"Why'd he have to put Adam in chains? Why'd he have to lock him up like dat? Adam wuzn't goin' run away. He has pride, Miz Marietta. Chainin' him like dat done—done make him feel like some worthless nigger. He's goin' die o' shame, and I'm goin' die, too. If they take my man away, I'm goin' die sure as faith—"

"Shut *up*, Cassie."

I felt wretched speaking to the girl like that, but I simply couldn't abide her sniveling any longer. Cassie retreated to the other side of the kitchen and stood wringing her hands, her eyes abrim with tears. I wanted to gather her in my arms and hold her close, comfort her, but I couldn't. This was no time for any kind of emotional indulgence. I had a great deal on my mind, a great deal to do, and it would take all the strength and courage I could muster. I knew I had to remain as cool, as calm as possible.

"It's wicked what he's doin'," Cassie sobbed. "Th'

master's always been good 'fore now, always been fair, and now—"

"I'm going out to see Mattie for a few minutes," I interrupted. "The master will be coming in any time now, and he'll expect his dinner to be ready. Set the table, Cassie, and then take the beans off and check on the cornbread. Have you sliced the meat?"

Cassie nodded wretchedly, and I felt like a traitor as I stepped outside and started across the yard toward Mattie's cabin. I hadn't revealed my plans to Cassie, nor had I said anything to Adam, afraid they might inadvertently give something away. I had confided in only two people: Mattie and Elijah Jones. Last night, at great risk, I had slipped out of the house after Derek had gone to sleep. I had walked all the way to Elijah's farm, returning just before dawn. Everything was ready. I just prayed that I would have the strength to go through with it.

Derek and I had had a violent argument this morning. I felt it unnecessary to put Adam in chains, but Derek insisted it was a precaution he had to take. Adam was dumbfounded when Derek led him to the shed and placed him in shackles, for neither he nor Cassie had had the least inkling that he was to be sold until then. Cassie had been wailing all day long, and when I had taken his lunch out to him Adam had been silent and sullen, desperately trying to conceal his anguish. As soon as I stepped out of the shed, Derek had taken the key from me and locked the door again. I had swept on into the house, refusing to speak to him.

Caleb was lingering outside Mattie's cabin, as stunned and frightened as all the other slaves. They found it hard to believe that Adam was locked up in the shed, that tomorrow he would be taken away, never to return. A tense atmosphere prevailed. No half-naked children played on the steps. There was no warm, friendly chatter among the women as they went about their work. A great pall had fallen over everything, the silence broken only by the clucking of the chickens and the grunts of the pigs in their pen behind the cabins.

The curtains were drawn inside Mattie's cabin, and it was so dim I could hardly see. Mattie climbed heavily out of her chair and came toward me. She was nervous, her eyes wide with fear as she handed me the tiny packet.

"Is this it?" I asked.

Mattie nodded. "You just puts it in his coffee."

"It—it won't hurt him, will it?"

"Won't do nuthin' to him but make him feel drowsy an' tired. He'll be fast asleep 'fore an hour goes by, an' when he wakes up late tomorrow mornin' he won't even have a headache."

"You're sure?"

"I'se sure, Miz Marietta. I was pickin' herbs an' grindin' 'em up long 'fore you wuz even born. He'll just get sleepy, an' he'll sleep like a lamb all night, wouldn't even wake up if there wuz an earthquake. You just puts it in his coffee like I says. He won't even taste it."

"I hope you're right, Mattie."

"I knows my herbs, gal."

"You haven't—said anything to anyone?"

The fat old slave shook her head. "When he finds them two niggers gone, th' master's goin' be furious, goin' question us all, thinkin' we wuz onto it. None of 'em but me's goin' know a thing, and I can keep my mouth shut. Long as none of 'em see you or hear you tonight, none of 'em's ever goin' know you had anything to do with it."

"That's the way I want it," I told her. "He—he mustn't find out."

"You's doin' a mighty risky thing, gal. Mighty brave, too. Reckon I'd be scared clean outta my breeches. Them two's lucky to have someone like you on dere side."

Derek was coming back toward the house as I crossed the yard. He looked weary, his old white shirt clinging across his back damply, his breeches dusty. I hurried on into the house, not deigning to speak, and later on, as I served his dinner, I maintained my silence. He had cleaned up and changed, but he still looked exhausted. I knew this was very difficult for him, knew he hated to part with Adam, and I had to steel myself to keep from

202

sympathizing. I was concerned about Adam and Cassie now. Later on I could be concerned about Derek. My hand shook ever so slightly as I carried the pot of coffee into the dining room. The liquid was thick and hot, steaming as I poured it into his cup. I was relieved to find that I experienced very little guilt.

He was already yawning when I returned with the rice pudding I had made for dessert. His eyelids were heavy, and I could see that he was struggling to stay awake.

"Are you all right?" I inquired. "You seem—unusually tired."

"I must have worked harder than I thought. I can hardly keep my eyes open. I'll skip dessert, Marietta. I'll —just go on up to my room, get to bed early."

Half an hour later I crept into his room. He was stretched out across the bed on top of the covers, sound asleep. He had pulled off his boots and shirt, but he still wore his breeches, and he had left the lamp burning. I blew it out, and as the moonlight poured into the room I swung his legs around and propped his head on the pillows. Derek moaned and made a face as I spread a light quilt over him, but he didn't awaken. I left him there in the darkness and hurried down to the kitchen where Cassie was washing the dishes.

"I want you to listen to me carefully," I said. "Don't ask any questions, just do as I say. Go to your cabin and bundle up your things. Adam's, too. Do it quietly. Don't let anyone see you or hear you. Then meet me at the side of the barn, in the shadows."

"I—I don't understand, Miz Marietta. What—"

"Don't ask questions, Cassie! It's important you do exactly as I say."

The girl understood then. She looked incredulous, then frightened, and then she nodded and gave me a quick hug, holding me tightly for a moment as the tears spilled down her cheeks. I blew out the lamp in the kitchen, and Cassie slipped out under the cover of darkness. With luck, all the other slaves would already be in their cabins. Peering out the window, I could barely see the girl as

203

she moved across the dark yard, keeping to the shadows. I suddenly realized the enormity of what I was doing, and doubts besieged me. He would indeed be furious when he discovered the couple gone. He would mount an extensive search. What if he discovered I was responsible . . . Again I steeled myself. I couldn't afford to think about possible repercussions, not at this point.

Moving quickly down the hall, I stepped into the study. The lamps were burning, filling the room with a mellow golden light, and all the draperies were open. Guiltily, I closed them so that no one could see into the room, and then I stepped over to the desk and opened the bottom drawer, taking out the cigar box. They would need a certain amount of money before they finally reached safety. I didn't intend to take much. Derek probably wouldn't even miss it, I told myself, gingerly removing several of the bills. I folded them up and slipped them into my skirt pocket, then put the box back and closed the drawer.

I was still nervous as I went outside and moved through the darkness toward the barn. Despite my resolution, despite the belief that right was on my side, I felt a tremulous quaking inside as I stepped into the pitch-dark barn and groped my way over to the shelf where I had placed the hammer and chisel earlier on. Chickens were roosting in the barn. They stirred noisily as I ran my hand over the shelf, finally locating the tools. I had been framed and sentenced for a crime I hadn't committed, and now I was committing a crime which, legally at least, was far more serious.

Clutching the tools, I left the barn with its fetid smell of old leather and hay and stole silently away toward the shed. There was too much moonlight, and the shed was far too close to the slave quarters. The horses moved restlessly in their stalls as I passed the stables and an owl hooted, giving me quite a turn. The front of the shed was bathed in luminous silvery moonlight and spread with lacy black shadows that shifted and swayed as the tree limbs moved in the breeze. Peering up at the sky, I could see that the moon was about to disappear behind a bank of clouds. I waited.

Each minute seemed an eternity, for time was of the essence. Elijah couldn't risk hiding them in his secret room, not in such close proximity to Shadow Oaks. He would have to transport them to a farm some fifteen miles away and then return to his own farm before morning. He couldn't afford to be away from his place, come morning, with so much suspicion already directed against him. It would take most of the night for him to accomplish his mission, and every minute that passed was cutting his chances of getting back before first light.

Wisps of cloud floated over the face of the moon, and the gleaming silver began to fade. In a few moments there was a deep velvety blackness, the cover I needed. I stepped to the door of the shed, inserted the edge of the chisel between the wood and the edge of the hasp and began to tap with the hammer, afraid to risk making too much noise. I couldn't have taken the keys, for Derek kept them in the pocket of his breeches, and even had it been possible I couldn't have risked it. This must look as though Adam himself had broken loose with Cassie's help. The hasp must be torn loose, the wood splintered as I was splintering it now.

It was slow work. My nerves were frayed, and I was dreadfully impatient. Taking a deep breath, I gave the chisel one mighty blow. It rang out loud and clear as though a blacksmith had struck his anvil, but the hasp tore free, at last. I opened the door and stepped inside the shed. It was pitch-black and smelled of damp and rotting feed sacks and tar. I couldn't see Adam, but I could feel his presence. I could feel his fear and humiliation. He moved. I heard his chains clanking.

"Who—who dat?" he growled. Although his voice was deep and harsh, there was a slight tremor that hadn't been there before.

"It's me, Adam. I'm going to get you out of here."

"Miz Marietta? You done come to—to help me escape?"

205

"That's right. I have everything arranged."

"No, ma'am, I cain't let yuh do dat. It's too dangerous. Th' master would—if he wuz to find out, he'd—"

"Don't argue, Adam!"

"You's an angel, a beautiful angel, and I'm thankful for what yuh wanna do, but I cain't let yuh. Th' master'd be wild with anger. He'd whup you, Miz Marietta. He'd—"

"He isn't going to find out. I'm going to have to pick the lock on your shackles, Adam. It shouldn't take long."

The moon came out from behind the clouds then. The shed filled with a misty silver haze. I could see Adam crouching on the floor, iron bracelets on both wrists, the chain fastened around a wooden post. He stood up as I approached, shaking his head. Taking a hairpin from my hair, I took hold of one of his wrists and inserted the pin in the tiny hole the key fitted into. Adam watched, scowling darkly.

"You ain't never gonna undo 'em with that li'l pin, Miz Marietta. It'd take all night."

"Don't bet on it," I retorted, and at that moment there was a sharp click and the bracelet opened, freeing his wrist.

"How—how'd you do dat?"

"There was a girl on the—the prison ship, a girl named Angie. She claimed there wasn't a lock made she couldn't pick with a hairpin, and she taught me how to use one. We'll just leave that other one locked for the time being. We must hurry—"

"Miz Marietta, I jest cain't let yuh—"

"Cassie's waiting for us beside the barn," I interrupted. "Both of you will be in a safe place before the night is over."

"You—you sure you wanna do this, Miz Marietta?"

"Of course I'm sure. Come. We—we'll have to be careful. No one must see us, not even one of the other slaves. No one knows about this but Mattie. I—I was afraid one of the others might talk."

Adam hesitated just a moment, and then he followed me to the door. We stood waiting for the clouds again, and when it was dark enough we hurried out of the shed and toward the barn, Adam gripping the chain in his hand so that it wouldn't rattle. Cassie was waiting for us in the shadows, clutching a large bundle in her hand. She dropped the bundle and sobbed and hurled herself at Adam. He crushed her to him so fiercely that it seemed her bones would crack. Cassie continued to sob, her shoulders shaking. Adam held her away from him, scowling.

"Hush dat bawlin', woman! You wanna wake up all them niggers?"

"I—I'm jest so happy."

"Did anyone see you, Cassie?" I asked.

Cassie shook her head. "Not a soul, Miz Marietta. I snuck into our cabin like a thief an' moved around quiet as could be. I—I waited till no one was stirrin' 'fore I slipped out here. Dat Caleb, though—he done gone past a minute ago on his way to th' half-moon house. He's likely to be comin' back—"

Before she had finished speaking we heard the boy sauntering back toward the cabins, shuffling his feet and humming to himself. He moved with infuriating slowness, seeming to deliberately dawdle. The owl hooted again. Caleb stopped and cocked his head.

"Where you at, hoot owl?"

Although we were deep in the shadows, the moonlight spilled over the rim of the clouds again, and we could see the boy clearly. He frowned, peering at the trees in an effort to locate the owl. As minute followed minute and he still didn't move, I thought I would scream. Adam sensed my alarm and muttered a curse beneath his breath. Caleb's ears actually lifted. He whirled around to peer into the shadows concealing us, his eyes wide with fright, his mouth hanging open.

"Wh—what dat? Who—who dat I hear?"

"He mustn't see us, Adam!" I whispered frantically.

Adam nodded and reached down to pick up a rock. He hurled it across the yard. It hit the trunk of a tree with a sharp impact. Caleb jumped at least a foot and whirled back around to face the direction of the noise, his back to us now. Adam darted out of the shadows and fell upon the boy from behind, clapping a hand over his mouth and slinging an arm around his throat. Caleb struggled violently, flailing his arms, kicking his legs out, but it was futile. Adam reared back, lifting the boy off the ground, his arm tightening brutally, and in a moment or so Caleb went limp, his whole body sagging as Adam dragged him over to where we were standing.

"You—you didn't—"

"Naw, I didn't kill him. I jest squeezed mighty hard till he lost all his fight an' went out. His neck'll be sore, but he'll be all right, should be comin' round in jest a few minutes."

"He'll raise an alarm—"

"Reckon he would," Adam agreed. "There wuz a rope in dat shed. I'll take him back dere and tie him up good— reckon I'd better gag him, too, or he'll squeal like a pig. There's some rags on one of th' shelves."

"Hurry, Adam," I urged.

Adam heaved the boy up and slung him over his shoulder as though he were a bag of potatoes, then moved quickly toward the shed. Cassie and I leaned against the side of the barn, waiting. She was shivering with fear, and I took her hand, squeezing it tightly. I was frightened myself, my calm resolution completely gone now, replaced by a nervous apprehension I found difficult to control. The moon disappeared again. The yard was shrouded in darkness. Adam returned so silently that both Cassie and I were startled when we heard the chain rattle quietly directly in front of us.

"Lawd!" Cassie exclaimed. "You done scared me half to death."

"I tied him up real good, Miz Marietta," Adam told me. "He wuz startin' to come 'round just as I got done. He opened his mouth to yell an' I crammed a wad o' rags in it and tied a gag 'round him good and tight. He ain't goin' do no squealin', ain't goin' no place, either."

"I—I suppose he'll be all right."

208

"Be a mite uncomfortable's all. 'Fore I come back, I stuck that hasp back up, pressed th' nails back in th' holes so's it looks like it did 'fore you broke in. Ain't no one goin' suspect nuthin' till they gets right up to it. Reckon they're goin' get a surprise."

"I imagine so. We—we'd better go while it's still dark. Mr. Jones will be waiting for us in his wagon up the road a ways."

We moved quickly and silently past the slave quarters, Adam holding the chain securely, Cassie clutching the bundle. We moved past the side of the house and down the drive through layers of blessed darkness. I stumbled once. Adam clasped my arm firmly. My eyes were growing accustomed to the darkness now, as were theirs, and we were able to move even faster, almost running. The moon came back out as we reached the road, but the trees growing on either side afforded excellent cover. Shadow Oaks safely behind us, we slowed down, finally stopping for a moment to catch our breaths.

"I'd better unlock that other bracelet now," I said. "You don't want to drag that chain around with you."

I performed the task with great ease. Cassie was as startled as Adam had been earlier.

"How you do dat, Miz Marietta?"

"Adam will tell you about it later on," I replied.

Adam hurled the chain and bracelets across the road. They landed in the ditch with a noisy clatter.

"I—I feels like—like a free man," he said, and there was awe in his voice. "I ain't a slave no longer."

"You *are* free, Adam," I told him. "You and Cassie both. Your child will be born up North. You'll find a job and earn a living and—and everything is going to work out fine."

"'Cause o' you, Miz Marietta," he said quietly. "You's a great lady, an' we'll always be grateful—"

"Here," I said, reaching into my pocket and withdrawing the money. "You'll need this."

"You—you *stole* that from th' master!" Cassie exclaimed. "Lawd, Miz Marietta, if he finds out—"

"He won't," I assured her. "We'd better move along now. The wagon should be up there around the bend."

We hurried along, keeping to the shadows. Elijah had pulled the wagon off the road, and it was almost invisible in the shadows. Had one of the horses not shied, we might have passed it. The preacher climbed down and waited for us to join him.

"We're a little late," I told him. "There were—complications. No one saw us, though. This is Adam and his wife, Cassie. Cassie, Adam, this is Mr. Jones. He's going to drive you to a farm fifteen miles from here. The man there will hide you, keep you safe until he can take you farther on. A whole lot of people will be helping you in days to come."

Cassie began to sob. She flung her arms around me and held me close.

"I—I hates to leave you," she wailed. "You's been so good an' kind. Ain't never known a lady like you. I'm goin' worry 'bout you—"

"There's no need to worry, Cassie. Just—be happy."

Cassie nodded, hugging me tightly. Elijah Jones took her arm gently and helped her up onto the wagon seat, climbing up beside her. Adam stood looking at me, and then he took both my hands in his and squeezed them. He was moved, too moved to speak. There were tears in my eyes, and I smiled a tremulous smile. When he let go of my hands, I touched his cheek with my fingertips.

"Take care of her, Adam. Take care of yourself, too."

"I'll do dat, Miz Marietta. We—we's never goin' forget you."

"Come on, boy," Jones said impatiently. "We've got no time to dawdle."

Adam climbed up beside his wife and curled his arm around her shoulders. Jones took up the reins and clicked them, and the horses moved back onto the road, into the moonlight. In a moment the wagon was moving rapidly down the road as the horses broke into a fast gallop. Cassie turned around to wave, and I waved back, although I was still in the shadows and knew she couldn't see me.

I could hear the horses' hooves pounding, hear the wheels spinning after the wagon rounded the bend, and then the noise grew fainter and fainter until finally there was just the raspy song of the crickets and the soft crackle of leaves rustling.

I walked slowly back to the house, sad, exhausted, proud of what I had done. Derek would be in a rage, and he would be in a desperate situation financially, but I felt sure he could work that out somehow. Adam and Cassie were going to be together, and that was all that mattered at the moment. As I entered the kitchen, I thought about Caleb tied up out in the shed, wishing I could help him. It was out of the question, of course. He would simply have to be uncomfortable for a while. I went on upstairs and paused to peer into Derek's room. He was still sleeping soundly. I stood there in the doorway for a moment or so, watching him sleep, knowing I had betrayed him, and finally I moved wearily down the hall to my own room, dreading the morning to come.

XI

It was after eight o'clock, and Derek still hadn't come in.
The slaves had had their breakfast much earlier, had already gone out to the fields. Ben Randolph would be arriving around nine-thirty or ten, and I thought it would be wise to go ahead and prepare breakfast and take it up to his room on a tray, as it would seem suspicious if I let him sleep too long. I would awaken him and be very concerned, disturbed that he had slept so late, inquire if he were feeling bad.

The bacon sizzled and curled as it cooked. I broke eggs into a bowl and whipped them with cream, getting them ready to scramble. The biscuits were baking in the oven, the coffee filling the room with a rich, aromatic smell. It was a beautiful day, the sky a hazy blue-white, sunlight pouring down. I was unable to appreciate the splendor. I hadn't slept at all, had tossed restlessly in my bed, plagued with apprehension. Just before dawn I had heard a wagon on the road and knew it must be Elijah returning. Cassie and Adam were safe now, I told myself, and now I must brace myself for the repercussions.

I took the bacon up, drained most of the grease from the skillet and poured the eggs in. I had just finished scrambling them and was putting them on the plate when I heard footsteps in the next room. My hands began to shake. My throat was dry. I fought to control myself as Derek sauntered into the kitchen.

"I—I was just coming up to awaken you," I said. There was a slight tremor in my voice. "I was beginning to worry—thought you might be ill. I can't remember your sleeping so late—"

"Don't know what came over me," he replied. He frowned, shaking his head. "I just seemed to pass out last night."

"You were very tired," I said quietly. "I—I came to your room before I went to bed. You were all sprawled out. I straightened you up and put a quilt over you."

"I figured you must have."

I took a pot holder and opened the oven door, removing the biscuits. Derek stood watching me, still a bit groggy, his hair spilling untidily over his brow. There was a tiny nick on his jaw where he had cut himself shaving, and he still wore the breeches he had slept in, his white shirt tucked loosely into the waistband.

"Are you feeling all right?" I asked.

"Feel fine—just a bit dazed. Haven't slept that long in months. I suppose I needed it."

"You've been under a great deal of stress."

"Guess that's it," he agreed. "I'm ravenously hungry."

"Breakfast is ready. I'll just set a place in the dining room—"

Derek sat down at the battered old wooden table. "I might as well eat in here. Where's Cassie?"

"I—she didn't come in this morning, and—well, I didn't go get her. She was naturally upset. I thought I'd just let her stay in her cabin for a while until—until it's all over."

"I don't imagine she'd be much help to you this morning, anyway," he replied, leaning back in his chair as I placed the plate of food in front of him. "I'm sorry about all this, Marietta. I know how you feel."

"It's—I suppose it's something that can't be helped."

"If there were any other way—"

213

"I know, Derek." I set butter and strawberry jam on the table. "You don't have to justify yourself."

"Indeed I don't," he retorted, frowning again.

I poured coffee for him and began to clear things up as he ate. When everything was put away and the dirty dishes were stacked on the drainboard, I poured coffee for myself and leaned against the drainboard, sipping it. He ate slowly, savoring the food, eating three biscuits with jam after he had finished the eggs and bacon. I refilled his coffee cup, hoping to keep him away from the shed as long as possible. Poor Caleb still hadn't been discovered, was still bound and gagged and no doubt terrified.

Derek finished his last biscuit, took up his coffee cup and leaned back in his chair, looking much better than he had earlier. The grogginess was gone, the shadows under his eyes less pronounced. He sipped his coffee slowly, gazing at me all the while. That didn't help my state of mind one bit. I was totally wretched, consumed with guilt when I thought of what I had done to him. I knew he would never forgive me if he discovered the part I had played in Adam and Cassie's escape. Derek set down his empty cup and yawned, stretching his arms out.

"Feel better?" I asked.

He nodded, climbing to his feet. "Delicious breakfast, Marietta. I enjoyed it. I think I'll go on into the study and do some figuring until Randolph gets here. He should be arriving soon now."

He strolled out of the room, and my heart sank. What if he discovered the missing money? What if he checked to see how much he had left and discovered several bills had been taken? It was an unreasonable fear, I knew, for there was no reason why he should open the cigar box this morning, yet I couldn't shake my apprehension. I cleared the table and washed all the dishes, and then I swept the floor and began to polish the silverware, determined to keep busy, knowing that was the only way I could endure the suspense.

I heard the wagon pulling around the side of the house sometime later. Derek left the study, went out the front door, and circled around the verandah to greet Randolph as he alighted from the wagon. I heard them talking and, stepping to the window, saw them standing together in the back yard. Randolph was a large man, powerfully built, looking like a rugged middle-aged pugilist incongruously dressed in glossy black knee boots and an elegantly cut maroon suit. His face was battered and worn, the large mouth set in a sullen curl, the eyes dark and cold. Although rich and abundant, his hair was the color of old pewter, a tarnished silver-gray. Even from this distance I could sense his innate brutality.

My pulses leaped as they started toward the shed. It was only a matter of minutes now. They moved behind the oak trees and out of sight, and I waited, so weak I could hardly stand. He would discover the broken hasp. He would find Caleb trussed up on the floor of the shed. He would be unable to believe his own eyes at first, and then filled with an all-consuming rage. The yard was silent, everything hushed and still. Then I heard him yell. He let out a curse that carried all the way to the kitchen. Unable to contain myself, I dashed out the back door and hurried toward the shed.

Derek was still cursing as he dragged Caleb out of the shed and began to untie him. Randolph stood with his hands on his thighs, his legs spread wide, an ugly expression on his face. Still gagged, Caleb squirmed excitedly as Derek tried to undo the ropes.

"Be still, boy!" he shouted.

"What—what's happened?" I cried.

"He's gone. Adam's gone. Someone broke into the shed."

"Cassie—" I whispered hoarsely. "She didn't come in this—"

"I found a hammer and a chisel in the shed. She must have used that to tear the hasp loose. Goddammit, Caleb, I said be *still*!"

215

"Looks like we're gonna have us a nigger hunt," Randolph remarked.

Derek tossed the ropes aside and untied the gag. Caleb spat out the rag Adam had stuffed into his mouth. Derek's eyes were flashing with anger, his cheeks flushed. Caleb was so frightened he couldn't stand still. Derek seized his arms, gripping them savagely.

"What happened?"

"I—I doan rightly know. I wuz on my way back from takin' a leak an' I heard dis owl—" Caleb hesitated, gulping, trying to control his fear.

"Go on!"

"You's hurtin' me," Caleb whined. "You's hurtin' my arms—"

"I'll do more than that! Who tied you up? Who put you in the shed?"

Caleb shook his head. "I—I doan know. It wuz a spook—"

Derek released one of his arms and slapped the boy across the face with such force that Caleb's head snapped back. He wailed loudly, and Derek slapped him again.

"Stop it!" I cried. "Can't you see he's—"

"You stay out of this!" Derek warned.

"You're too upset to do any good, Hawke," Randolph said calmly. "Let me question the boy. I'll get the information out of him."

Derek thrust the boy toward him. Randolph smiled and, seizing Caleb's left wrist, jerked it straight out, gave it a brutal twist and shoved it up between the boy's shoulder blades, grabbing hold of his hair with his free hand. Caleb let out a bloodcurdling scream.

"Derek! You must stop—"

"Shut up!" he ordered. "Go tell Mattie I want all the slaves in their cabins in fifteen minutes."

Caleb screamed again as Randolph wrenched his arm up even higher.

"You're gonna talk, boy," Randolph crooned, almost as though he were speaking to a lover. "You helped him get away, didn't you? You helped him get loose, then had

216

him tie you up so no one would think you were involved."

"No!" Caleb shrieked. "Massah, massah, make him let go! He's breakin' my arm!"

"I'm gonna break your neck next, boy," Randolph promised, jerking Caleb's head back.

"Derek!" I cried. "You can't let this—"

"Get out of here!" Derek thundered. "Do what I told you!"

Caleb's screams filled the air as I rushed away, unable to bear it, unable to watch, knowing I was responsible. The boy continued to scream, and then he sobbed and gasped and made spluttering noises. Mattie was on her front porch. She took one look at my face and hurried down the steps to fold me in her arms, holding me firmly against her great bulk, rocking me as though I were a little child. Caleb was silent now. I wondered if he had passed out.

"It's my fault," I whispered, my voice hoarse, barely audible. "It's all my fault. That terrible man—"

"Hush, chile," Mattie said. "They ain't gonna kill him. Reckon he'll jus' get a good shakin' up."

"He—doesn't know anything. He was coming back from the outhouse last night and heard us. Adam distracted him and grabbed him from behind, and Caleb never knew—"

"It's all right," Mattie crooned. "He's done stopped hollerin'. You have to pull yourself together now, chile. You gotta be strong now. Now's th' time you gotta be strongest."

I nodded and brushed the tears from my eyes. When I gave Mattie Derek's message, she released me and called one of the women from the smokehouse and told her to summon all the men from the fields. A few minutes later Caleb came stumbling toward the cabin, his right arm held painfully at his side, his eyes rimmed with pink and awash with tears. Mattie put her arms around him and shushed him when he started whimpering.

"I didn't do nuthin'," he whined. "Dat man wuz gonna kill me. He's a devil. He done broke my arm an' yanked

217

my hair somethin' awful. I'se *hungry*, Mattie. I ain't had nuthin' to eat an' I'm 'bout to die!"

Mattie gave a disgusted sigh and lifted her eyes heavenwards. I was relieved to see that the boy was more frightened than anything else. Mattie led him into her cabin, and I walked slowly back to the shed. Both men ignored me. Derek had control of his anger now. Although I could tell that it still seethed inside, he maintained an icy composure that was far more frightening than his violent outburst had been.

"There's nothing I like better'n a good nigger hunt," Randolph was saying. "It's something I feel right strongly about. Guess you heard two of my niggers ran off a while back. We never *did* catch up with those two, but one of McKay's bucks ran away no more'n a month ago. Now *that* was a hunt! Took us two full days."

"You caught him?"

"Finally found him hiding in some woods damn near thirty miles from home. You shoulda seen that boy crawling around on all fours, trying to hide in some bushes. We turned the dogs loose on him. You never *seen* such excitement!"

Randolph shook his head, smiling at the memory. "You're gonna need some help, Hawke," he continued. "While you question the rest of your niggers, I'll go round up some of the men. They'll be glad to help, love a good hunt as much as I do. We'll all ride after your two. With any luck we'll catch 'em before sundown."

"How long will it take you to get back here?"

"No more'n an hour or so. I'll stop by McKay's place, have him send for Johnson and Arnold. Barnett'll come, too, and Roberts. You be saddled up and ready to go in an hour, and we'll start after them coons."

Derek nodded curtly. Randolph beamed, greatly anticipating the sport in store.

"Reckon the first place we're gonna look is Elijah Jones's place. I still figure he had something to do with my niggers gettin' away like they did. We're gonna search

218

that place uv his top to bottom, and if I even so much as *smell* a nigger I'll personally set a torch to it!"

Randolph hurried back to his wagon and drove away. Derek watched until he was gone, and then he turned to me, his eyes hard and determined.

"You gave Mattie my message?" His voice was like steel.

"They—they'll all be in their cabins waiting for you in just a few minutes. What did Caleb say?"

"He didn't know anything. Adam jumped him from behind. He never even knew what happened."

"Derek—" I hesitated, summoning strength.

"What is it?"

"Do you have to go after them?"

"I have to," he said tersely.

He learned nothing from the slaves. None of them had seen or heard anything. He ordered them back to work, told one of the men to saddle the chestnut stallion, and went inside to change. I waited for him outside, standing under one of the oaks, watching patterns of sunshine and shadow flickering over the ground and feeling absolutely miserable. Derek came back out a few minutes later. He was wearing his black boots and heavy blue cord breeches and jacket, the material worn with age. His face was a granite mask as he strode briskly across the yard toward me.

"I'm leaving you in charge while I'm gone," he said. The words were crisp. "I don't know how long it'll take, perhaps a day, perhaps even two or three. I assume you can manage."

I nodded, and he moved on toward the stables without another word. I could hear horse hooves pounding on the road in front of the house. Derek mounted the chestnut and galloped away to join the planters. I heard boisterous laughter and hearty male voices, and then they all rode away. Mattie moved ponderously across the yard to join me, each step requiring an effort because of her great girth. Her black skin glistened with moisture, and her faded old blue calico dress was damp. As she joined me

219

under the tree, I saw the concern in her velvety brown eyes.

"He's gone," I said. "I don't know when he'll be back."

"You go on in now, chile. Get yoreself some sleep. You's done enough. Ain't nuthin' else you can do."

"I'm just so worried . . ."

"'Bout dem niggers? Don't you worry none. Dat 'Lijah Jones done took 'em off an' got 'em safely tucked away. Dem men gonna hoot an' holler an' have theirselves a good time, but dey ain't gonna find no niggers. Cassie an' Adam is safe."

"I hope so, Mattie."

"Ain't no use you frettin', chile."

Mattie was right, of course, but I continued to fret all that day, all the next. I prayed that Elijah Jones had done his part properly, prayed that Cassie and Adam were indeed safe. When Derek still hadn't returned by morning of the third day, I began to feel relief. Surely if they were going to find the runaways, they would have found them by this time, I told myself. Feeling that Derek was bound to return that afternoon, I went down to the river and took a long, luxurious bath, washing my hair as well, and when he did indeed return around two o'clock I was wearing the red dress printed with tiny black flowers, the dress I had worn to the fair.

His clothes were dusty and rumpled. He looked incredibly weary, and his expression was grim. I knew immediately that the hunt had been a failure, and it took considerable effort to conceal my relief. Derek didn't say a word to me. He went straight upstairs to wash and change clothes, and later on I heard him come down to the study and close the door behind him. I knew what he must be feeling. I felt very bad about that, but I was proud of what I had done. When he still hadn't come out of the study by four o'clock, I couldn't contain myself any longer. I had to see him, had to find out what had happened. Stepping to the study door, I knocked lightly, and he called out sharply, bidding me enter.

He was sitting at the desk, poring over a stack of

papers. I could see that he had been adding up figures, had wadded up several sheets of paper and tossed them to the floor. He turned around in the chair to face me, and I noticed that three of the desk drawers had been pulled open, including the bottom drawer containing the cigar box. My heart jumped when I saw that. Derek scowled angrily, his mood clearly thunderous. I hesitated, wishing now I hadn't interrupted him.

"Well?" he snapped.

"I thought you might be hungry. I thought perhaps you might like me to . . . bring you something."

"How very thoughtful," he said. His voice was sarcastic. "You're lying, Marietta. You came to gloat."

"That isn't true."

"You'll be happy to learn we couldn't find a trace of them. No one had seen hide nor hair of them. I finally realized it was futile, told Randolph and the others we might as well give up. Cassie and Adam are long gone by this time. I'll never get them back."

"I'm sorry, Derek."

"I still can't understand it! How did Cassie break open the door without anyone hearing? How did Adam get free of the shackles? We found them on the side of the road a quarter of a mile from here. They'd been opened, and I had the key in my pocket the whole time. Somehow or other he managed to pick the lock." He shook his head, muttering something under his breath.

"We'll get by, Derek," I said quietly. "You'll find a way to—"

"Don't play the hypocrite!" he interrupted. "You're glad they got away. There's no need pretending you're not!"

"Derek—"

"You won't be so damned glad when we all starve!"

Seeing that it would be useless to try to reason with him in his present frame of mind, I turned and left the room. I refused to let his mood disturb me, and, stubbornly, I refused to feel guilty. I had betrayed his trust, yes, and he was going to have a hard time because of

221

what I had done, but the ultimate good far outweighed the wrong I had committed. Derek would get over his ugly mood, and he would find a way to save Shadow Oaks. In the meantime, two human beings had been released from bondage and were on their way to a free life.

I was at peace with myself as I stepped outside. The day was warm and sultry, the sky a yellow-white without a trace of blue. The oak trees cast deep shadows over the ground as I strolled toward the storehouse. Chickens clucked as they wandered about the yard. Caleb must have left the gate to their pen open again, I mused. Responsible for seeing that they had feed and water, he frequently forgot to close the gate properly. I'd have to scold the boy and have him round the hens up, for in Derek's present state it wouldn't do for him to find the fowls roaming freely. First, though, I would fetch the basket of apricots on the shelf in the storehouse. I would make a cobbler for supper this evening. Apricot cobbler was one of Derek's favorite desserts.

As I neared the storehouse, I heard a peculiar noise in the distance. It sounded like a mule braying. Intent on getting the apricots and planning the rest of the meal, I paid little mind. After he ate, after he got some rest, Derek was bound to feel better. The storehouse was dim, filled with a variety of tangy smells. I moved over to the shelf and took down the basket of apricots. The shelf was dusty. Cobwebs stretched across the corners of the ceiling. The place needed a thorough cleaning. I would have to get around to it one day soon. As I stepped out into the sunlight, I heard the back door slam. Derek came down the steps and walked across the yard toward me, his jaw thrust out, his fists clenched.

I could feel the color draining out of my cheeks. I seemed to go numb, paralyzed in front of the storehouse, unable to move. He knew. He had counted the money in the cigar box, and he knew I had taken several pounds. He knew why. Chickens clucked noisily and flapped out of his way as he strode toward me. He didn't even notice them. His cheeks were ashen. I could tell that he was possessed with an icy, murderous rage.

"It was you!" he said, stopping in front of me.

"I—I don't know what you're—"

"Don't lie to me, Marietta! You did it! You helped them escape!"

I shook my head, terrified. His dark-gray eyes were blazing. His hands were tight balls, the knuckles white. All the blood seemed to drain out of my body. I felt dizzy and faint, yet still I couldn't move. I was rooted to the spot, clutching the basket of apricots. He took a deep breath, his chest heaving. He was actually trembling with rage, and it was a full minute before he could speak again.

"I opened the cigar box to count the money. Thirty pounds are missing. You're the only one who knew I kept my money there. You're the only one who could have taken it!"

"Derek—" I pleaded. "You—you must—"

"I knew then. I knew immediately! You helped them. You had to, else they couldn't have pulled it off so smoothly. Cassie would never have had the guts to break into that shed!"

I looked up at him, silent. Everything seemed to go slightly out of focus. I seemed to be standing a long way off, watching the scene with a curious detachment. This wasn't real. It was a dream, hazy, blurred, not really happening. My mind registered the sound of a mule braying, much nearer this time, but that seemed unreal, too, part of the dream.

"That night," he began. "I fell asleep right after supper. I was so sleepy I didn't even pull my breeches off. I passed out on the bed. You gave me something, didn't you? You got some kind of powder from Mattie and put it in my food!"

Derek seized my arms and shook me violently. I dropped the basket. Apricots rolled all around us.

"Didn't you? Didn't you!"

"Y-yes," I stammered. "Yes, I did."

223

"Goddamn, Marietta! Why? Why!"

"Mattie—Mattie had nothing to do with it. I . . . I told her I was having trouble getting to sleep. She gave me the powder, but . . . she had no idea I intended to—"

"You wanted to make sure I was asleep so I wouldn't hear!"

I nodded, and he slapped my face, slapped me so forcefully that I reeled backwards, stumbling, almost falling. I hardly noticed the pain. Through my tears I saw the man in buckskins leading his two mules around the side of the house, but I paid no attention. Everything was lost. I knew that. Derek would never forgive me.

"How could you do it to me?" His voice was calmer now, hard, laced with icy rage. "You knew I had to sell him. You knew how important that money was to me. Goddammit, Marietta, you *knew*."

"I had to," I said quietly.

"You've ruined me. You know that, don't you?"

"Derek—"

"You've ruined me!"

The man moved slowly across the yard, his hair burnished with sunlight, the fringe on his jacket swaying as he tugged the reins, forcing the mules to follow. His dark-brown eyes were amiable. He wore a merry grin. One of the mules balked. He sighed and heaved on the reins, causing the offending mule to bray loudly. Derek turned around, aware of Rawlins for the first time.

"Afternoon, folks," Rawlins called. "Thought I'd stop by and see if I could do a little tradin'."

He let go of the reins and sauntered toward us. His expression altered as he saw my tears, saw the look on Derek's face. He stopped, a tiny frown creasing his brow.

"I say, it . . . uh . . . it looks like I came at the wrong time," he apologized. "I reckon I . . . reckon I'd better came back later."

"You couldn't have come at a better time," Derek said. His voice was steely.

"Derek," I whispered. "Derek, no—no, you can't—"

"You still interested in buying her?" Derek asked.

224

Rawlins looked dumbfounded. "Hey, you're not serious?"

"Dead serious! I paid twenty-one hundred pounds for her," Derek informed him. "Do you have that much on you?"

"Afraid not, Hawke. Tradin's been a mite slow. Eighteen hundred's all I got to my name. I got it in one of the packs."

"Very well, I'll sell her for eighteen hundred."

Rawlins shook his head, unable to believe what he was hearing. He looked at Hawke. He looked at me. And then he grinned.

"You got yourself a deal," he said.

PART TWO:

The Trace

XII

The trail was rough and rugged with trees pressing close on either side, their trunks gnarled and choked with under-underbrush, leaves brown and green. The mules plodded along patiently. I rode one, Jeff Rawlins rode another, and he led a third laden with packs behind him. He was fairly casual about the Indians, but I half expected a band of bloodthirsty savages to fall upon us at any moment. I would almost have welcomed it. Almost two weeks had passed, and still I was in a state of shock, trance-like, totally without spirit.

We had been traveling hard every day, all day long, frequently into the night. It had been exhausting, but I never once complained. Nothing mattered any longer. I simply didn't care. I obeyed Rawlins passively, rarely speaking. From the first he had treated me with the utmost respect, handling me as though I were some precious cargo. He made camp at night. He took his rifle and shot game and cooked it over an open fire. He ordered me to eat. He chatted pleasantly, and my lack of response didn't seem to bother him at all.

He had made no attempt to sleep with me. He seemed to respect my grief, and he tolerated my lethargy and lack of spirit with remarkable patience. I wasn't a very pleasant companion, but Rawlins paid no mind. Still good-humored, he kept up his merry chatter, apparently enjoying himself immensely. Under other circumstances I would have found him delightful, for he was undeniably engaging, a hearty rogue with his fringed buckskins, boyish grin, and lively brown eyes.

"We should be reaching Crawley's Inn before night," he informed me. "It's gonna be nice to sleep in a real bed. This roughin' it, sleepin' in blankets on the ground—it ain't been much of a treat to you, I'm sure."

I did not reply. Undaunted, Rawlins continued in the same cheery vein.

"You'll be able to have a bath, too. Reckon you'll welcome that. And a home-cooked meal. That'll be a relief after all this wild game. Crawley's Inn is the last bit of civilization we'll see for a long time. This is Daniel Boone country."

"Daniel Boone?"

"Ol' Dan started explorin' these parts 'bout ten years ago. This land used to belong to the French, but they ceded it to the British back in '63. Reckon the British'll lose it 'fore too long—likely to lose everything the way things are shapin' up back east. Tennessee's a wilderness now, but William Bean built him a cabin on the Watauga River just a year ago. I figure there'll be a regular settlement soon. Them folks up east don't like all them rules and restrictions and taxes the British impose. They keep pushin' on to get away from 'em."

I paid little attention to what he was saying. I kept remembering that terrible day and Derek's anger, a nightmare I lived over and over again in memory. Rawlins had given him the money, and Derek had handed over the Articles of Indenture, and I had been numb with grief and shock ever since. I could barely remember packing my few clothes up.

We were on the Natchez Trace now, and in a few weeks we would be in New Orleans and Rawlins would sell me to one of the brothels for a huge profit, and I simply couldn't care. Life was over. Life without Derek was unthinkable. This deadening numbness had held on for days, and even my grief was something distant and removed, an emotion I observed objectively, as though someone else were feeling it. I wondered if I would ever be able to feel again.

"It's sometimes called the Chickasaw Trace," Rawlins was saying. "We pass through Chickasaw country—I told yuh that before—and then as we get furtha south we enter the land of the Choctaws. The Indians mostly leave us alone, but I've had a couple scrapes. Almost lost my scalp one time, year or so ago. Some of the younger braves resent us passin' through their land. They can be pretty vicious when they get riled up."

The mule I was riding stumbled, throwing me forward. I clung to the reins, regaining my balance. A small animal streaked across the road. The birds sang lustily. Leaves rustled. I could hear water in the distance. The sky was a pale blue-gray, the sun a blazing silver ball pouring down heat. I was still wearing the red dress. I hadn't bothered to change. It was deplorably soiled now, the hem ragged, and my hair was a wild auburn tangle. I felt certain my face must be streaked with dirt, but I was beyond caring.

"Not the Indians, but the robbers," Rawlins continued. "The Trace is a solid nest of 'em, cutthroats ready to rob and plunder at the drop of a hat. Soon slit a man's throat as look at him, that lot. Many a man's left Natchez and started for Nashville and was never heard of again. It's a real problem, but don't worry—I'll protect you. They have better sense than to fool with ol' Rawlins, know I'm even more onery than they are. I've been travelin' the Trace for quite a spell, and those boys know me by sight, know they'd better steer clear."

After a while he suggested we stop for a few minutes. Dutifully, I dismounted. Rawlins stretched and rubbed his backside, grinning. The mules stood in the shade of a tree, placid. A squirrel chattered at us from the branch of a tree, and a beautiful red cardinal swept through the air like a crimson arrow. Deep forest surrounded us, the narrow trail hewn out of the wilderness, already beaten flat and rutted with hundreds of hooves and wagon wheels.

"The men who floated their flatboats down the Mississippi, they had to get back upstream by land," Rawlins said. "That's how the Trace got started in the first place. It's become a regular thoroughfare—everyone uses it now. Ordinarily there's lots uv traffic—pioneers, settlers, traders, dandies, ladies of fashion—anyone who needs to get cross country. This time a year there ain't so many people usin' it, but I reckon we'll run into some interestin' types 'fore we get to Natchez."

I brushed a twig from my skirt, paying little attention to his talk.

"I meant what I said back there. You're gonna have to snap out of it. I know you ain't exactly happy 'bout the turn of events, but you can't just shut yourself out forever. I know how you feel, but—"

"You've no idea how I feel," I said coldly.

"Reckon I do, wench. I'm not the brightest chap on earth, but I know you fancied yourself in love with Hawke. A man like that—he ain't capable of appreciatin' you. Me now, I—"

"I don't care to discuss it, Mr. Rawlins."

"I've been pretty damned patient—I'm a patient chap, have the disposition of a saint—but it's been two weeks now. You're gonna have to get over it. You've been draggin' your tail like a dejected pup. Truth to tell, I'm gettin' pretty fed up."

"I'm sorry if you feel you wasted your money."

"Oh, I don't feel *that*. You were worth every penny. Once you get some of your spirit back, I reckon you're gonna be a handful. I'm lookin' forward to some rousin' fights."

"I don't care what happens to me."

"You say that now, but you'll feel different about it 'fore long. We get over things, you see. Takes a while, but we get over 'em every time. I reckon you'll feel better after we get to the inn and you have yourself a bath and a good meal."

When I did not reply, Rawlins merely shrugged, grinning that wide, boyish grin that was so disarming. I wished I could resent him, wished I could dislike him, even, but I

232

felt nothing. He was simply someone who was there, a part of the dreamlike world that existed outside my numbness. The heat, the exhaustion, the discomfort of riding all day on a mule, the tough, too-tangy meat he cooked and ordered me to eat—none of it was quite real, none of it aroused any response.

"Well, I can see you're not a-mind to be friendly yet," he remarked. "I guess we'd better push on."

We rode again, the mules plodding along, occasionally balking, braying now and then. The road was rough, the hard-packed earth uneven, twisting through the forest persistently. The sun began to sink, splashing the sky with scarlet and gold, and the trees cast long shadows over the ground. There was a smoky haze in the air now, soft violet-gray, thickening as night drew closer. Rawlins was silent, riding a little ahead of me, the fringe on his jacket swaying, the fading rays of sunlight burnishing his sandy hair. I was miserably tired, yet I would have ridden all night long without protesting.

The last rays of sunlight vanished. The sky was purple-gray, not yet black, the haze thick now, like fog. The trees pressing so close were dark, tall black sentinels, and the forest noises seemed magnified. A wild creature called out hoarsely. The woods filled with rustling, crackling noises as the shadows multiplied, night almost upon us. Up ahead I saw a large clearing, and I could barely make out a stockade of sturdy logs with pointed tops. Threads of yellow light spilled out through the chinks.

"There she is!" Rawlins exclaimed. "I was beginnin' to fear we weren't gonna make it."

We rode up to the front of the stockade and dismounted. Rawlins called out and pounded on the huge solid oak door. After a moment there came a sound of footsteps, and then a tiny window set in the door flew back and a pair of eyes peered out at us.

"That you, Eb? It's me, Rawlins! Open up, fellow. Let us in. We're dead tired, and starvin' to boot, longin' for some o' Maria's cookin'. What you waitin' for?"

"Rawlins?" a husky voice growled.

"Course it's me! Can't you see? Goddammit, open up!"

There was the sound of a heavy bolt being drawn back, and then the enormous door opened. Rawlins stepped inside, leading his two mules, and I followed, tugging at the reins of my own mule. As soon as we were inside, the man who had admitted us closed the great door and slid the bolt back in place. He was gigantic, dressed in buckskin trousers and a coarse white shirt, his face ruddy, his dark eyes grim, his thick red hair decidedly unruly.

"What's all this about?" Rawlins said irritably. "You think we was goin' to rob the place?"

"There's been talk of Indian trouble," the man retorted. "Me and Maria, we learned a long time ago not to take no chances."

"Hell, man, there's always talk o' Indian trouble. Never known you to act so scared, Eb."

"Get whatever things you want outta the packs, Rawlins, and I'll take the mules on into the stable. You plannin' on stayin' long?"

"We'll be leavin' in the mornin'," Rawlins replied, removing one of the packs from his mule. "You gotta room?"

"The best," Crawley replied. "You-all go on in, tell Maria I said you was to have the suite. I'll just see to these animals."

The red-haired giant led the mules away toward the stables to one side of the inn, and Rawlins shook his head. Evidently such security wasn't ordinarily taken. I glanced around at the tall log walls that completely surrounded inn and yard and stables. There was a walkway built along near the top, ladders leading up to it at intervals, and I saw long, narrow slits where a man could fire his rifle without being exposed to marauders. The stockade was built along the lines of the old fortified castles in England, rough logs taking the place of heavy stone. Warm yellow light spilled out of the windows of the inn, making soft pools on the ground, and chickens clucked and scratched about the yard, looking like tiny white ghosts in the semidarkness. Horses neighed in the stables.

"Right homey, ain't it?" Rawlins remarked. "Eb and Maria run the best inn on the whole Trace—best food, best beds, best everything. They're some of my favorite people."

"Jeffrey!"

It was more a bellow than a shout, and I was startled to see a woman in white blouse and vivid red skirt come tearing out of the inn, her heavy black braid flying behind her. Rawlins grinned and held his arms wide. The woman threw herself at him, and he gave her a bear hug that by rights should have cracked her ribs. Maria Crawley was almost as large as her husband, as tall as Rawlins and twice as stout. Her black eyes snapped and sparkled as she stepped back to look at him.

"You look just the same!" she exclaimed.

"Hell, Maria, it ain't been more'n a couple months since you saw me last."

"I *miss* you," she pouted. "Every day seems an eternity."

"You still got a yen for me? I swear, we're gonna have to do something 'bout that one of these days. If we could just get rid of Eb—"

"Honey, if I thought you was serious I'd poison him tomorrow. There ain't *nothin'* I wouldn't do to get a buck like you in my bed." The woman grinned, and Rawlins reached up to pinch her cheek. She slapped his hand, as playful as a girl.

"Stop your nonsense now," she scolded. "Hell, a rascal like you wouldn't know what to *do* with this much woman on your hands. Who's this you brung with you?"

"This is Marietta—Marietta Danver."

"I hate her," Maria said. "Any woman looks like *that*, I hate her on principle. Dress torn, face dirty, hair all tangled, and she *still* looks like a dream. Hi, honey. I'm Maria Crawley."

"How do you do?" I said stiffly.

Maria lifted her brows, startled by both words and accent. She gave Rawlins a questioning glance, and he merely grinned. The woman looked at me again, studying

235

me closely, obviously mystified, and then her innate good manners took over. Smiling, she took my hand, leading me toward the porch.

"Come along, honey. You look all tuckered out. A good hot bath's what you need, that and a decent meal. I figure Jeffrey here's been feedin' you wild game and parched corn for days now."

"You got somethin' good on the stove?" Rawlins asked, following us inside.

"Honey, I *always* have something good on the stove. Would you believe I baked apple pies this afternoon? Just hopin' you'd drop in. We're almost full up tonight—a dozen people stayin' with us. The suite's still available, though."

"The suite's always available. Ain't no one but me fool enough to pay the price you're askin' for it. Bloody robbery, that's what it is."

"Lita!" Maria yelled. "Take a tub up to the suite and then fetch plenty of hot water. Mr. Rawlins is here! Christ, Jeff, it's good to see you. I reckon Eb told you about the Indian trouble?"

Rawlins nodded. "Place was locked up tighter'n a tick. He stared out at me for a good ten minutes 'fore he'd let us in."

"I hear it's serious this time, Jeff. A lot of the men stayin' here have decided not to go on. I understand a party was massacred just two weeks ago. A family it was, travelin' in a covered wagon. Steve Benson found 'em. They was scalped, every last one of 'em, and the wagon was still smokin'."

"Aw, hell, Maria, I'm onto your tricks. You're just tryin' to scare us, hopin' I'll stick around a while 'cause you lust after my body. You don't fool me a minute. You take Marietta on up to the suite, why don't ya. I think I'll just pop into the taproom for a while, see if Eb's home brew is still as potent."

He sauntered on down the large foyer and pushed open a door. Maria shook her head and smiled, then motioned for me to follow her up the narrow, enclosed

236

staircase. The inn was quite large, and it smelled of wax and polish and ale. As we moved down the upstairs hall I noticed how neat and clean everything was, perhaps to compensate for the general roughhewn appearance. Maria opened one of the doors and led me into a small sitting room with hardwood floor and whitewashed walls. An open door led into the bedroom adjoining.

"It ain't much," she said, "but it's the best we've got. Most of the rooms ain't nothin' but cubicles. Hope you'll be comfortable, honey."

"I'm sure I will be."

Maria lingered, clearly reluctant to leave. She was the largest woman I had ever seen, and although she had to be nearly fifty, I could see that she must once have been quite pretty. That plump, ravaged face still bore signs of youthful good looks—the mouth small and cherry red, the dark eyes full of warmth, reflecting her amiable nature.

"You ain't like the others," she said. "I spotted that immediately, even before you spoke. Them others he's brung through—sometimes two or three at a time—they was tough-lookin', brassy. You're not like that at all."

"I . . . I suppose you mean that as a compliment."

"Sure do, honey. Are you Jeff's woman?"

"I'm an indentured servant, bought and paid for. I belong to him, yes, but I'm not his 'woman.'"

"Reckon that's your misfortune, honey. The woman who lands Jeff Rawlins is gonna be lucky indeed. We're mighty fond uv him, I don't mind tellin' you. They don't make many like him. He's rough and rugged, sure, and meaner'n a bobcat when he's riled up, but he's got a heart of pure gold."

"Indeed?"

"Don't ever let anyone tell ya different, honey."

"If he's such a paragon, why does he engage in white slavery?"

"White *slavery*! Jeff? Nonsense! Oh, he runs women from Carolina to New Orleans, sure. Buys 'em at auction, resells 'em for a big profit, but he's doin' the women a

237

favor. 'Stead o' workin' their tails off on some farm, they live in luxury, wear silks and satins, get paid good money for doin' what they do. And the women he buys—honey, they ain't lily-pure virgins. Most of 'em were walkin' the streets before they was well into their teens. Ain't a one of 'em wuzn't grateful to him—"

Maria cut herself short as a young girl came into the room carrying an enormous wooden barrel, placing it in the center of the bright, multicolored rag rug that covered most of the floor. Surely no more than sixteen, the girl was slender with delicate features and lovely indigo-blue eyes. Soft, silvery-brown hair fell about her shoulders in rich profusion. Barefooted, she wore a faded pink calico dress with a pattern of tiny blue flowers almost exactly the color of her eyes.

"This here's Lita," Maria said. "Lita, this is Miss Danver, a friend of Jeff's."

The girl smiled. "Hello," she said shyly.

I returned the smile. She was a beautiful creature, fragile, tender, poignantly young. Lowering her eyes, she scurried out of the room, her soft brown hair bouncing.

"Lita's got a cause to be grateful to Jeff, too," Maria continued. "Sixteen years old she is, thirteen when Jeff brung her to us. She an' her folks were goin' down the Trace three years ago. Th' Chickasaws fell on 'em, killed her parents and little brother, took Lita captive. A search party went after the renegades who done it, but they gave up after a week or so, said there was no chance of findin' the girl, said she was prob'ly already dead anyway. They gave up the search, but not Jeff Rawlins. No, he kept on after the Indians, all by himself. It took him two and a half months, but he found 'em. There was half a dozen of 'em, renegades who'd broken away from the tribe. Jeff rescued the girl, had to kill three braves in the process."

"That was a very brave thing to do."

"He didn't take her and put her in no whorehouse, honey. He brought her to me and Eb, asked us to take care of her. You shoulda seen him with her. Gentle as a

238

lamb he was, talkin' real soft, tellin' her not to be afraid. If you coulda seen him—" Maria shook her head, her dark eyes pensive as she recalled the scene.

The girl came back into the room carrying two enormous kettles of steaming water. She gave me another shy smile as she poured the water into the barrel. It was appalling to think that such a lovely, gentle creature had been in the hands of savages for almost three months. She must have endured horrors, I thought, but they had left no visible signs. The girl seemed to radiate a blissful contentment. Taking up the empty kettles, she left again. Maria sighed.

"Jeff Rawlins is a fine man, and don't you forget it. I don't know what kinda plans he has for you, but you can bet you'll end up the better for 'em, whatever they might be. He's a rogue, all right, but he ain't got a mean bone in his body."

She left, and I was surprised to find that some of my numbness had worn off. I had been quite touched by the story of Lita, by the girl herself, and I found myself admiring Jeff Rawlins for what he had done. How many men would have risked their lives to rescue a young girl everyone else had already given up on? I was beginning to see him in an entirely new light. I realized that Maria was prejudiced in his favor, and I didn't for one minute accept her version of his nefarious trade, yet I realized that no one was all bad. Rawlins undoubtedly had many redeeming qualities. The story of Lita proved that.

The girl returned again with another kettle of water, soap, a large white towel, and the pack Rawlins had taken from the mule. Setting the other things on a chair, she emptied the water into the barrel. It was more than half full, the water steaming visibly.

"Your bath is ready now," Lita said. "If you need anything else, you just let me know."

"Thank you, Lita. Is Mr. Rawlins still downstairs?"

Lita nodded. "He gave me the pack, said your clothes were in it. I imagine he'll be down in the taproom for

239

quite a spell, talking with Eb and the other men." Her eyes seemed to glow as she spoke of him.

"You're very fond of him, aren't you?" I asked.

The question seemed to surprise her. "I love him," she said. "Doesn't everyone?"

The girl left the room then, closing the door behind her. The water needed to cool a bit, so I stepped into the adjoining bedroom. It was small, with a low, sloping roof. There was barely enough room for the bed with its patchwork quilt and the dressing table with a musky, tarnished mirror hanging over it. If these were the best rooms in the inn, I reflected, the others must be small indeed. The furniture was all obviously homemade by Crawley himself, the quilt, the rag rug in the other room no doubt Maria's handiwork. There was great charm nevertheless, a snug, homey atmosphere that was most welcoming.

Catching a glimpse of myself in the mirror, I frowned. My face was streaked with dirt, my hair wildly disarrayed. I couldn't believe I had let myself fall into such a wretched condition. Something stirred inside of me as I stood there, a will to survive, a will to succeed, and the last vestiges of that deadening numbness seemed to melt away. I would never see Derek Hawke again. Heartlessly, he had thrust me into the hands of a man he knew would sell me to a brothel, and I had given up, had accepted my fate with meek submission, not caring what happened. How could I have been so passive?

The spirit seemed to swell up inside of me, and I knew then that I was going to fight. I had been dejected, mentally and emotionally destroyed by what had happened, but that was behind me now. I would never get over what had happened, would never be able to forget Derek Hawke or what he had done to me, just as I would never be able to stop loving him, but I was no longer prepared to give up. I was going to fight. I felt alive for the first time in two weeks, gloriously alive. Perhaps it was merely the contrast to the lethargy that had gripped me before, but it seemed every fiber of my being vibrated with life, and I had never felt stronger, more determined.

Stepping back into the sitting room, I opened the pack and pulled out the Italian peasant blouse and the leaf-brown skirt I had worn that day of the auction, such a long time ago it seemed now. Laying the garments out on the chair, I undressed and, clutching the bar of soap in my hand, climbed into the enormous barrel. It was exceedingly uncomfortable, but there was enough room to sit if I drew my legs up. The water was marvelously warm, and the liquid warmth seemed to steal through me, relaxing me, driving away all tension and care.

I bathed thoroughly and washed my hair, reveling in the warmth, the rich lather, the sweet scent of lilac soap that seemed to fill the room. My body seemed to glow with cleanliness as I rinsed away the suds and let warm water spill over my shoulders and breasts. I had been in the tub for almost half an hour and was just getting ready to climb out when the door opened. Jeff Rawlins strolled casually into the room, quirking one brow when he saw me in the barrel, arms crossed over my breasts. He grinned then, closing the door behind him.

"You look better already," he remarked.

"I should have locked the door!"

"I'd have broken it down. My, my, you are a sight. Never seen so much wet flesh in my life. Makes a man hungry to see even more."

"Are you going to just stand there?"

"No. Reckon I'll hand you the towel. Want me to help dry you off?"

"You—"

"Ah, your cheeks are burning. Your eyes are flashing with anger, full of blue fires. You don't know how glad I am to see that, wench. Thought I was going to have to take strong measures to snap you out of your—"

"Hand me the towel!"

"Yes, ma'am. Here you are."

Defiantly, I stood up and stepped out of the tub. Rawlins watched me, warm brown eyes dancing with amusement, that infuriating grin still curling on his wide pink mouth. I wanted to slap it off his face. Dripping on the rag rug, I wrapped the towel securely around me.

"Reckon I'll take a bath myself," Rawlins remarked. "No sense wastin' all that water."

"Go right ahead!"

I dropped the bar of soap back into the barrel and reached for the skirt and blouse I had spread over the chair. As I did so, the towel slipped, almost dropping to the floor before I caught it. Rawlins guffawed and began to pull off his buckskin tunic. I hurried into the bedroom and was dismayed to discover that there was no door I could slam shut between the two rooms. I discovered, too, that I had forgotten to get my petticoat from the pack. My cheeks were still burning, but, strangely enough, the anger was almost pleasant. Anything was better than that terrible numb lethargy.

There was a loud splash as Rawlins climbed into the barrel. Hesitating only a moment, I stepped back into the sitting room, the towel tucked securely around me. Rawlins was in the tub, scrubbing himself vigorously, his hair soaking wet and plastered over his head in pointed locks. He reminded me of a frisky puppy splashing about, and I almost smiled in spite of myself. Opening the pack again, I pulled out the multilayered petticoat I needed. Rawlins let out a little yelp as the bar of soap slipped out of his hand and went skittering across the room.

"Damn! Be a dear. Fetch me the soap."

"Get it yourself!" I snapped.

"You really want me to? You want me to climb out and—"

"I'll get it!"

He smiled as I handed it to him. Why did I feel myself warming to this man? I had every reason to hate him. Why did I want to smile back at him and smooth those damp locks away from his brow? He intended to sell me to a brothel in New Orleans. Despite his engaging manner, despite his charm, he was my enemy. I had to remember that. I had to keep that in mind at all times. To succumb to his charm would be a fatal mistake. Rawlins looked

242

up at me with those merry brown eyes, utterly disarming.

"I don't know what happened," he said, "don't know what caused you to come back to life, but I sure am glad to see you comin' round. Meek women bore the pants off me. I have a feelin' I ain't gonna be bored no longer."

"I'm hungry, Mr. Rawlins. I suggest you hurry with your bath so we can go downstairs and eat."

"Righto," he said. "Won't take me more'n a few minutes."

Leaving him to his bath, I went back into the bedroom and, standing well out of sight of the open doorway, dried my body thoroughly and then vigorously toweled my hair, ridding it of most of the dampness. I could hear him splashing away as I dressed. He was humming a jaunty tune, enjoying himself immensely.

"Hey!" he cried. "I need that towel."

I took it in to him and fetched my shoes.

"It's all damp," he protested.

"I'm sorry about that. You'll just have to make do."

"Inconsiderate wench," he grumbled.

He heaved himself out of the barrel, dripping rivulets of water all over the rug. I hurried back into the bedroom and put on my shoes. There was an old hairbrush on top of the dressing table and, sitting down in front of the mirror, I began to brush my hair. Soon it was almost dry, soft and feathery and wonderfully clean. The glow I had felt earlier still remained inside. The grief, the desolation were there as well, but they were tightly contained, locked away. I was no longer willing to let them render me helpless.

Rawlins stepped to the doorway and peered in at me. He had tied the towel clumsily about his waist. Seeing him like that reminded me of pictures I had seen of the early Roman gladiators. He was superbly built, lean and muscular, exceedingly virile and emanating a hearty confidence much as the gladiators must have done before entering the arena. Hearty, audacious, he grinned at me, those wet, sharp-pointed locks covering his head like a sleek helmet.

I put the brush down and stood up, looking at him with calm blue eyes.

"Just thought I'd tell you I'm almost ready," he remarked. "All I have to do is slip into some fresh buckskins. You look stunning, Marietta. Uh . . . we don't *have* to go down for supper . . ." His eyes took in the bed.

"I think we'd better," I said coldly.

Rawlins gave a good-natured shrug and stepped back into the sitting room to put on fresh buckskins identical to those he had been wearing before, only cleaner. Instead of boots, he wore soft buckskin moccasins. As we went down to the taproom, he seemed as jolly and exuberant as an Oxford youth turned loose on the city with a pocketful of money. Hair still damp, eyes merry, he led me into the dimly lighted, smoke-filled taproom. There were well over a dozen rough-looking men gathered around the tables, and all of them watched with considerable envy as Rawlins led me to a corner table.

"Hey, Rawlins," one of them called, "you in a sellin' mood?"

"No chance," he retorted. "This one's special."

"Keepin' her for yourself?"

"You're smarter'n you look, Benson."

Maria served us herself. The food was delicious: sugar-cured ham, hot bread, golden yams, greens. I was famished and dug into the food with great relish, as did Rawlins. He drank ale from a pewter mug with his food, and I wondered how much he had had before he came up to the room, how much of his jaunty humor was caused by the alcohol. Maria brought hot apple pie with cream after we had finished, and Rawlins leaped up to give her a mighty hug, claiming it was his favorite and she was a living angel. Maria blushed with pleasure, girlishly coy for all her great girth.

Eb Crawley came to sit with us for a few minutes after we had finished dessert. His ruddy face was grim as he took the mug of ale his wife brought.

"Another for me, too," Rawlins requested.

244

"You've already had enough, you rascal. You're not going to be able to get back upstairs!"

"Aw, don't get bossy, Maria. Just bring me the ale."

Maria moved away, red skirt swishing. Her husband's dark eyes were filled with grave concern as he inquired if we intended to push on tomorrow morning.

"Don't see why not," Rawlins replied. "Hell, there's always talk of Indian uprisin's. I ain't sayin' they didn't murder that family and burn their wagon, but it was probably no more'n half a dozen braves just feelin' their oats. They've probably left the area by this time."

Maria banged a pewter mug down on the table in front of him, foamy ale splashing over the rim. Rawlins scowled at her, then lifted the mug to his lips.

"If I was scared uv Indians, I'd never have ventured down the Trace the first time," he continued. "I got two powerful rifles, and a pistol as well, and there ain't a man around 's a better shot than I am."

"Be that as it may, I think you should reconsider. We got a whole slew of men here who're coolin' their heels, waitin' for things to calm down 'fore they go on. It ain't just the Indians, Jeff. I hear the Brennan boys are at it again. Talk is they waylaid a couple trappers not more'n fifty miles on down the road. Murdered 'em both."

"You mean them skunks is still loose and livin'? I'da thought someone would've put a bullet through their skulls 'fore this time. I knew Jim was outa jail, but I thought Billy was locked up in Natchez."

"He broke out. His brother helped him. They killed the jailer, shot another man, too. They don't make 'em any meaner'n the Brennans. If I had my choice of runnin' up against a pack of Chickasaws or runnin' up against the Brennan brothers, I'd pick the Indians every time. Didn't you have a run in with 'em a couple years back?"

"Sure did. Beat the shit outa Billy, put a slug of lead in Jim's shoulder. I'd welcome a chance to finish the job up proper. It's scum like them that gives the Trace such a bad name."

Eb Crawley frowned, clearly displeased. "If it was just

245

you, I'd say go on, get yourself scalped or shot up, but—hell, Jeff, you got the wench here to consider. You don't wanna take no chances with her along. If the Brennans got a-hold of her—"

"They ain't about to," Rawlins replied, finishing his ale. He slammed the mug down and climbed unsteadily to his feet. "I don't know what's gotten into you, Eb. You're talkin' like some frightened dude, and you one of the meanest critters ever drew breath."

"It ain't a jokin' matter, Jeff. These other chaps—"

"I'm tired talkin' about it," Rawlins interrupted. "Come on, Marietta, let's go on upstairs."

He took my hand and pulled me to my feet. All that ale had quite obviously gone to his head. He was weaving slightly as we left the taproom, and he stumbled as we climbed the stairs, crashing against the wall with considerable impact. When we reached the upper hall, he flung his arm around my shoulders, leaning heavily against me as we moved on down the hall. As soon as we stepped into the sitting room, he plopped down in the chair, looking flushed but still quite merry. The barrel was gone, I noticed, and so were our dirty clothes.

"Lita's launderin' 'em for us," he explained when I commented about it. "She'll have 'em all freshly ironed and ready to pack away when we get ready to leave in the morning. She always cleans my buckskins for me, has 'em smellin' like new."

"That's very thoughtful of her."

"Lita's a swell kid. I did her a favor once. This is her way of payin' me back. Hey, all that talk didn't upset you, did it? I mean all that jawin' about the Brennans and the Indians."

"Not—not particularly, but Mr. Crawley seemed—"

"Oh, Eb's always gettin' in an uproar about nothin'. You got no cause to be alarmed, gal. I been travelin' this trail for years and years, know it backwards and forwards. There ain't a man alive more capable of gettin' you safely to Natchez. You just put all that talk outta your mind, hear? It ain't worth thinkin' about."

246

"I'll try to," I told him. "I think I'll go to bed now."

"You go on. I'm gonna sit here a while and have me a cheroot."

"You intend to sleep here?"

"I sure as hell ain't gonna sleep out in th' hall. Don't you worry none. Go on to bed."

I went into the bedroom and, blowing out the lamp, undressed in the semidarkness. Soft rays of light from the other room filtered in through the doorway, leaving the rest of the room a hazy blue-gray. The window was open, and a cool breeze drifted in. I could smell tobacco burning as Rawlins smoked his cigar. Completely naked, I climbed under the covers. The coarse linen sheets were cool and clean, smelling of soap. I felt a certain apprehension. Thus far Rawlins had made no attempt to make love to me, but then we had never shared a bed.

Perhaps a quarter of an hour passed before he finally stepped into the doorway. He leaned against the frame with one shoulder, peering at me with a thoughtful look in his eyes. I gripped the sheets nervously, watching him. Rawlins noticed. He grinned sheepishly.

"Don't get yourself all riled up, wench. I ain't gonna do nothin' you don't want me to do."

He pulled off his buckskin tunic and tossed it onto a chair, slipped out of his moccasins, and kicked them across the floor.

"Aren't you going to blow out the light?" My voice was tight.

"Reckon I'd better, at that."

He stepped into the other room. A moment later there was only darkness. I heard him come back into the bedroom, heard him struggle out of the clinging buckskin leggings. Pale rays of moonlight slanted in through the window, tinting the air with a faint silver glow, and I could barely distinguish his naked body as he draped the leggings over the side of a chair. A moment later he sighed heavily and climbed into bed beside me. The springs creaked. The mattress sagged with his weight, causing me to roll over against him. I moved back over quickly, but his leg still touched mine. I could feel his warmth, smell flesh and perspiration and ale.

"You all snug and cozy?" he inquired.

"I—I'm almost asleep."

"Nice to be in a real bed, ain't it?"

I didn't reply. I was acutely aware of his nearness, and I experienced familiar sensations in spite of myself. Disturbed, I tried to make my mind a blank, tried to ignore the male body sprawled out beside me, but it was impossible. I remembered the time he had kissed me beside the wagon the day of the fair. I remembered the dizziness and the delight as his strong arms held me and his lips worked over mine, summoning an instant response. I had felt disloyal to Derek then because another man had been able to arouse the physical response Rawlins had aroused.

"I been lookin' forward to this for a long time," Rawlins said.

"Jeff, I—"

"Didn't wanna force myself on you before," he interrupted. "Figured I'd wait till you snapped outta your trance. You've been grievin' for Hawke, I know, and I was willin' to respect your grief."

"Please don't. Please just—"

"I know Hawke meant a lot to you, wench. I reckon you was near 'bout crushed when he sold you like he did, in a fit of anger. That's the past, over and done with. I'm gonna make you forget all about him, and that's a promise."

Shifting position, he pulled me into his arms and covered my mouth with his own. It was a long, leisurely kiss. He held me loosely, savoring my lips with his own, his right hand gently massaging my breast, and my head seemed to swim. Raising his head, he chuckled softly and stroked me with fingertips that tenderly explored.

"A man like Hawke—he don't know how to appreciate a woman like you. Me, I reckon I appreciated you the moment I first laid eyes on you."

"Jeff—"

And then he lowered himself on me as though I were

248

a cushion, and he kissed me again, lazily, and I found myself wrapping my arms around him, pulling him closer. I was alive with sensations I thought I would never be able to feel again. Rawlins entered me, moving slowly, savoring each second, savoring each sensation, using my body as a great musician might use a cherished instrument, tenderly. I seemed to be soaring through space, waves of ecstasy sweeping me further and further away from sanity and reason, and I forgot about Derek, forgot about everything but this man, this moment. He shuddered, sinking his teeth into the soft flesh of my shoulder, and I cried out, clasping him to me as I was swept into a realm of incredible pleasure like nothing I had ever felt before.

XIII

It was mid-afternoon, two days after we had left Crawley's Inn, and I was exhausted. We had been riding hard all day, with only a short break for lunch. I had grown to detest Jenny, my mule. She had balked several times already today, once in the middle of a small stream we were crossing. I had promptly tumbled off, landing in the water with an enormous splash. Nothing was hurt but my pride, and Rawlins's riotous laughter hadn't helped a bit. The heat was intense. We were traveling through real wilderness now, and the trail was much rougher than anything we had passed over before.

"I'm tired!" I protested.

"You'll never make a pioneer," he taunted.

"I've no *desire* to be a pioneer."

"Expect me to mollycoddle you, don't ya? If we stopped everytime you started gettin' tired, we'd never reach Natchez."

"Jeff, I mean it. I'm exhausted."

"Just keep forgin' ahead," he called amiably. "We'll take a rest 'fore too much longer."

I sighed and dug my knees into Jenny's sides, urging her on. My blouse was damp with perspiration, my skirt bunched up over my knees. A swarm of insects buzzed in the air. I slapped one of them off my arm. The sun beat down fiercely, slanting through the thick tree limbs to burn my skin. Crawley's Inn seemed a distant paradise. Rawlins moved on ahead, leading the third mule behind him, and I dared not lag too much. This wild, savage land was terrifying, unlike anything I had ever seen before, and, too, I couldn't forget the talk about Indians.

The trail wound through the dense woods, sometimes vanishing altogether, it seemed, hardly worthy of being called a trail at all. Although Jeff assured me the Trace was the main thoroughfare through the wilderness, we had encountered no one. This territory had been ceded to the English after the French and Indian War—Jeff had regaled me with tales of that conflict, most of them featuring hordes of howling savages—but I failed to see why anyone would want it. Although it did have a certain majestic splendor, it was much too vast, too wild.

At least Carolina had been partially civilized, with farms and plantations and settlements abounding, Charles Town a thriving port. I felt a stab of pain, remembering, and I forced all thoughts of Carolina out of my mind. I wouldn't think about it, I vowed. That was behind me. My life had taken another abrupt turn, and survival was all that mattered now. I was going to survive, and I wasn't going to end up in a brothel in New Orleans. Already I was contemplating my escape. It was out of the question now, of course. Where would I go? But once we passed through this wilderness, once we reached civilized country again, I would give Jeff Rawlins the slip at the first opportunity and, somehow, make a new life in the French and Spanish territory.

In the meantime, I could do nothing but stick closely to him until we left this wilderness behind. If one *had* to travel through this godforsaken country, I could think of no better traveling companion. For one thing, I was confident in his ability to get us through safely, and, for another, he was undeniably engaging and entertaining, constantly telling tall tales of his exploits and those of Daniel Boone. Boone, one of the first to explore these parts, was obviously one of his heroes. I might be exhausted, I might be uncomfortable and frequently irritated, but with Jeff Rawlins I was never bored.

There was the physical part, too. He was a superb lover. I couldn't deny that. Even on blankets spread over the rough ground, he was superb, and I gave myself to him willingly. It was all part of my plan. By the time we reached civilization, he would be completely sure of me, convinced I couldn't do without him, and he was bound to grow lax, seeing no reason to keep a close watch over me. It would make my escape all the easier. I justified it to myself this way, but the fact remained that I enjoyed our lovemaking as much as he. My mother's blood? Perhaps, but I wasn't particularly concerned. There was no place for moralizing in the middle of the wilderness.

We had been climbing the trail for some time, and soon we were on the crest of a hill, the trail winding down in front of us. Jeff came to a halt, and I drew Jenny up beside him. A spectacular vista unfolded before us. Against a pale-blue, sun-drenched sky we could see the tops of distant mountains, a hazy violet-gray, the slopes covered with trees, a patchwork of greens and browns. There was a stream below, sparkling silvery blue, now visible, now hidden by the trees, and the land itself was a rusty reddish brown. It was incredibly beautiful. I could sense Jeff's response. He loved this land. He was at home here. It was a part of him.

"It's really somethin', ain't it?" he said quietly.

"It's quite lovely. If you like wilderness," I added.

"Someday it's all gonna be ours."

"Ours?"

"It's gonna belong to us—the people. We're the ones who're gonna conquer it, settle it. The French, the British, all them bloody politicians with their grants and deeds— they're gonna have to pick up their papers and go back home."

"You don't consider yourself British?"

"Hell, no! My folks were, sure; they came to Virginia fifteen years before I was born. I was born there, in the American Colonies. I'm an American. That's what the

British call us, usually with a sneer. If things keep goin' like they have in Boston and Philadelphia and them parts, the redcoats ain't gonna be so disdainful. Reckon the 'Americans' will throw 'em out."

"That sounds suspiciously like treason," I remarked.

"Could be," he replied amiably. "Me, I couldn't care less about politics and such. I can get along wherever I happen to be—English territory, French, Spanish, don't much matter. But I hear talk. People up in that part of the country are gettin' fed up, tired uv bein' subjects of a distant king who's batty in the head."

King George was, indeed, quite mad at times. Everyone knew that. It was said he frequently had amiable chats with oak trees and claimed they chatted back, and he was kept confined for long periods of time, yet he was still our Monarch. I felt a fierce loyalty to the homeland, which was surprising after my experience with the English legal system. Still, here in the middle of this overwhelming wilderness, everything else seemed remote and unimportant. Men like Jeff were more concerned with living than law, and what took place in England and the eastern Colonies didn't affect them much one way or the other. He continued to gaze at the land unfolding before us, savoring its wild beauty as he would savor the beauty of a woman, and then he prodded his mule gently and started down the trail, leading the other mule behind.

Groaning, I followed. The trail was steep, and I bounced viciously, but soon we were on semilevel ground again, the lovely vista gone, trees growing thickly on either side, blotting out any view. It seemed an eternity before we finally reached the bank of the small stream. There was a grassy clearing shaded by trees, clusters of orange and reddish-orange wild flowers sprinkled over the ground. The stream was shallow, making a pleasant, melodic sound as it rushed over the large yellow-brown rocks scattered about the bed. There was at least two hours of daylight left, and I was surprised when Jeff suggested we stop for the night.

"Looks like a good place to camp," he said, "and I

253

don't wanna tire you out too much—for selfish reasons. We'll stop early, then get a good start in the mornin'."

"I've no intention of arguing," I retorted, eagerly dismounting.

Jeff swung himself off his mule and grinned. "You got a lot of stamina, ya know that? Oh, you complain a lot, always groanin' and beggin' me to stop for a while, but you keep right on pluggin'."

"There's not much else I can do under the circumstances."

"Some of the women I've hauled through these parts—you wouldn't believe the trouble they were."

"I can imagine," I said dryly.

As he fed and watered the mules, I thought of Maria Crawley and the way she had tried to justify the trade he engaged in. It was quite true that most of the women who came over on the prison ships were prostitutes, or worse, and I supposed any one of them would much prefer working in a brothel in New Orleans to doing the kind of hard manual labor they were likely to have to do otherwise. Angie, for example, would have jumped at the chance. That made it none the less unsavory. He knew that I wasn't a prostitute, yet he intended to sell me just as he had sold the others.

"How many women have you taken to New Orleans?" I inquired.

"Oh, couple dozen, I guess. No sense wastin' my time with them who ain't young and pretty, and not too many young and pretty women come over on the ships."

"I suppose some of them fell in love with you."

"Reckon a few of them did. Quite a nuisance."

"You've—never been in love?" I asked.

"Never had time, too busy makin' a livin'. I figure a woman's like a good meal or a glass o' fine whiskey—somethin' to be enjoyed wholeheartedly but nothin' to lose your head over."

"I'll keep that in mind."

"Say, you ain't fallin' in love with me, are you?"

"Not a chance," I retorted.

He looked relieved. "Wouldn't wanna complicate things," he said.

It would be all too easy for most women to fall in love with him. He was exceedingly attractive physically. Superbly built, he did indeed resemble an early Roman gladiator, one incongruously dressed in fringed buckskins and moccasins. There was the charm, too, and the jaunty, easygoing manner. He was, I knew, as rugged and virile as they came, yet there was a gentility about him as well. Rawlins would not be afraid to show tenderness. Though he delighted in teasing me, he had been extremely considerate from the first. So unlike Derek in every way . . . I had loved, and I had been deeply wounded, and I was never going to love again, certainly not a man who intended to place me in a brothel for profit. Sleeping with him was one thing. Loving him was something altogether different, and there wasn't a chance of it.

"How'd you like some fresh fish for supper?" he inquired.

"Fish?"

"This stream's full of 'em, just waitin' to be caught. Tell you what, you build a fire—you've seen me do it enough times to know how—and I'll catch us some fish to cook."

Pulling his hunting knife out of his scabbard, he examined the branches of a tree growing nearby, selected one and cut it off, then began to sharpen one end. When he was finished, he had a crude but serviceable spear. Taking off his moccasins, he stepped into the stream and, spear held aloft, gazed intently at the water. A moment later he brought the spear down quickly. There was a mightly splash, and when he held the spear aloft again a large, silvery fish was writhing on the point. He gave a shout of triumph and slung the fish on the bank, where it flopped for a moment and then grew still.

"Trick I learned from the Indians," he called.

"Clever," I retorted.

He splashed about in the stream, as happy and excited as a boy, spearing three more fish while I fetched the shovel from the pack, dug a narrow hole in the ground, lined it with rocks and then placed wood on top of the rocks. After gathering up more wood and some dry brush, I attempted to light the fire with the flint. It wasn't nearly as easy as it looked, and it took me a good five minutes to ignite the brush with a spark. By the time I had finished, Jeff had decapitated the four fish and was scraping scales off. He deboned them and, looking inordinately pleased with himself, took an old iron skillet from his pack and began cooking the fish, turning them with a long metal fork he'd also removed from the pack. I watched, feeling quite relaxed and at ease.

"You're quite handy to have around," I remarked.

"Reckon I am," he admitted. "A wench could do worse."

"I imagine she could. You've done a lot in your life, haven't you?"

"I've knocked around quite a lot. Left home when I was thirteen, struck out on my own. Took a lot of odd jobs. In '55 I joined Captain Waddell's Carolina Militia. That's when I first met Daniel Boone. He was twenty-one, four years older'n me. Joined up as a wagoner, Dan did. Both of us went with General Braddock's expedition to drive the French from Fort Duquesne. We were ambushed by Indians as we were advancin' on the fort. The whole damn expedition was almost wiped out—me and Dan and a handful of others were the only ones to get away with our scalps. Lost any interest in the military life after that, I can tell ya for sure."

"You've already told me about the French and Indian conflict," I reminded him. "What did you do after that?"

"Did a bit of scoutin', bit of trail-blazin', but I didn't have the knack, not like Boone. I finally ended up in Louisiana Territory, great place for an ambitious young man. Spent most of my time in and around New Orleans. It belonged to the French then. They ceded all territory west of the Mississippi to Spain in '62, includin' New Orleans. Hell, this land changes hands so often a chap never knows who it belongs to."

256

"What did you do in New Orleans?"

"Did a bit of tradin'. Raised hell mostly. Then I started makin' these expeditions to Carolina to see what the ships brought in, peddlin' goods as I went along. Reckon this is my last trip. I'm gettin' tired of all this travelin' back and forth. I got plans—"

He looked up at me and grinned mysteriously, and I had the curious feeling that these mysterious plans concerned me in some way. He clearly had no intention of going into detail, and I was too stubborn to ask. He took the fish up, and after it had cooled we ate it. The meat was juicy and succulent, quite the best fish I had ever eaten, but perhaps that was because I was so hungry. I went over to the river to wash my hands when I had finished, and it was as I was drying them off that I heard the horse neighing.

I was startled, too startled to be frightened at first. I hurried back to Jeff. His face was grim. He looked like a different person, the amiable rogue replaced by a deadly sober man with tight mouth and hard, fierce eyes. He held the rifle ready to fire, the barrel pointing toward the area on the other side of the stream where the sound had come from. The fear gripped me then. I could feel the color leaving my cheeks.

"Get over there behind those trees," he ordered. "Stay out of sight."

"What—"

"Do as I say!" he snapped.

I quickly obeyed, darting behind the trees and peering around one of the trunks to watch, my heart pounding. The horse neighed again, and the sound of hooves rang loud and clear. A moment later a horseman rode into sight, a string of four pack mules trailing behind. Thin and rangy, the man had a long, pale face with beard as black and lanky as his hair. He wore a raccoon-skin cap with tail dangling down in back and buckskins similar to those Jeff wore, only much dirtier. Jeff held the rifle steady for a moment, and then he lowered it and let out an exuberant whoop that caused birds perching nearby

257

to break into flight. The man on the horse, showing no reaction, calmly walked his horse across the stream.

"It's all right, Marietta!" Jeff called. "You can come on out. Jackson's a friend of mine. Jackson, you ol' son of a bitch! What th' hell are you doin' in these parts?"

"On my way to Carolina," the man replied. "Got four mules here loaded down with goods. Aim to sell to them folks you ain't already cheated. If there are any," he added.

"Christ, man, you gave us a scare!"

Jackson dismounted. He was tall, taller than Jeff, even, and so thin he looked unhealthy. The buckskins seemed to hang limply on his bony frame. The straggly beard and long hair were very dark, emphasizing his pallor. He glanced about the campsite with lazy blue eyes, showing not the least surprise when I approached from the trees. As I drew nearer I could smell him. It was difficult not to recoil. He smelled of grease and sweat and leather and various other odors, all of them blending into an exceedingly pungent whole.

"Heard that yell an' thought I was ridin' into a camp of savages," he said lazily. "You got any whiskey?"

"You know I always carry a quart, you bastard. You probably have half a dozen bottles stashed away in them packs yourself—just wanna mooch offa me. Reckon I can spare a shot or two."

"Be mighty obliged," Jackson drawled.

Jeff pulled the bottle out of one of the packs, and the two men drank, tilting the bottle back with relish. Jackson's horse nibbled at the grass. One of his mules brayed. The bottle was half empty before Jeff finally put the cap back on and slipped it into the pack.

"Mighty good," Jackson remarked.

"Particularly as it didn't cost you nothin'."

"Could have somethin' to do with it. You-all headin' for Natchez?"

Jeff nodded. "Left Carolina 'bout two weeks ago. Hear there might be Indian trouble up the trail. Crawley was certain they was gonna attack at any minute. See any signs of 'em?"

Jackson hesitated, glancing at me. He scratched the side of his head, his blue eyes filled with indecision as he debated whether or not to speak. After a moment he frowned and spoke in a guarded voice.

"Band of renegades. Couldn't be more'n ten or twelve of 'em, I figure. The rest of the tribe's moved on up country, fifty miles or so from the Trace. This bunch— they ain't up to no good. The McKenney family was murdered. I reckon Crawley heard about that. These braves're out to kill any white they can get their hands on."

Jeff was grave. "You run into 'em?"

"I saw 'em," Jackson said. "I'd camped for the night, had the horse and mules tethered. I heard 'em in the distance, heard 'em whoopin' and hollerin'. I crept through the woods to investigate, hid behind some bushes on the edge of their camp. They was all painted up, wearin' their feathers, dancin' 'round their fire. Joe Pearson—" He darted another glance at me, the crease between his brows digging deeper. "Joe started out a couple days 'fore I did. He—he was *in* th' fire, lashed to a stake, screamin' his lungs out. Wuzn't nothin' I could do but get th' hell outa there quick as I could. I backtracked and made a wide detour."

Both men were silent for a while. I was horrified by what I had heard. The river continued to rush along with a pleasant gurgling noise. Insects hummed. Sunlight and shadow played on the ground as tree limbs swayed gently in the breeze. The spot that had seemed so peaceful and lovely just a short while ago seemed suddenly ominous, threatening. I felt vulnerable and exposed, felt hostile eyes were observing us even as we stood there.

"How long ago was that?" Jeff asked.

" 'Bout a week and a half ago."

"Chances are they've moved out of the area by this time."

"It's likely," Jackson admitted. "Still, if you intend

goin' on, you want to keep your rifle handy. You might make sure the woman has a gun handy, too."

Jeff nodded again. Jackson's expression was impassive. He was clearly a man who felt little emotion, a man long inured to hardship and horror. In his filthy buckskins and raccoon cap, with his lanky locks and shaggy black beard, he was nevertheless an impressive figure in a way I couldn't quite define. If there was such a thing as an "American" type, Jackson was uniquely so.

"Guess I better be pushin' on," he drawled. "Reckon there's another hour or so 'fore dark. Want to get as far up the road as I can."

"You haven't seen anything of the Brennans, have you?"

"You mean Jim and Billy?"

"Crawley claims they're in the area, claims they murdered a couple trappers."

"Wouldn't doubt it. Trappers were probably carryin' a rich load of furs. Them Brennan boys is bad news. I ain't seen 'em, but that don't mean they ain't around. If they are, you wanna watch out. Reckon they bear you a pretty strong grudge after the way you shot up Jim and whupped Billy."

"Reckon they might," Jeff agreed.

Jackson mounted his horse, swinging lazily into the saddle. "Don't wanna dawdle. Take care, Rawlins."

"You, too."

He walked the horse slowly out of the clearing, the mules trailing behind. Just before he passed out of sight behind a line of trees, he turned around in the saddle and gazed at us with a pale, impassive face, then lifted his arm in farewell. Jeff was silent for a long while, a thoughtful look in his eyes, and then, seeing my expression, he broke into one of those wide, merry grins.

"Aw, come on now, don't look so scared. I'll protect you."

"It—it's just so frightening."

"Hell, them Indians have probably cleared out—that was more'n a week ago. As for the Brennans, I reckon I could handle 'em any day of the week. If they know what's good for 'em, they'll steer clear. Don't you worry about it."

"That poor man—"

He looked puzzled. "Jackson?"

"Joe Pearson, the one the Indians—" I hesitated, shuddering.

"Burnin' at the stake's downright gentle compared to some of the things they do to captives. Usually they keep a man alive as long as possible. He dies a thousand deaths before—I'm upsettin' you. Tell you what, why don't we have a little target practice?"

"I don't know what you mean."

"You ever fired a rifle?"

"I've never even touched one."

"High time you had a few lessons. Not that you're likely to be usin' it against Indians," he added hastily. "I might get tired of goin' out for game one day, might decide to send you out to round up dinner. Everyone oughta know how to use a rifle. You'll soon get the hang of it."

Jeff fetched powder horn and rifle from one of the packs. He showed me how to load the thing, how to hold it. Unenthusiastic, I watched, and when he thrust it at me I held it nervously, afraid it would explode in my arms. Jeff stepped behind me and, reaching around, helped me get the proper hold. I leaned back against him, my arms shaking a bit from the weight of the rifle. His cheek was almost touching mine, and I could feel his muscles tighten as he lifted my arms up higher.

"Like this, ya see? Hold it like this. Let the butt rest against your shoulder. Relax, Marietta, it ain't gonna bite you. Okay, now look through the sight."

"The sight?"

"That tiny piece of metal stickin' up on the end of th' barrel. Don't you know anything? That's the sight. You get whatever you intend to hit lined up with it. Then you just pull the trigger—and if you ask me what the trigger is I'm gonna strangle you here and now."

"I know what the trigger is," I said wearily.

Jeff let go of my arms and strolled several paces away to my right. The rifle was much heavier than I had thought it would be. It was difficult to hold it steady.

"All right," he said, "you're ready to fire."

"What am I going to fire at?"

Still holding the rifle, I turned innocently toward him. His face turned ashen. His eyes widened in alarm. He gave a yell and almost fell over backwards getting out of the way. I realized that the rifle had been pointing directly at him and I was unable to resist a smile. Jeff scowled, not at all amused. Still shaken, he pushed his hair from his forehead.

"That thing's *loaded*. You coulda blown my head off!"

"This was your idea," I told him.

He came up behind me again, evidently deciding that was the safest place to be.

"See that log across the river there?" he said. "There's a great big branch stickin' up there on the end. Fire at it. You couldn't possibly miss it, not from this distance. Remember to get it lined up in your sight."

My arms were already aching dreadfully from the strain of holding the rifle, and I was even more nervous than before. Nevertheless, I took very careful aim, determined to show him I wasn't a complete idiot. My finger rested loosely on the trigger. Tense, my body rigid, I closed my eyes. I squeezed. The explosion was deafening. The recoil almost knocked me over. I would have fallen had Jeff not been there to throw his arms around me. He held me tightly as the smoke cleared, and then he gave an exasperated sigh.

"Did I hit it?"

" 'Fraid not," he replied, "but you sure as hell messed up that clump of flowers over there."

He handed me the powder horn and insisted that I load the rifle again. I hadn't been paying enough attention earlier. I botched it terribly, spilling powder all over the ground. Jeff jerked the rifle out of my hands and loaded it himself, showing me how all over again, threatening to beat me if I made a mess of it the next time. He handed the rifle back to me and made me hoist it up into position without any help.

Again I took aim. I was more relaxed this time, not letting the weight of the rifle bother me so much, not nearly so rigid as I had been before. I covered the branch with the sight. I pulled the trigger, keeping my eyes open this time, steadying myself against the recoil. There was another deafening explosion, another great puff of acrid smoke. A rock in the middle of the stream shattered into bits.

"You probably hit a *fish!*" he exclaimed.

"I'm trying!" I retorted. "I didn't want to fire the bloody thing in the first place!"

"You're gonna be a crack shot before I get through with you!"

"Is that right!"

"It damn sure is!" he thundered.

We glared at each other, tempers high, eyes flashing, and then, unable to maintain his anger, Jeff broke into a sheepish grin. I began to smile. We both laughed, and then he clapped me on the back good-naturedly and gave me the powder horn again. I didn't spill a drop this time. I shot at the branch. I missed. He merely shook his head. We continued target practice for another fifteen minutes, and although I never once hit the branch, I did manage to do considerable damage to the area nearby. Jeff cleaned the rifle and put it away.

"At least we're making some progress," he remarked. "You're not afraid of it any more. Tomorrow you might even be able to *hit* something."

The sunlight was almost gone. Thick shadows were beginning to spread over the ground. Jeff checked on the mules and then spread blankets out over the grass beneath the boughs of a tree. The fire had long since gone out. I smoothed back my hair, feeling much better now. Jeff took me in his arms and kissed me soundly, and then he led me over to the blankets. Darkness fell as we made love, wrestling lustily, enjoying each other immensely. Jeff fell asleep immediately afterwards, his arms still wrapped around me, his head resting on my shoulder. The stream gurgled. Leaves rustled. The forest was filled with night noises. Through the branches of the tree I could see the dark sky frosted with stars that blinked and glittered brightly.

Jeff stirred, groaning, tightening his grip on me. I stroked the back of his head, loving his weight, his warmth, wishing I could feel safe and secure here in his arms. I couldn't. Despite all my efforts to put it out of my mind, I kept thinking about that poor man lashed to the stake while the flames crackled and the Indians howled. No matter what Jeff might say, I knew we were going to be in constant danger until we finally put this savage country behind us.

XIV

I hadn't become a crack shot, not by any means, but after four days of lessons I handled the rifle with some assurance and could usually hit whatever target Jeff indicated. He was quite pleased with me. His spare rifle was now mine for the duration of the trip. Sheathed in a long, shabby leather holster, the rifle was affixed to Jenny's saddle and I had my own powder horn within easy reach as well. It gave me a certain feeling of security, for although four days had passed without the least sign of Indians, I couldn't rid myself of the fear we would encounter them before the jurney was over.

We rode hard. I found that I was growing accustomed to it and not complaining nearly as much. Although we got up before dawn and resumed our travel while the sunrise was still staining the sky, Jeff was usually content to stop for the night quite early, providing we had made good time during the day. I was growing accustomed to the land, too. It still seemed ominous and forbidding, but I was beginning to appreciate the savage splendor, the startling variety of trees, the sparkling streams strewn with gray and golden-gray boulders, the rough, ruggedly beautiful vistas we saw whenever we momentarily left the dense forest.

Five days after our encounter with Jackson, we spent the entire morning laboriously moving up the side of a vast mountain thickly covered with towering pine trees, the trail winding gradually and carrying us higher and higher. I was amazed that Jeff, or anyone else for that matter, was able to stay on the Trace, for ever since we had left Crawley's Inn, the trail had grown much less distinct, vanishing altogether at times, it seemed, invisible to all but the most trained eye. I would never have been able to keep to it on my own, would have gotten lost immediately. But Jeff was confident, and even when there seemed to be no trail at all, he forged on through the forest without the least hesitation.

The sun was directly overhead as we neared the top of the mountain. I was exhausted, my white blouse damp with perspiration and clinging to my bosom, my brown skirt limp and dusty. I had caught my hair on a low-hanging branch earlier on, and I knew my auburn tresses must resemble those of a witch. We moved on up through the dense maze of pines, trunks a grayish-brown, needles a vivid green, each branch studded with rich brown cones. The reddish earth was strewn with dry needles and spread with soft blue shadows, a few brilliant yellow-white rays of sunlight slanting through the branches. Birds called. The scent of pines was glorious.

"How much further?" I called.

"Just a little ways," Jeff retorted. "We should reach the top in fifteen minutes or so. From there on it's easy going."

"I believe *that*," I said ruefully.

"You complaining again? I thought I broke you of that."

"Jenny keeps stumbling. She's exhausted, too."

"We'll take a rest once we reach level ground."

The top of the mountain was amazingly flat. The land seemed to stretch straight ahead to the distant horizon, and Jeff explained that we would be traveling along the crest of a small range of mountains for the next two or three days. True to his word, he dismounted and then, taking my hand, helped me dismount. I was so weary I almost fell. He clutched me to him, grinning, and then

266

he gave me a hearty kiss. His buckskins were slightly damp, too, and his hair was wet with perspiration, making it an even darker gold. I clung to him a moment, savoring his strength, and then he pushed me gently away.

"Time for that kinda thing when we stop for the night," he teased.

"I wasn't even—"

"Wasn't cravin' my body?" he interrupted.

"Not in the least. You're filthy and sweaty and smell like—"

"You ain't a bloomin' rose, yourself."

"I don't imagine I am. I haven't had a bath since we left the inn, and these clothes—"

"There's a dandy little stream a few miles up ahead, runs right over a bunch of boulders and makes a small waterfall. We'll stop there. Maybe we'll bathe together."

"I thought we'd never reach the top," I said wearily.

"Yeah, it was pretty rugged. You're holdin' up well."

"Think so?"

He nodded, his warm brown eyes merry. "I'm beginnin' to admire you so much I'm thinkin' I ain't gonna be able to give you up. I'm gettin' used to havin' you around, gettin' to like it."

I made a face and went to stretch out under the shade of a tree. Jeff tethered the three mules under yet another tree, and then he came to flop down on the ground beside me, stretching his legs out and cradling his arms behind his head. The trees were much less dense here, and we could see great patches of sky as pale and lovely as pale-blue silk. I closed my eyes, relaxed, content to be here, content to have him beside me, warm, friendly, comforting. I thought of what he had said about not being able to give me up, and I wondered if he had been serious.

I didn't love him. I never would, never could, not after Derek, but I realized that I *liked* Jeff Rawlins in a way I had never been able to like Derek. I had never been able to chat with Derek, to be completely natural and at ease with him as I was with Jeff. Jeff was a playful scamp who loved to tease me, loved to argue, yet this made him none

267

the less virile, a manly man who was a superb lover. It would be so much easier to be in love with him than it had been to be in love with Derek. Eyes closed, body weary, I forced the thought of Derek out of my mind, struggling to contain all those bitter, painful emotions that threatened to surface again.

I must have fallen asleep, for the next thing I knew, I was struggling up through heavy blue-black clouds, moaning as something soft and fuzzy tickled my nose. I opened my eyes to see Jeff's face inches from my own, his brown eyes dancing with amusement, his wide pink mouth stretching into that familiar grin as he ran the fuzzy leaf across my nose one more time. I slapped at it irritably, frowning at him. Jeff tossed the leaf aside and lowered his mouth over mine and turned his head to one side in order to make our noses fit. Against my will, I lifted my arms and ran my palms over his broad back, rubbing the rough buckskin and feeling the muscles beneath as he continued to kiss me, lazily, thoroughly.

He raised his head and peered into my eyes. His own were filled with affection.

"Figured it was time we got a move on," he said in that lovely, softly slurred voice.

"I've been asleep."

"Darn near half an hour you've been sleepin'. I just let ya. Ya know what?"

"What? I asked.

"Your face is dirty. There's a streak of dirt right there." He touched my jaw. "Your hair's all tangled, too, and your clothes are a mess. And ya know what? You ain't never been more appetizin'."

"Is that a fact?"

He climbed to his feet and peered down at me, shaking his head. "It's a fact. If I didn't have such a strong will—"

I sat up, brushing pine needles from my hair. "Yes?"

"If I didn't have such a strong will, we'd *never* get to Natchez."

Reaching down, he took hold of my wrist and pulled me to my feet. I was still a bit groggy, and I still felt a warm, comfortable glow from that prolonged kiss. He held me cradled against him for a moment, smiling a lazy, satisfied smile. Jeff was still feeling a glow, too. When his thighs touched mine, I felt tangible proof of it as he pressed against me.

"Damned if you ain't bewitchin'! I'm gonna have ta watch you, wench, I'm gonna have ta be strong and purposeful. A man could dally with you all day and never get nothin' done."

"You want to dally?"

He chuckled and whacked me lustily on the backside, giving me a shove toward the mules.

"Get on with you! I'm onto your tricks, wench. We got a long trek ahead of us 'fore we reach that waterfall I was tellin' you about, and you ain't gonna trick me into wastin' no more time."

I felt good as we continued on our way. I enjoyed his teasing, enjoyed his peculiar, roughhewn gallantry. He *was* strong, and he was purposeful, too, yet he had let me sleep for a full half-hour. He was considerate, and . . . and he was strangely tender. Robust and lusty, yes, but there was tenderness, too, the kind of tenderness Derek Hawke had never once displayed. Jeff Rawlins claimed to equate a woman with a good meal and a fine glass of whiskey, something to be enjoyed but never taken seriously, yet . . . that kiss had been so very tender, expressing an emotion he probably wasn't even aware of himself. I wondered if he could possibly be falling in love with me.

I was imagining things, I told myself. Surely. He had gone for thirty-two years without falling in love, and he wasn't fool enough to let himself fall in love now, not with an indentured wench he planned to sell to a whorehouse as soon as we reached New Orleans. He . . . he was just naturally affectionate, and that warmth, that tenderness meant nothing. He would turn me over to the madam and walk away and never give me another thought. I was nothing more than a piece of merchandise to him. He enjoyed me, yes, just as he must have enjoyed a number of other women he had transported over this same trail, for the same purpose. He might joke about not being able to give me up, but he would give me up soon enough when enough pieces of gold changed hands.

We were riding along a ridge now, the trail narrow, pine trees dense on our right. On our left the land sloped down steeply to a valley far below. I could see more mountains across the valley, tops a hazy purple in the distance, more like soft violet, looming up against the pale-blue sky. The valley was a patchwork of greens, tans, and brown, shot through with the silver sparkle of a stream. A large brown bird swirled lazily in the air, gradually circling down to the valley. Jeff told me it was an eagle. We stopped once to watch two furry black bear cubs gamboling down the side of the slope, an enormous black mother bear moving ponderously behind them.

"I didn't know there were *bears*," I said.

"Lots of 'em," he replied. "Don't worry. They won't bother you if you don't bother them."

"Those cubs are so adorable. Look, they seem to be skipping, and then they'll curl up and roll. The mother bear looks so patient—"

"She'd tear you to shreds if you so much as touched one of her young 'uns. Riled up, a bear can be deadly. Claws like steel. Wouldn't want to tangle with one myself."

The bears disappeared from sight, and we moved on. A short while later the trail turned sharply to our left, into the forest, and we left the ridge behind. We might be on top of the mountain, but the ground was as level, the forest as dense as it had been before. Although there were still many pines, most of the trees had large, leafy limbs. Jeff named half a dozen kinds for me, none of which I had ever heard of before. How different this forest was from the forests in England, so much wilder, so much larger. Would anyone ever be able to tame all this wilderness? I doubted it, despite what Jeff said to the contrary. There were far too many civilized places for people to settle in for anyone to waste time and effort trying to live amidst all this rugged splendor.

It was still early, perhaps four o'clock, when we reached

the clearing where we would spend the night. Situated beneath a small but exceedingly steep wall of gray rock down which the waterfall cascaded, it was surrounded on three sides by woods and intersected by the narrow stream, the bed golden brown and just deep enough for wading. No more than fifteen feet high, the waterfall splashed and splattered into a shallow pool, spraying thin mist. It was a lovely spot, the ground grassy and soft, the trees making living green and brown walls. Vines covered with pendant-shaped purple flowers climbed up the gray rock on either side of the waterfall.

Jeff and I dismounted. He removed the packs from the mules and, after drinking from the stream, they began to graze under the shade of the trees. I stood near the waterfall, watching the sunlight play in the mist and causing rainbow-hued patterns to shimmer. Jeff came up to stand behind me, resting his hands on my shoulders.

"Like it?"

"It's a charming place," I replied.

"Ready for a bath?"

"I'd rather eat first. I'm hungry."

"There're a lot of wild turkeys 'round here. Heard one gobbling just a minute ago. I'll go shoot us one in a little while. I'm thinkin' I'd like to cool off first—"

"Go right ahead," I told him.

Suddenly I felt his hands on my shoulder blades. He gave me a mighty shove. I cried out, stumbling, and a second later I found myself splashing into the pool directly beneath the waterfall. I was soaked immediately, of course, and when I tried to stand up the waterfall knocked me back down. He stood a few feet away, laughing uproariously. I was not at all amused. Finally getting to my feet, I stepped out from under the waterfall. Skirt and blouse clung wetly, and my hair was plastered to my skull in wet strands. I took off my shoes and tossed them onto the grass, staring at him with an expression that should have killed.

"That wasn't funny!"

"You look like a drowned rat."

271

I held my hand out. "Here, help me out—"

And when he took hold of my hand I gave a mighty tug and his eyes widened in surprise and he came crashing into the water on all fours. Now it was my turn to laugh. Jeff spluttered and coughed and then wrapped his arms around my knees and toppled me back down into the water and, like two children, we wrestled and splashed each other. Then we were standing directly under the waterfall and he was kissing me, kissing me furiously, and we both fell down into the pool and the water pelted us as his lips continued to cover my own. He released me and laughed again and clambered out of the water to dig a bar of soap out of one of the packs. He tossed it to me, then kicked off his soggy moccasins and pulled off his wet buckskin tunic and began to wriggle out of the clinging breeches.

Naked, he lunged into the water again, knocking me over on my back, and I struggled furiously as he undressed me, slinging the wet clothes onto the grass. The bar of soap was bobbing around in the pool. Jeff grabbed it and handed it back to me and ordered me to wash him, and I did. Delighted, standing up in the pool, covered with suds, he washed me in turn, and pulled me into the waterfall again so that the suds was rinsed off both of us. He kissed me once again, and once again we lost our footing and went tumbling into the pool. Wrapping one arm around my throat, he ducked me under the water, roaring with laughter when I came up spluttering and coughing. I dug my elbow into his ribs, sending him crashing backwards, and he caught hold of my foot and pulled me down beside him.

We spent another ten minutes in wildly abandoned frolic, and then he pulled me out of the water and shoved me down on the soft grass.

We made love explosively, a furious, passionate wrestling match unlike anything I had ever experienced before. I fought him, deliberately, and he was much rougher than he had ever been, crushing, clasping, spearing me with his passion while I struggled and kicked and, finally, permit-

272

ted him to subdue me as our energetic tussle came to an explosive climax. Jeff held me then, held me tenderly in his arms, kissing my nipples, my shoulders, nuzzling my throat as minutes passed, and after a while he lowered me back onto the grass and made love to me again with incredible tenderness, slowly, gently, giving himself completely even as he took, and I knew then that I had not been mistaken earlier on. He was in love with me, even if he wasn't aware of it himself. This was love, not sex, love expressed in a manner far more poignant and meaningful than words could have expressed it. As I caressed his shoulders, his back, his buttocks, as I rose to meet him and held him to me, every fiber of my being told me I was right, told me Jeff Rawlins loved me in every sense of the word.

We bathed again, briefly, and the sun quickly dried our bodies, and then we dressed, Jeff getting into the set of buckskins the girl Lita had cleaned for him at the inn. I struggled into fresh petticoats and put on an old yellow cotton dress with short sleeves and a square-cut neckline. Jeff looked sheepish now, grinning, and when both of us were dressed he gave me a tight hug and a quick, smacking kiss. I touched his cheek, looking into those merry brown eyes and wishing we had met long ago, under entirely different circumstances.

"Reckon I'd better go after that turkey now," he said lazily. "Shouldn't take me long to pick one off. You behave yourself while I'm gone."

"There's a little soap left. I'm going to wash our clothes. Does buckskin shrink?"

"A little. You can't hurt 'em none. They're already soaking wet."

He fetched his rifle and, crossing the stream, sauntered on into the woods on the other side, buckskin fringe swaying as he rolled his shoulders jauntily. Pensive now, still filled with that delicious glow that was the aftermath of love, I gathered up the wet clothes and the remains of the soap and took them over to the stream, kneeling on the bank. I heard Jeff's footsteps receding in the distance, and then there was silence but for the constant soft splatter of the waterfall. As I washed the clothes, I thought about what had happened and what it meant, and I was sad, for I didn't want him to love me. It could only complicate matters.

I intended to escape at the first opportunity, and, ironically enough, I found myself thinking how much that was going to hurt him. He trusted me, already. He had invested all his money in me, and when I was gone he would be penniless . . . I mustn't let myself think that way. I was too fond of him, much too fond, and even though I didn't love him, I felt closer to him than I had ever felt to anyone, even Derek. It was nothing but the enforced proximity, I told myself. I had to harden my heart. I had to be on guard constantly. He might love me, but that wouldn't prevent him from selling me. Not for a minute.

Wringing the clothes out, I took them over to one of the thorny shrubs growing at the edge of the clearing and carefully draped them on the branches. There was still plenty of sunlight, and with any luck they would be dry before nightfall. As I readjusted the skirt so that it would hang more evenly, I thought I heard a footstep in the woods directly behind the shrub. I paused, listening closely, but the sound was not repeated. It had probably been some small woods creature, I thought, as I strolled on over to the pile of packs Jeff had taken off the mules.

Digging through them until I found my hairbrush, I sat down on the lumpy pile and began to brush my hair. It was almost dry now, soft and feathery, only slightly damp at the ends. It was nice to be clean again, to be rid of the dirt and grime, to smell of soap. My yellow dress was the color of buttercups in the sunlight, and even though it was old, the bodice too tight, the full skirt neatly patched in half a dozen places, I knew that it emphasized my bosom and slender waist and went well with my auburn hair. I wanted to look nice for him for a change, even though I didn't love him, even though I intended to betray his trust in the near future.

As I finished brushing my hair, I had the impression

that someone was watching me. It was a very strong sensation, and I gazed nervously toward the trees where I had imagined I heard a footstep. It couldn't be Jeff. He had gone off in the other direction, on the other side of the stream. I saw only trees and thick shrubbery, the clothes strewn over the thorny bush already beginning to dry in the strong sunlight. The sensation persisted and grew stronger. I could actually feel eyes staring at me, watching my every gesture. I knew I wasn't imagining it. I put the brush aside and stood up, my heart beginning to palpitate rapidly.

A twig snapped loudly, so loudly it could be heard over the splatter of the waterfall. Shrubbery moved, leaves shaking. I was paralyzed with fear, expecting a tall bronze savage with feathers and war paint to leap out with a bloodcurdling cry. The rifle! Where was the rifle? Jeff had taken his, of course, but mine was . . . He had taken the sling off Jenny and put it down behind the packs. It was behind me then, on the ground, not two yards away. I must get it at once. I was terrified now as another twig snapped and heavy footsteps crushed twigs and leaves. I couldn't move. I was frozen in place, unable to do anything but stare in horror at the shrubbery that was parting, branches separating to make way for the man behind them.

He was tall and lean. His dark-brown hair was wildly unruly, his features roughhewn, blue eyes half concealed by drooping lids. His nose was humped, obviously broken at some time and improperly set. His boots were black, as were his clinging trousers. His vivid blue shirt was of some silky material, open at the throat, bagging slightly over his belt. The sleeves were full-gathered. A hunting knife hung in a scabbard on his right hip, and a long pistol was jammed into the waistband of his trousers. He stood there at the edge of the clearing, gazing at me, and I felt waves of relief sweep over me.

"You—you frightened me out of my wits—" I said hoarsely. "I thought you were an Indian—"

"Did you now?"

"I heard something in the woods, and—and I'm just glad to see you're not carrying a tomahawk."

The man allowed a wry grin to curl briefly on one side of his mouth. "I was kinda alarmed myself, if you wanna know the truth. I heard something human movin' up ahead—that's what I thought, too, thought it was a redskin. I crept up real quiet and peered through the bushes. I was mighty relieved to see it wuzn't a Chickasaw."

His voice was a lazy drawl, slurred like Jeff's, but coarser. There was a rough, raspy quality, as though it hurt his throat to speak. He looked like a highwayman with that broken nose and those drooping lids, but then I imagined most men out here looked that way. Jackson, for example, would have frightened little children.

"Always keep an eye peeled for redskins," he continued. "My brother and I had a run-in with three braves four days ago. Bastards stole one of our horses, would've made off with the other one if we hadn't spotted 'em and started shooting. Now we just got one horse between us."

"Are you traveling on the Trace?"

"More or less," he replied. He looked beyond me at the mules. "Them look like Rawlins's mules."

"They are. Do you know him?"

The man nodded slowly, a peculiar look in his eyes. "Reckon I do," he drawled. "You must be one of his women. He about?"

"He went off into the woods to shoot a turkey, but he should be back in a little while. I'm sure he'll be pleased to see you. We ran into another friend of his a few days ago—Jackson, a trader. Perhaps you know Jackson, too. He—"

I cut myself short. The man was clearly not listening. That peculiar look was still in his eyes. He seemed to be contemplating something, weighing the pros and cons. I didn't like that. I didn't like it at all. There was something disturbing about this stranger. His manner was . . . guarded, and he seemed to be keeping something from me. Why had he been wandering in the woods like that? Why had he been spying on me for so long before making his presence known? My uneasiness returned. The man looked up, noticing my expression. He lifted the corner of his mouth again, casually stroking the hilt of his hunting knife.

"So Rawlins has gone off, has he? Mighty convenient."

"He—he'll be back any minute now."

"I ain't heard no rifle fire. He's still trackin' down his turkey. He ain't gonna be back for a good long while—"

I took a step backward and glanced down at the rifle. That was a mistake. Quick as lightning, the man had hold of my right arm, twisting it, forcing it up between my shoulder blades. Before I could scream he clamped his free hand over my mouth, forcing my head back against his shoulder. Excruciating pain shot through my arm and shoulder as he tightened his grip brutally. I could feel his breath against my cheek.

"We're gonna play us a little game," he drawled. "We're gonna give ol' Jeff a surprise. He's gonna come back and find his little girl gone, and he's gonna come lookin' for her. Me and Billy're gonna be waitin' for him."

I knew who he was then. I should have known immediately, of course, after all that talk about the Brennans. This would be Jim, the one Jeff had shot in the shoulder. He had helped his brother Billy escape from a jail in Natchez, and they had killed two men in the process. "They don't make 'em any meaner'n the Brennans," Eb Crawley had said. "If I had my choice of runnin' up against a pack of Chickasaws or runnin' up against the Brennan brothers, I'd pick the Indians every time." These words raced through my mind as Jim Brennan gripped my arm tightly and held his palm pressed over my mouth.

"Yeah, reckon it'll be a regular set-up," he continued. "He'll come stumblin' through the woods, lookin' for his property, and me and Billy Boy will be waitin'. Come on, move. You're gonna make dandy bait."

I tried to struggle, tried to kick his shin. He gave my arm a savage wrench. I almost passed out from the pain. Whirling me around, he forced me to walk ahead of him through the shrubbery, still gripping my arm, covering my mouth. I stumbled. He wrenched my arm again. There was nothing I could do but walk. Branches slapped at me, tearing at my skirt, my hair. I couldn't endure the pain much longer. If he didn't let go of my arm soon, I knew I was going to faint.

When Brennan finally stopped, we had come a good way from the clearing. I could no longer hear the waterfall. He removed his hand from my mouth and curled his arm tightly around my throat, causing me to gasp and splutter. He leaned backwards, applying even more pressure. Dark wings were fluttering in my head as consciousness slipped away. His lips were against my ear.

"I'm gonna let go of you now, wench," he drawled. "And you're going to behave yourself. Understand? If you try to scream, if you try to run away, I'm gonna take out my knife and cut you bad. Understand? If you do, if you intend to behave yourself, nod."

Somehow or other I managed to tilt my chin forward in what might pass for a nod. Brennan hesitated for a moment, a moment that seemed to stretch into an eternity, and then he uncurled his arm from my throat and let go of my arm. I stumbled forward and would have fallen had he not grabbed my shoulder. I coughed. I rubbed my sore arm. He waited patiently for a minute or so, then gave me a vicious shove.

"You're all right now. Keep moving."

I stumbled against a tree trunk. Brennan frowned and took hold of my wrist, moving ahead with a brisk stride, forcing me to trot along beside him. They were going to set up a trap, using me as bait, so they could kill Jeff in cold blood, and then they would probably kill me. This man was utterly ruthless. He would kill as quickly, as casually, as another man might swat a fly. His brother was undoubtedly the same. I tripped, falling to my knees. Brennan jerked me back up, not so much as glancing at me, hardly breaking his stride. I wasn't a human being, not to him. I was a thing to be used and then disposed of. I knew he hadn't been merely trying to scare me when he mentioned the knife. I knew if I screamed, if I tried to break loose, he would kill me immediately.

We pushed on through the woods. We must have come half a mile from the clearing. I had lost all sense of direction. We moved down a gulley, stepped over a rotting log, climbed up the other side. The sky was gray now. The sunlight was thinner. The ground seemed to slope upward gradually, leafy limbs stretching overhead, thick tree trunks a maze around us. We came to a stream, and Brennan scooped me up into his arms, carrying me across. I looked up at his face. It was devoid of expression. He set me down on the other side of the stream. I realized this must be the stream that made the waterfall in the clearing. We were at least a mile away now. Had Jeff returned to the clearing yet?

"Come on," Brennan said.

"Let me—won't you just let me catch my breath?"

"There'll be time for that when we reach camp. Reckon it'll take Rawlins a while to track us down. Couple hours, at least. It'll be good and dark by then."

"Why—why are you doing this?"

"I got me a score to settle."

"How can you just—"

Brennan slapped me across the face with such force that I fell to the ground. He stood over me with his hands resting lightly on his thighs, his face expressionless. His vivid blue shirt billowed slightly as a small breeze blew across the stream. The full sleeves fluttered, the silky material flapping. I sobbed, shaking my head. I had never been so frightened in my life.

"I don't like women," he drawled, "particularly women who jabber. If you know what's good for you, you'll keep your mouth shut. Dead bait's as good as live. If it wasn't for disappointin' my brother, you'd be dead already. Billy's got a weakness for women. He's gonna be glad to see you."

He pulled me to my feet and, keeping hold of my wrist, strode on into the woods. I stumbled along beside him, swerving to avoid tree trunks and thorny branches.

279

Shadows thickened all around. Sunlight was fading quickly now. The woods seemed to be filling with dark blue-gray mist, brown tree trunks, and dark green leaves losing color, merging into black. Perhaps fifteen minutes passed, perhaps more, and then I saw orange flames flickering up ahead, through the maze of trees. Three or four minutes later Jim Brennan dragged me into a small clearing. Heavy tree limbs met overhead, making a leafy ceiling through which it was impossible to see the sky.

It was dark now, but the fire cast a wavering light. The man standing beside it was blond and sturdily built, not as tall as his brother, not much taller than I, but muscular. He looked as though he would have the strength of a young bull, the hump of his nose giving him a belligerent, pugnacious appearance. He wore black boots and black breeches identical to his brother's, but the loose-fitting, silky shirt was bright crimson.

"What the *hell*?" he exclaimed.

"I thought you'd be pleased, Billy Boy."

"Where'd *she* come from?"

"You know when we were standing on that bluff this morning and you said you thought you seen some mules moving down the trail? Well, I figured if there was someone traveling they'd probably stop for the night at that waterfall. Sure enough, they did."

Billy stared at us angrily. He seemed uneasy, even jumpy. Whereas his brother was unlikely to display any emotion, Billy Brennan was obviously volatile, explosive. Fists clenched, jaw thrust forward, shoulders hunched, he seemed about to charge and snort.

"Where's the man? She sure as hell wuzn't travelin' alone."

"He was out shootin' turkeys. I reckon he'll be payin' us a call before too long."

Billy moved closer, peering at me. He might have a weakness for women, but he was none too happy to see me. That much was clear.

"Christ, Jim! You don't mean—a woman looks like this, she can only be travelin' with Jeff *Rawlins*. You snatched her from his camp! He'll come back and find her gone and—Jesus Christ!"

"What's the matter, Billy Boy? You ain't scared, are you?"

"That Rawlins—"

"I got a score to settle with him. So do you."

Billy was even more upset, his cheeks ashen. "He's dangerous, Jim! There ain't a tougher man in the whole territory. I just wanna steer clear of him. We tangled with him once, and once was enough. That time we jumped him on the Trace—he put a bullet through your shoulder, busted my jaw, damn near broke my neck!"

"All the more reason we should set up a little trap for him. There are practical reasons, too. We need them mules of his. We got one horse between us, and we ain't gonna get nowhere that way. Relax, Billy Boy. I got it all figured out. He'll come looking for us, and he'll find us, and we'll be ready for him."

"What about *her?*"

"I more or less brung her along as a present for you, brother. I thought you'd be a bit more enthusiastic. After we get rid of Rawlins, you can amuse yourself with her. Hell, you can even keep her if you want to. Then when you get tired of her, we can sell her to one of them whorehouses, just like Rawlins was planning to do."

Billy examined me with belligerent blue eyes, scowling as he did so. He began to warm to the idea. Lifting his lips at one corner, Jim Brennan shoved me toward his brother. Billy caught hold of my arms, gripping them tightly, studying me as he might study a horse he was thinking of buying. Some of his anger vanished, replaced by lust. He crushed me to him, slinging one arm around the back of my neck, the other around my waist. He attacked my lips like a madman, forcing them open, thrusting his tongue into my mouth, all the while holding me so tightly I thought my bones would crack. I tried to struggle. It was futile. His arms merely tightened, his mouth working even more furiously over mine.

"Easy, Billy Boy. *Easy*. Save it for later, after we've killed Rawlins."

Billy Brennan lifted his head and loosened his grip on me, still holding me against his chest. He was breathing heavily, a virile young bull eager to stud. His brother, amused by the lusty exhibition, gave a dry laugh.

"You do like the women, Billy Boy. Ain't never seen nothing like it. Save it, fellow. After Rawlins is dead you can go at all night long, and if I know you, you will."

"She's a dandy, Jim. A real dandy. What's her name?"

"Wouldn't know."

"What's your name, wench?" Billy growled.

I tried to speak. I couldn't. My throat was dry. My lips were sore. I was so terrified I could only shake my head. Billy caught hold of my hair and jerked my head back.

"When I ask a question, I wanna answer!"

"I reckon she's stunned, Billy Boy. Hell, man, you went after her like a pack of starving wolves. Her name ain't important. What's important is she's Rawlins's property, and Rawlins is gonna be looking for her. Knowing him, it ain't gonna take him all night to find us."

Billy looked nervous again. His forehead was moist. He released me and stepped back, his eyes filled with uncertainty.

"I still don't think this is such a good idea, Jim. That Rawlins is one mean bastard. So he comes lookin' for us and we hear him comin'? What's to stop her from yellin' at him, warnin' him to watch out?"

The older Brennan sighed and gave his head a little shake. "You're my brother, Billy, and you got lots of brawn, but when it comes to brains—" He shook his head again. "We'll tie her up, gag her. There's some rope looped around the saddle horn and a couple of rags in the pack. Get 'em."

Billy strode across the clearing, past the fire. I noticed the horse for the first time, tethered to a tree in the shadows, the saddle still in place. I saw the blond take down the rope and open the pack. His brother stood with his arms crossed over his chest, looking both weary and bored. Billy returned. He was perhaps twenty-five years old. While his brother possessed a cool native shrewdness, Billy was plainly both slow and dense. He was the kind of man who blasted his way through life with blazing temper and flying fists, leaving the thinking to someone else. Each man was dangerous in his own way. Together, they were deadly.

"You want me to tie her up, Jim?"

Jim Brennan sighed. "If it ain't too much trouble, Billy Boy."

His sarcasm was wasted on Billy. He seized my arm and dragged me over toward the trees. I was still stunned, and I knew it would be foolish to struggle. My knees were weak. I felt faint. This was a nightmare, a terrible nightmare that surely must end. I told myself that, over and over again, willing myself to hold on. Billy wrenched my arms behind me and crossed my wrists, binding them so tightly I could feel the rope cutting into my flesh. He jerked and tugged, securing the knots, and I winced, gnawing my lower lip to keep from crying out at the pain. When the job was done to his satisfaction, he caught hold of my shoulder and whirled me around.

"There," he said gruffly. "You ain't gonna get loose uv that."

"You—you're not going to get away with this," I whispered. "Jeff will come. He'll kill you both."

"Shut up!"

"He'll know it's a trap. He'll—"

"My brother knows what he's doin'!"

"He'll never fall for it. He's too—"

He jammed a wad of cloth into my mouth, cutting me short, causing me to gag. He was angry again, his blue eyes flashing savagely as he tied the other rag around my mouth, knotting it in back. Then, scowling darkly, he spread his palm over my face and pushed hard. I tumbled over backwards, falling against a tree trunk. My head seemed to explode, and then I was whirling through a black void, spinning dizzily into oblivion.

I don't know how long I was out. When I finally opened my eyes, it was to see the Brennan brothers sitting before a fire that was little more than a heap of glowing orange coals. Jim perched on a log, and Billy sat on a large rock nearby, gripping his knees tensely. Their faces were shadowed, Billy's blond hair gleaming in the semidarkness. I could see the horse behind Billy moving restlessly. Beyond the circle of light from the dying fire there were layers of darkness. The forest seemed to close about the clearing ominously, trees pressing nearer.

"When's he gonna *get* here?" Billy exclaimed.

"Should be soon now," his brother replied. "It's been dark for nigh on two hours now. He's gonna be real careful, and he's not gonna do anything impulsive because of the woman. Keep your britches on, Billy. When he gets here we'll know it."

"What if he shoots first?"

"Rawlins don't play it that way. He'll step right into the clearing. He'd be afraid to do anything before he sees the woman's all right. Don't worry."

"You gonna—"

"Soon as he steps through them trees, I'm gonna lift this here pistol and blow his head off."

"Man 'ud be a fool to just come marchin' into—"

"I told you, Billy, I got it all figured out. We ain't gonna hear him, see? We're gonna be sitting here real casual like, like we're not expecting him at all, and he'll think he's taking *us* by surprise."

"I still don't like it!"

"Shut up, Billy," his brother said patiently. "Just think about the woman. Think what you're gonna do to her after Rawlins gets his."

My head was throbbing viciously. The rope was biting into my wrists. I desperately needed to swallow, but I was afraid to, afraid I would strangle on the wad of cloth Billy had crammed into my mouth. When I had fallen against the tree, I had slumped on down to the ground, and I was leaning against the tree now, my legs spread out in front of me. Jeff would come. He would be here any minute now, and he would do exactly as Brennan predicted. He would see them sitting there, and he would step into the clearing with his rifle raised, thinking he was taking them by surprise. Then Jim would raise his pistol, quickly, before Jeff could see what was happening. That was why they had let the fire die down, so he wouldn't spy Jim's hand gripping the pistol at his side.

Several minutes passed. An owl hooted in the night. A frog croaked. Leaves crackled as a breeze stirred through the trees. Jim sat as still as a statue, waiting. Billy shifted about nervously. He was obviously terrified of Jeff. Jeff must have given him a terrible beating, and that wouldn't have been easy to do. Billy was stocky and strong. It would take an incredibly adept fighter to get the better of him. There was a side to Jeff I had never seen. It was hard to believe that the raffish charmer could be the same man who made Billy Brennan tremble, the man who had risked his life to rescue Lita from the Indians. Now he was going to step right into the trap Brennan had set for him, and I was responsible. I couldn't let it happen. There had to be some way I could prevent it, some way I could warn him.

I tensed. There was something behind me. I could sense a presence, feel it strongly, even though there hadn't been a sound. Someone was there, just behind the tree. I could hear breathing now, soft, so soft, and the faint sound of a body inching nearer. Fingers touched my own, and his whisper was so low I had to strain mightily to catch the words.

"I'm going to cut you free. Don't make a move. Keep looking straight in front of you. When I've cut the rope, keep your arms in back of you and keep still—"

My heart started to pound. It pounded so loudly I felt sure the Brennans could hear it beating against my chest. Neither of them so much as glanced at me. They thought I was still unconscious. I could feel the cold metal sides of the knife rubbing against my wrists as he sawed at the ropes with the razor-sharp blade. I could feel the rope giving as strand after strand was severed. He cut swftly, silently. A moment later the ropes fell away. It was all I could do to keep from flexing my wrists and rubbing them, but I dared not make a single movement that might draw their attention.

"Just sit there like a good girl," he whispered, "and then, when the shooting starts, I want you to jump up and dart behind this tree. You got it? Don't make a move till I fire."

I had to warn him! Somehow I had to warn him. Yet I couldn't possibly do anything now. If I tried to reach up and unfasten the gag, the Brennans would see. I heard the faintest scraping noise, and I knew he was gone. The sense of presence was missing. How long had he been there? Long enough to hear their talk? He was planning something. That's why he had cut me loose. What was he going to do? The tension was almost impossible to bear. Several more minutes passed, and then there was a loud crash on the other side of the clearing.

Both men leaped to their feet, turning to the sound. Billy was shaking. Jim had his pistol ready, aiming into the trees.

"Brennan!"

The shout came from another direction, and Jeff stepped into the clearing even as they whirled around. There was a thundering blast, a streak of orange flame, a huge gust of smoke. A man screamed. I leaped to my feet, and through the smoke I saw Jim Brennan clutching his chest. Blood seeped through his fingers, and his face was a mask of incredulity. Eyes wide with shocked disbelief, he gave another anguished cry and toppled to his knees, showers of scarlet blood spurting as he threw his arms out and flopped over the log he had been sitting on only seconds before. The barrel of Jeff's rifle was still smoking, but he looked calm, almost bored.

Billy Brennan tore the reins loose from the tree where they had been fastened and leaped into the saddle, his red shirt billowing wildly. Digging his knees into the horse's side, he gave its rump a resounding slap, and

286

horse and rider tore into the woods before the smoke had even cleared. As I pulled the gag off and spat out the rag in my mouth, I was trembling violently and my knees threatened to give way. It had been less than sixty seconds since the rock Jeff had hurled had crashed into the woods.

He strolled over to the fallen man. Putting his foot against Brennan's side, he gave the body a shove, and Brennan rolled over like a limp, bloody rag doll. Jeff examined the corpse without emotion. I shuddered, turning my head away from the grotesque sight. We could hear horse hooves pounding through the woods, the noise fading in the distance.

"That's brotherly love for you," Jeff remarked. "He didn't even wait to see if Jim was dead or alive."

"You're not going after him?"

"No need to. He won't bother us none. Besides, without his brother to do his thinking for him, he won't last a breakfast spell out here. Are you all right?"

"I—"

When I couldn't continue, he stepped over to me and pulled me into his arms, holding me loosely against him. I was still trembling, going through a delayed reaction that was even worse than the initial horror, and Jeff murmured soft words, comforting me. I clung to him, sobbing now, and he stroked my hair. It was several minutes before I grew still. I looked up into those warm brown eyes. He grinned, touching my cheek.

"You thought I was a goner, didn't you? Thought I was gonna walk right into their trap? Not likely. I knew something was up. It was just too simple. I hung around out there for a good twenty minutes before I finally decided how to play it."

"I was brushing my hair, and—at first I thought it was Indians, and then—I was so relieved to see it was a white man. He and his brother had seen us earlier. He came to investigate. But when I suddenly realized who he was, he grabbed me and—"

"It's over now," he said quietly. "You're shaken up, but you're going to be all right."

287

"It was *you* I was worried about. I thought——"

Jeff placed his hand over my mouth, and then he squeezed me tightly and held me like that for a moment before releasing me. He picked up Brennan's pistol and thrust it into the waistband of his breeches, then glanced around the clearing as though to see if there was anything else worth taking.

"Reckon we'd better mosey on back to our own camp now," he said casually. "It's a good long walk, and we still haven't eaten. Billy Boy'll probably sneak back to bury his brother. You all right now?"

I nodded. It was over. The nightmare had ended at last.

Jeff grinned, and then he put his arm around my shoulders, leading me out of the clearing. He was his old self again, chattering blithely as we moved through the dark woods.

"Know what? I shot me the biggest, fattest gobbler you ever seen. I'm gonna clean it, and then I'm gonna roast it, and we're gonna have us the dandiest meal we've had yet. Talk about workin' up an appetite——"

XV

I awoke with a start. There was no grogginess, no period of transition. One minute I was asleep, the next I was completely awake, and I sensed immediately that something was wrong. I could feel it in my bones. I sat up, pushing the blankets away. Jeff was gone. He had been nestled under the blankets with me, and now he wasn't here. I had the feeling that he had been gone for some time. Why had he left me alone like this? It had never happened before. I got to my feet, deeply alarmed.

The sky was an ashy gray, the stars gradually dimming, barely visible behind a misty haze. The sun would be coming up quite soon now. I could see the campsite clearly, see the heap of charred logs that had been our fire last night, the pile of packs Jeff had removed from the mules. The mules were tethered to a tree at the edge of the woods. Jenny was nibbling the grass, and . . . one of the mules was missing. The third mule, the one that carried most of the packs, wasn't there. Why should Jeff leave like this, taking one of the mules with him? It didn't make sense.

None of it made sense. I was beginning to grow even more alarmed. Could Billy Brennan have crept up and stolen one of the mules and Jeff have gone after him? No, that was absurd. Five days had passed since Billy had torn off into the woods on his horse, and there had been no sign of him. He was terrified of Jeff, and creeping up to our camp was the last thing he would dream of doing. There was little chance we would ever see him again. He could make much better time on horseback than we could on mules, and he was probably two hundred miles away by this time.

But where had Jeff gone, and what had happened to the mule? If there had been any noise, I would have awakened. I felt certain of that. Jeff had slipped out from under the blankets and crept away into the woods, deliberately making no noise for fear of waking me. There was probably some very simple explanation, I told myself. Perhaps the mule had chewed through the tether rope and wandered off. No doubt I was being foolish, feeling this alarm, but I couldn't shake it. No matter how hard I tried to reason with myself, the alarm remained, mounting as more and more time passed and Jeff still didn't appear.

The dense forest surrounded me, seemed to engulf me. I was acutely aware of every noise, acutely aware of being alone. The last star flickered out, and the misty haze vanished to reveal a pearl-gray sky. As the pink and orange stains began to spread on the horizon, color began to appear around me, black and gray and silver giving way to the green of leaves, the blue of wildflowers, the tan and brown of tree trunks. Pale sunlight streamed over the treetops, growing stronger. We were usually on our way by this time. My alarm increased. I was on the verge of tears now, frightened, feeling lost. Where was he? What . . . what if he didn't come back?

A mockingbird began to sing in the trees. A raccoon peered out at me from behind a clump of bushes and quickly disappeared when I turned to look at him. The mules stirred restlessly. I heard something far, far away in the woods. It sounded like a shriek. A wildcat? The noise was not repeated. I took up my rifle. It was already loaded. It gave me some feeling of security. That feeling vanished after a while. What good was my rifle if Jeff was gone? Without Jeff I would be . . . I refused to think about that. I had to be sensible. I couldn't panic.

I put the rifle down. I gathered up wood and dry brush and placed it over the charred logs, and after two or three minutes with the flint I had the fire going. Jeff had walked to the stream and filled the old kettle with water before going to bed last night. I took the tin of coffee out of one of the packs and scooped coffee into the kettle, not bothering to measure it as I usually did. Coffee was precious, and this was our last tin, but I didn't let that bother me this morning. When the fire had died down enough, I set the kettle on it. I took out the battered tin mugs. I folded up the blankets and put them back in the packs.

I fought the alarm. I forced back the tears. I wouldn't let myself go to pieces. The sunlight was strong now, the clearing bathed with radiant yellow-white rays. Birds were singing all around. Fifteen minutes had passed since I had heard that peculiar noise in the distance. A wildcat. Of course it had been a wildcat. I wouldn't let myself believe it had been anything else. There had been no sign of Indians. Jeff had assured me they were well away from the area.

The coffee was boiling vigorously, filling the air with a rich, pungent aroma. Another five minutes passed. I fetched a cloth and took the kettle off the fire, setting it down on a rock, and it was then that I heard the footsteps approaching. I seized the rifle again, aiming it in the direction of the noise, and then the bushes parted and Jeff stood there with a surprised look in his eyes. I lowered the rifle. Looking relieved, he strolled on into the clearing.

"Hoped I'd get back 'fore you woke up," he remarked. His voice was casual. Much too casual.

"Where were you?"

"Uh . . . well, you see . . ." He hesitated, obviously trying to think up a plausible story. "I woke up, and I . . . I noticed that one of the mules had broken loose and just . . . wandered off. I went to look for it."

"Where is it?"

"Couldn't find it," he replied. "It musta wandered off

291

early, right after we went to sleep. Musta been gone for hours before I went out lookin' for it."

His manner was definitely too casual. He was keeping something from me. I sensed it immediately.

"You could track down the Brennan brothers," I said, "but you couldn't find a mule that wandered away from camp."

"Yeah. I feel kinda stupid, but—"

"You're lying, Jeff."

He gazed at me with hurt brown eyes, managing to look like a particularly virile choirboy. It was then that I noticed the cut on his leg. The buckskin was slit perhaps four inches alongside his right thigh. The edges of the slit were stained red, still wet.

"What happened to your leg? You're hurt—"

"Aw, it's nothin', Marietta. Nothin' to get into a stew about. I ran into a thornbush, long, sharp thorns. Caught my breeches on one of the thorns, scratched myself. Say, is that coffee?"

"Jeff—"

His manner was suddenly stern, irritable, and a deep frown creased his brow. "The mule's gone, Marietta," he snapped. "Forget about it. I'm back now. Everything's all right."

"I heard a shriek in the woods. I thought it was a wildcat. Jeff, I want to know the truth. The mule didn't just wander off. You're keeping something from me."

"I said forget it!"

He had never spoken to me so sharply before. I knew that he was worried, and I suspected the reason why. He poured a cup of coffee and banged the kettle back down so sharply that hot liquid spurted out of the spout and burned his hand. He let out an outraged cry and then glared at me as though I were responsible. I turned away from him, angry myself. I could hear him digging through the packs, cursing volubly when he was unable to locate whatever it was he was looking for.

"Where the *hell* is that ointment?"

I sighed wearily and stepped over to the packs, shoved

292

him aside, pulling out the ointment almost immediately. Taking hold of his hand, I smeared it with the clear, sticky gel. He watched closely, a petulant expression on his face.

"I think you'll live now," I said coldly, putting the ointment away.

"You're in a bitch of a mood this morning."

"How do you expect me to feel? I wake up while it's still dark and find myself alone in the wilderness. I hear a strange noise in the woods. One of the mules is missing, and you come back with some cock-and-bull story a child of three wouldn't—"

"Look, let's not argue. Okay? I just might hit you. I don't usually beat my women, but you're sorely temptin' me."

I poured my coffee and drank it, ignoring him. Jeff kicked dirt over the fire, dousing it, then poured the rest of the coffee out over it to make sure no sparks were still burning. Then he saddled the mules and began to arrange the packs on them. Jenny and his mule were going to have to carry a heavier load now. Coffee finished, I stood up just as he was fastening the final pack on his mule.

"Will they be able to carry all that and us too?" I inquired.

"They're sturdy beasts. They'll manage."

He was still sulking, and I strongly suspected that it was a deliberate ploy to keep me from asking more questions. I opened one of the packs and put the mug away. I noticed that the blood had dried on his thigh, and the cut was no longer bleeding. It couldn't be very deep, I thought. He wouldn't be moving about so briskly if it were. I didn't buy the story about the thorn bush. The slit had been made by a blade of some sort.

My suspicions were confirmed when, once we were under way, Jeff casually informed me that we wouldn't be following the Trace today but would be taking a "shortcut" instead. Leaving the trail behind, we moved down a small hill covered with blue and purple wildflowers, then into a stretch of dense woods. Limbs arched overhead, cutting off all but a few wavering rays of sunlight, and it was like riding through narrow green-brown tunnels. My nerves were on edge, and Jeff was edgy, too, frequently turning around to look back. His usual jauntiness was missing. He couldn't conceal his apprehension, and after a while he no longer even tried.

I guessed at what had happened. The mule hadn't wandered off. An Indian had crept through the trees, untied it, and led it away. A single Indian, probably, for had there been more, we would have been attacked. Jeff had awakened and followed the thief into the woods. There had been a fight, and Jeff had been cut with the Indian's blade. I remembered the shriek. Had Jeff murdered the Indian? He wouldn't have dared use his pistol for fear of drawing even more savages to the area. Had the Indian gotten away, taking the mule with him?

I resented his not telling me the truth, even though I appreciated the fact that he didn't want to alarm me. Did he think I was so dense that I couldn't figure out what must have happened? If there had been one Indian in the area, there were bound to be others. I remembered what Jackson had told us and found it hard to contain my apprehension. I tried not to think about the man screaming in agony and writhing on the stake as the flames crackled and the Indians danced and hollered. We rode quickly, making as little noise as possible. Jeff didn't chatter as he usually did. He said nothing at all, and he kept close to me, not riding on ahead as was his habit.

The forest abounded with noises, just as it always did, but now each time a bird cried out, each time a shrub rustled, I gave a start, certain a band of Indians was going to fall upon us. An hour passed, two, three. We rode up a hillside covered with scrubby trees, passed through more dense woods, crossed a stream shaded by enormous trees, without once stopping for a rest. I was weary, my bones aching, but I was hardly aware of it, my fear overshadowing everything else. The sun was directly overhead now, and both of us were perspiring freely. We had

294

come miles and miles, and I was beginning to relax just a little, although I still jumped at each unexpected noise.

It must have been around two o'clock when Jeff finally suggested we take a short break. I dismounted eagerly. Jeff tethered the mules to a slender tree and then took out the canteen he had filled at the stream. He passed it to me, then drank himself. His sandy locks were damp with sweat. His features were taut, brown eyes dark and grim. This new Jeff seemed much stronger, much more capable, than the engaging clown, and it was difficult to believe they were the same person.

"Did you kill him?" I asked.

He looked at me, frowning, debating whether or not he should tell me the truth. After a moment he sighed and began to brush at a smear of dirt on his tunic, still silent.

"I'm not a child, Jeff. I have a right to know."

"I killed him," he said. His voice was flat.

"He—that's how you got the cut on your thigh."

Jeff nodded. "I heard him creepin' through the woods. He made hardly any noise at all, but I—over the years I've developed a sixth sense about these things. I heard him, and I woke up, and I lay very still, watchin' him step into the clearing. I always sleep with the pistol beside me. I had it in my hand, ready to fire if necessary."

"What did he do?"

"He just stood there like a shadow, trying to make up his mind if he should kill us. Thing is, he wasn't certain there were just the two of us. It was still real dark, and there were three mules. Coulda been someone else sleepin' behind that pile of packs. He finally decided not to risk it, just untied one of the mules and led him off into the woods. I waited three or four minutes, then went after him."

"Leaving me alone," I said bitterly. "You could have been killed. It was a foolish risk to take just to get back a—"

"Took me a while to catch up with him," Jeff continued, interrupting my tirade. "It was almost dawn by

295

that time. I had my pistol with me, of course, but I was afraid to use it, 'fraid it might alert any other Indians roamin' about the woods. I circled around, got ahead of him, waited behind a tree. When he came by, I jumped him."

"You got cut. He—"

"He was quick, and he was strong, wiry. He grabbed hold of my wrist before I could plunge the knife down, whipped out his own knife, managed to nick my thigh. We were rollin' on the ground by that time, wrestlin' furiously. He slammed my wrist down on a rock, slammed it down hard, and I dropped my knife. He was straddlin' me, but I threw him off. He got to his feet and drew his arm back to hurl his knife at my chest. I rolled to one side—the knife missed me by inches. I grabbed my own knife off the ground, threw it. He let out a shriek—"

"I heard it."

"Then he crumpled over, dead as a doornail. I pulled my knife out of his throat and wiped it off, wonderin' if I should try to catch the mule—it had raced on off soon's the Indian dropped the reins. But I—uh—thought I should get on back to camp, see if you were all right. That's when I got the biggest scare of all—seein' you shakin' like a leaf, the rifle pointed directly at me. Scared me more than any Indian, I can tell you for sure."

"Was he traveling alone?"

"Wuzn't anybody with him at the moment, no, but—"

Jeff hesitated, looking indecisive again, wondering how much he should tell me, how much he should hold back. I managed to maintain a calm expression that belied the apprehension inside. There was a hollow feeling in the pit of my stomach, and it was all I could do to keep from trembling, but Jeff saw only the composed features, the level eyes. When he finally continued, his voice was flat, his eyes grim.

"I might as well level with you, Marietta. I feel pretty sure the fellow was headin' back to his own camp. He was movin' along like he knew exactly where he was

296

goin'. Don't think his buddies heard his shriek—I doubt their camp was that close—but by this time they're gonna have missed him, they're gonna have found him with a great hole in his throat, and they're gonna be lookin' for whoever did it."

"That's why we're not on the Trace?"

He nodded. "They'll go racin' down the Trace first thing, assumin' that's how we're travelin'. One good thing, they ain't found us by this time, chances are pretty strong they aren't gonna. We're miles away from the Trace, and it's a great big forest. I'll feel even better when we get several more miles behind us. If we ride hard, I think we can make the cave by nightfall."

"The cave?"

"Place I know. It's small, just a hole in the side of a hill, really, but it's big enough to hold us and the mules, and the entrance is completely hidden by bushes. I hid there once before when the Indians was lookin' for me some years ago. We'll be safe there."

We resumed our ride, moving on through the forest. It was dim and shadowy, trees close all around, only the faintest amount of sunlight sifting through the heavy, leafy limbs overhead. Sound seemed to echo strangely, the steady clopping of the mules thrown back at us, distorted. A vivid red cardinal burst out of a thicket, wings flapping vigorously. I gave a little cry, almost falling off the mule. Ordinarily Jeff would have laughed and made some teasing remark. He didn't now. On and on we went, twisting this way and that to avoid the trees. I had long ago lost all sense of direction. I prayed that Jeff knew where he was going and could get us back on the Trace eventually. The woods seemed so ominous and forbidding.

Hours passed. I had never been so weary, but I didn't complain. Jeff was tired, too. His face looked drawn. There were faint gray smudges beneath his eyes, slight hollows under his cheekbones. Healthy and robust as he was, he was showing signs of the hard push and the worry. We had never traveled so hard, so long, and neither of us had had a bite of food all day. The mules, at least, had been able to nibble at the grass when we had taken our break. I was ravenously hungry, but I wasn't going to complain about that, either.

The sun was going down now. The trees cast long black shadows over the ground, shadows that stretched and merged together in a dark network. The sky was a deep-violet gray, the air filling with a thickening blue haze as the final rays of the sun vanished. We were in a less densely wooded area now. Although there were still hundreds of trees, tall, gigantic trees that reared up like leafy giants, they weren't growing so closely together, weren't choked with underbrush. There was a stream up ahead. I could hear the water gurgling over sand and rocks. I wondered how far we were from the cave.

"I guess we'd better stop for a few minutes, catch our breath," Jeff said. "It's at least another hour to the cave. Too, I want to fill the canteens and let the mules drink."

There was a small clearing perhaps fifty yards from the stream. We dismounted. Jeff stretched, flexing his arms, and then he looked at me in the fading light and saw my grim expression and smiled. It was a beautiful smile, tender, not at all like the engaging grin he so frequently wore. He stepped over to me and placed his hands on my shoulders.

"I think we're in the clear now," he said. "I think we've foxed 'em. They're probably still chasin' up and down the Trace on their ponies, huntin' for us."

"You really think we're out of danger?"

"Not completely, o'course. I'd be lyin' if I said that. We'll keep to the woods for a couple more days, then turn back on the Trace."

"You're sure you can find it again?"

"We ain't more'n a quarter of a mile from the Trace right now. We circled around, and we've been runnin' more or less parallel to it for quite a while. How're you feelin'?"

"Tired. Hungry, too."

" 'Fraid we're gonna have to make do with beef jerky

and parched corn tonight—emergency supplies I got in the pack. Can't risk a fire, not even in the cave. We'll have us a nice long rest and see what tomorrow brings."

"All right."

"You've been terrific, keepin' right along with me, never complainin', showin' true mettle. Most women—but, hell, it ain't even fair to try 'n compare you to anyone else. You're pretty unique, ya know that?"

"Am I?"

"Ain't never encountered another woman quite like you. I'm right proud of the way you've been holdin' up. You're a magnificent wench, no question about it."

He squeezed my shoulders, still smiling, and then he gave me a quick kiss. I placed my hand on the back of his neck, feeling closer to him than I ever had before. Jeff drew back, eyes twinkling mischieviously.

"I'll take the mules down to the stream and water 'em, fill up the canteens, and then we'll move on to the cave. I'm hungry, too—and not just for food. I'm gettin' a mighty strong yen—"

"You're incorrigible," I teased.

"Reckon I am," he admitted.

"We've been riding since dawn, expecting Indians to attack at any minute. We're exhausted, bone-weary, and we haven't had a thing to eat all day, and you think about—"

"I'm *always* thinkin' about it."

"Go on," I said, "go water the mules. After we get to the cave, after we've eaten your wretched beef and parched corn, we'll see what happens. I'm not making any promises."

" 'Fraid you ain't got a *choice*," he told me.

Jeff grinned, slipping back into the jaunty manner as he would slip into old clothes. He pulled my rifle out of its leather pouch and handed it to me, explaining that he wouldn't want it to slip out and fall into the water, and then he took out his own rifle, gathered up the reins and led the mules down the sloping ground to the stream. Tall trees arched heavy boughs over the water. There was a particularly heavy oak tree with thick boughs just a few yards from the spot where Jeff stood with the mules, pulling the canteens out of their packs as they greedily drank. I held the rifle at my side, watching them, feeling relaxed for the first time.

It had been a hard day, but it was almost over now. The immediate danger was behind us. Jeff was relaxed, too, and that was a good sign. He had been so tender and affectionate, treating me like someone very precious, and I had been deeply moved. I was very fond of him, and I wished I weren't. It was impossible not to respond to that warmth, try though I might to resist. Later on, when we reached civilization, I could harden myself against him. Right now I could only consider myself lucky that he was the man he was.

The light was almost completely gone, just a faint afterglow remaining. Jeff and the two mules were in silhouette. He was kneeling, filling up the canteens. One particularly thick bough of the oak tree stretched almost directly over his head. As I stood there, feeling pensive, feeling at peace, I saw the leaves of the bough move ever so slightly.

Something moved in the tree. I couldn't believe my eyes. One minute the thickness was there, and then it started to move, edging back toward the trunk of the tree. The stream rushed along, splashed over the rocks with a pleasant noise that was loud enough to drown out the faint noise of the body inching slowly backward on the bough. Jeff capped one of the canteens, slung it on the ground behind him, kneeled down to fill up another. In the bough I saw a silhouette, rising now to its knees, and then it dropped softly to the ground and stood poised there for a moment, not more than six or seven yards from where Jeff was kneeling.

I saw a tall, powerfully built body, and I saw a muscular arm raising back, saw the tomahawk, all black, in silhouette, and I was so stunned I couldn't cry out. The savage crept slowly toward the kneeling man. I was screaming inside, unable to make the screams audible, and then I realized I was holding the rifle. I reared it up into position and covered the silhouette with the sight and pulled the trigger. There was a blinding orange flash and a puff of smoke and the silhouette moved crazily like a puppet on jerking strings, then fell on the ground in a broken heap.

I dropped the rifle. I raced toward Jeff. He caught me in his arms. I began to sob. He held me tightly, peering over my shoulder at the Indian on the ground, and, ironically, the mules continued to lap up the water, unperturbed by the explosive blast. I turned in Jeff's arms, glancing down at the body sprawled out there on the ground, arms and legs akimbo. The light was stronger here and I could see the bronze skin smeared with war paint, the bear-tooth necklace, the feathers. The Indian was naked but for a thin loin cloth and moccasins. Half of his face was missing, and I was glad the light was no stronger.

"Good shootin'," Jeff said. "Now we've got to get the hell away from here."

"He was in the tree. I—I couldn't believe—"

"We've no time to waste, Marietta. If he's here, the others can't be far away. They're probably on the Trace. He was probably an advance scout. In less than ten minutes this place is going to be swarmin' with Indians—"

"Jeff, he was going to *kill* you. He had his tomahawk raised and—"

"Come on! You can tell me about it later. That rifle shot could be heard for miles around. Pull yourself together! Here, help me with the mules—you've had enough to drink, you little bastards! Don't you dare try to balk now—"

Moments later we were on our way again, and in the distance we could hear hooting, yelping noises that caused my blood to turn cold. We urged the mules on, tearing away through the woods, and my heart was pounding so loudly I couldn't hear the yelps any longer. Ten minutes passed, fifteen, and still we rode. We were racing down a hill now, and then we turned the mules and were

301

moving along the bottom of the hill. Thick, scrabbly bushes grew there, half-concealing the face of the hill. Jeff came to an abrupt halt and swung off the mule. He hurried over to help me dismount.

"Okay, follow me. It's tricky. I'll lead the mules."

He took the reins and started toward the bushes, pushing them aside as he reached them. I followed close behind, my heart still pounding. In a moment or so we were completely surrounded by bushes, and Jeff simply disappeared. The mules disappeared, too, and I stumbled on through the bushes. They slapped my arms, tore at my skirts. I saw the narrow opening then and, stepping through it, found myself swallowed up in darkness. The air was damp and cold, the ground soft, spongy. I could hear something stirring, but it was impossible to see.

"Here we go, fellow," Jeff said quietly. "Hate to do this, hate to put a muzzle on you, but can't have you decidin' to bray. There, that comfortable enough? Now it's your turn, Jenny."

"Jeff—"

"Be with you in a minute."

"It's so *dark*."

"Your eyes'll soon get accustomed to it. There you are, Jenny. Snug, but not tight enough to hurt. I know it's humiliatin', lass, but that's the way it has to be. Marietta?"

"Over here."

He moved toward me, reached for me, pulled me up against him, wrapping his arms around me. I rested my cheek on his chest, the buckskin rough and scratchy against my skin. Cold air swirled around us in clammy currents, and there was a noise like heavy breathing as some force sucked the air toward the rear of the cave.

"Guess I can thank you for savin' my life now," he said.

"I—I just shot. I didn't even remember I had the rifle in my hands for a moment. I was terrified, so terrified I couldn't even scream, and then I just—just swung the rifle up and fired—"

"I'd uv been a goner if you hadn't. The water was rushin' along and the mules was makin' so much noise drinkin' that I couldn't hear him. I liked to jumped outta my skin when I heard the blast, saw that redskin leapin' up in the air with half his face gone. Glad I taught you to shoot, wench."

"They won't find us, will they?"

"Not a chance," he told me. "If you didn't know this cave was here, you'd never be able to find it. I—uh—I gotta leave you alone for a little while, Marietta."

"You're not going back—back out there?"

" 'Fraid I have to," he replied. "We left some pretty obvious tracks, and I've got to hide 'em. Don't worry, I won't let 'em catch me. I'll be back 'fore you know it. Here—I want you to take this."

I felt him fumbling, and then he took hold of my hand and placed something cold and heavy in it. As my fingers closed around it, I realized it was his pistol.

"If anything should happen—not that anything *will*, mind you—I want you to use the pistol, Marietta. Do you understand what I'm saying? If I shouldn't come back, if the Indians should find you—you're to use the pistol on yourself before they can take you."

"Please don't go out there," I whispered. "Please!"

"It's something I gotta do, Marietta. As it stands right now, we might as well paint a big arrow pointing to the cave entrance. Ten, fifteen minutes of work, and our tracks'll be gone."

"It's insanity. They—even now they're probably—"

"I know my way around. Don't you worry none. I've been eludin' Indians for years. They won't see hide nor hair of me, won't hear me, neither. There's just enough light for me to see how to erase our tracks. If I wait any longer—"

"I won't let you go!"

But Jeff had already gone. I realized that I was alone in the pitch-blackness, and I was terrified, afraid for Jeff more than for myself. I heard the bushes rattling softly as he moved through them, a faint, barely audible rustle I

303

wouldn't have heard at all had I not been listening for it, and then there was only the soft swoosh of the air, as though the cave itself were breathing. Minutes crept past, and gradually my eyes grew accustomed to the darkness. A faint suggestion of light seeped in through the opening, and the dense, impenetrable blackness melted into a deep gray, enabling me to make out the damp stone walls and the mules standing placidly at one side, muzzles in place. I heard tiny squeaking noises coming from above me. Peering up, I could barely discern the furry brown masses hanging from the rock. There must have been two dozen bats. I could see their eyes glowing.

I leaned against the wall, breathing heavily. The bats frightened me almost as much as the Indians. My cheeks were damp with tears I hadn't even known I had shed. I had never felt so utterly defenseless. I felt like a small, abandoned child, and the tears continued to flow down my cheeks. He pretended there was no danger, claimed he had been eluding Indians for years, but if there was no danger, why had he given me the pistol? They would catch him, kill him, burn him at the stake as they had burned Joe Pearson, and then they would come after me. Would I be able to use the pistol? If they came, if they found me, could I put the gun to my head and pull the trigger?

The mules stirred restlessly. The bats squeaked. Fifteen more minutes passed, at least that many, and still he didn't come. The light seeping in through the opening was tinged with silver. The moon must be unusually bright. Far, far away I heard a gobbling noise, like a wild turkey, and then there came an answering gobble from another direction, then a third, and I knew it was the Indians, knew they were signaling each other in the woods. Had they spotted him? Was that what the calls were about? I prayed, silently, fervently, and then I heard the shrubbery rustling and my heart leaped.

"Marietta—"

"Jeff! Thank God!"

"Took me a bit longer than I expected. Our tracks are

all gone, and I left some new ones to take their place, tracks leadin' down to the stream. I broke a few branches, left a bit of handkerchief on a thorn, dropped an old powder horn on the bank. They're gonna think we moved up the stream a ways and then crossed over to the other side."

"Thank God you're back."

"Almost walked smack-dab into a brave," he said, jauntily, bragging just a bit. "He was standin' there with his back to me, still as could be. It was dark as hell, and I thought he was a *tree!* Then one of his buddies let out a turkey gobble and he gobbled back and I popped behind some shrubs. It was a pretty close call!"

Jeff reached for me, pulled me into his arms. He touched my face and felt the tears.

"Hey, you've been cryin'."

"I couldn't help it."

He kissed the tears away and wrapped his arms more tightly around me. "It's all right now. They're gonna do a lot of prowlin' around, and they'll make a little noise, but they ain't gonna find us. Hey, no need to tremble. No need at all. It's all right."

He stroked my hair and then wrapped his hand around my chin and tilted my head back and kissed me. I clung to him, savoring his strength, his warmth, his goodness.

"You still hungry?" he asked after a moment.

"I'm too frightened to eat anything."

"Reckon we'll wait a while then. Here, we'll just make ourselves comfortable."

Holding on to my wrist, he sat down and pulled me down beside him. Leaning against the rock, he pulled me over until I was snuggled against his chest. He held me loosely, stroking my arms, comforting me as one might comfort a child, and after a while my trembling ceased and I grew still. He had taken the pistol from me earlier, and now he set it down on the ground beside him, within easy reach. I turned in his arms, resting the back of my head against his shoulder. He curled his arm

305

around my throat, gently, leaning down to brush his lips against my temple.

"All right now?" he whispered.

"I—I think so. I—I didn't mean to be so—so weak and all. I hate women who cry, women who fall to pieces. I don't usually—"

"I know, wench. You're a tough, feisty hellcat, full of spunk and spirit. I kinda like you like this, though. Makes me feel strong and protective and manly. Makes me feel somethin' else, too, but I reckon I'll just have to forget about that for the time bein'."

"You certainly will."

"And I was plannin' such a celebration. *Damn* these Indians."

"They'll soon go away, won't they? They'll—"

I cut myself short. Stealthy footsteps were moving outside the cave, and the bushes were rustling. I let out a gasp, and Jeff clamped a hand over my mouth, lightly but firmly. The footsteps stopped. There was a loud gobble, an answering gobble from across the way. In a minute or so there were more footsteps, and we could hear the Indians talking to each other, their voices low. Then they stopped talking and began to search through the shrubbery. Jeff reached out and clasped the pistol. My heart seemed to stop beating. The footsteps were so close, the branches right outside the opening moving with crisp, rustling noises. There was a moment of agonizing suspense, and then a shrill, excited cry shrieked in the distance. The shrubbery rattled noisily as the Indians searching it left to join the one who had cried out. Jeff moved his hand from my mouth.

"One of 'em must of found the new tracks," he said.

"I thought they were going to find us."

"Yeah, for a minute or two there I was kinda worried myself. They'll be huntin' down by the stream now."

"I hope your ruse works."

"It'll work. Just relax. Even though we've just been whisperin', I reckon we'd better shut up for a while, just in case one of 'em comes back to have another look at them bushes outside."

"I'm so frightened."

"Relax. I ain't gonna let 'em get you."

His arm was still curled loosely around my neck. He put the pistol down and curled his other arm around my waist. I leaned against him, trying to conquer the fear that gripped me like a tangible force. The Indians were no longer being stealthy. We could hear feet slapping against the ground as they raced about. They called to each other in harsh, excited voices, and then they seemed to be arguing among themselves. Jeff held me, and I closed my eyes, praying they would go away.

Then he was shaking me and I opened my eyes to see the cave filled with misty yellow-white light. I had fallen asleep. I couldn't believe it. The Indians had been jabbering and I had been terrified and I had actually fallen asleep. I was stretched out on a blanket, another blanket pulled up over me. Jeff was grinning. He looked cocky and very pleased with himself. I sat up, rubbing my eyes. My whole body ached, and I was hungrier than I had ever been in my life.

"Must say, when you sleep, you sleep soundly. Thought you'd *never* wake up. It's nigh on ten o'clock in the morning."

"Did they—are they gone?"

"They're gone," he said, "long gone. They went splashin' off down the stream just a little while after you dropped off. I've already been out, had me a good look 'round. They ain't gonna be lookin' for us any longer, Marietta."

I climbed to my feet. "How can you be so sure?"

Jeff frowned, reluctant to speak. There was something he hadn't told me. I sensed it at once. His brown eyes were dark, his mouth tight at the corners. He still hesitated, looking at me, and finally he sighed, grimacing before he spoke.

"They found who they were lookin' for," he said, "or who they *thought* they were lookin' for. Billy Brennan

307

was camped 'bout a quarter of a mile up the stream, Marietta, on the other side. They found him. They had a bit of fun. I . . . uh . . . I heard 'em at it last night, after you dropped off to sleep. I heard him, too. I was damned thankful you weren't awake. No one oughta have ta hear anything like that."

I was silent. I knew my cheeks were pale. Billy Brennan had been a dyed-in-the-wool villain, a thief, a murderer, but no man should have to die like that. Jeff looked at me with worried eyes.

"I shouldn'ta told you," he said quietly, "but in the long run it's best you know. I found Billy, what was left of him. I buried him before I came back here to wake you up. The Indians are gone, and they won't be back. We don't have to worry about them any longer."

"That poor man."

"Yeah," Jeff said, and then he changed the subject. "The mules are already outside, eatin' all the grass in sight. I suggest we have some breakfast, too, and then—then what say we push on to Natchez?"

"That sounds like a splendid idea," I told him.

XVI

As we neared Natchez the land became incredibly verdant, rich and green, and the trees were majestic, great oaks that spread their boughs as though luxuriating in the fresh air, the rich soil, the clear blue sky. It was still early morning. Jeff told me we would reach Natchez shortly after noon. I should have been relieved, should have been eager to reach the comfort of civilization at last, but I wasn't. I was curiously sad, for it was over now, this long, hazardous, grueling journey, and the warm, satisfying intimacy must end, too. I would not be able to relax and revel in Jeff's nearness any longer. I had to steel myself against him. I had to escape at the first opportunity.

"Natchez really began way back in 1716," Jeff informed me. "Chap named Jean Baptiste Le Moyne, Sieur de Bienville, built a fort high on the bluffs, Fort Rosalie, near the villages of the Natchez Indians. He and his men had a lot of trouble with the Natchez, but he managed to subdue 'em—forty-nine men against the whole Natchez Nation. A great settlement grew, Frenchies pouring in from all over. The land was cleared, plantations established, merchants and artisans arrived. Ten years or so passed, and then the Frenchies got greedy and tried to take even more land from the Indians." He paused, shaking his head.

"What happened?"

"One of the bloodiest massacres in history. The Natchez came to the French with reports that the Choctaws were going to attack, claimed they wanted to help fight 'em off. The French were frightened and let the Natchez come pouring in with weapons—Indians entering every house to 'help' fight off the Choctaws. At four o'clock in the afternoon—this was November 28, 1729—their chief gave the signal. The killing began. The French were butchered, decapitated, their heads piled up in the public square. The women and children who weren't butchered along with the men were taken captive. The whole settlement was razed to the ground."

"How—dreadful," I said with a shudder.

"There was retaliation, of course," Jeff continued. "The Choctaws were old enemies of the Natchez, and the French got 'em to help. Soldiers and savages came pourin' up from New Orleans, and the Natchez Nation was destroyed in a spree of bloodlettin' that made the massacre seem pale by comparison. A few of the Natchez survived and fled through the wilderness to join up with the Chickasaws. The settlement of Natchez was reclaimed by the wilderness, swallowed up as though it had never existed. Then, at the close of the French and Indian Wars, it passed to the British."

"I thought the French ceded this territory to the Spanish?"

"Most of it was—Natchez bein' the exception. It's the only English outpost in these parts. A few years back, settlers started pourin' in, folks who couldn't make a go at farmin' back east, folks who were dissatisfied with the politics of the Colonies, others who simply wanted a taste of adventure. They've done wonders in the past five-six years. It's still pretty rough and rugged, of course, but it's growin' all the time. The land's some of the richest I ever seen, and men like Helmut Schnieder are establishin' plantations that are gonna become the glory of the territory."

"Helmut Schnieder? That sounds like a German name."

Jeff nodded. "Teutonic to the core. Grim chap,

310

Schnieder. He arrived a couple of years ago, a man of mystery, loaded with gold. He bought all the land he could get his hands on, built him a cabin, and then sent for his sister, a mousey little thing, scared of her own shadow. They say Schnieder's buildin' him a mansion now, say it's gonna be a showplace that'll make them fine homes up east look like shacks."

There was a high bluff up ahead. Jeff looked at me, grinning, his brown eyes twinkling as though he were planning a surprise. We rode side by side toward the edge of the bluff, passing under oak trees, emerald-green land sloping away on either side. I heard a soft, rushing noise; then we were at the edge and the land dropped away abruptly in a steep, rocky cliff and I had my first glimpse of the Mississippi River.

It was large, unbelievably large, a vast blue-gray expanse of water that seemed to divide the continent in half. I stared at it in awe, for I had never seen anything like it. It made the rivers in England seem like paltry streams, made even the mighty Thames seem insignificant in comparison. As we watched, a huge flatboat loaded with wooden crates moved past, and two men poled a crude log raft piled high with bundles of fur. There were several canoes, as well, the great river carrying them all along as though indulging these tiny specks bobbing on its enormous back. Jeff sat there on his mule, grinning, delighted that I was impressed. One would have thought he had invented this majestic spectacle.

"Thought you'd be impressed," he said.

"It's overwhelming."

"Flows all the way down to New Orleans and then out to sea. It's more'n a mile wide in places—has to be one of the biggest rivers in the world, maybe *the* biggest. It's really somethin', ain't it?"

I nodded. The river seemed to sparkle in the sunlight, silvery-blue reflections dancing on the surface. The banks were a reddish-brown mud, and on the other side another cliff rose, rocks golden brown, jagged, the land above as green as on this side, the great trees dwarfed in the

311

distance. It was one of the most beautiful sights I had ever seen. I gazed, and the sadness that had been lingering grew stronger. I wanted to cry. Jeff sensed my mood.

"It's been good, hasn't it?" he said.

I knew what he meant. I nodded again, not trusting myself to speak.

"We've had some rough times, true, and a couple of pretty scary days, what with the Indians and the Brennan boys, but . . . it's been good. I ain't ever enjoyed a trek so much."

"It's over now," I said.

"Yeah, I guess all good things gotta come to an end."

"And now—" I began.

"Now we'd better push on to Natchez," Jeff interrupted. "I got a lot of business I wanna take care of this afternoon, and then, tonight, I'm gonna treat you to the grandest dinner you've ever had. The inn's got a dandy taproom, real elegant. All the best folks in Natchez dine there."

"When will we leave for New Orleans?"

"Tomorrow morning."

"There'll be a boat?"

"Traffic 'tween here and New Orleans is constant. There's always a boat leavin', always one pullin' in filled with goods. The docks are a regular beehive of activity every day."

We rode on then, the wind whipping my hair and lifting the skirt of my red dress. It was the dress I had worn to the fair, the dress I had been wearing the day Derek sold me to Jeff. That seemed such a long time ago, a lifetime ago. Carolina . . . I mustn't think about that now. I must concentrate on making my escape. It would have to be this afternoon or tonight. Jeff was in love with me, but he still had every intention of taking me down to New Orleans. Love was one thing, business another. He would probably make an enormous profit, enough to give up these treks and go into some other kind of work. He had mentioned wanting to open his own place, had

312

mentioned it several times, though he hadn't been specific about what kind of "place" he had in mind.

We reached Natchez three hours later. It was indeed a bustling, growing settlement with dozens of sturdy, squared-timber houses, a number of shops, new ones going up. Perched on a bluff overlooking a river, it was impressive, and I found it difficult to believe that, just a few years ago, it had been a wilderness with only a few rusty French cannon and the ruins of the fort. As we rode toward the inn, I could see the docks down below, crowded with boats, dozens of men busily unloading crates and barrels. There seemed to be another small town down there, too, the buildings ramshackle, already run down. When I inquired about it, Jeff shook his head, making a clicking noise with his tongue.

"Natchez-under-the-hill," he said. "It's already got the reputation of bein' the wickedest spot in this whole territory. Settlers come, decent, hard-workin' folks who wanna establish homes, open businesses, get a new start in life —they're the ones who're makin' Natchez an important town that's gonna rival New Orleans one of these days. Other folks come, too—riff-raff, men fleein' the law, thieves, murderers, whores. The decent folk want nothin' to do with 'em, so they settle down there."

"I see."

"Man can indulge any kinda vice down there—drinkin', whorin', gamblin', you name it. A lot of the so-called 'respectable' men help keep it goin'. Some claim Helmut Schnieder owns half the property, includin' the biggest whorehouse. Wouldn't surprise me none if he did."

"You keep mentioning him. He must be an important figure."

"I suppose he is, if by important you mean powerful. I don't like the man, not many folks do, but he's rich— gettin' richer every day, it seems. There's somethin' about him . . ." Jeff hesitated, frowning.

"Yes?" I prompted.

"He's cold, grim, likes to intimidate people. He never smiles, and you never know what he's thinkin'. You get the idea he's plottin' something all the time, and whatever it is he's plottin' ain't healthy."

We reached the inn a few minutes later. It was a large, two-story building with a gray slate roof. The verandah in front was supported by a row of slender white columns in an attempt at New England elegance. A neatly clad black man hurried to take the mules around to the stables in back, agreeing to bring in the packs Jeff indicated he wanted. Jeff led me up the steps and onto the cool verandah, proudly opening the front door.

Inside, it was even cooler, dim. A small hallway led into the main room where the proprietor stood behind a long mahogany counter. The walls were off-white and brass chandeliers hung from the ceiling. A blue carpet covered the floor, and there was a tapestry sofa, matching chairs, and a low table with blue and lilac flowers in a large white bowl. A curving staircase led to the rooms above, and an archway opened into the large dining room adjoining. Though it might have been considered pitifully second-rate in the large cities up east, the inn was like a haven of luxury after so many weeks trekking through the wilderness.

The proprietor greeted Jeff effusively and personally conducted us to our room. There was a large mahogany fourposter with a rather worn violet satin counterpane, a matching dresser with tall oval mirror, and a roomy mahogany wardrobe as well. A carpet with faded gray and rose patterns covered most of the polished hardwood floor, and soft violet curtains hung at the windows. The furniture was all old and looked as though it had been over many a rough trail, but everything was neat and clean, and the room had an undeniable charm. When the packs arrived, Jeff stowed them away in the wardrobe, and then he eyed the bed and beamed happily.

"Sure beats sleepin' on blankets under the stars, don't it?"

"It certainly does."

"You tired?" he asked.

"A little. I'd like to rest a while."

314

"Tell you what, why don't you take a nice long nap? I gotta take care of some business, like I said, and when I get back—" He paused, grinning that sheepish grin I had grown so fond of. "When I get back, we'll celebrate in style."

"That'll be nice. How long will you be gone?"

"Oh, maybe three hours, maybe four. Long enough for you to have a good rest."

He stepped over to the wardrobe and took out one of the packs, opening it on the bed. I moved to the window and pretended to gaze out at the gardens back of the inn, but by turning my head slightly to one side I could see him in the mirror. I was surprised to see him taking a roll of bills out of the pack. I hadn't known he had any money, had thought he gave it all to Derek. Jeff peeled off several bills, thrust them into his pocket, and put the rest back in the pack, stowing it away in the wardrobe again. I turned around to face him. If things went well this might be the last time I ever saw him. The sadness welled up again, try though I might to control it. Jeff cocked his head to one side, peering at me.

"Somethin' botherin' you?" he asked.

"No, I'm just tired."

"You look like you just lost a loved one."

"That's silly."

His fringed buckskins were incredibly dirty, and there was a streak of dirt on his jaw. His sandy hair was dirty, too, and he smelled of sweat and leather and woods, and he had never looked more endearing, those warm brown eyes gazing at me with affection, those wide lips ready to spread into another grin. I wanted to rush to him, wanted him to hold me close, wanted him to stroke my hair and croon to me and banish the nervous tremors inside. I hated what I was going to do to him. I actually felt guilty.

"Everything's gonna be all right, Marietta," he said.

"Is it?"

"I got a big surprise planned for tonight."

And I have one for you, I thought.

315

"You go on and get some rest," he said. "Tonight's gonna be a night you'll never forget."

He turned to leave. As he moved toward the door, my heart seemed to be pulled with every step he took. I called his name. He turned, puzzled. I hurried over to him. He grinned, slipping an arm around my wraist, drawing me to him. The lips curled at the corners. The eyes were filled with pleasure.

"Just can't let me go, can you?" he teased. "Can't stand for me to be out of your sight."

"I . . . I just wanted to say . . . goodbye."

"I'm only gonna be gone a few hours, wench."

"I know, but . . ."

"You'll miss me?"

I nodded, and he put his other arm around me, lowering his mouth over mine. He kissed me, firm, moist lips caressing mine, and I wrapped my arms around his shoulders, savoring each second, sad, hating myself, sorry when he drew back and released me.

"There'll be more when I get back," he promised.

"Goodbye, Jeff." The words were barely audible.

He left then, and I stood there staring at the door he had closed behind him, bracing myself, trying to hold back the tears. I finally sat down on the bed, leaning against one of the heavy posts, too weak to do anything just yet. I kept remembering. I remembered the waterfall and our riotous bath together and the explosive bout that followed, the achingly tender lovemaking that followed that. I remembered the cave and my fear and the way he had held me, so very gently, stroking my hair, his lips brushing my temple every now and then. There had been so many good moments, and against my will I had grown very fond of him, fond of him in a special way that had nothing to do with real love, the kind I still felt for Derek, even after all that had happened.

It was nothing short of incredible. Jeff was a rogue, however amiable, and he planned to sell me to a brothel, however reluctantly, and I was the one who felt guilty because I was planning to flee while I had the chance.

316

Where was my spirit? Where was the will to survive and succeed? I stood up, thrusting all tender thoughts out of my mind. He was in love with me, but he still intended to take me to New Orleans, and I was fond of him, but I couldn't let that prevent my doing what I had to do. He would be disappointed and angry and hurt, but . . . but to hell with him! The man was a white slaver. He probably didn't love me at all. I had probably imagined the whole thing. How could he love me and still plan to take me to New Orleans?

I was filled with determination now, that hard core tightening inside, all tender feeling and emotions vanished. He said there were boats leaving every day for New Orleans. There would probably be one leaving this afternoon, and I would be on it. I had planned to stow away at first, but now I could pay my fare. He had lied about the money, had told Derek eighteen hundred pounds was all he had to his name, and just a few minutes ago he had peeled bills off a large wad. How many other things had he lied about? It served him right to lose me. I would go to New Orleans, and then I would take another boat as soon as I could. Perhaps I would go to Paris or . . . or Spain. Great ships left New Orleans all the time, I knew, and I would take the first one available and leave this raw, sprawling land full of hazard and unrest. If there wasn't enough money to pay my fare, I could earn it easily enough. New Orleans was full of wealthy men.

I took the pack out. I didn't bother to count the money. I placed the whole roll in my skirt pocket, slung the pack back into the wardrobe, and slammed the door shut. Resolution gave way to anger, and that was good. It strengthened my resolve, made this all the easier. How dare he treat me with such affection when he planned to deposit me in a brothel! He was sly and deceitful and I had allowed myself to be taken in by his charm. It had made the journey much easier, but the journey was over now and it was time to face reality.

How to get down to the docks without him seeing me? I didn't dare step out the front door and walk through

317

town. He might be anywhere, just down the street, in one of the shops, anywhere. I stepped to the window again and looked down at the gardens. They stretched to the very edge of the bluff, and a steep, rocky incline would spill down to the stretch of land below. Perhaps I could climb down the incline. It might be dangerous, but I couldn't possibly risk getting down to the docks any other way. If the incline were too steep here, I would simply walk along the bluff until I found a spot where descent would be possible.

I left the room. Coming up, I had noticed a flight of stairs at the end of the hall, obviously backstairs used by the servants. I moved down them and found myself in a small back foyer, one door leading into the kitchens, another leading out into the gardens in back. My anger had dissolved. I was nervous now, and there was a hollow sensation in the pit of my stomach. I stepped outside and strolled as calmly as possible to the foot of the gardens and peered down. Directly below, there was a grassy strip, then a narrow dirt road, then more grass leading to the muddy bank of the river. The incline was steep but not impossibly so. It was perhaps a hundred feet down to the land below, and there were heavy vines growing down over the rocks. It wouldn't be pleasant, but I felt sure I could make it down without too great a risk.

I took a deep breath, frightened, trying to quell my fear. There were bound to be a lot of footholds, and I could hold on to the vines. I had to do it. I simply couldn't risk going through town, not knowing where Jeff might be. I sat down, dangling my legs over the edge, and then I turned, inching my way down, grabbing hold of one of the vines as my feet touched a narrow ledge of rock. I was over now, clinging to the face of the cliff, and it was insanity, sheer insanity. I realized that immediately. The wind whipped at my hair and tossed my skirts about my legs. I was terrified, but I forced myself to move down, finding another ledge, holding to the vine. I made the mistake of looking down. The land seemed far, far below, and I knew I would be killed if I fell. Insanity!

318

I closed my eyes, leaning against the rock as my heart pounded away.

Several moments passed before I was able to ease myself down further. My right foot found a root jutting out of the rock. My left foot dangled out in space, but I had a firm grip on the vine. As I lowered myself, the weight of my body caused the root to tear loose. I slipped a good ten feet, would have fallen had I not been clinging to the vine. My feet banged down on another ledge, not a foot wide, and I paused, catching my breath. Staring out, I could see the river. A large boat moved slowly past and I could barely make out the tiny figures standing on deck. They must have been startled to see a woman in a red dress flattened against the face of the rock, clinging desperately to a vine as the wind ripped at hair and skirts.

I peered down, saw another foothold a few feet below, to my left. I let go of the vine I had been holding and caught hold of another, moving down slowly, touching the jutting rock with my right foot. Little by little I descended, and when I paused again I saw that I was halfway down. It wasn't so difficult, I told myself. I was lying, but I didn't dare give way to the sheer panic that threatened to demolish me. Gripping the root with both hands, I started to move down some more, and suddenly there was a ripping noise, a shower of dirt, and the vine swung out into space and sailed to the ground. I tottered for a moment. This was it! I was going to fall! Then a great gust of wind struck me, flattening me against the rock. My fingers gripped the rock, but there was nothing to hold on to. I was poised on a tiny ridge or rock no more than eight inches wide, and as soon as the wind died down I was going to tumble over backwards.

Wild, disconnected images flashed through my mind, the kind a drowning man is supposed to see just before he goes under for the last time. My mother was laughing, serving ale, basking in the admiration of the men at the inn, and I reached for a mug, which turned into a wineglass, and then I was sitting before the fireplace, elegantly

319

clad, demure, smiling as my father told me about the wonderful plans he had for me. The image blurred, dissolved, and I saw the house on Montagu Square, saw Lord Mallory leering at me, handsome, demonic, destructive, and his face disappeared and I was in that dank, dreadful cell, in shackles. Angie grinned, perky, defiant, showing me how to pick the lock on the shackles, and then Derek was in bed, delirious with fever after the snakebite, and I touched his cheek and he was storming across the yard toward me and I was holding a basket of apricots and they spilled and Jeff and I were riding through the dense green and brown forest.

The wind died down. Abruptly. The images had flashed and flickered in a matter of seconds. The wind was gone and I hadn't fallen. Out of the corner of my eye I saw another thick vine spilling down perhaps two yards to my right. If I could gradually edge over, catch hold of the vine . . . I prayed for strength, and after a while it came and I began to inch over toward the vine, cautiously, and then the ridge gave out and I could move no farther. I reached for the vine. My fingers were inches away from it. I would have to swing over and catch hold of it. I couldn't. If I missed, if I failed to get a firm purchase, I would fall. Panic swept over me, and there was one dreadful moment when I didn't care, when I knew I was going to fall crashing to the ground and simply didn't care. Not caring, I lunged for the vine and caught hold of it with both hands. I swung out into space and my hands slipped down the vine and then I swung back toward the rock and landed on a wide ridge several feet below.

The vine held. It was strong, sturdy. I moved on down, finding footholds to my left, to my right, and I was calm now, concentrating, fear gone at last. My feet touched the ground. I let go of the vine and stepped back and looked up at the cliff looming in front of me. I had to tilt my head back in order to see the top. I knew I was mad to have attempted to climb down it in the first place. I was down now. That was all that mattered. I shoved long, tangled locks of auburn hair away from my cheeks, brushed the dirt and dust from my red skirt. It must have taken me almost half an hour, but I had made it. I had an impulse to burst into gales of laughter, an impulse I curbed immediately. There was no time for hysterics, no time to dwell on what I had done. I turned and started walking up the road in the direction of the docks.

The ramshackle buildings up ahead were all clustered together as though for support, and they looked even more sordid close up. I heard riotous laughter and bawdy music. Someone was banging on a piano. Someone was singing, off key. Even now, in the middle of the afternoon, Natchez-under-the-hill was alive with activity. I could imagine what it must be like when nighttime came. I passed three taverns and a two-story brown frame building with a wide verandah in front. Brightly clad women were sitting on the verandah, drinking, laughing, and more women leaned out of the windows upstairs. They called out to me. I hurried on, trying to ignore the lascivious remarks, the lewd suggestions.

A man staggered out of a tavern, clutching a half-empty bottle. He saw me and let out a great whoop, staggering down the steps, stumbling toward me, waving the bottle. He was big and burly, his brown hair growing down to his shoulders. I quickened my step, but he soon caught up with me, grabbing my shoulder, whirling me around. I was furious, hot flashes of anger preempting the alarm I might have felt otherwise. The man chuckled, his breath reeking of alcohol, and as he tried to pull me toward him I gave him a mighty shove. Drunk, already finding it difficult to maintain his balance, he toppled over backwards with a cry of dismay.

The girls on the verandah cheered. Amazed at what I had done, I moved on, shaken now, feeling the alarm I hadn't felt before. Keeping my eyes in front of me, I passed the rest of the buildings, ignoring the catcalls, the boisterous hoots, and a few moments later Natchez-under-the-hill was behind me, the docks ahead. Three huge ships and at least a dozen smaller craft were bobbing on the water, brawny men moving up and down gang-planks, loading and unloading. The docks were crowded with boxes, barrels, coils of rope, men scurrying about, others barking orders. So brisk was the activity that no one paid me the least attention. The men were much too busy to greet my arrival with any show of interest.

I paused beside a stack of boxes, wondering how I should go about getting a berth. I finally stopped one of the men hurrying past and asked him if one of the ships would be leaving for New Orleans this afternoon. He nodded, pointing to the largest ship, the *Royal Star*. Men were pushing barrows down the gangplank filled with what looked like pink brick. As I drew nearer, I saw that it was indeed brick, a soft, delicate pink like faded roses. Other men were loading the brick into a large wagon, and as I watched, another wagon, already loaded, pulled away from the docks and started up the gradually sloping road that led to the town above. The four horses strained mightily as the driver cracked his whip in the air.

A large, heavyset blond man seemed to be in charge of unloading the *Royal Star*. He stood back with his arms folded across his chest, watching the activity with a severe expression. He thundered at one of the workmen who lost control of a barrow and nearly dumped the lovely pink brick into the water. The offending man grimaced, steadied the barrow, and rolled it on down the gangplank and over to the wagon. The heavyset man frowned, highly displeased. I wondered if he was the captain of the ship. If so, he could probably arrange a berth for me. As I approached, he looked up, observing me with cold steel-blue eyes.

Something in those eyes made me hesitate. He was a formidable figure, exuding power and authority, easily dominating the scene even though he stood perfectly still. He had incredible presence, presence so strong it was alarming. Powerfully built, he was elegantly attired in highly polished black knee boots, snug gray trousers, and a loosely fitting white silk shirt. His features were blunt, the jaw square, cheekbones broad and flat, and there was a knot of flesh on his nose that made him look belligerent. His hair was a pale yellow-blond, cut short, a monk-like fringe falling across his jutting forehead. Probably in his mid-forties, I thought as I came closer to him.

"You want something, woman?"

His voice was deep, guttural, his manner definitely harsh. I realized I must look frightful, my hair all atangle, my dress streaked with dirt, my face probably dirty, too. I had come from Natchez-under-the-hill, and he probably thought I was a harlot come to ply my trade. A man like this would be utterly disdainful of such women, consider them dirt beneath his feet. He stared at me with those hard blue eyes, looking as though he'd just as soon knock me down as not, and it was a moment before I could bring myself to speak.

"I—I want to go to New Orleans," I stammered.

My accent surprised him. One of those heavy brown brows lifted.

"Where are you from?" He didn't ask. He demanded to know.

"I really don't . . . think that's any of your affair," I retorted.

"Answer me, woman!"

"Or what?" I asked defiantly.

"Or you'll wish you had," he threatened.

"I suggest you go straight to hell," I said calmly.

His brows drew together. His mouth tightened. He wasn't used to back talk, that was quite clear. He was used to snapping orders, having them obeyed immediately. His size, his strength made him a ntaural bully, and I sensed a streak of cruelty in the curl of his mouth, in the hard, steady glare of those intense blue eyes.

"You're new around here," he said. "I've never seen you before."

"I arrived in Natchez this morning, as a matter of fact."

"And you want to go to New Orleans. On this ship."

"I understand it's leaving soon."

"As soon as these incompetents finish unloading."

"Are—are you the captain?"

323

"I own the ship. The captain's my employee."

"Then you can arrange passage for me."

"If I wanted to, yes."

Although his manner was still sullen, that first angry disdain was missing now. Those eyes seemed to assess me, taking in every detail, and he was extremely interested. No longer intimidated, I could feel my cheeks begin to color. I wanted to shove him over backwards just as I had shoved the pathetic drunk who had run after me on the road a few minutes before. I knew that my eyes must be flashing as I spoke.

"I can pay," I snapped. "I can pay whatever you ask. I need to leave Natchez . . . as soon as possible."

"Before Rawlins finds you, you mean."

"How—"

"You're not one of the whores from under-the-hill, and you're damned sure not one of the good women from town. I heard Rawlins had arrived, heard he had a stunning wench with him."

"News travels fast," I said bitterly.

"In a community like this it does. So you want me to help you get away? Where did you get the money you're so eager to pay me? The women Rawlins bring down the Trace don't have money."

"I—"

"You stole it," he said. "Even if I were inclined to help you, it's too late now, I'm afraid."

He was peering over my shoulder. I turned to see Jeff strolling toward us, his manner as jaunty as ever. He didn't seem at all surprised to see me standing here on the docks with this surly giant. He acted as though it were perfectly natural, as though we had arranged to meet here. He gave me a friendly nod, nodded at the man with less warmth.

"Schnieder," he said.

"Rawlins. I was expecting you."

"Heard you were unloading building material. They say two shiploads of lumber arrived 'fore I started up the Trace to Carolina. Hear you brung in a fancy architect

324

from New Orleans. Your house must be comin' along right well. Nice-lookin' brick, unusual pink."

"I'm going to call the place Roseclay."

"Nice name. Bit fancy, perhaps, but then I imagine the house is gonna be somethin' to behold."

Helmut Schnieder did not reply. The two men disliked each other intensely. That had been obvious from the first. Although Jeff's remarks had been spoken casually, there had been a suggestion of mockery. Schnieder seemed to be holding himself in tight control, looked as though he'd like nothing more than to knock Jeff flat with one mighty blow. The air seemed to seethe with animosity. Jeff turned to me ever so casually.

"You ready to go back to the inn now, Marietta?"

Schnieder spoke up before I could reply. "How much did you pay for her, Rawlins?"

"Plenty."

"I'll double it."

" 'Fraid she's not for sale, Schnieder."

"Name your price," the German said. "My money's as good as any whoremonger's. Better. I'll pay in cash, any price you name."

"That's mighty generous of you, Schnieder, but what I said still goes. 'Sides, what you need with another woman? I hear you got a whole house full of whores under-the-hill, hear you own the place."

"I want her, Rawlins." There was menace in his voice.

"That's too bad, fella."

There was a tense silence as the two men eyed each other. Schnieder was an inch or so taller than Jeff and much heavier. Beneath that civilized façade lurked the brute strength of a German peasant, and I was worried for Jeff's sake. Schnieder's facial muscles were taut, his eyes dark with hostility. Jeff appeared utterly relaxed, the suggestion of a grin playing at the corner of his mouth. He seemed to be inviting the larger man to start something. Several moments passed, and Schnieder finally backed down, scowling.

"If you ever change your mind—"

"I ain't plannin' to. Come along, Marietta."

He took my arm and led me away from the *Royal Star*, past the docks and up the gradually sloping road toward the town above. Neither of us spoke. He didn't seem to be at all angry or upset about my attempted escape. We might have been taking a pleasant stroll. Reaching the bluff, we turned, walking through the town toward the inn. Jeff nodded to several people, stopped once to exchange a few friendly words with a man in black, holding my arm all the while. It was only when we were on the front verandah of the inn that he released me. He grinned and held out his hand. I took the roll of money from the pocket of my skirt and placed it in his palm. He shook his head slowly in mock disappointment.

"Just outta curiosity—how'd you get down there? I kept my eye peeled every minute, never saw you pass."

"I climbed down the cliff in back of the inn."

"You did *what*?" he exclaimed.

"I climbed down the cliff."

"You coulda broken your bloody neck!"

He took hold of my arm again, tightly this time, his fingers squeezing viciously. He took me inside and through the main room and up the curving white staircase. By the time we reached our room his anger had dissipated. He let go of my arm and looked at me with perplexed brown eyes. I rubbed my arm.

"You knew I'd try it," I said.

"Hell, you practically drew me a picture—tellin' me goodbye like that, fightin' back the tears, holdin' on to me like you didn't wanna let go. I'd uv had to be blind not to know what you was plannin'."

"Then why did you leave?"

"I figured the exercise'd do you good, knew you wouldn't get no further than the docks. I *didn't* know you was gonna do anything as damnfool stupid as climbin' down a cliff or I'd uv left you tied to the bed. I could *beat* you for that."

"Go ahead. I—I just don't care."

"Christ! Look at you. You look like some kinda

326

wretched waif. There's dirt all over your dress, all over your face. Your hair looks like—like you oughta be stirrin' a kettle full of frogs and cacklin'."

"Thanks!" I snapped.

Jeff grinned, delighted to see my spirit returning. He stepped over to the wardrobe and took out the pack. He peeled a few more bills off the roll and then put it back in the pack, slung the pack into the wardrobe, and kicked the door shut. As I looked around, I noticed the stack of boxes on the bed. There were three of them, all white, two extremely large, the other small. He must have brought them back here before coming after me. He was so insufferably sure of himself!

"I still got a lot of things to tend to," he told me. "I'll be back here around seven. You be ready to go down to dinner. Better yet, be waitin' for me downstairs. I'll tell 'em to arrange for a bath as I go out."

He sauntered out of the room then, leaving the door wide open. I slammed it shut, wondering why I wasn't really upset, wondering why I was almost glad he had come after me and found me so easily. I wasn't going to try to escape again. Both of us knew that. I resented his knowing it, resented his blithe, airy manner, putting the money back into the pack, leaving the door open like that. It was infuriating. It also gave me a poignant, aching feeling inside and made me want to dissolve into tears.

Stepping over to the bed, I opened the boxes. When I saw what was inside them I felt even more like crying. I was amazed that he had been able to buy such things in Natchez, for the undergarments were elegant and the gown one of the loveliest I had ever seen. The high-heeled slippers that matched were gorgeous, too, a perfect fit. I realized that he must have taken one of my old dresses and a pair of shoes from the pack that hadn't been brought up and carried them to the shop with him in order to make sure everything was the right size. Damn him, I thought. Damn him for doing it, for making me feel this way—happy, beholden, defenseless.

A few minutes later there was a brisk knock on the

327

door. I opened it to discover an exceedingly plump young girl with tousled blond curls and jolly brown eyes. She wore a blue cotton dress, a starched white apron and, incongrously enough, a pair of dangling jet earrings. Merry, effusive, she identified herself as Lizzie, confessed that she was the proprietor's daughter, and added that she detested being a maid and longed to be an adventuress.

"My, you *do* need a bath, don't you? It's ready—that little room at the end of the hall. Here's the key. Don't dawdle now. The water's good and hot. There's a big fluffy towel and a bar of the sweetest smellin' soap! I wish *I* had hair that color."

"Your hair is lovely, Lizzie."

"Wish I had a figure like that, too. I'm giving up sweets, I swear it. That Mister Rawlins—I wish I had a man like him sleepin' in *my* room. He's ever so excitin'."

"I'll tell him you said so."

"Cripes! You wouldn't? He'd think I was awful!" And she scurried off down the hall, giggling merrily.

I felt marvelous after the long, hot bath in the huge white porcelain tub filled with steaming water. Later, wearing the lovely new petticoat with its billowing, lace-trimmed skirts, I spent over an hour working with my hair, using the brush and the pair of tongs Lizzie had brought to me with a brazier of burning coals. I was quite pleased with the results, hair pulled up sleekly and fastened in back, a mass of long, perfectly shaped sausage ringlets spilling down to my shoulders.

I was ready to go downstairs a few minutes before seven, and I took a final look at myself in the mirror. The gown was a rich brown satin with great puffed sleeves dropping off at the shoulder. My breasts were caught up in an inset of dark beige lace, a blue velvet bow centered beneath, and the skirt was composed of huge puffy brown flounces adorned with blue bows, parting in front to reveal the underskirt covered with row upon row of beige lace ruffles. It was the kind of gown the ladies in

328

the French court were wearing, a magnificent creation that made me feel like a queen . . . or an extremely elegant courtesan. Du Barry herself would have been jealous, I thought, sweeping out of the room and moving down the curving staircase.

Jeff was nowhere in sight. The main room was empty but for a slender, nervous-looking girl with light-brown hair and violet-blue eyes and an unusually handsome young man who seemed to be upbraiding her about something. The girl, who wore a white silk gown sprigged with tiny blue and violet flowers, was obviously from a wealthy family. The young man had unruly black hair and angry brown eyes. His black boots were old, poorly polished, his brown suit beginning to grow shiny with age. He was an appealing figure, nevertheless, aglow with youth and vitality. The girl was pale and would have been plain but for those lovely, tormented eyes and the hair so light a brown it had a silvery sheen. She kept glancing over her shoulder toward the crowded dining room, and she seemed to be on the verge of tears. Immersed in their intense, intimate private drama, neither of them so much as looked up when I moved down the last steps and entered the room.

"I don't *care* what he says!" the man protested. "It's your life, Meg, your decision. I'm almost twenty years old! When Pa died I inherited everything. Oh, the plantation isn't much now, I grant that, but in a few years, with a lot of hard work—"

"James, you—you don't understand. He would—" The girl cut herself short, again glancing toward the dining room. "We'll have to wait. I'll be eighteen in two years, and then—"

"I want you now!"

How bold and impetuous he was, fiery with the passions of youth and eager to assert himself. The girl loved him, too, desperately. That was quite evident. Seeing them together made me feel a curious sadness. Although both were more or less my contemporaries, I felt immeasurably older, wiser, and it was not necessarily a pleasant feeling. The innocence, the wonder, the surging intensity of young love as they knew it had been denied me. How beautiful it was, how sad.

"After we're married there's not a thing he can do," the handsome youth continued. "You may be scared to death of him, but he doesn't frighten me one bit! I want you to come with me now, Meg, tonight, this minute! I don't intend to sneak around any longer!"

The girl looked up at him with anguished violet-blue eyes, and then she shook her head mournfully and hurried on into the dining room. The young man slammed his fist into his palm, emitted a colorful curse, and stalked out of the room and down the short hallway leading to the front door. He was just a few months younger than I, yet he seemed like a frisky pup compared to the men I had known. I wished I could be young and dewy-eyed again, wished there were still beautiful illusions to cling to.

"I see the gown fits," Jeff remarked. "Woman who sold it to me assured me it would. You look gorgeous."

"Jeff. I didn't hear you come in."

"Almost didn't make it. Young James Norman swept out the door just as I was about to enter—damned near knocked me down. Didn't even apologize. If I didn't like him so much I'da given him a good shakin'."

"Who is he?"

"Norman? Owns a plantation outside of town, right next to Schnieder's. His folks died of the fever a year or so ago, and Norman's runnin' the place all by himself, tryin' to make a go of it. Refused to sell out, even though Schnieder offered him a small fortune."

"He's very good-looking."

"Reckon he is," Jeff agreed.

He was silent. He seemed to be waiting for something. Finally he shook his head in exasperation, took several steps backward, and turned around slowly. I had been so immersed in thought that I hadn't even noticed his new clothes. No wonder he was exasperated. Gone were the dirty buckskins. He wore shiny new black boots, a splendid blue suit, and a blue-and-brown-striped waistcoat. His brown silk stock was impeccably folded, and for once his hair was neatly brushed, not a lock out of place. I hardly recognized him. I told him so. He made a face.

"Took you long enough to notice! I coulda been stark naked for all the attention you paid. James Norman is handsome, but me—me, I'm an old shoe you don't even pay any mind to. These duds cost me a pretty penny, I don't mind tellin' you, and I had to wait hours while they took the breeches up."

"You look extremely dashing."

"Feel like a fool," he grumbled, "but I've worn buckskins for the last time. From now on, it's Jeffrey Rawlins, gentleman, at your service. Think you can stand me like this?"

"I think so."

"Then let's go on in to dinner. I'm starvin'."

The dining room was crowded, but Jeff had reserved a table. As we took our seats, I noticed the girl with light-brown hair sitting at a table across the way. I recognized the man with her immediately. Helmut Schnieder had donned a blue waistcoat and the gray jacket that went with the breeches he had been wearing on the docks. Catching sight of us, he stared openly, as though amazed at the transformation both of us had undergone.

"Who is that woman with Schnieder?" I asked.

Jeff glanced across the room. "His sister, Margaret. I mentioned her to you earlier."

"You said she was a mousy little thing. She's almost pretty. Lovely eyes, and that hair—"

"Look, Marietta, would you mind payin' just a little attention to *me* for a change?"

"I'm sorry. Have I hurt your feelings?"

"Don't be bitchy! I sold the mules this afternoon. Hated to part with 'em, I'll admit, but that phase of my life is over. Soon as I get to New Orleans I'm buyin' a place. It's kinda run down now, but after I spend a little money on it, it's gonna be plush as all get-out."

"What kind of place are you talking about?"

"Gamblin' hall," Jeff said. His voice was sharp with enthusiasm. "It's gonna be somethin'. There'll be all kinds of tables, a roulette wheel, a fancy bar, the works. There'll be a ballroom, too, for dancin'—this'll be the kinda place the ladies can come to—well, a certain kinda ladies. No whores, mind you, but the men can bring their lady friends. There'll be white marble and gold curtains and—"

"How do you intend to pay for all this?" I interrupted.

"Didn't I tell you? I'm a rich man—well, fair to middlin' rich. I got a lot of investments, and I've been savin' all the while, savin' for the day I could open my own place, be a gentleman."

"Gentlemen don't own gambling houses," I informed him.

"Hell, you really are a wet blanket tonight, aren't you? Here I have all these excitin' things to tell you and—oh, forget it! Let's order dinner!"

He was like a petulant little boy, and I couldn't help but smile. Feeling sorry for having teased him, I reached across the table and gave his hand a pat. Jeff jerked his hand away, scowling. He continued to sulk for a few moments, and then he looked up and grinned his sheepish grin, waved the waiter over to the table, and ordered our meal. Though plain, the food was excellent, and there was a bottle of sparkling wine to go with it. Jeff continued to talk enthusiastically about the gambling house. I tried to be an appreciative audience, but it was difficult. Although Jeff didn't seem to notice, I could feel Helmut Schnieder staring. I turned once, glancing in the direction of his table. He didn't bother to lower his eyes, simply stared, openly and rudely. I was relieved when he and his sister finally left the dining room.

When we had finished our meal and drunk the last of the wine, Jeff suggested we take a stroll in the gardens out back. He was in a thoughtful mood as we stepped outside, his hands thrust into his pockets, his exuberance released. I had paid little attention to them this afternoon, but now the gardens seemed lovely. The moon was almost full, the pink and white roses silvered with moonlight, the small, neat shrubs casting velvety black shadows across the flagstones. We strolled slowly, my skirts rustling softly, Jeff's new boots squeaking ever so slightly. Reaching the foot of the gardens, we stood looking at the Mississippi below, a vast silver ribbon shimmering in the night, banks shrouded in darkness.

"You really climb down this cliff?" he asked.

I nodded. "Right over there. It was . . . rather frightening."

"Fool, you silly little fool."

"I almost wish I had fallen. It would make things so much simpler."

"Hey, this is supposed to be a celebration. We're supposed to be happy."

"I'm afraid I don't feel very happy."

"I wonder why."

"Jeff—"

Before I could continue he pulled me to him, slipping one arm around the back of my neck, the other around my waist and drawing me even closer. He kissed me for a long, long time, with incredible tenderness, his lips pressing and probing with a delicious languor that had little to do with passion and everything to do with love. After a while he released me and, reaching into his jacket pocket, pulled out a much folded square of paper and showed it to me.

"Watch," he said.

He tore the paper in two, then tore it again, continuing to tear until the paper was a handful of tiny pieces. These he tossed into the air. The wind caught them, and for a moment they fluttered in the moonlight like frenzied white moths, then disappeared into the night. Jeff sighed and turned to me, grinning again.

"You're a free woman," he said.

"I don't understand."

"That was your Articles of Indenture, purchased by me from Derek Hawke for a whopping eighteen hundred pounds. You're free, Marietta. You belong to no one."

"You . . ." I was too moved to continue.

"Aw, I know what you thought. You thought I was gonna sell you to a brothel. I never told you any different, but I never intended to do that. You see, I was thinkin' about the place all the time, thinkin' I ought to have a gorgeous woman to . . . well, kind of act as hostess. A sort of special attraction, you might say."

"Why didn't you *tell* me?"

"I was savin' it for a surprise."

"That's—"

"Wretched of me, I know. I didn't intend to set you free, Marietta, not at first. And then—somethin' happened. I reckon you know what I'm referrin' to. I reckon you know I'm in love with you. Don't guess you could help but know."

"I—I'm not in love with you, Jeff."

"You think you're not. You think you're still in love with Hawke. I think differently. I gave you your freedom, Marietta, but now I want to take it back again. I want you to marry me. 'Stead of bein' my hostess, you'll be a partner. Christ, what a team we'll make!"

He was standing behind me now. He wrapped his arms around in front of my waist and, leaning forward, rested his cheek against mine. Below us, far below, the river shimmered, silver and black, silver-blue, and I stared at it and felt his cheek resting on mine and felt something hard inside that I recognized as determination. I didn't love him, but he loved me and I could use that love. I was going to succeed. I was going to have all the things a woman could desire, and because Jeff Rawlins loved me he would help me begin to acquire them.

"I won't marry you, Jeff," I said. "I'll go to New Orleans with you. I'll act as hostess at your gambling house, but I don't intend to marry you."

334

"Reckon I'll have to persuade you to change your mind."

"Don't. You'd only be wasting your time."

"We'll see," he replied.

PART THREE:

New Orleans 1774

XVII

Jeff didn't like me to go out without an escort, and it really wasn't safe, even in our section of the city, but the shop was only a few streets away and I was completely out of perfume. Jeff was in his office, going over the accounts, and Kyle was down in the cellar, taking inventory of the wine. One of the servants could have fetched the perfume, true, but it was an unusually sunny day and I looked forward to the walk. I adjusted the bodice of my dress, a tan silk sprigged with orange and brown flowers. Then, taking out a long brown velvet cloak lined with orange taffeta, I slipped it over my shoulders. I was wearing very grand clothes these days, and it was most satisfying.

Leaving my bedroom, I passed through the small, elegantly appointed sitting room and on into the hall. Jeff's room was across the way. I had insisted on separate bedrooms from the very first, and he had agreed with considerable reluctance, grumbling that all that going back and forth would wear him out. Of late there had been very little of it. I knew that he was seeing a beautiful, honey-skinned quadroon with dark luminous eyes and luxuriant black hair. Her name was Corinne. She always wore pink. She was one of the most celebrated courtesans in New Orleans and one of the most expensive. I wished that I could be jealous. Jeff wished so, too.

I moved down the hall and down the gorgeous white marble staircase that curved so gracefully to the entrance hall below. The place was silent, and as none of the shutters had been opened, there was very little light. On impulse, I toured the rooms downstairs. On the right, as one entered, there were three spacious gaming rooms, one leading into the other, and on the left there was an opulent ballroom, the ceiling two stories high, crystal chandeliers hanging from the sky-blue ceiling traced with patterns in gold gilt. The ballroom was only used as such once a month, when we gave the balls for which Rawlins Palace had become famous. The rest of the time it was filled with white silk sofas and gilded white chairs and tall green plants in white porcelain urns, a social area where customers could eat, drink, flirt, groan about their losses or boast of their winnings. A kind of gentleman's club as well as a gambling house, Rawlins Palace offered all the amenities.

What a ruin it had been when Jeff first bought the place, I thought as I strolled through the gaming rooms. He had converted all his holdings into cash, had poured all his money into the place, running out before we had finished renovations. He had been able to borrow at steep interest rates, and we had finally finished, had finally opened. The first year had been extremely difficult, but the place had caught on and the money had been paid back. Now, after three years, we were making a very good profit, although Jeff was constantly complaining about costs. We served the finest food, the finest wine, and the atmosphere was undeniably luxurious. The ivory walls, gold carpets, gold velvet draperies, the gleaming white marble bar made it truly a palace. Rawlins Palace catered to the highest strata in a city where wealth, not birth, distinguished a man.

It was a shade more respectable than most establishments of its kind. Although the men could bring their mistresses, and usually did, we did not allow unescorted women. Our dealers were sharp, adept at their jobs, but they were honest. Some of the young blades occasionally grew a bit too boisterous, some of the customers grew quarrelsome when they lost too much or had too much to drink, but Kyle was more than capable of handling them. He was six feet five, lean and muscular, a sober, grim-faced chap who ousted potential troublemakers with firm efficiency.

I paused at one of the tables, fingering the green baize cloth, wondering how we were going to replace Laval. He had been caught holding money back two nights ago. The amount had been trifling, but Jeff had dismissed him immediately. Laval wouldn't be dealing anywhere for quite some time. Kyle had followed him out into the street, had pulled him into a dark alley and broken both his arms. I was horrified when I heard about it, but Jeff merely shrugged, saying Laval had it coming, claiming it would keep the others from attempting to skim a little off the top.

"You let one get away with somethin' like that, they all try it," he informed me.

It was going to be difficult to find a replacement, but I would let Jeff worry about that. Stepping into the back room with the enormous gilt mirror hanging behind the bar, I heard domestic noises coming from the kitchen and the servants' quarters below. Kyle had a small room upstairs next to Jeff's offices, but the rest of the household staff lived in the basement rooms. We had a very good staff. I had trained them myself. Our French cook was rather temperamental and the maids were terrified of Kyle, but the place was usually run with harmony. All the staff adored Jeff, were intensely loyal, and they received very handsome wages. The dealers and footmen who came in nightly to manage the gaming tables and serve food and drink, respectively, also received generous wages. Laval was the only one who had ever given us any trouble.

We had come a long way in three years, I reflected. Rawlins Palace was a huge success. Jeff and I had both worked at it, worked hard. Strolling into the back hallway, I paused before the open doors leading into the

341

spacious courtyard in back of the building. The blue tiles were a bit warped, with tufts of grass growing up between some of them, and the high tan stucco walls that enclosed it were flaking and smeared with dirt, but it was nevertheless charming with the lily pond and fountain, the ragged dwarf palm trees, the white wrought-iron tables and chairs. A marmalade cat lounged on top of one of the tables, stretching indolently in the sunlight. He belonged to Pierre, our cook, and judging from his plumpness and sleek orange coat he received his fair share of gourmet food. He didn't even bother to look up when a bluejay swooped down and began to splash in the fountain. Although the courtyard looked a bit shabby and run down in the bright sunlight, it was extremely romantic by moonlight, usually filled with the music of rustling skirts and hushed voices in shadowy corners. Many an assignation was made in the courtyard of Rawlins Palace, many a new romance begun.

Moving back down the hall to the front door, I stepped outside and began walking slowly down the street in the direction of the apothecary shop. The cobblestoned street was narrow, with rows of buildings on either side, and although the sun was bright, little direct light streamed through. Everything was blue and gray and shadowy tan. Black women with voluminous white aprons over their dresses and red bandanas atop their heads strolled leisurely toward the market place with their baskets. A tipsy young man staggered down the street with a dazed look in his eyes, his fine clothes rumpled after a night on the town. A painted, over-dressed prostitute stepped out of a courtyard and turned to wave at a man standing on an ornately patterned black iron balcony. Turning a corner, I moved down a much busier street. Carts and carriages rumbled past. The sidewalks were crowded. The noise was deafening as hawkers cried their wares and stray dogs barked and women argued in shrill voices.

I kept a firm grip on my orange velvet reticule. Up ahead I saw a pair of nimble thieves lift the wallet from a plump, smartly attired middle-aged man who lingered in front of a shop. The pickpockets hurried on, grinning widely, and the plump man had no idea he had been robbed. Two beautiful courtesans came out of the hat shop and stepped into the elegant black open carriage that stood waiting for them. One of the women wore a pink velvet gown, pink and white plumes curling down on one side of her wide-brimmed white hat. I recognized her at once. Corinne recognized me, too, peering at me with dark, resentful eyes as the liveried coachman cracked his whip and drove on down the street. She was a gorgeous creature, desperately in love with Jeff and eager to provide the slavish devotion I withheld. I felt rather sorry for her, knowing he would soon drop her just as he had dropped all the others.

Before Corinne there had been Thérèse DuBois, a wealthy, aristocratic Frenchwoman with the morals of an alley cat. Well into her forties, Thérèse had fallen under his spell, too. Thin, tense, volatile, she had tried her best to take him away from me. Jeff had amused himself with her, had treated her rather shabbily, leaving her abruptly, causing the poor woman considerable anguish. There were so many women ready to give Jeff the love he wanted only from me, and none of them realized that it was his love for me and the frustrations it caused that drove him to them in the first place.

I turned another corner, nearing the open marketplace. I could smell fish and bloody carcasses and spoiling fruit and flowers. This street was even darker, narrower. A handsome Spanish soldier was strolling hand in hand with a nubile young girl, and another soldier was ardently kissing a brunette in red in a darkened doorway. Romance. New Orleans seemed to be obsessed with it. Perhaps it was the hot, sultry climate, the warm winds constantly sweeping over the city. Perhaps it was the too-fragrant perfume of too many exotic flowers that overlaid the reek of filthy canals and congested slums. If people in Boston and Philadelphia were ardently concerned with freedom from tyranny or loyalty to the

Crown, people in New Orleans were as ardently concerned with pleasures of the flesh.

It was unlike any place I had ever been to, an over-ripe fruit of a city that had passed from hand to hand, nationality to nationality, retaining its own personality all the while. Where else could pirates and smugglers mingle with aristocrats and officials who were rogues at heart? Where else did convents share the same street with brothels, sordid slums stand back to back with gracious buildings featuring wrought-iron balconies, enclosed courtyards and patios and opulent gardens? The city was too rich, too flamboyant with its crowded waterfront, its industry, its wickedness. Inbred and isolated from the events that kept the English colonies in a constant upheaval, New Orleans was both seductive and alarming, totally unique.

Leaving the narrow street with its strolling lovers, I walked across a busy, bustling square flooded with sunlight. The smell of fish from the marketplace one street over was strong here. A bell jangled loudly as I stepped into the apothecary shop. It was cool and dim, crowded with tables and shelves holding bottles of colored liquid, packets of powder, and boxes full of dried roots and herbs. The apothecary was not in, but his apprentice hurried forward to wait on me. A lad no more than seventeen, he was tall and well built with glossy brown hair, wide, innocent blue eyes, and a full pink mouth that suggested a very sensual nature not yet explored. The lad blushed when I told him who I was and what I wanted, yet those wide indigo eyes looked at me with a calf-like longing. He was obviously still a virgin, frustrated and eager to explore.

"Number 93," I said politely. "It should be ready."

The lad nodded and hurried into the room in back of the shop. Highly skilled at his work, the apothecary had created a perfume especially for me, a subtle, barely discernible scent quite unlike the too strong, too sweet perfumes both men and women used to camouflage body odor. Most of the more refined citizens of New Orleans took a bath at least once every two or three months, relying on their perfume the rest of the time. My daily baths were a great eccentricity, but I refused to give them up even though they were considered both unhealthy and highly dangerous.

The lad returned, handed me the small bottle, and took my money. I put the bottle in my reticule and, smiling warmly, thanked the boy in a quiet voice. He blushed again, looking terrified and, at the same time, looking as though he wanted to leap on me in a frenzy of passion. The bell tinkled again as I left the shop. I could feel the boy watching me from the window as I crossed the square. It wouldn't be long before his frustrations were relieved, I reflected. New Orleans was filled with bored, restless women who would enjoy nothing more than initiating so handsome a youth. In a year he would probably be a profligate young rake ruining himself over someone like Corinne or Thérèse DuBois.

As I neared the narrow side street that I had come down a few minutes earlier, a loud commotion broke out nearby. A man yelled. Horses shrieked. I whirled around to see two handsome grays still rearing, forelegs dancing in air, a husky, rough-looking man waving his arms directly in front of them. The coachman tugged on the reins, trying his best to calm the horses. The man who had almost been run down was shouting vile abuse, and a crowd began to gather, almost trampling a black woman who had dropped her basket of apples and was crawling about nervously trying to gather them up.

"You friggin' bastard! Why'n't ya watch where you're goin'! I've a mind to wring your neck!"

"Out of the way!" the coachman called. "Out of the way, I say, unless you want a taste of my whip!"

While the two men continued to abuse each other, I stared at the woman who sat back calmly in the carriage, utterly bored with the furor. She wore long black lace gloves and a gown of sky-blue silk, the bodice cut extremely low, the very full skirt adorned with row upon row of black lace ruffles. She was small and looked a bit frail, her full pink mouth wry, her nose turned up, her brown eyes enormous. There was a scattering of light golden freckles across her pale cheeks, and her silky blond hair was elaborately arranged in sculptured waves, long ringlets dangling down in back. There was something vaguely familiar about her, I thought, yet I couldn't quite place her.

She sighed. She tapped the coachman on the shoulder with the tip of a furled blue silk parasol, silencing him immediately. Calmly she stepped down out of the carriage, her skirts rustling crisply. The crowd grew silent with anticipation as she walked around to confront the scowling, belligerent pedestrian who still shook his fist, still refused to move.

"What have we here?" he asked sarcastically. "Come to give me a few coins and send me on my way? You bleedin' rich! You damn near run over me with your bleedin' carriage, and you think—"

"I think you'd better move on *toot sweet*, mate, or I'm going to take this umbrella and shove it up your ass!"

The crowd roared with laughter. The black woman was so startled that she dropped her basket of apples all over again. The man was dumbfounded, so dumbfounded that he couldn't speak. The blond in blue glared at him, eyes flashing, and after a moment he made a face and hurried away. There was more laughter, and the crowd began to disperse. The blond sighed and began to scramble on the ground, helping the woman gather up the evasive apples. When they were all back in the basket, she stood up, brushing her skirt. I smiled, a great rush of joy swelling inside. The blond felt me watching her and whirled around, ready to snap.

She stared. Her brown eyes grew wider, her cheeks turned even paler. She shook her head in disbelief, then took a step nearer, peering at me. I nodded.

"It's really me," I told her.

"My Gawd! I—I can't believe it!"

346

"I couldn't either, not at first. I thought I was mistaken, thought it couldn't possibly be you, and then you opened your mouth."

"Marietta!"

We fell into each other's arms then, hugging, sobbing, laughing there in front of the carriage. The coachman watched with horrified disapproval. When the first burst of excitement was over, she stepped back and grinned that wry, saucy grin I remembered so well, the same old Angie—sumptuously gowned, elegantly coiffed, but Angie nevertheless. She took me by the hand and helped me into the carriage, climbing up beside me. Our skirts spilled over the side.

"To the market café, Holt!" she ordered. "I still can't believe it," she said, clasping my hand. "I have so much to tell you! What on earth are you doing in New Orleans?"

"I'm hostess at Rawlins Palace. It's the most elegant gambling house in the city."

"And the owner is madly in love with you, showers you with jewels and gifts! I *knew* it! Remember me tellin' you, remember me sayin' we'd both end up on top?"

"I remember. You—you're so—"

"Piss-elegant," she supplied. "What about this carriage, this dress? I 'ave . . . uh . . . *h*ave dozens more at home. Only been in New Orleans for three weeks, but it's already my favorite town. So many opportunities!"

"Are you—is there a man?"

"Is there bloody ever. He's a bloomin' Spanish grandee, forty-five, tall and dark and rich as the devil. *Very* peculiar in the bedroom. Met him on the boat. I had to leave Boston in a bit of a hurry."

"Boston? You were in Boston?"

"I've been all over, luv. Wait'll we get to the café. I'll tell you all about it. Just let us out here, Holt. We'll walk the rest of the way. You can take the carriage back home."

The coachman looked disturbed as we climbed down.

"What am I going to tell Don Rodriego?" he asked.

"Tell him I'm screwin' a sailor and don't know when I'll be back," Angie snapped.

The carriage drove on, and Angie and I passed stalls laden with baskets of fruit, carts full of flowers, wooden sheds with bloody carcasses hanging on racks, counters covered with heaps of glittery silver fish and long black eels. There were lobsters in wooden cages, tubs filled to the brim with shrimp. The market was a kaleidoscope of color and movement, the noise ear-splitting, the odors overwhelming. Flies abounded. The cobbles were littered with filth.

The café was on the edge of the market, tables and chairs sitting out in the open with only a tattered green awning to ward off the sun. We sat at one of the tables and ordered the marvelously strong coffee that had to be taken with cream. Angie sighed and shook her head again, gazing at me with those saucy brown eyes.

"That husky young farmer—" I began.

"George Andrews. Had him eatin' out of my hand in less than a week, had him marryin' me a month later. Couldn't keep his hands off me, George couldn't. As randy and robust a buck as I ever hope to meet. Had quite a large farm, lots of land. Poor George. Gored to death by a bull not more'n nine months after we were married. I *told* him that bull was vicious, told him not to buy it. He went ahead anyway, and two days later . . ." Angie hesitated and her eyes were sad.

"So you became a wealthy widow," I remarked.

"I sold the farm and all the land and took off," she replied. "I had a lot of unusual experiences, let me tell you! A year later I was penniless again. Damned scoundrel named Peter. Handsome as all get-out. Sneaked out of the inn with his shoes in one hand, my reticule in the other. Never saw the bastard again. Served me right for trustin' him. Then this distinguished British colonel came along, spent three days at the inn. When he left for Boston, I was in the carriage with him."

"A colonel?"

"Bleedin'. redcoats! Man was a wretched bore, always talking about rules and regulations, giving the citizens a hard time. No wonder they're so unruly with sods like him snapping orders all the time. I stuck with him for almost a year, though. He was so prim and official and stern in public, so bloody high-falutin' in his uniform, but when it was off, when he was alone in the bedroom with me, you'd of thought the bed was a bloomin' battlefield and me the enemy!"

"What happened eventually?"

"I got bored. Bastard was tight as hell, didn't like to spend money on me. Began to think I was some kinda servant. Actually expected me to polish his bloody boots! He got more and more difficult to live with, and after the Tea Party he was downright impossible. We got in a fierce argument about the tea that was dumped—"

"The famous Boston Tea Party? We heard about that even down here."

"Happened last December. These three big ships sailed into the harbor filled with tea—they were British East India Company vessels, and all that low-priced tea was gonna wreck havoc, establish a monopoly for the company and deprive the colonists of a lucrative source of revenue. They were riled up, I can tell you! Felt it was another example of British interference in colonial trade."

Angie paused as the waiter brought our coffee, a pitcher of cream, and a plate of doughy fried cakes sprinkled with sugar. She took a sip of the potent brew, grimaced, and then poured a generous amount of cream into her cup.

"Anyway, the rebels—that's what my colonel called 'em, 'damned bloody rebels'—they smeared themselves with dye and dressed up like Indians, rowed out to the ships, and dumped all the tea into the harbor, hootin' and hollerin' all the while. It caused *quite* a furor. The port of Boston was closed and'll stay closed till the tea's all paid for. I sided with the rebels, said they were only

349

protectin' their interests. Colonel Bates went into a rage, roarin' at me like I was some lowly private he intended to clap into irons after administerin' twenty lashes. I let him rage on, and that night while he was happily snoring away I picked the lock on his safe, filled my bag with lots of money, and slipped off into the night. Like a thief," she added, saucy grin flashing. "That was four months ago, and now here I am in New Orleans."

She reached back to pat the long silvery-blond ringlets dangling down to her shoulders. "I was fed up with the Colonies, to tell you the truth. Everyone's always so bloody worked up over things—the citizens rebellin' against the government, the soldiers damnin' the rebels. It's all going to explode one day soon. I decided to get out before the *real* fighting commences."

"Is it really that bad? We hear rumors, of course, but we're so far removed."

"It's bloody tiresome," Angie replied. "The soldiers are gettin' much stricter. The farmers are hidin' guns in the hayloft. But who wants to talk about that! I've told you all about me, and I'm dying to know how you ended up in New Orleans, lookin' like a bloody duchess. Come on, Marietta, tell me."

I stirred more cream into my coffee and gazed down at the cup, wondering how it would be possible to tell her all that had happened during these past four years. Pensive now, I told her about Derek and the plantation, Cassie and Adam and my helping them escape, Derek's rage and his selling me to Jeff Rawlins. Angie listened quietly as I continued, giving her a brief account of our journey down the Trace, telling her about the gambling house and that first difficult year before the place caught on.

"And?" she said when I had finished.

"And now it's very successful and . . . and Jeff and I are still together."

"And you still love this bloke Derek?"

"I'm afraid I do. I shouldn't. I have every reason to

350

hate him. I've tried to hate him. I can't. I . . . I don't actively think about him as much as I used to. Sometimes a full week will go by without my thinking of him at all, and then . . . then I'll find myself alone and suddenly he'll be in my mind and the pain will be as . . . as fresh as it was that day he sold me to Jeff."

"I guess I've been lucky," Angie reflected. "I've never been in love, not really. I was fond of George Andrews, and I was wildly taken with Peter Jamison, the bastard who ran off with my money. When he snuck off like that I missed him terribly, missed his handsome face, his gorgeous body and teasin' ways, but I missed the money a hell of a lot more, I can tell you for sure! What about this Jeff fellow?"

"He's good-looking in a rugged sort of way, and he's the most charming man you'll ever meet. He's a superb lover, and he worships the ground I walk on."

"But you don't love him?"

I hesitated a moment before answering, gazing across at the colorful marketplace. Black men wearing only ragged blue breeches were bringing in more baskets of shrimp. An old woman in black was examining bright-yellow lemons and golden oranges. An organ grinder with a monkey perched on his left shoulder strolled along eating bits of fried fish from a curled paper, sharing the tidbits with the monkey. How could I explain the way I felt about Jeff? It was so very complicated.

"I love him, yes," I said quietly. "But not in the way he'd like me to love him. It's a very special kind of love, more than just fondness. I enjoy sleeping with him, and the rest of the time I feel . . . almost maternal, protective. He needs me. He loves me quite desperately, and without me he'd be lost."

"You've been faithful?"

I nodded. "That's the least I can do. I wouldn't hurt him for the world."

"But still you won't marry him."

"It wouldn't be fair to him, Angie. Jeff deserves so

much more."

"Is *he* faithful?"

"There've been several women. He has one right now. None of them mean anything to him. He'll ask me to marry him again and I'll refuse again and then he'll feel angry and frustrated, feel he has to prove something. He'll go out and find another woman. But he invariably tires of them and comes back to me with that damned sheepish grin on his face."

"You've never considered leaving him?"

"I couldn't. I owe him a great deal, Angie. He—after Derek, he was my salvation. He gave me my freedom, gave me a whole new life. He needs me. One day he'll meet someone else and transfer all that love to her, and then I'll leave. Until that day comes I . . . I'll stick by him."

Angie sighed, and I could see that it was all too much for her to fully comprehend. Angie was one of the lucky ones, able to squeeze through life with jaunty aplomb, taking the good with the bad and considering it all a delicious joke. She had gone through just as many hardships as I since arriving in America, had had tragic and harrowing experiences left and right, yet she had changed very little. Her speech was a bit more refined, she wore beautiful clothes and had elegantly styled hair, yet she remained the feisty, audacious little cockney prostitute at heart. I had become a completely different person.

"It's getting late," I said. "I'd better get back. Jeff will be worried sick if I don't show up soon."

Angie made a face. "Guess I'd better get back to my bloody Spaniard, too. He's not much, but he's all I've got at the moment."

"You met him on the boat?"

"It was a dreary trip, I don't mind tellin' you. Don Rodriego livened it up a bit. The captain was shocked when I moved into Rodriego's cabin. He's a diplomat, rich as the devil, has a grand house here in the city and more servants that I can count."

"What's he like?"

"Tiresome," she admitted. "He's got this Latin temperament, you see. Seethin' with passion and rage. One minute he's threatin' to kill me, and the next he's smotherin' me with kisses. He's got some mighty funny ideas about what should take place in bed, too, but I won't go into that. He's generous, bought me all these gorgeous gowns soon as we landed, keeps me in grand style, but . . . it's not much fun! I'd leave him in a minute if I had any place else to go."

I suddenly had an idea. "Angie, do you really mean that?"

"Course I do. Who needs all that aggravation?"

"Tell me, do you know anything about cards?"

"Playing cards? There's nothing I *don't* know! The colonel had a passion for them. He and his cronies would sit up half the night, playing for high stakes. I sat in, learnin' all the tricks. Couple of months later I was cleanin' up. They finally refused to let me play, said I was a bloomin' sharp."

"How would you like to be a dealer?"

"At Rawlins Palace?" Angie's eyes flashed with excitement. "That'd be fantastic!"

"You know you'd have to be honest."

"I guess I could try," she said.

"You'd receive a regular salary, of course, and there's a guest room upstairs, right down the hall from mine. You could move in. We'd see each other every day."

"Done!" Angie exclaimed. "When do I start?"

"Tonight. We desperately need a dealer. We lost one two nights ago. I'll have one of the other dealers show you the ropes late this afternoon before the customers start arriving."

"What will your man Jeff think?"

"He'll be delighted," I assured her.

Ten minutes later we entered the still dim main entrance hall and walked up the marble staircase to the private living quarters. Angie was a bit nervous. She wasn't about to part with all those lovely gowns Rodriego

353

had bought her, and she feared he would fly into one of his wild Latin rages when she went back for them. I told her I would send Kyle along with her, explaining that he was six feet five and had the kind of grim, formidable expression that made the strongest men grow pale.

"Your Don Rodriego won't say a word," I promised, "not with Kyle at your side. Come on, I'll take you upstairs and introduce you to Jeff. He's probably still in the office."

He was indeed, sitting at his mahogany desk and frowning over a stack of papers. His dark-gold hair was unruly, a deep line dug a furrow above his nose, and his brown eyes were perplexed. Jeff handled all the business transactions, and of late he had been investing profits in various shipping ventures, none of which had yielded anything yet. I sometimes worried about that, but I assumed he knew what he was doing. He looked up irritably as we entered and then, spying Angie, got to his feet, reaching for the jacket he had discarded earlier.

I introduced them. Jeff was charming and gallant. Angie was enchanted. He was slightly taken aback when I told him she was to be our new dealer, was going to move into the guest room, but he quickly recovered, agreeing that it was a dandy idea and graciously adding that having such a pretty dealer at the table was bound to stimulate business. Angie expressed her delight in ribald terms, her choice of words causing Jeff to grin. We left him with his paperwork and went downstairs to find Kyle.

He was just coming up from the cellar as we reached the bottom of the stairs. Kyle had been one of Jeff's cronies during the old days, had fallen upon hard times and, when Jeff finally located him, had been living in a sordid room on the waterfront, sick, hungry, resigned to his fate with the deep melancholy that was part of his nature. He was the first employee hired, the highest paid. He opened the door for guests with impeccable servility, never spoke except to answer a question, and barred the way to anyone who didn't meet the standards of Rawlins Palace. When he had to remove one of the guests, he did so firmly, silently, rarely finding it necessary to employ his awesome strength.

Kyle was intensely loyal to Jeff, would have killed for him without a moment's hesitation. Cheerless, intimidating, he doubled as coachman during the day and frequently helped out by doing things like taking inventory of the wine cellar, which had occupied him for most of the day. Kyle had nothing to do with any of the other employees; he kept to himself. His job and his devotion to Jeff left room for little else.

When Angie saw him approaching us down the shadowy hallway, she gasped and gripped my hand.

"Christ!" she exclaimed. "He's a bloody giant! That face would make small children shriek in terror."

Kyle gave no indication that he had heard. Incredibly tall, with wide shoulders and a lean, muscular frame, he wore black boots, black breeches, a white cambric shirt with full sleeves, and a brown-and-white-striped satin vest. He had pale, sober features, extremely dark eyes, and sleek black hair brushed severely to one side. Although his manner toward me was invariably polite and formal, I was still a bit uncomfortable around him. Most people were. He gave the impression of a man with great violence pent up inside, and he had never been known to smile. I had the feeling that Kyle disapproved of me, that he disapproved of everyone but Jeff.

"Hello, Kyle," I said pleasantly. "This is Angie. She's a friend of mine, and she's going to be our new dealer."

Kyle didn't speak. Neither did Angie. They sized each other up, his expression bleak and morose, hers saucily defiant, as though she were about to thrust her tongue out at him. Kyle frightened the maids. Pierre broke into a fit of nervous tremors whenever the giant stepped into the kitchen. Angie wasn't at all intimidated. Kyle clearly presented a challenge. I had visions of a small, scrappy terrier nipping and snarling at a gigantic, bored mastiff.

"Angie needs to go fetch her things," I continued.

"She's going to move into the extra room upstairs. I'd like for you to take her in the carriage and go inside with her. It might be a bit uncomfortable."

"Not bloody likely!" Angie cried. "Don Rodriego will take one look at 'im and crawl under the bed. Are you sure it's safe for me to go traipsin' off with him? I've been raped before, but never by anything this size! I'm not sure I wouldn't take my chances with Rodriego's wrath."

Kyle's dark eyes hardened with disdain, and his wide mouth curled contemptuously at one corner, but he still made no comment. Instead he fetched his jacket, put it on, and held the front door open for her. Angie winked at me, emitted a delighted titter, and sashayed out with high heels tapping and ruffled skirt swishing noisily. Kyle followed her out like a sober martyr. I rather fancied that he had met his match.

Three hours later I was in my room getting ready to dress for the evening when Jeff came sauntering in. I was in my petticoat, but he was already elegantly attired in a dark-brown frock coat, matching trousers, and a rather dashing vest of dark-orange satin embroidered with leaves in brown silk. His boots were polished to a glossy sheen, his hair neatly brushed. Curiously enough, the dandified attire emphasized his masculinity instead of detracting from it. I stepped over to adjust his brown silk cravat.

"You look quite handsome tonight," I remarked.

"Don't I always?"

"Always," I agreed.

"You're a lucky wench," he teased. "You look pretty damned fetchin' in that petticoat, too. If it hadn't taken me so long to get into these fancy duds, I'd get right out of 'em and give you a treat."

"Oh? That would be a change."

"Hey, do I detect a note of resentment? An important chap like me can't spend *all* his time pleasin' the ladies. I know I haven't come visitin' your bedroom for the past few nights, but . . . uh . . . I've been busy."

"Indeed," I said dryly, moving over to the dressing table.

I sat down in front of the mirror. Jeff stepped over to stand behind me, resting his hands on my bare shoulders, peering at me in the glass. I picked up a sable brush, dipped it into a pot of rouge, and began to brush a faint suggestion of pink on my cheekbones. He watched, his fingers gently squeezing my flesh. I put down the brush, picked up the powder puff, and began to powder my face. Jeff continued to watch, and I tried to ignore him. It wasn't easy.

"You're not mad, are you?" he asked.

"Of course not."

"I'll be gone for a while tonight. Won't be missed. That's the nice thing about the place. It almost runs itself, no need for me to hang around all the time."

I put down the powder puff. "No need at all."

"Fellow can take a night off every now and then, take care of business, see his old friends once in a while."

I brushed my lids with light mauve shadow and applied a touch of cinnamon-brown paste to lashes and brows with a tiny brush. Jeff's fingers dug into my shoulders, not gentle, not quite hurting.

"You know, I wish I could believe you really were jealous. I don't know why I even bother looking at another woman when I have someone like you right here at my fingertips. It's just—"

"You don't owe me any explanations, Jeff."

"You could stop it. You could put an end to it once and for all. With two words—'I will.' "

I did not reply. He was frowning now, his brown eyes dark. He let go of me and stepped over to the table to pour himself a brandy from the crystal decanter. I touched up my lips with coral, patted my hair back in place and got up, moving over to the wardrobe to take down my dress, pale-yellow silk, the skirt aglitter with flowers embroidered in silver and gold. Jeff gazed into his glass of brandy, still frowning.

"I'm sorry, Jeff," I said quietly. "I told you in the

357

beginning I wouldn't marry you. I appreciate everything you've done for me. You know that. You're very dear to me. You know that, too. Any time you want me to leave I'll—"

"Don't talk nonsense!" he said harshly. "You know I don't want you to leave."

I slipped into the dress, sure his bad humor would pass, as it always did. These moods came over him rarely, but when they did they usually resulted in some noisy brawl on the waterfront with the rowdy companions he still saw regularly. He would drink himself silly, come staggering home in the middle of the night, and feel wretched and apologetic the next day. And I would feel terribly guilty, knowing I was to blame, yet unable to do the one thing that would prevent these periodic outbursts. I would sit by the bed and bathe his temples with a cloth dipped in cologne, and I would smile and gently scold and reassure him of my affection in a thousand little ways, giving him affection when he wanted undying love.

"Sorry," he said. "Didn't mean to bark like that."

He downed the brandy and set the empty glass down.

"Jeff, promise me you won't drink too much."

"Fellow needs to loosen up once in a while."

"I always worry about you."

He lifted a brow. "Really?"

"You know I do."

"I guess that's one consolation," he said wearily.

I finished fastening the dress and stepped back from the full-length mirror to adjust the puffed sleeves that fell off the shoulder. The yellow went extremely well with my auburn hair, gleaming with coppery highlights in the bright glow of the candles. Satisfied, I turned away from the glass, deciding not to wear the diamonds tonight.

"How's your little friend doin'? She get moved in all right?"

I nodded. "She's downstairs at one of the tables right now. Frank and George were supposed to be giving her instructions, showing her how to deal. There was a huge

358

pile of chips in front of her. Frank and George both looked a bit perturbed."

He grinned at that. "I like her. She oughta work out just fine."

"I'm a bit worried about Kyle," I remarked.

"He scare her?"

"Not at all. I think she scares *him*. She was cocky and insulting when they first met, and when they came back she had him carrying her things up like he was her own personal lackey, bossing him about outrageously. Kyle looked thunderous."

Jeff chuckled. "It's about time someone shook Kyle up a bit. Chap's much too gloomy. Well . . . uh . . . I reckon I'd better get goin'. I don't know when I'll be back. You behave yourself while I'm gone, hear?"

"You behave, too."

"Not much chance of that," he said jauntily.

He left then, and I sighed. He would pay a call on Corinne, would make love to her and feel manly and strong as she yielded, and then he would join his gang of friends and they would make a round of the taverns. He had done it innumerable times in the past . . . . why should I be so concerned now? It wasn't just Jeff, I realized. Standing there in the middle of the beautifully appointed room, the soft candlelight causing my skirt to shimmer, I realized it was something more. Although I couldn't determine the reason, I was curiously disturbed. It was . . . it was almost as though I had a premonition. Something was going to happen. I could feel it in my bones.

Nonsense, I told myself. I was tired. It had been an unusually stimulating day, what with meeting Angie and talking so much about the past. I had been thinking of Derek a lot, and that was never good. Picking up my fan of yellow ostrich feathers, I left the room and walked down the hallway to the white marble staircase. As I started down, Kyle was just admitting the first customers. They were laughing, ready to have a good time. One of them saw me on the stairs. I smiled, the beautiful hostess, beautifully gowned, but try though I might I couldn't shake the feeling that something catastrophic was going to happen . . . quite soon.

XVIII

Lucille examined the sketch and knitted her brow in disapproval, immediately suggesting a bow here, a row of ruffles there, but I was adamant. She threw her hands in the air and then scrutinizing the sketch again, she finally began to nod vigorously.

"Yes, yes, I see. I see! The simplicity—it's cunning! The gown shall be cloth of gold—it'll cost you the earth, you know—and with all that gold you don't *need* the ruffles, the bows. You're a genius, Marietta! It will be the most stunning gown I've ever made."

"The skirt must be very, very full," I reminded her, "like a great golden bell, the sleeves narrow, off the shoulder, just as I've indicated in the sketch."

Lucille nodded briskly. I was her only customer this afternoon. Her assistants were in the cutting room, unpacking bolts of cloth and gossiping like merry magpies. Gray hair piled atop her head in a mass threatening to spill down at any second; thin, sharp face heavily rouged, she was a spry, brisk, frequently dictatorial creature in her late fifties who had devoted her life to the creation of beautiful gowns. She invariably wore a long-sleeved, high-necked black taffeta dress and dangling garnet earrings. She smoked thin black cigars, an eccentric habit her more respectable customers found utterly shocking. She lighted one now, exhaling plumes of smoke, flicking ashes into a white porcelain saucer she kept on top of the counter.

"I only hope you never open a shop of your own," she exclaimed, peering at the sketch once more. "You'd soon run me out of business! Most of my customers have no idea what they want—you always bring a sketch, never let me do anything but run up the gown you've already designed. You have a genius for it. I mean that sincerely. There's not a woman in New Orleans so splendidly dressed, and the gowns are all your own creation. I'm surprised you even let me make them for you."

"If I had time to sew, I probably wouldn't," I admitted. "I'm quite good with a needle."

Lucille threw up her hands again, wispy strands of gray hair slipping down over her brow. "It's a waste! A shocking waste! You should be doing it for a living—though I hope you never decide to. Playing cards in a gambling house! A shocking waste," she repeated. "If only you'd been born pinched and plain like me. You'd have *had* to put your genius to use. The cloth has already arrived—" Lucille's conversation darted hither and yon with abrupt changes of subject that frequently dismayed those not used to her. "Do you want to see it?"

I nodded. Lucille gripped the cigar in the corner of her mouth, clapped her hands and, when one of the girls hurried out, instructed her to bring out the cloth of gold. When it came, Lucille draped a swath across the counter. It shimmered richly, gleaming like molten gold liquid. Lucille flicked an ash in the general direction of the saucer.

"All the way from Paris," she informed me. "That's a secret, by the way. God knows what I'd do if it weren't for Valjean and his crew! My very best goods are smuggled in through the bayous in the dead of night. They're our salvation, these smugglers. New Orleans would be lost without them. Of course, the Spanish are *livid*, but there's nothing they can do about it. Valjean and his ilk are much too clever."

"If it weren't for smuggled goods, half the shops in

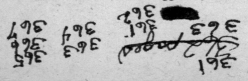

the city would be empty of merchandise," I said, "and the wine cellars would be empty, too. Jeff gets a monthly consignment of bottles. The men always come in the middle of the night, long after the place has closed."

"Making a fortune, the smugglers are! Charge the earth! I've no doubt they'll own the city one day. Romantic figures, too. The man who delivered this cloth—if I'd been thirty years younger!"

I smiled, knowing she longed to tell me about him. "What did he look like?" I asked.

"Tall," she said, "and ever so grim! The cart pulled up in the back alley—it was well after midnight. I was expecting them, was waiting at the back door with a candle. He stepped out of the shadows wearing a long black cloak and pirate boots. Gave me quite a turn! As cold as an iceberg he was, with windblown raven hair and piercing gray eyes. There was a thin pink scar from his temple to the corner of his mouth, made him even handsomer. Handsome as a lord, that man, and just as aloof. He had two lackeys with him, didn't say a word, just stood there in the alley with his cloak flapping in the wind while his men carried in the bolts of cloth. Acted as though he loathed what he was doing, didn't even count the money when I paid him."

"They're a strange lot," I remarked. "A necessary evil. Are you sure the gown will be ready in time?"

"Positive. Have I ever failed you? You'll wear the diamonds with it, of course?"

I nodded. Lucille sighed and shook her head. More gray hair spilled down, and three or four hairpins clattered to the floor. She put her cigar out, jabbing it viciously into the saucer.

"Such a generous man, that Mr. Rawlins," she said. "He came in just a few days ago—Oh Lord! I shouldn't have—" She looked up at me with distressed black eyes.

"I would imagine he came in with Corrine," I said calmly. "I know you make all her gowns, too."

"That one!" she snapped. "No imagination! It's always pink, pink and more pink! Pink satin, pink velvet, pink silk! She looks marvelous in it, of course, but you'd think—" Lucille waved her thin hands, disgusted. "I don't know what he sees in her."

"She's a very beautiful woman."

"You're so calm about it."

"Jeff will tire of her sooner or later."

"Sooner, I fancy. She's a sullen, moody thing, always pouting, always looking tragic and forlorn. She was in one of her moods when they came in the other day, complaining to him in that husky voice, threatening to kill herself if he—"

"I really don't care to hear about it, Lucille," I interrupted.

"I just babble away, never stop and think. Forgive me, dear. He *is* a charmer, isn't he? You've very fortunate. I just hope you don't have to sell those diamonds he gave you!"

"What on earth are you talking about?"

Lucille frowned and looked distressed again, and then she lighted another cigar, her thin face suddenly hard, all business.

"The fact is, dear, that he owes me a fortune. Hasn't paid the bill in months. He was always a bit late, of course, but I never actually worried until recently. You see, he's supposed to be paying for all *her* gowns, too, and what with the bill you run up every month—" She hesitated. "I really shouldn't have mentioned it, I know, but—"

"Give me a copy of the bill," I said. "Both bills, hers and mine. I can assure you they'll be paid tomorrow."

"Oh Lord, you're not angry?" Her distress was genuine.

"Of course not," I said quietly. "I'm embarrassed, Lucille. I had no idea Jeff hadn't been paying you every month. He—he's so busy with all his investments and such. I'm sure he just let it slip his mind."

Lucille stepped into the back room and returned a minute or so later with two long sheets with every purchase neatly itemized. Before folding them up, I glanced at the amount shown at the bottom of each sheet. The total owed was a staggering amount. No wonder Lucille had finally spoken up. I was furious with Jeff for letting the bills go for so long a time.

"Now don't you fret," Lucille told me. "Gentlemen never pay a single bill on time. It's against their principles! I'm not really worried about the money, but . . . well, I *do* have to keep the place going."

"I understand. It won't happen again."

"And now we'll just forget it. So unpleasant! Pompadour had a gown made from cloth like this. I didn't make it, of course. My shop was much too humble—never really came into my own until I left France." She began to roll the gleaming material back on the bolt. "Frigid woman, Pompadour. Don't know what the king ever saw in her. She was little more than a procuress, actually, had a whole bevy of nubile young girls ready to keep him amused when he grew bored with her constant chit-chat."

Kyle was waiting for me with the carriage as I stepped outside. Expressionless, silent, he helped me into the seat upholstered in dark-blue leather, then took his place in front, cracked the whip, and drove away. The carriage was open, and I was assailed by the sights, sounds, and smells of New Orleans. We were near the waterfront. I could smell the tar, the oil, the bales of cotton. A short while later we were driving through one of the better residential areas and there was the splash of fountains behind walls, the scent of exotic flowers, the beauty of iron balconies and marvelously designed iron gates.

Kyle let me out in front of Rawlins Palace, then drove on to put the carriage away. I stepped inside, angry with Jeff, determined to speak to him immediately. As I went upstairs, I felt again that curious, subtle feeling of vague alarm I had first experienced over a month ago, the day Angie had arrived. It had never left, really. It had been with me all the while, just beneath the surface. A premonition, I had called it. A month had passed and that catastrophic event hadn't occurred, yet the feeling remained. I tried to tell myself it was pure nonsense, a matter of strained nerves and discontent, but as I walked down the

365

hall to Jeff's office, the sensation of impending doom was stronger than ever.

The office was empty, desktop littered with papers, the smell of whiskey strong. A half-empty bottle sat on a small table beside the desk, glass beside it. Frowning, I stepped to the door of his room and knocked. A merry voice called out, bidding me enter. Jeff was dressing for the evening, tucking the white cambric shirt into the waistband of his snug tan breeches. He looked up and grinned, eyes full of pleasure and delight.

"Just in time," he told me. "I can manage the waist-coat and jacket, but I doubt I can fold my neckcloth properly. Gotta look dandy for th' customers—" His voice was slightly thick, his cheeks flushed.

"You're drunk," I said coldly.

"Aw, not drunk, love, just a mite tipsy. Feelin' good. Man needs to feel good ever now an' then."

"Jeff—"

"Now look!" he interrupted. "I don't want no naggin'. I can drink if I want to. Those bloody accounts—'d take a wizard to keep 'em all straight in 'is head. Figures an' numbers, so much here, so much there—drive a man up the wall. Oughta get a bookkeeper. That's what I oughta do."

"Perhaps you should."

"Acid. I detect acid in your voice. My, my—we're cold an' haughty, ain't we. Just 'cause I had a couple. Come on, love, be a love. Be my gentle, understandin' Marietta."

"I think perhaps I've been too understanding."

"I love you, ya know. That's why I made all them 'vestments, 'cause I love you and wanna be rich, really rich. I get rich enough, you'll marry me an' we'll live happily-ever-after—" The last three words slurred together into one.

Shirt tucked in properly, he reached for the rakish yellow waistcoat patterned with brown and bronze flowers. He staggered just a little as he stepped over to the mirror.

366

He put the waistcoat on and smoothed it down, stepping back to examine himself.

"Good-lookin' man," he said, addressing his reflection. "Damned handsome. Gonna be rich, too, soon as them investments pay off. Rich an' handsome."

He turned to face me then. His grin was lopsided. He peered at me, and the grin vanished. The merriment went out of his eyes. He pressed his brows together in that irritable scowl that was becoming increasingly familiar.

"All right," he said sullenly. "You got somethin' on your mind. What is it?"

I took the bills out of my recticule and handed them to him. He peered down at them, still scowling, finding it difficult to focus.

"What're these?"

"They're bills, Jeff. From Lucille. Two. One for my dresses. One for Corinne's."

"So you found out about that?"

"I've known about Corinne for months. It isn't that."

"*She* loves me. Did ya know that? Loves me. Been beggin' me to leave you, beggin' me to marry her. Ain't just th' money either. She's had lotsa men richer'n me, could find one twice as rich tomorrow. Thinks I'm th' most wonderful man—"

"I'm not interested in that," I said sharply. "The bills haven't been paid, Jeff. You've let them go for months. I was humiliated. Lucille works very hard, and—"

"I'll pay them tomorrow!"

"See that you do, Jeff."

I turned and left the room then before either of us could say words we would regret later on.

Reaching my own bedroom, I sighed, forcing myself to calm down and forget the scene just enacted. Jeff would pay the bills, would be humble and apologetic, and I would forgive him, just as I always did. I couldn't help worrying, nevertheless. How many other bills remained unpaid? Was he running short of money? We made a good profit here every week after expenses, and I had assumed there was a large amount in the bank. Was there? Jeff

367

never discussed finances with me, had given me only a sketchy description of the investments he had been making, assuring me they would bring in piles of profit in just a little while. I wondered just how much he *had* invested. Jeff fancied himself a shrewd businessman. I wasn't so sure of that.

I took my time getting ready, and it was almost an hour before I was ready to go downstairs. My auburn hair was arranged in waves in front, long ringlets dangling down in back, and I was wearing the dark-blue velvet gown that was one of my favorites. I decided to wear the diamond necklace Jeff had given me two years ago, when we had known for certain that Rawlins Palace was going to be successful. The diamonds rested against my skin in a web of glittering pendants alive with silver and violet fires. Inspecting myself in the full-length mirror, I was satisfied with my appearance. I only wished I felt as serene and composed as I looked.

I went down to the kitchen to check with Pierre. He was in a flurry as usual, slamming pots and pans, snapping orders at his underlings, complaining that the hams weren't properly glazed, the roast not sliced thinly enough. I flattered him outrageously, assured him everything would be done to perfection. He begged me to sample one of the tiny frosted cakes. I did so as the marmalade cat watched resentfully. Pierre reminded me that we were running out of the expensive French wine our customers had come to expect. I told him it was supposed to be delivered tonight, after the place was closed. Pierre made a face to indicate his disdain of the smugglers, and then he began to stir the cheese sauce vigorously.

I went back up to the main floor. The young waiters who would serve food and drink in the ballroom had all arrived and were standing at attention as Kyle inspected them with a severe expression. The crystal chandeliers shed dazzling light over the gaming rooms. The tables were all ready, cards in place, and the dealers in their handsome uniform jackets were waiting for the first customers to arrive. Angie hurried over to join me as I entered. She was wearing a lovely white silk gown adorned with violet ribbons. There was a mischievous look in her eyes.

"That bloody Kyle," she said. "I guess I gave him what for. He told me I'd better watch myself, said he had his eye on me! I've been as honest as the day is long since the day I arrived, haven't cheated once! I told him to go get laid. He was terribly upset."

"When are you and Kyle going to stop this constant bickering?"

"Soon as he makes up his mind to *do* somethin'," Angie replied. "Oh, he *wants* to all right. I guess I know that much. You should have seen the look he gave me when I met him in the hall this morning—I know what's on his mind. He thinks he's too high and mighty to tumble to a bit of goods like me, thinks he might demean himself, but he's dyin' to have me."

I smiled. "You've been teasing him again."

"Bloody right I have," she admitted. "He's going to break down any day now and pull me into the first handy broom closet. Truth to tell, I can hardly wait!"

"You're incorrigible, Angie."

"I know," she sighed. "When I see a man I fancy I just can't seem to help myself. Kyle's ever so intriguin'—never met a man so hard to get. He's so bleedin' solemn and so *big*. Gives me goose bumps just thinkin' about it!"

"Poor Kyle. He doesn't stand a chance."

"Not bloody likely. You look smashin' tonight, Marietta. That blue dress, cut so *low*. Goes well with your hair, too. And those diamonds! You look like a duchess."

"Thank you," I said, distracted. "Angie, have—have you seen Jeff?"

"He came down almost an hour ago," she replied. "I smiled at him and said 'Good evenin' ' and he just walked right on past, like he wasn't aware I was there."

"He went out?"

Angie nodded. "Looked like he was ready to tear one on. Looked like he'd already started, if you want to know the truth. The smell of whiskey almost knocked me over."

I shook my head and gave a weary sigh.

"Did you two have words?" she asked.

"It was foolish, really. He'd been drinking, and it wasn't terribly pleasant. I spoke rather sharply. We didn't really argue, but I do wish he hadn't gone off like that."

"He'll be all right. Always is, isn't he? Oh, he'll have a wretched hangover tomorrow, of course, but then he'll be a bloomin' prince for two or three weeks, charming as can be, trying to make up for slipping again."

"I know it's silly to worry. It's just—I've had this curious feeling, as if something dreadful is going to happen."

"Nonsense. He'll probably be back before we close. Cheer up, luv. Oh dear, here come the bloody marks. Got to get to my table. Old Langley looks full of mischief, must have a big roll on him. Don't you worry now. Have a glass of champagne."

Angie hurried over to her table, greeting Charles Langley with a ribald remark that caused him to bellow with laughter. She was vastly popular with the customers, saucy, spirited, enjoying herself immensely every night. That enjoyment was infectious, and her table was always crowded. The place began to fill up rapidly with merry, optimistic gentlemen who would become tense as the evening progressed, with lovely, amoral women who would become quickly bored and prowl restlessly. I immersed myself in my duties, greeting the regular customers, smiling at new ones, circulating around the rooms. I let one of the regulars buy me a glass of champagne and agreed to play a hand for another. An hour passed, then two, and still I couldn't get Jeff off my mind, couldn't stop worrying about him.

I took a second glass of champagne and wandered into the ballroom. It was filled with guests who weren't playing. Women in gorgeous gowns sat on the sofas, gossiping and flirting. Men in elegant attire talked about their winnings, their losses, drinking steadily to give themselves courage to return to the tables. Food was being served. Corinne was holding court in one of the corners, sumptuous in pink satin, her dark, lustrous hair gleaming. Although she was surrounded by attentive men, she kept glancing around restlessly, making no effort to conceal her boredom. So Jeff isn't with her tonight, I thought. He and his boisterous friends were probably in some waterfront tavern, getting ready to wreck the place.

A gruff, noisy voice assailed my ears as I stepped back into the hallway. Kyle was standing in front of the door, barring the way to a tall man with powerful shoulders. His brown suit was decidedly shabby, his yellow stock creased and stained. His mouth was too wide, his nose hawk-like, his blond locks tumbled.

"Ain't my bleedin' money good enough for you?" he cried huskily. "See here, I got five pounds. Who do ya think you are, mate? I'm warnin' you better step aside or fists are gonna fly! You may be a bloomin' giant, but that don't bother me one bloody bit. Reckon I could take you on with no trouble. Shove off now, mate. Don't wanna hurt you."

I stared at the man, unable to believe it, and then I felt a rush of pleasure. I hurried over to the door. Kyle had been patient enough, but I could tell he was ready to take the necessary measures. The blond had his fists doubled up.

"Let him in, Kyle," I said.

"I think not," Kyle replied grimly. "He's riff-raff. A troublemaker as well."

"Riff-raff, am I! No one calls Jack Reed names like that without gettin' a bloody nose!"

"Let him in," I repeated.

Kyle looked at me with dark, resentful eyes, but he stepped aside nevertheless. Jack Reed sauntered into the hall with that swinging, bouncy walk that betrayed his years at sea.

"Bloody lackey," he said. "You'd think he owned th' bloody place. Thanks for the help, ma'am."

"Hello, Jack," I said quietly.

371

"I say, how'd ya know my—" He cut himself short. He stared at me, eyes wide with dismay. "Sweet Jesus!" he exclaimed. "It *is* you, isn't it?"

I nodded, smiling warmly. Jack's wide mouth split into a grin.

"I knew it! I knew you'd end up wearin' fancy gowns an' diamonds! A lass like you, it was bound to be. What's it been—four years? Five? I say, this is bloody wonderful, seein' you again."

"Come to lose your money, Jack?"

"Come to *win* is more like it. Five pounds is all I got to me name, but once I get to them tables that's gonna change. I'm feelin' real lucky, and runnin' into you's gotta be a good omen. I still can't believe it!"

"Have you had supper yet, Jack?" I inquired.

He shook his head. "Didn't wanna waste any of my money on food. Asked 'em what was th' best gamblin' place in New Orleans and they give me this address. Then your bleedin' lackey tried to keep me out. I'm rarin' to get to them tables."

"Perhaps you'd like a little food first," I suggested. "We could dine together. You could tell me what you've been doing. You'll be my guest, of course."

"Wouldn't mind a bite or two," Jack admitted. "You own this place?"

"I help run it. My—my good friend owns it."

"I see," he said, eyes twinkling. "Always figured you'd get yourself hooked up with someone important. Knocks me over to see you doin' so well. Sure you wanna waste time talkin' to a rowdy bloke like me?"

I smiled and took his hand. "Quite sure," I told him. "Come along. We'll have a lovely chat and some food, and then I'll turn you loose in the gaming rooms. I've the feeling you *are* going to be lucky."

Kyle watched with stern disapproval as I led Jack down the hall and into the ballroom. I summoned a waiter and asked him to bring food and wine, then led Jack over to the alcove where Jeff and I usually dined. There was a small table, covered with a snowy white cloth, and two comfortable chairs. Although it opened directly onto the ballroom floor, an urn of tall greenery gave us some privacy. Jack was a bit uncomfortable now, awed by all this splendor, aware of his shabby suit, his shaggy, uncombed locks. The waiter brought champagne in a silver bucket and returned a few moments later with our food. I smiled warmly at Jack, doing my best to put him at ease.

"What brings you to New Orleans?" I inquired.

"On my way to Natchez," he explained. "Done my last bit o' seafarin', I 'ave. Thought it was time for a bit of settlin' down. They say Natchez is th' comin' spot. Up in th' Colonies ain't nothin' but bleedin' rebels stirrin' up trouble and bein' disloyal to England. Lotta folks loyal to th' King 've been movin' down to Natchez, sendin' their possessions down by flatboat."

I had heard about that. A General Lyman had brought a group of military people to Natchez and laid out several townships in the vicinity, and it was estimated that over four hundred families had emigrated to the budding city in the summer of '73 alone. Jeff had predicted that it would soon grow to rival New Orleans, and it looked as though his prediction was going to come true sooner than anyone expected. Actually, Natchez was a fourteenth colony of Britain and, because of its remoteness, blessedly removed from the conflicts boiling in the other thirteen.

"Reckon I can find work easily enough," Jack continued. "New buildings are springin' up every day. They need men to help build. Friend o' mine told me all about it, urged mc to come."

I opened the bottle of champagne. The cork popped loudly. Jack shook his head, sighing, as I poured the sparkling beverage into our glasses. He smiled, studying me with fond eyes.

"Lotta time 'as passed since we had our little tussles on board ship. You've become a grand lady."

"Hardly that," I told him.

"'Deed you 'ave. Surprised you'd even speak to a shaggy ruffian like me."

"Don't be silly."

"I'm happy for you," he said. "Does me good to see you such a bloomin' success."

"I'm sure you'll be successful, too, Jack."

"Aw, bloke like me'll never amount to much, but if I can win enough to pay my fare to Natchez and keep me from starvin' till I get a job, I reckon I'll get by. Bloke like me doesn't require much."

As we drank our champagne and ate the delicious food, Jack began to relax, no longer intimidated by the splendor surrounding us. He related some of his experiences during the past four years. He had been through a hurricane and a mutiny, and had helped harpoon a whale. Finally weary of the seafaring life, he had jumped ship in Jamaica and had worked in the cane fields there until he had enough to pay his passage to New Orleans. He had arrived only this morning and wasn't at all taken with the city. It was too bloody big, for one thing, and it smelled like a cesspit. He couldn't wait to get up to Natchez where there was clean air and good British folks who didn't jabber in Spanish and French.

When the meal was finished, I took him into the gaming rooms. A few of the customers looked askance at his shabby apparel, but most of them were far too engrossed to pay attention to anything but the cards they held. Jack wanted to know if we would take English pound notes. I assured him we would, leading him over to Angie's table.

"This is Angie," I told him. "She was on the ship, too."

"Christ! This is like old 'ome week."

"Jack Reed!" Angie exclaimed. "I remember you. Handsomest sailor on board. Sit down, sailor. I have a feeling this is going to be your lucky night."

"So do I," I said meaningfully.

Angie understood at once. She gave me a tiny nod. The other players were a bit disgruntled by the attention she paid to him, and they were dismayed by his incredible luck. Angie was very subtle. He didn't win too much at once, he lost a little now and then, but the cards were definitely in his favor. Jack was elated, and as his winnings steadily mounted he grew more and more excited. A crowd gathered around the table. There was an air of excitement, people urging him on, giving advice. Everyone liked to see a winner, and Jack's lusty cries and boyish exuberance made him a favorite with the crowd. They enjoyed his success vicariously, were stimulated to try and match it. It was well after midnight before he finally got up from the table, over two hundred pounds richer.

"Pretty good for one night's work," he admitted.

"I'm worn out," Angie declared. "I've never seen such bloody luck!"

"Serves you right," one of the players teased. "You're always taking us. It's high time you were took yourself."

"Piss off, Dalton. Everyone knows you're helpless in bed and hopeless at cards!"

Dalton roared with laughter along with the others. Angie's insults were a token of esteem. The regulars delighted in them. Her silvery-blond hair was slightly disarrayed now, her gown a bit crumpled. She gave Jack a long, hard look, knitting her brows together.

"If you didn't have such innocent blue eyes I'd swear you were a bleedin' sharp!"

"Mighty obliged to you," Jack said, flashing a cocky grin.

"Get on with you! I've got to win some of that money back or I'll be sacked for sure. Come on, men, place your bets! We've only got an hour or so left to play. So long, sailor."

"Be seein' you," he called.

Jack put his money away in a thin leather pouch, and I walked out front with him. It was a sultry night with a full moon half-hidden by dark, drifting clouds. Moonlight gilded the cobbles with a silvery sheen and intensified the heavy black shadows. Jack sighed wearily, gazing up at the moon for a moment, then looking at me with a rueful smile.

"Reckon it was my lucky night after all," he remarked.

"It certainly was."

"You didn't have to do that, you know."

"Do what?" I asked innocently.

"Oh, I saw what the two of you were up to, saw right from the start. I'm lucky, but I ain't *that* lucky. I'm pretty good at cards, you know. I probably could've won fair and square."

"I didn't want to take any chances."

"No?"

"You were very kind to me once, Jack. Let's just say this was my way of repaying some of that kindness."

"You're a real lady," he said, "as fine a lady as I ever 'ope to meet. I always knew you was, even when we was on the boat."

"I suppose you'll be leaving for Natchez now," I said, changing the subject quickly.

"First boat I can get," he replied. "Reckon I'd better get back to my room now, took one this mornin' down by the waterfront, stored all my gear there."

I peered down the dark, deserted street, a nest of sinister shadows broken only here and there with wavering rays of moonlight. I was apprehensive, for New Orleans was filled with footpads and thieves who would slit a throat for much less money than Jack was carrying. Sensing my concern, he reached under his jacket and pulled out a long, narrow club bound with leather strips. He slashed the air with it, grinning.

"Any man fool enough to tangle with Jack Reed'll get a bashed 'ead for 'is trouble. Don't you worry. I can take care of myself."

"Do be careful, Jack."

"I will. Maybe we'll run into each other again, lass. Never can tell. You might get down to Natchez one o' these days. I might see you there. I wish you 'appiness."

"And I you, Jack."

He nodded and started down the street with that jaunty, dipping sailor's walk and was soon swallowed up by the shadows. I stood there in front of the steps for a few moments, listening to the echo of his footsteps, and finally there was silence.

I went back inside and resumed my duties. Customers were beginning to leave now, and an hour later only the most persistent remained, determined to make up their losses. The ballroom was empty, the waiters clearing up, carrying trays of dishes down to the kitchen. Two of them carefully lowered the chandeliers until they almost touched the floor and held the ropes steady while another snuffed out all the candles. Candles still flickered in the wall sconces, but the room was now awash with shadows. I strolled back into the gaming rooms. The hangers-on were leaving, cheerfully shooed away by a weary, wilting Angie.

"What a night," she said. "We made a killing. I more than doubled what Jack won. All the chaps were eager to match his luck. Fancy him showin' up like that."

The other dealers were putting things away. Ordinarily Jeff acted as cashier, taking charge of all the money. Now Kyle was counting it in his absence, tallying figures on a sheet of paper and finally carrying it all up to the safe in Jeff's office. The dealers left. Angie and I stood together in the main gaming room.

"You're still worried about Jeff, aren't you?"

I nodded. "I can't help it. He didn't go to see Corinne. She was here earlier, holding court, looking disappointed because he wasn't around. He was in one of his moods when he left."

"He'll be all right, Marietta."

"I suppose so. I just wish I could shake this feeling."

Kyle came back downstairs to supervise locking up. I asked him if he knew the places where Jeff and his cronies usually spent their evenings on the town. Kyle gave me a solemn nod.

"She's worried," Angie said. "Why don't you take the carriage and go look for him, see that he gets home safely? You don't have anything *else* to do tonight."

"Would you, Kyle?" I asked. "I'd feel so much better knowing you were with him."

"The men with the wine will be here in half an hour. I have to let them in the back gate, pay them for the goods."

"I can attend to that."

Kyle was clearly reluctant. Angie gave him an exasperated look.

"Come on, Goliath. I'll go with you, keep you company. While we're lookin' for him I'll tell you the story of my life."

"The places I'll be going aren't suitable for a woman."

"Suitable? That's a bleedin' laugh. There's not a place in New Orleans I haven't been in one twice as bad. Besides, I'll have you to protect me, won't I? Don't just stand there lookin' like a dunce. Go get the carriage and bring it round!"

Kyle glowered at her with menacing eyes, but he obeyed nevertheless. Angie trotted upstairs to fetch her cloak and came merrily back down a few moments later, all traces of weariness gone. When the carriage pulled up in front, she blew me a kiss and dashed outside, white silk skirts fluttering. I locked the door and went upstairs to Jeff's office. The smugglers always demanded to be paid in gold coin. Opening the safe, I found the small chamois bag of gold that had been set aside for them.

When I went back downstairs some twenty minutes later, the place was silent and still, the rooms dark, only a few candles left burning in the hall. I hadn't bothered to get a cloak, and my blue velvet skirt rustled softly as I moved toward the back doors that opened onto the courtyard. I should have removed the diamond necklace, I thought. It might not be wise to let the smugglers see me wearing such valuable gems. They were bound to be ruffians. I would simply have to risk it, as there was no time to return to my room. I took up the lantern kept in a wall niche by the door, lighted it, and stepped out into the courtyard.

The moon was behind a bank of clouds. The courtyard was shrouded with thick, heavy shadows thrown into even sharper relief by the flickering glow of the lantern. There was a strong wind that caused the palm fronds to rustle with a stiff, rattling noise. The fountain splashed as I moved past it toward the small gate in an archway set into the back wall. As I set down the lantern and unlocked the gate, I could hear a cat yowling in the alley beyond, but there was no sound of the smugglers' cart. I stepped over to one of the white marble benches to await their arrival, all my senses alert. Something was going to happen. Now. Tonight.

A gust of wind swept through the courtyard and blew the lantern out, and there was a moment of total darkness. Then the moon came from behind the clouds and turned the courtyard into a world of blue and black and silver, the tiles gleaming as though wet with moonlight, the shadows soft now, not so dense. I heard the cart approaching, heard quiet, surly voices. Stepping over to the gate, I pulled it open and stood looking out into the alley. The cart stopped. There were three men, two of them roughly dressed and burly, but the third was slender and wore a long black cloak. The cloak billowed out as he climbed down. He gave instructions to the other two men, and they started to unload the cases of wine. The man in the cloak turned around, looking at me for the first time, and I was paralyzed with shock.

I could see him clearly in the moonlight. I saw every remembered feature, saw the scar that hadn't been there before. I looked at him, unable to speak, unable to breathe, it seemed. He showed no surprise. He stepped toward me, the cloak belling out behind him like demonic wings. I was numb, unable to feel any of the emotions I should have felt.

"Hello, Marietta," he said. "It's been a long time."

I might have been in the middle of a dream. The man, the moonlight, the blue-black shadows that filled the courtyard: all seemed part of that dream, without real substance. The palm fronds rattled. The fountain splashed, and crickets made scratchy, clicking noises between the tiles.

"You've brought the wine," I said.

My voice was calm, without the least shading of emotion, yet it seemed to come from a long way off, seemed to belong to someone else. I saw him standing there not ten feet away, saw the men behind him lifting the cases of wine out of the back of the cart, and none of it was real. It was an illusion, like the soft shimmer of moonlight, like the shadows brushing the walls.

"It goes in the wine cellar," I said. "The back door is open. There's a stairway to your right as you enter. It goes down past the basement and on into the cellar."

"Aye, I know where it is," one of the men growled. "I brung th' goods last time."

"Snap to it!" Derek said sharply.

Each of the men picked up a case of wine and carried it through the gate and across the courtyard toward the back door. Derek stepped into the courtyard, out of the wind, and the cloak settled over his shoulders in silky folds that almost touched the ground. I was standing in a shaft of moonlight, and he studied me with a cool, indifferent gaze.

"You seem to have done quite well for yourself," he remarked.

"Yes."

"Velvet gown. Diamonds. Quite well."

"So you're the man with the scar."

"I got this in Jamaica over a year ago. There was an altercation over a load of goods."

"What happened to the man who gave it to you?"

"He died."

I was as cool, as poised as I had ever been in my life, but I knew the numbness would wear off soon now, knew violent emotions would begin to stir inside. I had to hold them at bay, had to maintain the poise at all costs. I knew it was my only defense.

"Rawlins Palace," he said. "Jeff Rawlins. I should have

made the connection. I've only been working this end for three weeks now. Before I was in Jamaica."

"You lost the plantation," I said.

"Three months after you left, I had to sell out."

"I'm sorry to hear that, Derek."

"It's just as well. The place was a losing proposition from the first. There're easier ways of making money."

"Like smuggling," I said.

"Lots of money in smuggling," he replied. "I've made a small fortune. In six weeks or so I'll be giving all this up. I'll be leaving for England to settle matters there."

The men came back out and moved past us on their way to fetch the other two cases. The horses stamped restlessly in the alley, and one of the men cursed as he heaved a case up into his arms. Bottles rattled. The men came back through the gate, casting long shadows over the silver tiles as they moved past us toward the building.

"At the moment I have rooms here in the city," Derek continued. "The apartment belongs to Valjean. He's letting me use it while he's in Martinique. It's quite near here, as a matter of fact."

I was silent. Derek continued to study me.

"You're as beautiful as I remember."

His voice was flat. It was a statement, not a compliment. His face was all planes and angles in the moonlight, the scar a thin, jagged line running from his left temple to the corner of his mouth. It added a sinister touch and, strangely enough, enhanced his looks, an imperfection that made the rest seem all the more attractive. His eyes revealed nothing.

"So you're still with Rawlins," he said. "He didn't sell you to one of the brothels."

"He's been very good to me."

"I've thought about you, Marietta."

"Have you?"

"You've been on my conscience all these years. I acted in a moment of anger. I regretted it bitterly later on. When I thought about what I had done to you, I was filled with remorse."

"You needn't have worried. As you can see, it worked out very nicely for me. I . . . I'm wearing velvet and diamonds. I'm a free woman, and I have everything I always wanted."

"Do you love him?"

"That's none of your concern," I replied. "I don't belong to you any more. You sold me. You collected eighteen hundred pounds. You assumed Jeff would put me in a brothel, but that didn't stop you."

"I hated myself for what I'd done," he said in that flat, emotionless voice. "I hated you, too, because you had ruined me financially—and because I finally realized what you meant to me."

"Indeed."

"I hated you for that most of all."

"Your men are coming back, Derek," I said calmly. "Here. Here's your gold. You might want to count it."

Derek took the bag of gold and handed it to one of the men. The two of them went on out into the alley and climbed up onto the cart. A thin cloud passed over the face of the moon. Derek made no move to join his men. I knew I couldn't take much more of this without breaking down, and I had too much pride to let him know how he affected me. I looked at him with cool dignity, and when I spoke my voice was like ice.

"You delivered the wine. I paid for it. Our business together is over, Derek."

"Is it?" he asked.

"I must go inside. Goodbye, Derek."

"I intend to see you again."

"That's out of the question."

"I'll be in touch, Marietta."

I didn't reply, but turned and started across the courtyard. I could feel his eyes following me until I finally reached the back door. Safely concealed by the darkness, I turned and looked back, and I saw a dark flutter as his cloak lifted in the breeze. He stepped through the gate, and a moment later I heard the cart pulling away.

I gripped the side of the door, so shaken I could hardly stand, and as the emotions swept over me I prayed for strength. I was going to need it as never before.

XIX

Angie tapped on the door and stepped into the sitting room, turning around slowly to show off her gown of sky-blue tulle, the wide, full skirt caught up with dark-blue velvet bows. This would be her first ball at Rawlins Palace, and she was very excited.

"You look enchanting, Angie," I told her.

"I thought so, too, till I saw you. That gown—I've never seen anything like it. It must be solid gold!"

"Lucille did a fine job with it," I remarked.

"You look like a bloody queen! Only a queen wouldn't wear a gown cut quite so low, I'm sure. Golden gown, diamond necklace, hair so superbly arranged—you're gonna dazzle 'em. They won't know there's another woman in the ballroom."

"Nonsense."

"I can hardly wait for Kyle to get a glimpse of me. I'm gonna just sweep right past him with my nose in the air, and I'm gonna let him see me dancin' with all the gents. Tonight may be the *night*."

"You mean he hasn't—"

"Hadn't laid a hand on me," Angie said, exasperated. "We've spent an awful lot of time together, it's true, ever since that night we went lookin' for Jeff, but he's been a perfect gentleman. He's Welsh, of course, and everyone knows the bloody Welsh are a bit slow."

"Don't despair, Angie. He'll get around to it."

"I just wish he'd hurry up a bit. You want to know somethin'—I think I'm gettin' fond of him. No man's ever treated me like this before, like I was someone special and not just another piece of tail. When we go out for a drive together or take a stroll in the public gardens, he's solemn as a preacher, never has much to say, but I get the feelin' bein' with me means somethin' to him."

"Do you two still argue?"

"Worse than ever. He told me I was to stop flirtin' with the customers, told me I was to mind my tongue and stop usin' certain words so often, and I told him—well, never mind what I told him, but for a minute there I thought he was gonna knock me down! I think he actually *cares*."

"Perhaps he does."

"I think I'm beginning to care about him, too. He gives me a funny feelin' I've never felt before. I feel all tingly and aglow. I want to aggravate him and stir him up, and at the same time I want to kiss him somethin' awful. Do you think I might be fallin' in love?"

"It sounds like it."

"With a bloody Welshman big as a mountain and cheerful as a graveyard? Christ!"

"One can't always control these things," I said quietly.

"I've never been in love before. I'm not sure I like it."

Angie shook her head, silvery-blond ringlets bouncing in back. She looked both dismayed and delighted as she contemplated the possibility, and then she sighed, putting Kyle out of her mind for the time being. She looked at me closely, a small, worried frown creasing her brow.

"Are—are you all right, Marietta?"

"Of course I am. What a silly question."

"It's not silly at all. Somethin's botherin' you. I can tell."

"You're imagining things."

"Not bloody likely, luv. I know you. You've been nervous as a cat for the past three weeks, all jittery and

385

tense, not yourself at all. Been distracted, too, like your mind was on somethin' else all the time."

"Indeed?"

"Is it Jeff?" she asked.

"Jeff's been perfectly marvelous. He paid the dress bills. He's been attentive and—utterly endearing. He's cut down on his drinking and hasn't had a night out since the night you and Kyle went to look for him. He hasn't even been to see Corinne. I imagine she's frantic."

"Then—"

"It's something else, Angie."

"And you don't want to talk about it."

"I'm not sure."

"Sometimes it helps, luv."

I hesitated for just a moment, still indecisive, and then I sighed. I knew I could trust her, and I simply couldn't keep it to myself any longer. As calmly as possible, I told her about my encounter with Derek. I had been unable to think of anything else since the night it happened, and it was a relief to be sharing it with someone at last. Angie listened without betraying any reaction, but when I finally finished she gave a low whistle, looking at me with dismay.

"No wonder you've been upset," she said. "Has he attempted to see you again?"

"The next day he sent a boy over with an envelope addressed to me. I just happened to be downstairs. And Jeff, thank God, was in his office when the boy arrived. There was no message, just a slip of paper with an address scribbled on it—and a key."

"Bloody arrogant if you ask me!"

"I know he expected me to come at once."

"You haven't gone, have you?"

I shook my head. "I've wanted to, God knows, but . . . I can't see him again. I mustn't. Things are bad enough as it is."

"You still love him. That's plain as houses."

"The moment I saw him, it all came rushing back. I tried to hide it, tried to be cool and indifferent, but— he knew at once. Every night I've expected him to walk

386

into the place, demanding to know why I haven't used that key. I've been terrified that Jeff would find out Derek's in New Orleans."

"That wouldn't set too well with him," Angie agreed.

"I've got to think about Jeff. I . . . I owe him so much. I love Derek, but I know it would never lead to anything. He'll be leaving for England soon. He has money now. He'll be able to win his inheritance through the courts—have a title and a stately mansion and all the things that mean so much to him. Once he gains his rightful place among the aristocracy, he'll marry into his own class. There'll be no place in his life for someone like me."

"I can see your point."

"I could have a few weeks with him, yes, but that would just make it harder on me when he finally left. I'll never get over him, not entirely, but I can't risk destroying everything just . . . just for a few weeks."

"You're being very sensible."

"It hasn't been easy," I said. "You don't know how I've longed to throw caution to the winds. I *have* to be sensible. I have to be strong. If I gave way to temptation it could only mean disaster. Jeff is in some kind of financial trouble, I fear. He won't explain it to me, but I know enough to see that it could be bad. I've been faithful to Jeff from the beginning, and if I were to betray his trust at this point and he were to find out about it—"

I left the sentence dangling in air. Angie understood. There was a long silence while we looked at each other, and then I sighed wearily. I felt much better after discussing it with her, and I told her so. She gave me a wry smile and squeezed my hand.

"You'll make it, luv," she promised.

Angie went on downstairs to parade around in her gown in front of Kyle, and I stepped into the bedroom to take a final look at myself. The gown was perfection, simple, narrow sleeves off the shoulder, snug bodice leaving half of my breasts exposed, the skirt belling out over the hoop, but not a ruffle or bow anywhere. The gold made my hair seem a richer, deeper coopery shade, and the diamonds flashed and glittered. I looked so very calm, so serene, yet the strain I had been under was visible if one looked closely enough. The skin over my cheekbones seemed taut, and there were faint mauve shadows under my eyes.

Sighing, I turned away from the mirror. I would smile. I would be gracious. I would dance with all the men and make polite conversation, and no one would even suspect the turmoil inside. Unburdening myself to Angie had done me a great deal of good. I felt stronger now, more determined. Merely putting it all into words made it seem clearer, less confusing. I wouldn't see Derek again. I had resisted temptation thus far, and I would continue to resist. He would be gone soon. If he had intended to take any kind of aggressive action, he would surely have done so by this time. He had sent the key, had expected me to come. I hadn't. Perhaps he intended to let it go at that. I hoped so. Fervently.

I left my rooms and started downstairs, moving slowly down the wide white staircase. The guests wouldn't be arriving for another quarter of an hour, and the front hall was deserted. I could hear Angie's voice in one of the empty gaming rooms, and Kyle's low, somber voice admonished her in reply. He was evidently telling her how to behave tonight, not that it would do any good. The capricious minx would do as she pleased, mischievously taunting him with her misconduct. Kyle was bewitched by her, and Angie was more a little bewitched herself. I suspected that the flighty London sparrow was soon going to have her wings clipped permanently.

Skirt rustling with a soft crackle, I moved on into the ballroom. Two hundred candles burning in the chandeliers and wall sconces shed a dazzling light. Gold gilt patterns glittered in the sky-blue ceiling high above, and the vast parquet floor gleamed. The white silk sofas and gilt white chairs had been arranged around the wall, separated by tall white wicker baskets of long-stemmed roses, white, yellow, yellow-gold. Partially concealed by the bank of plants, the musicians were tuning up their instruments, and the neatly uniformed waiters were chilling bottles of champagne. Everything was in readiness.

These monthly balls at Rawlins Palace had become a regular feature in New Orleans demimonde society, so popular that they were already being imitated elsewhere. Tickets were shockingly expensive, but there was always a large crowd. Men could bring their quadroon mistresses, could drink and dance and dally in an atmosphere of total discretion. Champagne would flow. A buffet would be open, the tables laden with superb food. There would be no gambling tonight, the emphasis on romance. Gorgeously gowned courtesans would make new conquests. Dashing young rakes would flaunt their virility, hoping it would compensate for the lack of plentiful cash. Intricate games of love would be played to the lilt of music, enhanced by the perfume of roses, the glow of candlelight.

Hearing footsteps, I turned to see Jeff strolling into the ballroom. He paused a few feet away, looking at me with warm brown eyes that gleamed with admiration.

"You look a vision," he said. "I've never seen anything so lovely."

"Thank you, Jeff."

"I can't believe it."

"Can't believe what?"

"Can't believe you're real, that anything so breathtaking actually belongs to me."

"I'm quite real, I assure you."

"And you belong to me."

"More or less."

He grinned. "I should never have given you your freedom. Then I could be sure."

"You're not sure now?"

"I keep thinkin'—what if I lost you? What if you left me? What would I do?"

"I'm not going to leave you."

"I wouldn't blame you if you did," he said. "Chap like

389

me—always actin' up, drinkin' too much, gettin' into mischief. I just wish I was worthy of you."

He tilted his head to one side, looking thoughtful now. He was elegantly attired himself, in black trousers, black frock coat, and a white satin waistcoat, his shirtfront frilled. Sandy hair neatly brushed, burnished by candlelight, wide mouth curling in the familiar grin, he looked like a naughty lad dressed up in grownup clothes. I stepped over to him and touched his cheek, letting my fingertips linger there.

"Don't be silly," I told him.

"Hey, you actually *like* me."

"Very much."

"Guess I should be satisfied with that."

"You know what I wish?"

"What's that?"

"I wish the ball were over," I said. "I wish the two of us could go upstairs right now."

His grin widened. The brown eyes danced.

"Reckon that's one hold I have on you. You love makin' love with me. I reckon I'm still about the best in that department."

"If not the most modest," I teased.

Jeff drew me to him and gave me a long, lingering kiss, his mouth caressing my own gently, firmly. He made a moaning noise in his throat, drawing me closer, gentility giving way to greed. I pretended a response I was too tense to feel, melting against him, letting him drink his fill. When he finally released me, his eyes were aglitter with desire. A lock of hair fell over his brow; I reached up and brushed it back. Jeff sighed deeply.

"Shouldn't have done that," he admitted. "Now you got me all stirred up and there's no time to do anything about it."

"You'll just have to wait."

"I'm gonna be thinkin' about it all evening."

"Good."

"I reckon you'll be thinkin' about it, too."

"Perhaps."

"We got an appointment, then?"

I nodded, and suddenly I felt very pleased with myself, proud even, for I had resisted temptation, had been faithful to him. I felt a great rush of affection for this good-looking scamp who loved me so inordinately. I smiled and touched his cheek again, and he looked both pleased and surprised, as though I had just handed him a beautifully wrapped present. It was such a little thing, and it gave him such pleasure. He gave me a quick hug, rough, clumsy, and it was at that moment that I vowed I was going to relent at last. Jeff deserved happiness, and I had the ability to make him the happiest man alive. The next time he asked that familiar question, I was going to say the word he had wanted to hear for such a long time.

"I hear folks comin' in," he said. "Guess we'd better go greet 'em. I feel *good* tonight."

"So do I."

"I'm gonna feel even better when this shebang is over with and I get you alone. I'm gonna feel terrific then — and so are you. That's a promise!"

Guests arrived in a continuous flow, and soon the place was filled with the rustle of silken skirts, the popping of champagne corks, the sound of husky laughter. Jeff and I greeted people as they arrived, as though it were indeed merely a social occasion, and finally, when most of the guests had arrived, a grim-faced Kyle took our place so that we could open the ball. Angie was chatting vivaciously with a handsome young Spaniard who devoured her with his eyes. Kyle didn't like that a bit. I smiled and shook my head as Jeff led me into the ballroom.

The musicians began to play. The dance floor cleared. Jeff slipped his arm around my waist and took my hand and grinned, whirling me onto the floor with great gusto. I almost tripped, my skirt flying. He gripped me tightly, sweeping me around, and the candles seemed to spin and the guests standing around the floor blurred into a swirl of color. As the other couples joined in, the dance floor became a garden of colored skirts spinning, swaying in ever-shifting patterns. I felt flushed, elated, secure with his arm like an iron band holding me against him, his face inches from my own, brown eyes merry, wide mouth curving in the inevitable grin.

"Sorry," he said as he stepped on my foot.

"You really *are* a wretched dancer, Jeff."

"You like it, though. I can tell."

"I feel like you're going to break me in two. Must you hold me quite so tightly?"

"Pardon," he said as he crashed into another dancer.

"Why they all long to dance with you I'll never know."

"They like me. They'll be linin' up soon."

"We're *dancing*, Jeff, not trying to escape a band of Indians."

"Shut up," he said amiably. "Know what I want to do?"

"I'm afraid to ask."

"I wanna sink my teeth into your shoulder."

"Don't you dare."

He chuckled, holding me even closer when the music permitted, whirling me about as though I were a rag doll, and he was right, I liked it, liked his enthusiasm, his boisterous zest. When the dance ended, he gave me a quick, clumsy kiss and chuckled again. He had rarely been so relaxed, so carefree. Did he perhaps suspect I was going to capitulate? Was that the reason for that robust glow, that jaunty manner of old? Breathless, feeling bruised, I informed him that I desperately needed a glass of champagne. He took hold of my hand and half-dragged me over to where a waiter stood with tray in hand.

"Here," he said. "The best stuff. Those smugglers may ask the earth, but they always deliver the goods. I'll have one, too. This is a champagne evening."

"You're in rare form."

" 'Cause I've been behavin'," he confessed. " 'Cause I've been doin' a lot of thinkin'."

"Indeed?"

"I've been thinkin' what a bloody fool I am to drink so much, to carry on like a spoiled schoolboy just 'cause

I can't have everything my way. I've decided to devote all that energy to *gettin'* my way."

"Oh?"

"I . . . uh . . . haven't seen Corinne for three weeks. I don't intend to see her again. She's too fond of me, gettin' too possessive, and me, I've merely been usin' her. From now on, I'm not gonna see anyone but you. I'm gonna see you every night, all night long, and I'm gonna wear you down. I'm gonna keep after you and keep after you till you give in."

"And if I don't?" I teased.

"I'll either throttle you or take you to the altar with your arm twisted up behind your back, and I'll keep twistin' it until you give the proper responses. I don't intend to fool around any longer. It's time I started gettin' mean about it."

"You could never be mean," I told him.

He looked at me with mock ferocity. "No?"

I shook my head. He grinned.

"Guess I couldn't," he confessed, "but I can be mighty persuasive. I intend to be from here on out. I got methods in mind that'd make you blush."

I smiled, feeling that rush of affection again, and the anguish I had gone through these past three weeks seemed totally absurd. Perhaps this affection was even better than love. There would be no pinnacles of bliss, but neither would there be bleak despair. I could make Jeff happy, and he would never be able to wound me, no matter what he did. I wondered why it had taken me over three years to see things this way.

Jeff set his empty glass down on a table. "Guess I'd better go make the ladies happy," he said. "They're pantin' to have a go-round with me. That's why most of 'em come, to dance with me."

"They're welcome to you."

"I'll get back to you, don't you worry. And don't you forget out little appointment. I'm gonna start usin' those new methods I was tellin' you about soon as I get you out of that dress."

Jeff sauntered off and was promptly snapped up by a dark-eyed blond in honey-colored satin. I finished my champagne, thoughtful now, almost happy about my decision. Jeff would be very, very good to me, just as he had always been. Most women would envy me. Why had I been so stubborn? He was sweet and engaging and virile, and he loved me like few women were ever loved. Derek . . . Derek thought I was a whore, had always thought so. Damn him for sending that key. Damn him for thinking I'd come running. I hated him for his arrogance, and I prayed he would stay away.

"Dance, Marietta?" Raoul DuBois asked.

"Hello, Raoul. I'd love to."

"Festive night tonight," he said.

"Isn't it. My, you look quite dashing in that waistcoat."

I flirted instinctively as I danced with Raoul, with Jonathan Barkley, with Jamie Perez, making light conversation and smiling, playing my role with ease. An hour and a half passed, and I was beginning to grow a bit weary, thankful for the opportunity to take a short break from dancing. Jean Paul Etienne fetched a glass of champagne for me. A handsome young Frenchman with wavy black hair and moody brown eyes, he wore a wine-colored suit, and his right arm was in a black silk sling. When I inquired about that, Jean Paul made a face, looking disgruntled.

"It's only a nick. I'll be out of this sling in a week or so."

"Another duel?" I asked.

Jean Paul nodded. "You should see Guy Nicholas. I put a bullet through his kneecap. He'll walk with a limp for the rest of his life."

"One of these days you're going to kill someone," I admonished.

"I intended to kill Nicholas. The duel took place three mornings ago, at the Oaks. Devereaux was my second. It was foggy, and I couldn't see properly. I aimed for his heart, hit his kneecap. Rotten luck. I had to be satisfied, though."

I shook my head. Dueling was a regular feature of New Orleans society, and hardly a morning passed that there wasn't a duel of some sort under the oak trees outside the city. So many duels had been fought beneath a certain group of trees that they were known as the Dueling Oaks, a dubious landmark where countless men had been wounded or killed. Hot-blooded youths like Jean Paul bragged of their exploits beneath the Oaks, and even the most trifling arguments were settled there with pistols or swords. It was a deadly sport I couldn't comprehend.

"More champagne?" he asked as I set my empty glass aside.

"No, thank you, Jean Paul. I think I'll circulate and give some of the other women an opportunity to question you about your wound. I've noticed a number of them casting glances your way."

Jean Paul curled his lip, looking bored with the idea, but I could tell he was eager to dazzle the ladies. He had come by himself, but he had no intention of leaving alone. As soon as I moved away, two women rushed over to question him, fluttering like beautiful moths about a seductive flame. Candles burned brightly, bathing the walls with golden shadows. The music rose and fell as dancers swept around the floor. Courtesans held court, sitting on the white silk sofas, surrounded by admirers, and groups stood all around the floor, talking quietly, flirting. Many couples had already adjourned to the courtyard for more intimate conversation.

As I moved from group to group, I saw Corinne entering the ballroom on the arm of a swarthy young Spanish officer in full-dress uniform. She paused, said something to him in a sharp tone and sent him on his way, his purpose fulfilled, as unaccompanied women were not permitted to attend. While the officer retreated with snapping black eyes and a fierce expression, Corinne glanced around the ballroom trying to spot Jeff. Her dark hair was worn in a bun in back; a magnolia blossom was fastened above one ear, and her pink silk gown was sumptuous, with its full skirt in layers like pink rose petals. There were shadows under her eyes. She looked tense. I hoped there wouldn't be trouble.

Jeff was talking with a blond in blue velvet across the room. Looking up a moment or so later, he saw Corinne, and I could tell that he wasn't at all happy about it. He scowled, brows pressing together. When Corinne finally spotted him and started in that direction, Jeff turned to the blond, asked her to dance and swept her onto the floor, quickly guiding her to the other end of the room, away from Corinne. Corinne took a glass of champagne and downed it in one gulp, then drank two more in rapid succession, looking mutinous and ready to explode. The music stopped, began again. Jeff was dancing with another woman now, deftly avoiding the languorous brunette in pink.

Immersed in my duties, I soon lost track of both Jeff and Corinne. I smiled. I chatted. I danced with half a dozen men, sailing around the floor with my golden skirt belling out behind me, the candles ablaze above like flickering golden stars, the scent of roses mingling with the scent of sweat. My tension vanished. I was enjoying myself now, and I was anticipating the night to come, Jeff's body, his love, the present I intended to give him. I felt at peace with myself after such a long time, pleased with my decision, sure it was the right one.

I went into the gaming room where the buffet tables had been set up in splendor. Waiters were filling plates with slices of ham and roast and turkey, with exquisite chilled salads, steaming saffron rice and tender asparagus cooked in butter. I had a few oysters, another glass of champagne, and I complimented Pierre, who stood behind the tables looking resentful as his gorgeously arranged dishes were demolished. Jean Paul Etienne sauntered in with a sultry blond in bronze satin who fetched a plate for him, treating him like a wounded hero. He watched her with heavy-lidded eyes, contemplating pleasures to come.

As I was returning to the ballroom, I met Jeff in the

hall. He looked both exasperated and worried. When I asked him what was wrong, he scowled and indicated the staircase. Corinne was sitting on the bottom step, her layered pink skirt spilling over the floor. She clutched the banister with one hand, the other holding an empty champagne glass. The magnolia fastened in her hair was drooping limply. Tears streamed down her cheeks.

"I've got to take her home," Jeff told me.

"Is something wrong?"

"She's drunk. God knows how many glasses of champagne she's downed. I tried to keep away from her, but she finally caught me—started cryin', started threatenin' to kill herself. I got her out of the ballroom before she could make a real scene, but—" He shook his head in disgust. "Christ! Just what I needed!"

"Of course you must take her home, Jeff."

"I don't *want* to," he insisted, "but if I don't, God knows what she might do. Kyle's gone to fetch the carriage and bring it round. He'll be out front in a couple minutes. I . . . uh . . . I might have to stay with her a while, Marietta."

"I understand."

"She keeps talkin' about killin' herself. I'll have to sober her up, give her some hot coffee, keep her on her feet. I'd like to strangle the minx!"

"Don't worry about it."

"You're not *mad*?"

"Of course not. Jeff—be kind to her. You owe her that."

"I'll try," he groaned.

Kyle came in and told Jeff that the carriage was waiting. Jeff shook his head again and, stepping over to the staircase, took hold of Corinne's wrist and pulled her to her feet. As she looked up at him with tearful eyes, Jeff wrapped his arm around her waist and moved her toward the door. Corinne staggered, waving the empty glass in the air, demanding more champagne. Jeff clamped his free hand over her mouth and hurried her out into the night, cursing under his breath. I wasn't at all perturbed, was, in fact, rather amused. It served him right for treating her so shabbily. Poor Jeff and his women. After tonight there would be only one. He wouldn't need to look elsewhere for reassurance.

When I returned to the ballroom, the Spaniard in dress uniform who had come with Corinne asked me to dance. I nodded graciously. He was a superb dancer, and those dark, flashing eyes seemed to devour me. When the dance was over, he made a highly improper suggestion. I smiled, pretending to be flattered, and crushed his hopes with a polite refusal. He executed a formal bow, clicking his heels together, then sought out a more responsive partner. Someone else asked me to dance, then someone else, and it was wonderful to be desirable, to be dancing, to be wearing a golden ball gown and diamonds, to be at peace after three weeks of anguished indecision.

Another hour passed. It was after midnight, and the ball was officially over at one. The candles were starting to burn down, the roses beginning to wilt. Many people had already left for more private entertainment, Jean Paul with his blond, the Spaniard with a brunette in red. Angie had disappeared, too, and Kyle was no longer at his post. I imagined they had gone into the shadowy courtyard or perhaps even upstairs to one of their rooms. They would be good for each other, I thought. Angie would make Kyle less grim, and Kyle would keep her in line.

The musicians were taking a well-deserved break before the last session. No more than thirty people were left in the ballroom. Standing with a glass of champagne in my hand, surrounded by a small group of men who hadn't yet found partners for the remaining hours of the night, I smiled and chatted lightly. They teased me about Jeff's abrupt departure, volunteering to keep me company in his stead. It was all good-natured, relaxed, diverting.

Five gorgeously gowned women stood together at the other end of the room, near the door, gossiping, toying with their fans. Couples sat on the sofas or wandered up and down waiting for the music to resume. The floor was empty, gleaming still, reflecting the candlelight. Looking around, I saw the tall man with the scar enter the ballroom. The courtesans stopped talking, and then, as one, they moved toward him, colored skirts swaying. He paused, cool gray eyes searching, and when he saw me he started toward me, ignoring the fluttering beauties who fell back in disappointment.

I handed my empty champagne glass to one of the men and asked them to excuse me. They grumbled. Returned to their stand, the musicians began playing as I moved forward to greet Derek Hawke. Couples began to dance. And I paused to wait for him to reach me. My emotions were in wonderful control. I had made my decision. I would be polite. I wasn't scared, wasn't even nervous. I felt very strong.

He was wearing black, his waistcoat a deep maroon embroidered in black silk. The slight hollows beneath his cheekbones that I had noticed that night in the moonlight were still there, and he looked thinner, taller as well. That thin, jagged scar made him look like a handsome pirate, sinister and romantic. It was difficult to associate this elegantly attired stranger with the farmer in sweat-damp shirt, old breeches, and muddy boots.

"Hello, Derek," I said politely.

"I intended to get here earlier, but I had one or two errands I had to run."

"I'm glad you could make it."

"Are you?"

"We welcome all comers as long as they pay. I assume you bought a ticket."

He nodded. "There was no one at the door to collect it."

"Keep it. The ball is almost over. I'm afraid you're not going to get your money's worth."

"I imagine I shall."

"Oh?"

"Where's Rawlins?" he asked.

"Jeff had to leave some time ago."

"Shall we dance?"

"I'm rather weary, Derek. There are at least a dozen very attractive women who'll be delighted to dance with you. You might even persuade one of them to go home with you."

"We'll dance," he said.

He took my hand, wrapped his arm around my waist, and swung me into motion with one graceful swirl. I relaxed, letting him guide me over the floor. I had never danced with him before, and I was surprised at his expertise. His eyes held mine, cool, remote, revealing nothing. I refused to be intimidated, refused to show the least emotion.

"I've been expecting you, Marietta."

"Have you?"

"I felt certain you'd come."

"You were wrong, it seems."

"You wanted to," he said.

"Indeed?"

"I saw your face in the moonlight. I saw your expression when you recognized me. I'm sure. You don't love Jeff Rawlins. You're still in love with me."

"You're mistaken."

"I don't want to play word games, Marietta. We've already lost three weeks."

"You're terribly sure of yourself."

"I'm sure of you."

"Because of what you imagined you saw in the moonlight?"

"I didn't imagine it."

The music stopped. There was a faint scattering of applause. Derek released me. I moved away from him as the music began again. He followed me and took hold of my arm. I turned, my anger beginning to surface. People were staring at us. I let him lead me over to the side of the room. We stopped by a tall basket of yellow roses, the sofa beside it vacant.

"You're wasting your time, Derek," I said. "I mean that. Your—your arrogance is not to be believed. Whatever I might have felt for you is quite dead. I'm living with Jeff and I intend to marry him."

"Not now you're not."

"I suggest you leave, Derek."

"Come, we'll go out to the courtyard. We can't talk here."

"We've nothing to talk about."

"Are you going to come peacefully, or shall I drag you out? I will if necessary. Your friends are already staring at us. I'm sure they'd enjoy seeing that little scene enacted."

I could tell that he was serious. With as much dignity as possible, I left the ballroom with Derek beside me. The courtyard was clothed in deep blue-black shadows, moonlight illuminating the fountain and a section of the tiles. The two or three couples, whispering together in the darkness, paid us little attention. Taking hold of my hand, Derek led me over to one of the walls where tall shrubs concealed us from view.

"I hope you're satisfied," I said.

"You intend to keep playing games?"

"I just want you to leave me alone."

"No, Marietta. That isn't what you want."

"It's been over three years—"

"You want me, just as I want you."

I wanted to deny it, but I was afraid that if I tried to, my voice would betray the emotions welling up inside. My anger had been genuine, but it was gone now, replaced by those other feelings I wanted so desperately to hide from him. I stood with my back against the wall, and he stood directly in front of me, now two feet away, and as my eyes adjusted to the dark I could see his mouth was set in a determined line. I prayed for strength, for I knew I must resist him.

"I tried to forget you," he said. "I couldn't. After I had to give up the plantation, after I got into my new line of work, there were other women, one right after the other. I took them eagerly, hoping each one would cure me of you, make me forget. It was futile. They only

401

made it worse, made me realize all the more what I'd lost."

His voice betrayed no emotion.

"You didn't lose me, Derek. You sold me."

"In a fit of anger. I told you how much I regretted it the night I delivered the wine. I was filled with remorse for what I'd done."

"And now—"

"Now I want to make it up to you."

"You don't owe me anything, Derek. You—you did me a favor. I have everything a woman could possibly want. I have money, jewels, security, a man who loves me with all his heart."

"You don't love him."

"You'd like to think that. Jeff is charming and kind and—generous. He treats me like a queen. He's tender, too, not afraid to show his love."

"You don't love him," he repeated.

"That's not true."

"You love me. I knew. The minute I laid eyes on you I knew you hadn't been able to forget, just as I hadn't."

"So you sent a key, expecting me to come like—like some expensive harlot. You were disappointed, weren't you? You're so incredibly arrogant you actually believed that's all you had to do."

"I want you, Marietta."

"You want to sleep with me. You're not alone. There are dozens of men who'd give anything to be able to take me away from Jeff. Most of them have tried. I've never once been unfaithful to him." I gave him a piercing look, and asked, "You told me you're leaving for England shortly."

"That's true."

"And it would be nice to have a bed partner until it's time to leave, wouldn't it? Go find yourself a beautiful whore. New Orleans is full of them. I don't consider myself one of them."

Derek didn't reply. I tried to control the tremors inside, tried to deny the aching desire that grew steadily.

402

I longed to touch that jagged scar, that wide, determined mouth. I hated him for what he was doing to me, hated myself for feeling the emotions of old. The palm fronds rattled in the wind. From across the courtyard there came a throaty laugh, the sound of a brief scuffle, a moan smothered by a kiss.

"You're trembling," he said.

"I—I'm going back inside now. I have duties."

"You're not going anywhere," he said softly.

He pulled me toward him, sliding one arm around my waist and the other around my neck, tilting his head to one side as he leaned down, covering my mouth with his. I tried desperately to resist as those firm, moist lips pressed and probed, demanding the response I could withhold no longer. He parted my lips with his own, clasping me against him, and my head seemed to swim and the world seemed to recede. There was nothing but this man, that mouth, these emotions sweeping over me and rendering me helpless. My arms circled his broad shoulders, and I melted against him in total surrender.

It seemed an eternity before he finally released me. I leaned back against the wall, looking up at him with tears in my eyes. The wind ruffled his hair, and in the faint mist of moonlight his face was stony, the face of a victor, stamped with satisfaction. I actually hated him at that moment, hated him even as I longed for those strong arms to enfold me once more, longed for that mouth to resume its sweet torture. Derek knew, and he nodded. It was a while before I could speak. My voice trembled.

"I—I'll never forgive you for that."

"I imagine you will. You love me and want me as much as I want you. I'll leave now. I don't intend to force you to do anything you don't want to do. You still have the key."

"You actually think I—"

"You'll come," he said, "and I'll be waiting. There's just one more thing I want to say. I love you, Marietta.

There, I've used the words. I love you. I loved you from the first. I should have told you."

"Derek—"

"I'll be waiting, Marietta."

He turned then and moved away from me. I heard his footsteps sounding on the tiles, and then he was gone and I was alone in the courtyard. All of the others had gone inside. As I listened to the crickets, to the splash of the fountain, to the lilting music muted by distance, I knew that he had won. I was helpless against the emotions still smouldering inside. I wiped the tears from my cheeks and tried to compose myself, but several minutes passed before I finally had the strength to go inside and bid the last of the guests goodbye.

XX

Perhaps today would be the day. There wasn't much time left. Although he hadn't mentioned it, I had heard that the ship for England would be leaving New Orleans on Monday, only five days from now. He hadn't talked about it at all, hadn't given the least indication that he planned to take me with him, but in my heart I was sure that's what he intended. Perhaps today he would tell me. He would be very casual and matter of fact, would simply tell me that I was going with him and should start making arrangements. He had probably already purchased my passage.

He loved me. After all this time he had finally said the words, and although he had not repeated them, he had shown his love in a thousand small ways. Derek wasn't a demonstrative man, but he couldn't entirely conceal his emotions behind that stern façade. Each time I saw him he betrayed them with a look, a casual word, a gesture. He loved me, and when he left for England I would be with him. He would win his inheritance, would take his place among the aristocracy, and I would be his wife. How foolish of me to think my background would make the least difference. The opinion of his peers wouldn't matter in the least to him. He would be just as disdainful of them as he had been of his neighbors in Carolina.

I quickened my step. It was after two o'clock in the

405

afternoon, and Kyle had let me out in front of Lucille's only a few minutes ago. He would return to the dress shop at five. Derek and I would have almost three hours together in that sunny apartment, where we would talk, deliberately forestalling our trip to the bedroom, delaying it, savoring the anticipation. Then he would give me that drowsy look and I would smile and we would make love. Derek would express with his body, his flesh, all those things he found so difficult to express in words. Reluctantly, I would return to the dress shop, and Jeff would be none the wiser.

He would probably be in his office all afternoon, going over the books in an effort to make them balance. He still hadn't confided in me what the problem was, but his face was grim as he worked. He wasn't at all concerned about all my visits to the dress shop. Actually he seemed pleased that I was planning a new wardrobe and devoting so much time to it. I think it made him feel less guilty about seeing Corinne again.

Jeff hadn't returned the night of the ball, hadn't come back until almost noon the next day. Corinne had attempted to swallow a bottle of laudanum that night, he informed me, and he was going to have to break it off gently or the foolish creature would do something desperate. I could tell that he was flattered she had gone to such extremes. It bolstered his ego, made him feel dashing. He had been unusually affable and endearing during these past two and a half weeks, as though to compensate for his backsliding. The fact remained that he was seeing her again, regularly, and we hadn't kept our "appointment." Jeff had no idea how relieved I was about that.

I would have to tell him soon, of course. It wasn't going to be easy, but I would try to break it to him as gently as possible. It had been sheer folly even to consider marrying him. Seeing Derek again had made me realize all the more that I could never give Jeff the love and total commitment he deserved. Once I was gone, he would find someone else, someone who could give him all the devotion he was entitled to. He would be hurt, of course, but in the long run he would be much happier, I told myself.

I moved on down the street, my turquoise silk skirt fluttering in the breeze that cooled the air and laced it with the tang of salt. It was a glorious day, the sky a light, clear blue awash with silvery sunlight that threw flickering silver-gold spangles over the mellow brown walls. The city seemed to be charged with vitality, colors brighter, sounds noisier, its customary lethargy replaced by an atmosphere of joyous abandon.

I felt young and radiant. I felt like a girl again, and all because of the happiness welling up inside. I had never thought I would feel this way again. I turned a corner, nearing Derek's quarters. The street was lined on either side with carts of flowers, feisty old women in faded shawls standing beside them, urging people to buy. There were golden marigolds, yellow chrysanthemums, blue larkspurs, pale lilacs, scarlet azaleas, their colors offset by the brown stone walls. People strolled up and down, stopping to examine, to haggle over prices. A spotted dog was barking lustily, tail awag. A stout black woman in starched blue dress and white bandana moved purposefully along, holding the hands of two beautiful little girls with long blond ringlets.

I had told no one about these visits, not even Angie. Angie was immersed in her own affair, for Kyle had indeed succumbed the night of the ball and, to her horror and delight, declared that he intended to marry her, if only to keep her in line. She thought the idea outrageous, but she was beginning to warm to it day by day. The scrappy little sparrow was fast becoming a docile, devoted pet. Angie didn't suspect the true reason for my daily trips to Lucille's, and Lucille herself asked no questions. She knew I was using her shop as a blind and accepted it with cool sophistication.

Reaching the intricately wrought black iron gate, I pushed it open and stepped into the sun-drenched patio with its blue slate tiles and splashing fountain. Buildings rose on three sides, festooned with ornate iron balconies on two levels. A brilliantly crested white cockatoo strutted restlessly on a slender yellow swing suspended from one of the dwarf palms, cawing loudly as I took the key from my reticule and inserted it in the lock. Valjean's rooms were on the ground floor, facing the gate, spacious, expensively appointed rooms designed for comfort.

"Derek?" I called.

"I'm in here. In the sitting room."

I stepped to the door, smiling. Derek was sitting in one of the plush tan velvet chairs, sunlight spilling over him from the windows directly behind. His hair was disarrayed, and there were faint shadows beneath his eyes. I knew that he had made a delivery last night, and I suspected that he had just gotten out of bed and dressed. The deep coral draperies billowed behind him as the breeze swept into the room. He continued to lounge in the chair, looking at me with drowsy gray eyes.

"You're so gallant," I remarked. "A gentleman is supposed to get up when a lady enters the room."

"I'm no gentleman."

"I'm delighted you're so glad to see me."

"I'm glad to see you," he said.

"Are you?"

"I'm tired. I didn't get back until five o'clock this morning."

"Perhaps I should leave," I teased.

"I'm not that tired."

Lounging with one leg slung over the arm of the chair, he examined me with lazy appraisal. The turquoise dress was new, a deep, rich silk, and I knew it went well with my coppery auburn hair. The petticoats beneath were in varying shades of green and blue. Derek liked what he saw. I was glad I had taken such care in selecting the dress and arranging my hair. I wanted to be attractive for him. Lazily he contemplated me with lids drooping and gray eyes darkening with desire, and then he scowled and looked away, almost as though he were irritated with himself for wanting me.

I understood all too well. Derek loved me, but he did so grudgingly. He wasn't at all pleased to find himself a prey to the emotions I aroused. They made him feel vulnerable, and Derek equated that with weakness. One day, when he had his rightful place in the world, when he was at peace with himself, he would learn to accept his feelings. I was willing to be patient. Against his will or not, he loved me, and that was all that mattered now.

"You had a bad night," I said.

"I had a bad night."

"Something happened?"

"When we were bringing the boat through the swamp, we ran into a Spanish patrol. We exchanged fire. One of my men was wounded. We evaded the patrol, but Peters almost bled to death in the boat before I could get him to a doctor."

"Do things like that happen frequently?"

"It's a risky occupation. I've seen lots of men die. I've had to kill a man myself. That's why I have this scar. The chap who gave it to me intended to cut my throat. I had to run him through."

"It must have been dreadful."

"Some men can kill with ease. I'm not one of them. I'll have him on my conscience for the rest of my life."

"Even though he meant to kill you?"

"I'll never kill another man, no matter what the circumstances."

He got to his feet and stepped over to the sideboard to pour a glass of brandy from the crystal decanter. Leaning against the sideboard, he stared down at the glass in his hand as though contemplating whether or not to drink it.

"It was my last," he said.

"I don't understand."

"My last delivery. I'm finished with smuggling as of last night. My business in New Orleans is over."

"You've always detested it, haven't you?"

"It meant money."

"And now you have all you need."

"Now I have all I need. There'll be no more boat rides through swamps in the dead of night, no more fights with greedy employees who want to make a bit on the side, no more shady transactions with nervous customers who always believe you're cheating them."

"You never told me how you got into smuggling."

"There's a lot I haven't told you, Marietta."

"I didn't mean to pry."

"Before I went into smuggling, I signed on with a slaver. I met him in Charles Town, right after I'd lost the plantation. He needed a second-in-command. I agreed to take the job. We sailed for Africa. I saw things I hope never to see again. It changed my ideas about slavery entirely. On the journey back we docked in Martinique. I left ship, took what gold was coming to me, and left. I vowed never to own another slave."

I was silent, remembering Cassie and Adam. Derek was thinking about them, too. I could tell. He looked up at me with a grim expression on his face.

"I began to understand why you helped those two escape. I hated you for it at the time, but after sailing on the slave ship—" He cut himself short.

"I wonder what happened to them," I said quietly.

"I imagine Adam got a job in one of the foundries. His lot won't be much better than it was in Carolina, but at least he's a free man. Thanks to you. You did a brave thing, Marietta."

"I had help."

"Elijah Jones. I always knew he was involved, even though I could never prove it. Men like Jones will eventually see to it that slavery is abolished. I'll be on their side."

There was a moment of silence as both of us thought about the past, and then Derek drank his brandy and set the empty glass down, folding his arms across his chest.

"I met Valjean in Martinique," he told me. "That's how I got into smuggling. It hasn't been a pleasant occupation, but it's better by far than slaving."

410

"And now you'll return to England," I said.

He nodded. I waited. He said nothing about taking me with him. I stepped over to one of the windows and held back the coral drapery with my hand, peering out at the gardens in back, refusing to let myself doubt. Of course he would take me with him. I meant as much to Derek as he meant to me. I mustn't allow myself to doubt it.

"I'm going to win," he said.

"I'm certain you will."

I turned away from the window, letting the drapery fall back into place.

"I've worked so hard, so long, and at last it's about to pay off. I've been in touch with my lawyer in London, have kept in touch all this time. He's finally been able to verify the documents that prove my father married my mother. It took a lot of time and even more money, but he's finally got the proof we need."

"You told me once your uncle had a shrewd set of men working for him. You said they'd been able to keep it out of the courts. Won't they try to do the same thing this time?"

Derek smiled bitterly. "They'll try, but this time I have the money to fight back. *I* can bribe officials now. I can grease enough palms to make certain it goes before the magistrates."

"I see."

"It's a corrupt world, Marietta. Even those who are in the right have to acknowledge its corruptness and bow to it. It's taken me a decade, but I'm finally going to see justice done."

"And then you'll be satisfied?" I said.

"I'll be satisfied."

"I hope so, Derek. I hope you can start living."

"What's that supposed to mean?"

"I—nothing. It meant nothing."

"I'm not a very pleasant person, am I?"

"I wasn't implying—"

"I'm cool and aloof and utterly ruthless. I know. I've

411

been told so dozens of times. I've been obsessed with my inheritance. It's driven me, shaped me into the person I am, and that person isn't charming, isn't genteel, doesn't leap to his feet when you enter the room."

"Derek—"

"And yet you claim to love me. You're a fool, Marietta. I treated you wretchedly in Carolina, abused you, tossed you aside in a fit of rage. And still you're here, asking for more. I don't understand it."

He gazed at me, his eyes almost angry. He still leaned back against the sideboard, arms crossed. The beige cord breeches clung to his legs, and the white cambric shirt was so fine I could see the suggestion of skin beneath. Why, I wondered. Why must it be this moody, enigmatic man, and not some other? Why must he be the only one to set these tremulous emotions astir inside me? I didn't understand it, but it had happened and there was nothing I could do.

"You're beautiful," he said, and it was like an accusation. "You're the most beautiful creature I've ever laid eyes on, and you've haunted me like a witch."

"Have I?"

"I wanted to forget you. I tried. I wanted to hate you, and for a while I thought I did. The other women—I punished them. I treated them abominably, heartlessly. I was punishing you."

"Because I ruined you?"

"Because I couldn't get you out of my mind. When I saw you that first night in the moonlight, looking like a vision in your velvet and diamonds, looking like a witch, I wanted to strangle you."

"But you sent the key."

"And when you didn't come, I cursed you. I told myself I was glad, told myself I'd been a fool to send the key in the first place. Three weeks went by, and I realized I couldn't stay away any longer. I realized the only way I could exorcise you was to bed you and prove to myself that what I felt was purely physical."

"And now?"

412

"Now it's worse than ever."

Derek sauntered over to me and took hold of my arms, looking down into my eyes. His own were dark, filled with love and angry resignation. For a long time he peered at me, and then he shook his head as though in defeat.

"I suppose it was meant to be," he said.

"I suppose it was."

He tilted his head to one side. The jagged white scar moved as he slowly parted his lips. He leaned down and fastened his mouth over mine, catching it in sweet suction and working over it with lazy, sensual deliberation that caused my senses to reel. His arms folded around me, and I moved against him, tilting my head back as his mouth plundered leisurely. The muscles of his arms tightened, tightened until I thought my bones would snap, and I welcomed it, clinging to him.

He moved his lips down to the curve of my throat, lips firm, pliant, smooth. I curled one hand around the back of his head, running my fingers through those dark locks, leaning back against his arm as he planted his lips between my breasts. I could feel the sweet, liquid warmth stealing through me like honey filling a comb, and the familiar ache tingled as the blossom of my passion unfurled petal by petal, blooming inside at his nearness, his touch, his scent.

"Beautiful," he said.

"I'm glad."

"Mine. Mine still."

"Yes."

"Even more than before. Mine."

"Yours, Derek."

"Meant to be. It was meant to be."

Derek lifted me up in his arms and carried me down the short hallway to the bedroom. It was small, intimate, only a few misty beams of sunlight seeping through the louvers of the closed brown shutters. The whitewashed walls were brushed with blue-gray shadows. The bed and dresser were golden oak, the mirror a murky silver-blue. A rich brown brocade counterpane covered the bed.

Derek put me down and kneeled to pull off my slippers and peel off my stockings. As he tossed them aside, they drifted to the floor like wisps of smoke. He stood up, pulled me to my feet, arms encircling me as he unfastened the tiny, invisible hooks down the back of my dress. I drifted in a haze of sensation.

Derek stepped back and slowly pulled the bodice down, bending to ease the dress over the blue and green skirts of my petticoat. I shivered as the final petals unfurled, the blossom of my passion full blown, vibrant and lovely within me, urgently demanding to be plucked. Derek undressed me as though he were unwrapping a wonderful present, refusing to hurry, savoring the joy yet to come. He unfastened the bodice of my petticoat and freed my breasts, fondling them leisurely before slipping the garment down over my hips, and when he was finally finished, when my clothes were strewn over the dark golden carpet and I was completely naked, he kissed me yet again, folding me against him. I ran my hands over his back, feeling muscle and warm skin beneath the fine cloth.

"Witch," he said.

"Yours."

"I should cast you out."

"You won't."

"I'd like to. I can't."

"We need each other," I whispered. "Without you I— I'm not complete. I'm only half alive. And you. It's the same with you."

"Damn you."

"It's true."

"Damn you for what you've done to me."

He eased me onto the bed. I stretched languorously, the counterpane cool and silky beneath me. He perched on the stool in front of the dresser and pushed off first one boot, then the other. He stood and pulled off the thin white shirt and let it float to the floor. He undid his trousers and eased them down, stepped out of them, and then he was naked, too, a superb nude statue pulsating with life and readiness. As he moved toward the bed, I raised my arms. The mattress sagged as he kneeled over me, and I wrapped my arms around him and shifted as he lowered himself. I gathered the weight and warmth to me, trembling beneath him.

He entered with the softness of velvet, the strength of steel, and I rose to meet him. We were one now, no longer incomplete, together, as we were meant to be, limbs entwined, one. I ran my palms across his shoulders, down the smoothness of his back, over the swell of his buttocks, and slowly, so slowly, he filled me, caressing me as I caressed him, and wells of sensation overflowed, rising, ever rising, and the sweet tingle and the ache quickened. Caught up, he drove forcefully, seeking fulfillment now, passion mounting, caresses giving way to a savage frenzy. He thrust, and I clasped him and the wells became waves, great waves that swept over us both again and again, crashing now, carrying us to the crests. For one incredible moment we hung suspended in ecstasy, senses shredded, and he gave a hoarse cry as we went hurtling down into release.

Derek shuddered. Several minutes passed as I held him to me, shaken to the core by the splendor that slowly ebbed, leaving in its wake a residue of glowing warmth. Neither of us spoke. We never did. I stroked his hair, damp from his exertions, and finally he withdrew and the oneness was gone and the invisible barrier was in place once more. I closed my eyes, drifting into sleep. When I awoke, Derek was no longer beside me. His clothes were gone. He had dressed while I was still sleeping. I heard him in the sitting room, glass clinking as he poured another brandy.

It was twenty minutes before I finally joined him in the sitting room. I was fully dressed, and I had rearranged my hair. Derek was standing at one of the windows, looking out. His skin was still slightly moist, and the fine white cambric clung to his back and shoulders. He didn't turn as I entered the room. The rapturous unity might never have taken place. Each time we made love it was as though I had robbed him of part of his independence. One day he would be at ease with himself and his love, I thought. One day he would look at me with eyes filled with that love, and the invisible barrier would be gone forever.

I glanced at the clock. It was almost four-thirty.

"I'll have to start back," I said.

Derek turned. His face was expressionless. He hesitated just a moment before speaking.

"I . . . uh . . . I'll be out tomorrow afternoon, Marietta."

"Oh?"

"All afternoon," he said. "There's no point in your coming."

"I see."

"I'll . . . get in touch with you."

"Is something wrong, Derek?"

He frowned. I had the impression he was keeping something from me. I felt a tiny fear awakening inside. I curbed it, knowing I mustn't nourish it, let it grow. Derek stepped over to the sideboard to set down his empty glass, deliberately avoiding the question. It probably had something to do with the smuggling, I told myself. That must be it, must be why he couldn't discuss it with me.

"I'll see you the day after, then," I said lightly. "I . . . I really must be going. Kyle is supposed to pick me up at five."

Derek nodded and walked to the front door with me. He opened it and I stepped outside. He followed me. He was still frowning. He seemed to be indecisive about something, reluctant to let me go. Finally he drew me to him and kissed me a final time. He was trying to tell me something with that kiss. The lips covering mine seemed to convey a poignant message, one he couldn't put into words. He drew his head back, still holding me loosely, looking down into my eyes.

"Goodbye, Marietta," he said softly.

Neither of us had heard the gate opening. Derek looked up as footsteps sounded on the tiles. His face grew suddenly grim. He released me abruptly and stepped aside.

416

I turned. Jeff strolled casually toward us, a curious smile playing on his lips.

"Thought you might be here," he remarked.

I stood very still—paralyzed, it seemed. The expected onrush of emotion didn't come. After that first moment of shock I felt only a deep sadness, my concern for Jeff, not myself.

"I told myself you really were going to the dress shop every day," he said amiably. "I told myself it was foolish to entertain the least doubt, but I had to banish that doubt, you see. I had to prove to myself that you weren't seeing him."

"Jeff—"

"I knew he was in New Orleans, knew he'd come to the ball after I left, but I told myself you wouldn't do this. This—this afternoon I couldn't contain myself any longer. I finally went to the dress shop, and when you weren't there, I had to come here. I knew he was staying in Valjean's rooms. I prayed you wouldn't be here."

"I'm sorry, Jeff. I—I didn't want to hurt you. It—it's something I couldn't—"

Jeff cut me short with a gesture and then, ignoring me, he looked at Derek, nodding at him as though in greeting.

"I guess I'll have to kill you," he said.

"Hold on, Rawlins."

"Shall we say tomorrow morning? At the Oaks?"

"You're suggesting a duel?"

"It's customary, I believe."

"I won't fight you, Rawlins."

"No?"

"We can settle this some other way."

"You think so?"

"I've no wish to harm you."

Jeff smiled and shook his head, amiably, as though he'd just heard a not-too-amusing joke. Then he stepped over to Derek, drew back his hand, and slammed it across Derek's cheek with shattering impact. I gasped as Derek stumbled back toward the door. I seized Jeff's arm, trying to pull him back. He brushed me aside as though I were some worrisome insect and stood waiting for Derek's reaction. A moment passed. Derek drew himself up. The imprint of Jeff's hand burned on his cheek, but the rest of his face was deathly pale.

"You shouldn't have done that, Rawlins."

"Shall we say seven o'clock? Pistols?"

"Pistols will be fine."

"No!" I cried. "I'm not going to let you do this!"

"Shut up, Marietta," Jeff ordered.

"Both of you are insane!"

Neither man paid the least attention to me. They stared at each other, Derek grim, his gray eyes dark, Jeff superbly composed.

"I'll see you tomorrow then, at the Oaks," Jeff said.

Derek nodded. Jeff took hold of my wrist.

"We'll go home now," he said. "Till tomorrow, Hawke."

"Till tomorrow," Derek replied.

XXI

It was almost six, and still the sky was dark, sprinkled with stars, not even a hint of dawn on the horizon. I let the curtain fall back in place and resumed my pacing. I hadn't been able to sleep, hadn't even attempted to go to bed. All night long I had paced, frantic with worry, trying to think of something I could do to stop this insanity. At one point I had been on the verge of going to Derek, pleading with him as I had pleaded with Jeff, but that would have been futile. Derek would have been as deaf to my pleas as Jeff had been.

Jeff hadn't spoken a word during our ride home in the carriage, and I had been silent, too, shaken, upset, consumed with guilt yet knowing I must somehow keep calm. He had gone to his room as soon as we got back, closing the door firmly behind him. Somehow or other I had managed to change and perform my duties as hostess, and it had helped, for when the last customer had gone I was calmer, ready to discuss things with Jeff in a reasonable, civilized manner. He had stayed upstairs in his room ever since returning. I had expected to find him drunk, but when I finally knocked on his door and entered, it was to find him stone sober, sitting in his chair and staring into space like someone in a state of shock.

He refused to discuss it, refused to let me explain, re-

419

fused to listen to my pleas. He was calm—cool, even —and that had only made me feel worse. Finally, unable to help myself, I had cried, and that hadn't moved him, either. After almost an hour, I had finally come to my room. Four more hours had passed, and soon he would be leaving. The candles had all burned down, flames dancing now in pools of wax, casting shadows over the walls. The clock ticked monotonously, bringing the hour nearer and nearer.

What was I going to do? What was I going to *do*?

There were tears in my eyes, and I had never felt so wretched in my life. In just a little over an hour, two men were going to meet outside the city, under the oak trees, to fire pistols at each other, all because of me. It was insanity, pure insanity. What if one of them were hurt? My God, what if one of them were *killed*? I knew I couldn't bear that. I loved Derek with all my heart, and I loved Jeff, too, and if either of them . . . I thrust the image out of my mind.

The clock struck six. I must stop them. Somehow or other, I must make them see reason. But how? Jeff wouldn't listen to reason, and I knew Derek wouldn't either. He could not ignore the insult of the slap. He was a proud man. He had vowed he would never kill again, no matter what the circumstances, yet he was going to meet Jeff on the field. If there was an accident, if something happened to Jeff, Derek would blame me. And Jeff . . . Jeff intended to kill Derek. This wasn't a question of honor to be settled between two young hotheads. It went much deeper. I had to stop it.

First of all, I must get hold of myself. I was on the verge of hysteria, and that would accomplish nothing. I must calm down, and then I must dress, for I was wearing only my petticoat. I forced myself to sit down at the dressing table, forced myself to pick up the brush. In the flickering candlelight I brushed my hair until it fell about my shoulders in rich red-brown waves. The physical action was soothing, and I could feel some of the tension receding.

I dressed carefully, selecting a dark navy-blue dress with long sleeves. I stepped over to the full-length mirror. There was anguish in my eyes, and my lids were brushed with the blue-gray shadows of fatigue. The skin was stretched tightly over my cheekbones. I gazed at the reflection, forcing back the tears threatening to spring anew.

I should have gone to Jeff in the beginning. I should have told him that Derek had returned, that I was going to live with him, but I had been reluctant to hurt him, had put it off repeatedly. Instead of being open and honest and making a clean break, I had slipped off like a deceitful wife to meet Derek. Because I hadn't wanted to hurt Jeff, because I had delayed telling him for as long as possible, I had hurt him much worse. I alone was to blame for all this.

Turning away from the mirror, I heard voices in the hall. Jeff's voice was cool and precise as he gave instructions to Kyle, and Kyle replied in deep, sepulchral tones that caused me to shiver. I moved quickly through the sitting room and opened the door just in time to see Kyle moving down the hall toward the staircase. Jeff stood watching him. He hadn't slept, either. I saw that at once. His face was pale, his features drawn, and all traces of the raffish charmer were gone. His brown eyes were grim, and that wide pink mouth so ready to grin was set in a hard, determined line.

He turned to look at me. I might have been a stranger.

"You can't go through with this, Jeff," I said quietly.

"Kyle has gone to the livery stable to fetch the carriage."

"You must call it off."

"That's impossible, Marietta."

"You could be killed."

"I could be, yes. It wouldn't much matter."

"Jeff—"

"It's something I have to do," he said.

"This—this insanity will prove nothing. It will change

421

nothing. I love him, Jeff. I always have. I've never pretended with you."

"You've never pretended," he agreed.

"I—I didn't want to be unfaithful. It was something—something I couldn't help. When he came back, when I saw him again—"

"I don't care to discuss it, Marietta."

"I didn't want to hurt you. That's why I didn't tell you. I intended to tell you, but I kept putting it off, knowing what it would do to you. If there were any way I could have spared you this—"

"It's too late for words."

"How you must hate me," I whispered.

"No, Marietta, I don't hate you. I couldn't, no matter what you did. I love you with all my heart and soul, but unfortunately that doesn't seem to be enough."

We looked at each other for a moment. Jeff's eyes were filled with that love, with the pain it cost him, and my own filled with tears I could no longer hold back. He sighed and shook his head wearily, and then he drew me to him and kissed me tenderly on the lips, as though he were comforting a child. I rested my hand on his cheek, looking up at him with tearful entreaty.

"Please forgive me," I begged.

"I would forgive you anything."

"Don't go through with it, Jeff. Please don't."

"I must, Marietta. I'm afraid I can't salvage very much out of all this, but perhaps I can salvage my manhood, my pride."

"Pride—"

"I must have something left when this is all over."

"I'll give him up, Jeff. I'll never see him again. I'll even marry you. I do love you. In my way I love you. How I wish it could be—how I wish I could love you the way you love me. I . . . I'll learn. You'll make me. The night of the ball you said you were going to—"

"It's too late," he said quietly.

"What have I done?" I whispered. "I never wanted to hurt you. You must believe me."

422

"I believe you, Marietta."

He took me by the shoulders, gently moved me back, away from him, and then walked down the hall to his office and disappeared inside. I leaned against the wall. It was useless. I had failed. I had wounded him as deeply as a man could be wounded and, being a man, he had to fight.

The rooms were silent. The candles in the wall sconces flickered. I could hear the carriage coming down the street, hooves clopping lightly on the cobblestones. It stopped in front. Jeff came out of his office. He carried the leather box that contained his pistols. His long black cloak billowed and spread out behind him as he walked back down the hall toward me. He was no longer grim, merely resigned. He looked very, very tired.

He didn't even look at me. He moved on past and started toward the stairs, and my grief was so overwhelming that I thought I must surely die of it. I moved to the head of the stairs to watch him descend the last few steps. I seemed to be trapped in the middle of a terrible dream. Jeff walked to the front door and stepped outside. As he closed the door behind him, I stood there in a daze. Listening to the carriage pull away, I felt as if my heart were being wrenched from my body.

Several minutes passed, and I didn't even hear Angie approaching. She took my hand and squeezed it, and I looked at her with anguished eyes. She was fully dressed, even though it was only a little after six. She led me back down the hall into my sitting room and, as I sat on the sofa, handed me a glass of brandy.

"Drink it, luv. It'll help."

"You know," I said.

She nodded. "Kyle told me."

"I must go, Angie."

"You can't."

"I have to. I have to stop them."

"There's nothing you can do."

"I've got to go. Something dreadful is going to happen. I feel it. I've felt it for a long time. I—I had the feeling before. I felt something catastrophic was going to happen, and then Derek turned up and—and I thought that was it. It wasn't. It was *this*. This is the catastrophe. I've got to stop it."

"It's too late. There's no way—"

I set the brandy down and stood up abruptly. "I'll go to the livery stable. Someone will be up at this hour. Yes —yes, Kyle would have awakened them when he fetched the carriage. I—I'll hire a carriage."

"Marietta—"

"I've *got* to, Angie!"

Angie saw there was no way she could dissuade me. She sighed.

"Very well," she said. "You'd better let me go for the carriage. You're in no shape to do it yourself. I'll get that young Teddy Blake to drive us. He won't like the idea, not at this hour of the morning, but I imagine I can persuade him. I'll be back with the carriage in less than ten minutes. Wash your face. Pull yourself together."

"I'll try, Angie. Do hurry."

"I'll run all the way, luv."

She left, and I washed my face with cool water, and I did calm down. I forced back the emotions that had almost overwhelmed me. Jeff was determined to go through with it, and I was just as determined to stop it. I would. Somehow. Jeff was beyond reason, but there was still Derek. He would listen to me. He must. He hadn't wanted to duel in the first place, had refused to until Jeff slapped him. That slap had been a terrible insult, but I would make him listen to me. I would make him give up the duel.

I went downstairs and stepped outside to wait for the carriage. The sky was dark-gray now, no longer black, and the stars were gone. Up and down the street the buildings were shrouded with heavy shadows, and there was a thin, wispy fog that swirled slowly in the air like smoke. The chill of night hadn't yet vanished, and I shivered just a little, but I didn't go back in to fetch a

424

cloak. I waited, growing more and more impatient, fear and panic close to the surface again.

Two or three minutes later I heard the carriage pull out of the livery stable on the corner and start down the street. It was large and black, a closed carriage pulled by two stout dappled grays. Teddy Blake tugged on the reins to stop the carriage directly in front. His hair was mussed, his face flushed with sleep. His clothes had been hastily pulled on, and his cloak hung lopsided on his shoulders. Angie opened the door for me, drew me inside. Teddy called to the horses and clicked the reins. We were on our way.

"Can't he go any faster?" I said.

"Relax, luv. We'll get there. It's just now six-thirty. Shouldn't take us more'n twenty minutes to reach the Oaks."

"It's set for seven."

"I know."

"I'll make Derek see reason. I'll stop it."

"I hope you can."

"It's my fault, Angie. All this is my fault."

"Mustn't be too hard on yourself," she said. "I don't imagine you wanted to be unfaithful to Jeff. I don't imagine you could help yourself. I understand now, loving Kyle as I do."

"I tried to stay away."

"I know you did, luv. But it was inevitable. I can see that now."

"I *do* wish he'd go a little faster."

"Poor Teddy. He'd gone back to bed after Kyle left. I had to roust him out, and him naked as the day he was born. Blushed somethin' awful, he did. I stood there tappin' my foot while he dressed, orderin' him to snap it up. He'll get us there."

I leaned back against the leather cushion and stared out of the window as the carriage drove down dark, narrow streets, rocking slightly as it rumbled over the cobblestones. We passed a square where men in brown leather aprons were setting up vegetable carts. Small black braziers had been set on the ground, fires burning like bright orange blossoms that waved in the breeze. We drove on, down more dark streets, near the waterfront now. I could smell oil and tar and salty water. It seemed we would never get out of the city.

My calm had worn off. I was tense now, my nerves on edge. I wanted to shout at the driver, urge him to hurry, hurry, even though we were moving as fast as possible over the rough cobbles. Angie reached for my hand. Her pale-blue taffeta skirts crackled.

"We're almost out of the city," she said. "He'll be able to drive a lot faster once we're clear of these narrow streets. Do try to get hold of yourself, luv."

"I feel like I'm going to jump out of my skin."

"I know."

"What—what if we're not in time?"

"We will be," she assured me.

"Derek will listen to me. He must."

"I imagine he will."

"He—he hates killing. He told me. He had to kill a man once. The man who gave him his scar. He's never been able to forgive himself for taking another man's life, and now—now he's going to take a pistol and—"

"Try not to think about it. Try to relax."

"They'll already be there by this time. Kyle is acting as Jeff's second and—and I suppose one of Derek's men will act as his. They'll be going over the rules. Rules. How silly to have rules. They're going to try to *kill* each other."

"We'll be there in just a few minutes," she said.

She gave my hand a tight squeeze and settled back against the cushion. The carriage rocked as the wheels skimmed over hard-packed earth. We were clear of the city at last. The carriage picked up speed. We drove alongside a canal. There was a smell of swamp. The fog was thicker here. Trees seemed to take shape like dark phantoms emerging from the swirling, grayish-white mist. We turned, moving inland, away from the canal. It was growing lighter.

"Teddy does know the spot, doesn't he?" I asked.

"Everyone knows the Oaks."

It seemed an eternity before the carriage finally stopped. Angie and I climbed out. We were on the edge of a large field surrounded by giant oaks. Two other carriages stood at the edge of the field, half-concealed by the fog, which hadn't yet lifted. The sky was still gray, wavering rays of pale yellow-white sunlight streaming down over the field where five men stood in a cluster. I was so nervous now I could hardly keep from trembling. Angie took my hand once again, squeezing it.

"Calm and easy, luv. Mustn't fall apart now."

"Thank—thank God they haven't begun."

The men separated, two moving in one direction, two in the other. The fifth man shook his head and went to stand under one of the oaks. None of them had looked up, although they must have heard the carriage approaching. As we drew nearer, I could distinguish features. Jeff and Kyle were talking as Jeff removed his cloak. Derek stood with one of the smugglers, calmly examining his pistol, holding it out in front of him, testing the weight. The fifth man held a bulky black bag in his hand, and I knew he must be the doctor Jeff and Kyle had fetched after they left the gambling house. The fog was a fine mist in the air, gradually dissipating as the sunlight grew stronger.

Angie let go of my hand. Heart pounding, I hurried across the still-damp grass toward Derek, tendrils of fog parting before me. My skirts billowed in the breeze, dark red underskirts showing beneath the navy blue. I stumbled and almost lost my balance, and Derek looked up. He showed neither surprise nor displeasure, his gray eyes revealing nothing. He said something to his second, and the man moved away several paces, scowling. When I reached him, Derek lowered the pistol he had been examining.

"You shouldn't have come, Marietta."

"I had to. I have to stop this."

"It's rather late for that," he said dryly.

427

"Jeff wouldn't listen to reason. I tried to persuade him to give up this—this madness, but he wouldn't listen."

"And you think I will."

"You must, Derek."

"We've less than five minutes left, Marietta. You'd better get out of the way."

He was so very uninterested, as though this were all a rather tedious affair he would try to endure along with the boredom it entailed. I couldn't reach him. I realized that at once. He was as determined to go through with it as Jeff had been.

"Please, Derek," I whispered. "I beg you."

"A few minutes ago, just before you arrived, both of us were given an opportunity to call the duel off. Neither of us took it."

"You can still call it off. You can refuse—"

He looked at me with those bored gray eyes, and I knew that any further argument would be futile. I felt a terrible sinking sensation inside. I had lost. Derek frowned, and then he turned his back to me and signaled to his second. As the man approached, I left, moving across the damp grass and through the fog as though I were in the middle of a dream. I hardly noticed when Angie took my arm and guided me over to one of the oak trees. We stood there beneath the heavy boughs, and she slipped her arm about my waist.

"Try to bear up, luv," she said quietly.

"He wouldn't listen."

"It'll all be over in just a few minutes. There's so much fog they'll probably both miss. Everything is going to be all right."

I shook my head. I was numb, and the dream-like quality mercifully remained. I watched as the two men approached each other across the field, one in brown, his sandy hair ruffled by the breeze, the other in dark-blue breeches and white shirt, his manner still bored. Each held a long, deadly pistol. The fog was lifting rapidly now, though the trees surrounding the field were still wrapped in shadow.

They met each other. They turned, standing back to back, and then a somber voice began to count the paces. *One, two, three,* and they moved apart. *Four, five, six,* and the distance between them grew and I wondered why Kyle was calling the paces and not Derek's man. Had they drawn lots? Did it make any difference? A gust of strong wind swept over the field, blowing most of the fog away, and the oak boughs groaned overhead, tendrils of Spanish moss waving. Ten paces now, ten to go, and then they would turn and fire and one of them would die. I knew that for a certainty. I felt it in every fiber of my being.

"*Sixteen,*" Kyle called. "*Seventeen, eighteen—*"

I loved them both, each in a different way, and because of me one of them was going to die. There was nothing I could do, nothing, and I shook my head as Angie's arm tightened about my waist. It was real, *real,* not a dream at all. Kyle called the last two numbers and the men turned, facing each other again, forty paces separating them now, and each man raised his pistol. There was a deafening explosion and puffs of smoke. I saw a bright-red blossom bursting on Derek's white shirt and he staggered backward, still clutching the smoking pistol in his hand.

I tore free from Angie's grip. I raced across the field toward him, and he stood there with the same bored look in his eyes as the red blossom spread on his shoulder. The doctor! Where was the doctor? Why wasn't he hurrying over with his bulky black bag? The color had drained from Derek's face. His cheeks were ashen. He staggered again, swaying for a moment before maintaining his balance. I seized his arm. Derek pulled away, looking at me with cool hostility.

"It's over," he said.

"You're hurt!"

"It's only a flesh wound. The bullet passed through my shoulder. It's over, Marietta. My ship is leaving this afternoon. Go to him now."

"You're leaving—without me. You can't mean—"

"He's dying, Marietta. I aimed for his shoulder. His bullet struck me just as I pulled the trigger. My shot went through his chest. He's dying. You've caused me to kill a man. You've brought me to that. We have nothing more to say to each other."

"Derek—"

"Go to him!"

As he turned and strode briskly away from me, the impact of what he had just said suddenly hit me. I had been so stunned when he told me he was leaving that what followed had hardly registered, but now it was as though an arrow pierced my heart. I cried out and stumbled across the field to where Kyle and the doctor huddled over Jeff. I pushed them aside and fell to my knees to gather him in my arms. He looked up at me with puzzled eyes.

"Marietta?"

"I'm here, Jeff."

"It's you? Marietta?"

"I'm here, darling. I'm here."

He grinned that foolish grin. "It is you. You called me darlin'. I imagined it, didn't I? I must uv imagined it."

"No, darling. My darling."

"You said it again," he murmured.

"Of course I did."

"I wish—" The words were barely audible.

"Yes?"

"—wish I coulda been th' one. Wish it coulda been me."

I cradled him to me, gathering him closer, and he rested the side of his head on my shoulder and looked up at me with that grin still playing on his lips. His face was terribly pale, and damp, and I brushed a lock of hair from his forehead and rested my hand against his cheek. I could feel the warmth leaving his body and feel the chill stealing over him, and I knew.

I looked up at the doctor. He shook his head. There was nothing he could do. He and Kyle had stepped back, and Kyle had his arm around Angie. Tears were spilling

430

down her cheeks. Jeff shuddered. I tightened my arms around him.

"—only I'd had more money," he said. It was little more than a whisper. "That day—woulda all been different. If only—he'd 've lost and you'd 've been mine and—"

I realized he was talking about the auction. I stroked his cheek.

"I am yours, darling," I said. "Surely you know that. You—you're going to be all right. We're going to be married. We're going to be very, very happy—"

"Marietta?"

"I'm here, Jeff."

"I can't see you!"

"Darling—"

"Don't leave me!"

"Never. I'll never leave you."

He clutched me with amazing strength, looking up at me with eyes that could no longer see. He coughed. It was a hoarse, rattling cough, and his whole body shook with it. I held him, folding him against me, and when the cough was over, he blinked his eyes and peered up at me, and his eyes filled with joyous recognition.

"—didn't go away," he whispered.

"I'm still here, darling."

"—love you. Always did."

"I love you, too, darling."

He seemed puzzled. "You do?"

"I do, Jeff. I do."

I saw the happiness in his eyes and he tried to say something else, but the words wouldn't come. He frowned, and then he clasped me with desperate strength, trying to speak. The light went out of his eyes. The arms that had been clasping me dropped limply. I cradled him against me, rocking him gently in my arms as the tears streamed down my cheeks. Jeff was dead.

XXII

He examined them carefully, unable to conceal the acquisitive gleam in his eye. Mr. Dawson had been recommended as the man most likely to give me a fair price for the diamonds, but I saw at once that I was going to have to bargain hard. He was a plump, robust man with ginger-colored sidewhiskers and shrewd brown eyes. The sign on his door identified him as a merchant, and his office was indeed plush, but I strongly suspected that most of the merchandise he handled was acquired through dubious means.

"Lovely gems," he admitted.

"They're quite genuine, I assure you."

"And you want to sell them?"

"That's why I'm here, Mr. Dawson."

He set the diamonds aside as though they were baubles hardly worth considering. That was part of the act. He would denigrate them now. He would tell me how the market for diamonds had dropped. He would offer me a tenth of their value and act as though he were doing me a favor. I knew what they were worth. I knew approximately what I could expect to get. I intended to stand firm.

"I hear you've had a spell of bad luck, Miss Danver. It *is* Miss Danver, isn't it? You and Rawlins weren't married?"

"Mr. Rawlins and I were not married," I said coldly.

"Hear he made a lot of foolish investments, lost a fortune speculating. Hear there were so many debts the Palace had to be sold, all the furnishing auctioned off. Hear there still wasn't enough to pay all he owed. Seems he bought a lot of stocks on credit, lost 'em, still hadn't paid for all of 'em when he died."

"The diamonds belong to me, Mr. Dawson. They're my personal property. You have the bill of sale marked paid-in-full right there in front of you. Perhaps you'd better examine it again."

"Oh, no question but what they're yours. His creditors would've got 'em otherwise. They got everything else, I hear. Understand the new owners are going to take over the property tomorrow."

"Are you interested in the diamonds, Mr. Dawson?"

"I'm interested. Lovely gems, just like I said, but the market's not what it was. Gems like these, they ain't so easy to resell. Hardly worth my time making an offer. More trouble than it's worth."

"Perhaps I'd better leave, then. If you'll hand me the diamonds—"

"Hold on, hold on. I didn't say I *wouldn't* take 'em off your hands. I'm sure you need the cash—need it badly, if all I've heard's so. I'll give you five hundred pounds for 'em."

"I'm afraid that isn't enough."

"It's the best I can do, Miss Danver."

"Then I've wasted your time. Mr. Rawlins paid three thousand pounds for those diamonds. I won't take a penny less than a thousand for them."

"A thousand!"

"Take it or leave it, Mr. Dawson."

"I'll give you seven hundred," he said grudgingly.

"Sorry. I'm really in a bit of a hurry, Mr. Dawson. There are three other gentlemen on my list. I'm sure one of them will be more than willing to meet my price."

"Eight hundred. Not a penny more."

His cheeks were a bright pink now, his brown eyes

gleaming with greed. He wasn't about to let the diamonds go. He stood to make an enormous profit from them, would probably be able to resell them for more than Jeff had paid originally. I was well aware of that. I stood firm. He blustered and argued. He protested vehemently and finally resorted to personal abuse, informing me that he had no intention of being held up by a debtor's fancy lady. Calmly, I picked up the diamonds. They flashed and shimmered like chunks of frozen rainbow. I thought Dawson was going to have apoplexy.

"All right, all right, I'll *give* you the thousand!" he exclaimed.

"I'm afraid they'll cost you twelve hundred now, Mr. Dawson."

"Twelve hundred! But—"

"I don't appreciate pompous little crooks making personal remarks."

"You bitch! If you think—"

"Fifteen hundred, Mr. Dawson."

Dawson went through another siege of apoplectic gestures, cheeks flaming, but he couldn't take his eyes off the diamonds. I stood there in front of his desk with an icy expression, and he finally admitted defeat. He heaved a weary sigh and gave in. I demanded payment in cash. He opened the safe and counted out the money. I felt a terrible humiliation at having to deal with such a repulsive creature, but I had no choice. I needed the money. When I left his office a few minutes later, I had fifteen hundred pounds in my reticule, five hundred more than I had counted on. That helped considerably.

I could go ahead with my plans now. I could survive, on my own terms. Half a dozen men had rushed to the gambling house with generous offers, assuring me I needn't worry about a thing. All had been eager to take care of me, but I would have nothing to do with them. I didn't intend to be dependent on anyone. I would make my own way, and selling the diamonds had given me the means. As I walked down the bright, sun-splattered street, I felt a strong determination inside. I felt hard, too, and cold. I was going to fight back, and the encounter with Dawson had given me a great deal of confidence.

Three weeks had passed since that dreadful day when my whole world had fallen to pieces. Just three weeks, and it seemed a lifetime ago. There had been little time for grief, no time to give way to the guilt, the dreadful sorrow. Jeff was dead. Derek was gone. He had sailed that afternoon. After Jeff's funeral there had been an onslaught of creditors, and then there had been a public auction. Everything was gone now, and I was alone. I had my clothes, a few personal possessions, and I had the money in my reticule.

I was going to survive.

Someday, perhaps, I would be able to forgive myself for what I had done to Jeff, and perhaps someday I would be able to forgive Derek Hawke for what he had done to me. In a perverse way, I was almost glad, for I was free of Derek at last. He had murdered the love in my heart. It had been replaced by icy resolution. I had learned my lesson. I had let my heart guide me. I had been ruled by my emotions. No more. From now on, I was going to use my head, and never again would I permit my heart to dictate. The empty place that Jeff had left there would never be filled.

After the auction, I had taken a boat upriver to Natchez. I spent a full day there, investigating, asking questions, and finally selected a site, a small white frame building near the center of town. I signed a lease, promising to pay at the end of the month. Back in New Orleans, I had several long sessions with Lucille and made arrangements for goods to be delivered in Natchez. Now that I had the money, I could go ahead with complete confidence. I had waited until the very last to sell the diamonds, reluctant to part with them. Now the deed was done.

It was fifteen minutes before I finally reached the gambling house. It looked bleak and empty in the sunlight, as though the plundering within had left its mark outside as well. I unlocked the door and stepped inside.

The hall was dim, empty, stripped of its finery. The gaming rooms were empty, too, the vast ballroom like a shell, furniture and chandeliers gone. Tomorrow the new owners would take over. I had no idea what they intended to do with the place. I didn't care. It was already a part of my past, and the future was all that mattered now.

Hearing footsteps on the stairs, I looked up to see Angie descending. Angie and Kyle had stayed on, had stood by me. The man who had bought the furniture had kindly agreed to let us keep a few token pieces until our departure, so at least we had beds to sleep on. He would come for the rest tomorrow.

"Did you sell it?" Angie asked.

"I got fifteen hundred pounds."

"Fifteen hundred pounds! That's wonderful! You'll be able to open your shop with plenty to spare."

"I suppose I will."

"I know it'll be a grand success, luv. No one knows more about dresses than you do, and those ladies in Natchez will flock to your place. They'll be the best-dressed women in the territory."

"Is Kyle in?" I asked.

Angie shook her head. "He's gone to purchase our passage. The ship'll leave next Thursday. We'll stay in an inn until then. Lucky he saved his money these past three years!"

"Indeed," I said.

"Come on upstairs, luv. I've finished my own packing. I'll help you with yours. There's some brandy Kyle put aside. You look as though you need a glass. I know *I* do!"

My sitting room was bare, and in the bedroom only the bed, the wardrobe, and two chairs remained. A valise and two large trunks stood ready to be packed. Angie scurried off to her own room and returned a moment with a bottle of brandy and two glasses.

"I still can't believe it," she said. "Me, married to a Welshman, about to leave for Wales! It's supposed to be dreadfully gray and gloomy there. I just *know* I'll be utterly miserable."

"I doubt that, Angie."

"I do, too, frankly," she confessed. "As long as I'm with Kyle, I'd be happy anywhere. You know, I don't feel married. I suppose because it was such a dreary little ceremony in that dusty office with stacks of yellowing papers and that plump white cat snoozing on the windowsill. The bloody sod didn't even give me a ring! He says he'll buy me one later, after the pub is established and bringing in enough to pay for it."

"He's going to open a pub?"

"I didn't tell you? There's only one pub in that pathetic little village where he was born, and he aims to put it out of business. He's got a lot of relatives still living there, and there's even a cottage. It passed on to him when his folks died. It's been rented out all this time to a cousin of his. God knows what his people are going to think about me."

"I'm sure they'll find you enchanting."

"They'll probably be shocked speechless. A flashy little London whore who used to do tricks for tuppence! One husband already in his grave—poor George. That seems such a long time ago. I—I feel like a different person."

"You are a different person, Angie. The past is behind you. You're going to make Kyle a wonderful wife."

"I'm damn sure gonna try. If he can forget my past, I suppose I can, too. Here, luv, drink your brandy. We'd better get started if we intend to pack all these things. It'll take us forever—"

We drank our brandy, and then I began to pull dresses out of the wardrobe and spread them out over the bed. I had sold several in order to pay for the quick trip to Natchez. The splendid gold ballgown Jeff bought me was gone, as was the blue velvet I had been wearing the night Derek delivered the wine. I would never have been able to wear them again, and the used-clothes dealer had given me a reasonable price. I had sold others as well. I doubted that I would have need of splendid gowns in the future. Angie seemed to be reading my mind. Folding up a violet-blue silk, she gazed at me with a thoughtful expression.

"There'll be a man," she said.

"Oh?"

"In Natchez. There'll be a man, probably several. Oh, the shop will be all very well and good, it'll keep you amused for a while, but eventually—there'll be a man, luv."

"I'm not interested."

"Not just now, no, but a few months from now, after you've gotten over the initial stages of grief and disappointment—"

"If there is a man," I interrupted, "he'll be very, very rich. He'll be able to give me everything, and I'll give nothing in return."

"No?"

"I'll never love again."

"This has all made you very hard, Marietta. Very bitter, too."

"Perhaps it has. I won't deny it."

"This isn't you, you know. It's a role you're playing. You've resolved to become a cold, heartless opportunist, but it isn't you. You're much too sensitive to play that role for long. You're much too good at heart."

"I'll never let myself be used again, Angie. Derek used me. Jeff did, too, in his way. I was concerned for them, their feelings. From now on I'm going to think of myself."

"You say that. I've no doubt you believe it—at the moment."

I closed the lid of one trunk and open the other. Angie continued to fold dresses, eyes still thoughtful.

"Do you think he'll ever come back?" she asked.

"Derek? He'll win his inheritance, become an aristocrat. He'll marry a pallid blueblood with an impressive pedigree. He's out of my life for good."

"You still love him."

"I hate him!"

"You just think you do. He'll always be in your blood."

438

"I thought so, too. Once. I know better now."

We worked for a while in silence, filling the trunk, and at last the job was done, only a nightgown and the clothes I would wear tomorrow unpacked. Angie sighed and brushed her hair from her temples. She sat on the edge of the bed, her expression sad.

"I'm going to miss you, luv," she said quietly.

"I'll miss you, too, Angie."

"We'll write."

"Of course we will."

"And—you're going to be happy, Marietta. I feel it in my bones."

"Happiness no longer concerns me."

"It'll come, though. Eventually. Just like it came to me."

"Perhaps," I said dryly.

Kyle returned a short while later, bringing cheese and bread and fish with him. We ate in the sitting room, on the floor, candles burning in old chipped saucers. Although we tried to make it a light, festive affair, a pall hung over us. The empty rooms all around seemed to echo with ghostly voices. Kyle sat with his arm draped around Angie's shoulder, as grim and solemn as ever. I knew he blamed me for Jeff's death—that he had never approved of me—yet he had done all he could to help me these last weeks.

"I suppose I'd better take the trunks down now," he said after we finished the scanty meal. "We'll need to get an early start. Your boat leaves at seven, I believe?"

"That's right."

"I've already made arrangements with young Blake. He'll bring a carriage around at five-thirty. We'll strap your trunks on top and return for ours after you've gone."

"You've gotten us a room at the inn?" Angie inquired.

Kyle nodded, getting to his feet. In the empty room he seemed even larger than usual. The flickering candles on the floor cast a long shadow across the wall. Angie and I cleared up the things, and after Kyle had carried

439

all of the trunks down to the hall, they retired to their room.

In my nightgown, I folded the clothes I had been wearing and packed them in the valise along with my toilet articles. I blew out the candle and climbed into bed, knowing I would toss and turn for hours, just as I had done every night for the past three weeks.

I was up at five o'clock, dressing. Angie came in with a cup of steaming coffee she'd made down in the deserted kitchen. I could tell that she hadn't slept well, either. She was fully dressed, ready to leave, and she stayed with me, trying valiantly to be cheerful. We heard the carriage coming down the street. I picked up the valise, and we went downstairs where Kyle was waiting. In a matter of minutes the trunks were strapped on top of the carriage and we were on our way. A sleepy Teddy Blake drove us down the still dark streets toward the docks.

Kyle handled everything once we arrived. He saw to my berth, saw that my trunks were safely stored on board. The sun was just beginning to come up, staining the sky with orange. The ship was brown, as were the docks, the great Mississippi a dark, dark blue spangled with flecks of gold as the sun touched it. There was very little fog. It was going to be a clear day. Angie and I stood watching passengers going up the gangplank. She held my hand in a crushing grip, and just before Kyle joined us, she pulled me to her and gave me a mighty hug. There were tears in her eyes.

"Goodbye, luv," she whispered.

"Goodbye, Angie."

"I'll never forget you, Marietta."

"Nor I you. Be happy with Kyle."

She sobbed and turned me loose. I was thankful for Kyle's arrival, afraid I might break down myself. I kissed her cheek and shook his hand. Then, tearing myself from them, I climbed the wooden gangplank just before they raised it. I stood on deck, holding onto the railing as the ship pulled slowly away. Kyle's arm was around

Angie's shoulder again, and she was still crying. The sunlight was brighter now. I could see her tears glistening. She took out her handkerchief and waved it as greater and greater distance separated us. I waved back, filled with tremulous emotions I could no longer contain.

I waved goodbye to Angie, and to Jeff, and to all that had been. Tears welled up in my eyes, spilled down my cheeks despite my efforts to stem the flow. It was the first time I had cried since the day Jeff had died. It would be the last. Angie and Kyle were small specks on the dock now as the ponderous ship started slowly up the river. Angie waved her handkerchief one last time. I returned the wave, and then I brushed the tears from my eyes and turned away. That part of my life was over for good. I wondered what the future held in store.

PART FOUR:

Natchez 1775

XXIII

It was Sunday afternoon. I sat downstairs in the tiny office back of the shop, the heavy ledger opened on the desk in front of me. Going over the columns of figures slowly and carefully, I knew it was no longer possible to deny the obvious. The facts were there, neatly recorded on the pages in black ink. The expenditures had been heavy, the profits small. I had done little more than break even.

I closed the ledger with a sense of finality and put it away. I wasn't in debt, but almost all the money was gone, and I knew there would be very little coming in. Oh, I could make a living from the shop. If I went on working my fingers to the bone six days a week, I would continue to come out each month with some small profit, enough to live on. But after six long months I had to admit to myself that the shop was never going to be the success I had envisioned.

I knew that, and I knew why.

A ray of sunlight streamed through the window gilding the grainy leather pad and making a tiny silver sunburst on the black ink pot. I could go on sewing gaudy gowns for the prostitutes of Natchez-under-the-hill and sensible, serviceable garments for those friendly, hard-working women who were trying to establish roots for their families here in the unofficial fourteenth colony. But those affluent women who provided the very life blood for a business such as mine would continue to stay away.

Natchez wasn't New Orleans. It was a thriving, bustling British colony with carefully structured social levels. Thousands of people had poured into the isolated frontier settlement as the turmoil between rebels and Royalists took on impetus. Staunchly loyal families left the thirteen colonies bag and baggage to establish homes far away from the tense conflict that everyone predicted would soon erupt into an all-out revolution. A number of the families were quite wealthy, many with aristocratic connections back in England. They brought their wealth with them, and their rigid class consciousness. The women who could have made the shop a success had their own seamstresses, dowdy, aging spinsters who made a precarious living trotting from fine house to fine house in a desperate effort to please the grand dames and their spoiled, pampered daughters. They would have nothing to do with the scarlet woman from New Orleans.

My reputation had proceeded me. Somehow or other, these snobbish, self-satisfied women had learned that I had been hostess of a gambling house. It might as well have been a brothel as far as they were concerned. Morals in Natchez were as lax as anywhere else, illicit affairs rampant, but it was all concealed behind a solid wall of hypocrisy. There was no demimonde society in Natchez. There were the good citizens who lived on the hill and the dreadful social lepers who caroused in the taverns and brothels under-the-hill. Class distinctions were sharp, and the upper-class ladies had decided not to patronize my shop.

I smiled bitterly, remembering the early enthusiasm that had caused me to pour all my time, energy, and money into the place. My shop was in a small white frame building at the end of one of the main business streets, almost on the outskirts of town. A white picket fence enclosed the small yard, and three tall elm trees grew in front. My living quarters were on the second floor, above the shop, and I could see the Mississippi River from my bedroom

446

windows. Convinced smart ladies would soon be pouring in, I had hired two young assistants, bright, merry girls who had been as eager as I to make the place a success. One of them had to be let go after the first two months, and I was forced to dismiss the second last month. There simply wasn't enough business to justify full-time assistants.

Though my lease on the place was for a year, I seriously doubted that I would be able to survive another six months. I could make a living, but merely making a living wasn't enough. It was time to admit defeat and move on to something else. I didn't plan to grow old making inexpensive, durable garments for middle-class matrons and spectacular gowns for prostitutes. Even if the shop was a failure, it had served its purpose. It had helped me over a very difficult period, and it had taught me a lesson about social power.

The sunlight wavered on the desktop. Outside, the elm trees stirred in the breeze. The shop was silent. The bitter smile still played on my lips. I had come to Natchez to make a new start, to put my past behind me. I was going to become a respectable business woman. My shop would be the best of its kind in the whole territory, my conduct above reproach. I was going to make my own way, using the ability I knew I had. But the fine ladies of Natchez wouldn't allow me to make a new start. They had labeled me a scarlet woman from the beginning and had wrecked any chance of my success.

I tried not to resent it, but I did. I wanted to strike back at those self-satisfied, hypocritical dames. I wanted to *show* them. I would, too. Somehow or other I would make them come around. The shop was a failure, but they hadn't defeated *me*. I was going to fight back. A plan had already begun to take shape in my mind. It was utterly mercenary, and I didn't know whether I could go through with it or not. One thing was certain: I no longer intended to be a victim, passive, acted upon. I was going to take matters into my own hands.

Leaving the office, I went up the back stairs to my bedroom. It was after two o'clock. Bruce Trevelyan

447

would be coming to take me for a ride in his carriage shortly before three. We had gone for a ride almost every Sunday for the past two months. Bruce was twenty-two years old, a tall, slender young man with wavy brown hair and serious blue eyes. The Trevelyans had been among the first Royalist families to move to Natchez. Bruce's father was the second son of a duke, his plantation already one of the largest in the territory. His background, wealth and clean-cut good looks made Bruce easily the most eligible bachelor around. He was polite and formal and rather grave, and I feared that he was very much in love with me.

Apparently unaware that it was off limits to the respectable upper class, he had come into the shop two months ago to purchase a birthday present for his sister Cynthia. His elegant clothes and reserved manner immediately identified him as a member of the gentry. He looked bewildered by all the frills and fripperies surrounding him. Clearly at a loss, he smiled politely and silently beseeched me for assistance. I was touched by his youth, his vulnerability, the warmth of that polite smile. After suggesting a number of gifts, I sold him a lovely shawl. He thanked me and left, and I forgot about him. So, when he returned the following Sunday to inquire if I would care to go for a ride in his new carriage, I was completely taken by surprise.

I had hesitated, of course. Although he really wasn't a great deal younger than I, he was a mere youth by my standards. I thanked him for the invitation, intending to refuse, but in the end I hadn't the heart. I found his nervous uncertainty and youthful gravity quite endearing. Bruce proved to be a charming companion, and while I realized our weekly drives were causing a furor of gossip, I also realized that such gossip couldn't matter less to me at this point. Bruce was determined. He had told his parents that he was twenty-two years old and could see whomever he chose, adding that he didn't give a hang what people said. My reputation as an adventuress was considerably enhanced, but, while I firmly refused to see

Bruce during the week, I saw no reason to give up these innocent Sunday drives.

The white curtains in my bedroom billowed inward with the breeze, and I stared glumly at the worn gray carpet with its blue and rose patterns. The room was small and inexpensively furnished, as was the sitting room adjoining it. At first these rooms had been a snug haven, comforting me in my grief, but recently, as my loneliness and dissatisfaction grew, I had found them confining, almost prison-like. They seemed to symbolize my failure. I had never spent a happy night in that large brass bed with its dark rose coverlet. The first two or three months I had been unable to sleep peacefully because of my grief, and then, when that was finally under control, I began to worry about the shop. Nights of angry frustration followed the nights of grief, and always there was the loneliness that grew stronger, more tormenting, as the weeks passed. Had I not been so lonely, had I not been starved for some kind of social contact, I would never have accepted Bruce's invitation in the first place.

Still, I enjoyed the rides tremendously, enjoyed the fresh air, the gentle rock of the carriage as the horses moved along at a leisurely pace. It soothed me seeing the countryside, so lovely and verdant. And I could forget my problems for a while, in the company of the grave, polite young man who was so serious and earnest and endearing, who talked about his childhood in England, about books and music and life and what he hoped to accomplish. It was casual and relaxing and innocent, until I realized that Bruce was falling in love with me. I had not encouraged him, yet last time, when he stopped the carriage on the river road and pulled me into his arms, I hadn't protested, nor had I pulled away.

His kiss had been long and tender and surprisingly experienced. Bruce had the quiet, understated virility of the well-bred English gentleman, and I suspected his years at Harvard College in Massachusetts had not been spent entirely pouring over books. Though carefully controlled, the kiss had communicated a passionate urgency.

449

When he finally released me, he hadn't said a word, had simply looked at me with those serious blue eyes that expressed his feelings far more eloquently than words could have. His wasn't a boyish infatuation, nor was Bruce a randy young buck with seduction in mind. It seemed the wealthy, handsome only son of one of the town's most prominent families was in love with me.

Sitting down at the dressing table, I began to brush my hair vigorously. What superb irony, I though, not without a certain satisfaction. Bruce was the prize catch in the society that had so successfully thwarted all my plans. Those haughty, self-righteous matrons would give anything to nab him for their daughters, and, I knew, the daughters vied for his attention, constantly visiting his sister in hopes he would be on hand. Bruce wanted none of them. He wanted me, and I intended to use him to achieve my goals. I only hoped I could do it without hurting him too badly.

It was important that I look especially attractive today, and I chose my dress with care, finally selecting a soft beige muslin sprigged with tiny brown and blue flowers. The dress made me look younger and emphasized my full breasts and slender waist. It was a provocative garment, one I wouldn't have dreamed of wearing for Bruce before. Today, it suited my purpose ideally.

Giving a final pat to my hair, I went into the hall and moved down the stairs. Stepping outside, I locked the shop door behind me. It was a lovely spring day. There was a subtle perfume in the air that blended with the smells of mud and moss and river that were ever present. I felt strong and purposeful as I moved toward the gate. I had finally admitted defeat and was ready to give up the shop. Another chapter of my life had closed, a brief and frustrating chapter, and a new one was about to begin. I was going to be in control this time, I vowed. Marietta Danver was no longer to be a pawn of fate.

A light, elegant open carriage came bowling down the road a few minutes later, pulled by two sleek gray horses with silky manes that waved in the breeze. Bruce drove with practiced skill, handling the reins firmly without apparent effort. I smiled as he halted the horses and climbed down. I was genuinely glad to see him, and I wished I weren't so fond of him. It would be so much easier if he weren't such a serious, admirable youth. I didn't look forward to hurting him. Had there been some-one like Bruce. in my life six years ago, I mused, none of this would be necessary.

Although his generous pink mouth shaped a smile, I could tell that he was preoccupied, as though there were some very important decision he must make. I fancied it concerned me in some way. Not much taller than I, Bruce had the lean, finely muscled build of a young athlete, shown off to advantage by his superbly tailored pearl-gray breeches and frock coat.

The preoccupied look gave way to one of appreciation as he took in the details of my appearance. Manipulating him was going to be absurdly simple, I knew. He was so young and malleable that he'd be defenseless against my wiles. I wasn't particularly proud of myself, but what must be done must be done. As he handed me into the carriage, I wished I were an innocent eighteen-year-old girl whose only desire in life was to please him.

"It's a lovely day," I remarked.

Bruce nodded, taking up the reins. "You're lovely, too."

"Why—thank you, sir."

"You've never looked so fetching."

"I imagine it's the dress. I wanted to wear something appropriate for such a glorious spring day. You approve, I take it?"

"Very much."

Bruce drove us through the heart of the city on his way to the river road. I was still amazed at the changes that had occurred since the time Jeff and I stopped here on our way to New Orleans. Natchez was little more than a frontier settlement then, and in just four years it had become an impressive town with many fine buildings and an increasing number of elegant homes. It had a clean and graceful beauty quite unlike that of New Orleans. Perched high on the bluff overlooking the river, it had a spacious, airy charm all its own, and there was an aura of prosperity. Fortunately the bluff concealed that second city huddled under the hill. Bruce was silent, a slight frown creasing his brow.

"You seem preoccupied," I said.

"Sorry. It's Schnieder's ball."

What a stroke of luck, I thought. Bruce had brought the subject up himself. I knew he was referring to the ball Helmut Schnieder was giving at Roseclay the following week.

"I'm expected to attend," he replied.

"I understand it's to be the event of the season. Everyone in Natchez seems to be talking about it. Schnieder's never entertained at Roseclay before, they say, and this will be the first time anyone's had an opportunity to see the place properly."

"I don't like the man," Bruce said, "and I haven't the least desire to see the interior of his house."

"It's supposed to be magnificent," I said casually.

"It is," Bruce admitted. "It took him over three years to finish it to his satisfaction. He had a whole crew of foreign artisans working on the interior, and he spent a fortune having the gardens laid out. He just finished the place a few months ago, and then he took off to Europe to buy furniture. A whole shipload arrived last month."

"I heard about that. Mr. Schnieder must be very wealthy."

"He is. His plantation is the largest in the territory, and the most productive. They say he owns half the land in Natchez. He came here years ago, when it was a tiny settlement, and he was already a wealthy man. When the place started booming, he seemed to have his hand in everything. He's helped finance a lot of the building, helped get businesses started, made loans left and right."

"He sounds quite the philanthropist."

"Not at all. Schneider never does anything without a reason. He's been open-handed, yes, and as a result he's

452

got a tight hold on the entire town. Everyone's intimidated by him—with a good reason, I should imagine. Even my parents. That's why I'm expected to go to this damned ball. Can't risk offending the mighty Helmut Schnieder."

Bruce scowled, lapsing into silence, while I thought about the encounter I had had with the German almost four years ago on the waterfront. He had been supervising the unloading of pink brick for the mansion he'd recently finished. That day he had wanted to buy me from Jeff. I remembered the way he had looked at me, remembered his incredible presence, his strong, blunt features. One wasn't likely to forget a man who exuded such power. I hadn't. Only last week I had seen him driving past the shop, his large, heavyset body impressively clad in expensively tailored clothes.

That was when the plan first began to formulate in my mind.

I had heard a great deal of talk about him, of course. I knew that he was still single, and I knew that his sister Meg was attending school in Germany. I had frequently wondered about her and the adamant young man who had been trying to persuade her to elope with him. Evidently, Schnieder had sent the girl away shortly after I had overheard that fiery conversation at the inn. Young James Norman had lost his plantation soon afterwards, and many claimed Schnieder was responsible. After losing his place, Norman had left for New Orleans and hadn't been heard from since.

Gossips claimed that his sister was the only thing in the world Helmut Schnieder cared about, and they added that no man would ever be good enough for her as far as her brother was concerned. He had gone to visit her in Germany almost every summer since her departure. The girl was supposed to be returning to Natchez in just a few weeks, I understood. She would be twenty years old now. I remembered her pale, fragile face that would have been plain except for those violet-blue eyes which had been so tormented as she pleaded with her swain. I wondered if she were still as frightened of her brother as she had clearly been four years ago.

As a shopkeeper overhearing gossip and asking discreet questions, I probably knew far more about Helmut Schnieder than Bruce did, but I had no intention of letting him know that. Leaving Natchez proper behind, we turned down the sloping river road. I caught glimpses of the masts of ships that crowded the harbor, and then the road twisted and they vanished. Tall oaks trailing Spanish moss grew on either side of us now, and sunlight sifted through the canopy of limbs overhead. It was all very peaceful and lulling, but I wasn't ready to drop the subject of Helmut Schnieder.

"They say that now that he's finished Roseclay he's looking for a wife," I remarked. "Rumor has it that that's why he's giving this ball—he wants to look over the prospects."

"Could be," Bruce replied, uninterested.

"Aren't we near Roseclay?" I inquired.

"It's a mile or so up the road. You haven't seen it?"

I shook my head.

"Driving out to watch the progress on the big house used to be a favorite pastime for folks around here, but now that it's finished, Schnieder doesn't like anyone nosing about. We'll go by just the same."

"If you think we shouldn't—" I began.

"We'll have to trespass in order for you to see it properly, but Schnieder inspects his plantation on Sundays. He'll never know we were there. It can't hurt anything."

"I wouldn't want you to get into trouble."

"What's he going to do? Shoot me? I'm not afraid of Helmut Schnieder. If you want to see the house, we'll go by and see it." His voice was slightly defiant.

A few minutes later, we stopped before two tall pink brick pillars. The ornate wrought-iron gate between them was closed but not locked. Bruce climbed down to push the gate back. Getting back up beside me, he urged the horses up the private drive at a slow walk. The grounds on either side were beautifully laid out, the grass

454

neatly trimmed, trees casting long shadows in the sunlight. There were elegant flower beds as well, and as the drive curved around I had my first glimpse of Roseclay.

It was stunning. The pink brick was light and mellow, and there were white shutters at all the windows. The roof was a blue-gray slate, and six tall white pillars in front supported the portico and second-story verandah. The house was enormous, with deep, cool-looking verandahs surrounding both floors. Tall elms growing on either side of the house brushed the walls with hazy shadows. As the horses slowly trotted along the drive that circled in front of the house, I caught glimpses of the spacious gardens in back. Bruce stopped the carriage directly in front of the house, holding the reins loosely in his lap.

"There it is," he said.

His manner was slightly bored, and I could tell that he was determined to remain unimpressed. I gazed up at the house with something like awe, for it was quite overwhelming. Majestic without being ostentatious, the house's simple elegant lines gave an impression of graceful ease. Although it was not at all like the stately homes I had seen back in England, it had a grandeur all its own. How glorious it would be to be mistress of a house like this, I thought.

"Impressed?" Bruce inquired.

"Extremely."

"It's altogether too large," he remarked. "Schnieder has delusions of grandeur. He thinks he has the power of a king, and he's built himself a palace."

"Now all he needs is a consort," I said quietly.

Bruce made no comment. I continued to gaze at the house, my resolution growing by the moment. If I hadn't been sure of my plan before, I was now. Seeing Roseclay gave me an even greater incentive, and I was determined to go through with it at all costs. If I succeeded, the rewards would be staggering. If I failed, at least I would have made the effort. At this point, I had nothing to lose.

The horses began to stamp restlessly on the drive, and

I could see that Bruce was impatient to be gone as well. I was just about to tell him to drive on when the front door opened. Helmut Schnieder stepped out onto the verandah, pulling the door shut behind him. I couldn't believe my good fortune. Thank goodness I had selected this particular dress and taken such pains with my hair.

Where another young man might have been at a loss, or nervous and upset by Schnieder's unexpected appearance, Bruce was as calm as could be. Showing no surprise, he nodded at the German.

"Good afternoon," he said politely.

Schnieder stared at us with cold blue eyes, and then he moved toward the wide front steps. He was exactly as I remembered: tall, heavyset, his features strong and blunt. He still had a belligerent look, and the pale yellowblond hair still fell in a monkish fringe across his jutting brow. He wore brown breeches and a thin white shirt slightly damp with perspiration. His tall black boots were dusty. He had obviously just returned from inspecting his plantation.

"You wanted something, Trevelyan?" he inquired. His voice was deep and guttural, just as I remembered.

"I didn't think you'd be here," Bruce replied. "Miss Danver wanted to see the house. I thought I'd bring her by to have a look. I suppose I owe you an apology."

Ignoring Bruce, Schnieder stared at me. I met his stare with a cool, level gaze, not at all intimidated. I felt sure he didn't remember me. If he did, he certainly gave no indication. I was amazed anew at the presence this man possessed. He would easily dominate the largest gathering without any effort. Those cold blue eyes seemed to be offering a silent challenge, one I was all too ready to accept.

"It's my fault," I said. "I insisted. I've heard a great deal about Roseclay—and about you."

"Indeed?"

"The house certainly lives up to my expectations."

I placed the slightest emphasis on the word "house," subtly indicating that its owner did not impress me.

Schnieder didn't miss that. The eyes continued to challenge me. Bruce gathered up the reins. I had almost forgotten that he was there beside me, so strong was Schnieder's effect on me.

"You must see the rest of it," Schnieder said. "Let me show you around inside."

"We have to be going," Bruce replied.

"I'd enjoy showing you around," Schnieder said, ignoring Bruce and speaking directly to me."

"I'm afraid there isn't time, Mr. Schnieder."

"No?"

"Some other time, perhaps."

"You must come to my ball, Miss Danver."

"I—"

"Young Trevelyan can bring you."

"That's quite impossible," I said.

"Not at all," Bruce informed me. "It would give me great pleasure."

"It's out of the question, Bruce."

"You don't care to come?" Schnieder inquired.

"I hardly think it would be seemly, Mr. Schnieder. I'm a—a seamstress. I feel quite sure your other guests would be very perturbed if I were to appear."

"I shouldn't think that would bother you, Miss Danver."

So he did remember me, after all. I could tell from his tone of voice that he had recalled that tattered creature in the soiled red dress who had wanted to book passage to New Orleans. He remembered, yet he had invited me to his ball. There could only be one reason: Helmut Schnieder was interested. I observed him coolly, sizing him up as an opponent.

He had commanding presence, yes, but he did not appeal to me physically at all. He was too large, and that powerful, heavyset body suggested brutal strength he would employ mercilessly to achieve his ends. Those blunt, harsh features augmented that impression, and there was an undeniable cruelty in the curve of that wide mouth. He might not attract me physically, yet that combination of power and authority was intriguing. What

457

satisfaction it would be to use him as he used others. Schnieder awakened something hard and vengeful inside me. He would be a worthy opponent indeed.

"We'd better leave now, Bruce," I said. "We've already taken enough of Mr. Schnieder's time."

"I shall look forward to seeing you both at the ball," Schnieder said. "I feel sure you can persuade her to come, Trevelyan."

"I imagine I can," Bruce replied.

He clicked the reins and turned the horses around on the drive. The German's eyes never once left me, and even as we drove away I could feel them boring into my back. I could hardly believe how well things had gone. How simple it had been. I intended to go to the ball, of course, had had every intention of doing so before we even set out this afternoon. But I had anticipated a subtle and rather taxing campaign to bring Bruce around to asking me, and Schnieder's sudden appearance had saved me the trouble. As we drove back through the portals and Bruce alighted to close the gate, I felt a sharp sense of triumph.

Schnieder had been interested in me four years ago— had wanted to buy me—and I hoped to reawaken that interest. There could be no doubt about the fact that I had done so, today. He had thrown down the gauntlet, presenting me with a challenge no woman could mistake.

Bruce was silent for a long while after we resumed our ride toward the river road. Immersed in thought myself, I was pleased with the silence. After he took me to the ball, Bruce would be of no more use to me. I was pleased it hadn't been necessary to build up his hopes. As it was, he would be able to get over me much more easily. I sighed, brushing a strand of hair from my temple. We were driving alongside the river now, blossoming dogwood trees on either side of the road, pink and white and soft, pale red. Bruce let the horses slow to little more than a walk, holding the reins loosely and turning to me with solemn eyes.

"You will come to the ball, won't you?"

458

"I shouldn't, Bruce."

"Because of what people would say?"

"That's one of the reasons. I'm a seamstress with a terribly wicked reputation. You're a young man with . . . much to lose."

"I don't give a hang what people say, Marietta."

"Your parents—"

"I'm twenty-two years old, no longer tied to any apron strings."

"They'll be outraged."

"Let them be," he replied.

The blossoming dogwood branches reached out over the road, almost touching us. I reached out and gently moved aside a branch laden with fragile pink flowers. Bruce had a determined look in his eyes, and his mouth was set in a stubborn line.

"I'm in love with you, Marietta. You must know that."

"I know, and . . . I'm sorry."

"Sorry?"

"I never meant you to fall in love with me. It—it could never lead to anything, Bruce."

"Because you're a seamstress? Because you're a few years older?"

"Partly."

"That doesn't matter to me in the least."

"I'm not in love with you," I said gently.

"You will be. I'll see to that."

The horses had stopped of their own accord at the side of the road. We were almost engulfed in pink and white blossoms. The river was only a few yards away on the other side of the road, moving along with a pleasant music. A breeze caused the dogwood branches to tremble, and soft petals sprinkled down. Bruce was frowning. He looked so young and sincere. I wanted to smile and touch his cheek, but I knew I mustn't. I couldn't give him any sort of encouragement.

"I want to marry you," he said firmly.

"I couldn't marry you, Bruce. I . . . like you too much."

"That doesn't make sense."

"I suppose it doesn't—not to you."

"You're trying to tell me something."

"Yes, Bruce."

"Look, I know about your . . ." He hesitated, the frown deepening. "I know all about your reputation. When we started going for our drives any number of people made it their business to inform me of your 'past.' I know you worked in a gambling house, know there was some sort of scandal. It doesn't matter."

I did not reply. A bird warbled throatily in a tree nearby. Bruce studied my face, and I feared he would pull me into his arms at any moment. So, I sat up very straight, deliberately hardening myself, refusing to be moved by this wonderful young man who had come into my life much too late. I must keep my mind on the goal in front of me, must curb any tenderness that might stir in my heart. I had let my heart guide me before, and the results had been disastrous.

"I'd like to go back home now," I said crisply.

Bruce looked crestfallen. "But—"

"Please, Bruce."

"Very well," he said.

During the ride back to the shop, I could tell that he was both disappointed and hurt, but I couldn't think about Bruce. He was merely a tool, and my need for him would soon be over. He climbed down from the carriage and helped me alight, then held the gate open for me. I stepped inside and closed the gate, shutting him out. Bruce caught hold of it, looking at me with eyes that were once again determined.

"You're coming to the ball with me," he said. His voice was firm. "I won't take no for an answer."

"As you wish, Bruce. If it means that much to you, I'll go."

"And you're going to forget all this nonsense about— about class distinction and age differences and the past. I'm going to *make* you fall in love with me."

460

"Goodbye, Bruce. Thank you for the lovely ride."
"I'll be here Friday at seven-thirty. You be ready."
"I will be," I promised.

XXIV

I didn't keep my promise. I wasn't ready when Bruce arrived. Wearing only a robe, I let him into the shop and led him upstairs to the sitting room to wait. That was over half an hour ago. As I stood now in front of the mirror, making a final inspection, I could hear him pacing impatiently. We were already late, would be even later by the time we drove out to Roseclay, but that was my intention. I planned to carry this through with all the verve I could command, and it suited my purpose to arrive after all the other guests had already assembled.

I had spent the past four days working on my dress, finishing it just this afternoon. It was a deep brown, embroidered with floral patterns in glittering black and bronze beads. The shimmering beads drew attention to my full, swelling breasts more than half exposed by the daring neckline. The dress was bold and dramatic and pleased me immensely.

My hair was carefully arranged on top of my head in glossy, coppery waves, three long ringlets dangling down, and I had applied my makeup carefully. The good ladies of Natchez were going to see their scarlet woman at her best. And Helmut Schnieder was going to find her cool and composed and, I hoped, irresistible. I was playing for very high stakes, and I had every intention of winning.

Opening the door connecting the two rooms, I stepped

into the sitting room. Bruce was standing at the window, peering out at the night. He turned. He stared with something like incredulity, taken aback by the sight of me. I could see that he was most appreciative, but as he was essentially a conventional young man, he was also a bit dismayed by the amount of bosom the gown revealed.

"You're dazzling," he said. "It was worth the wait."

"It was wicked of me to keep you waiting like this. I wanted to look especially nice for you."

Flattered, convinced that I had gone to all this trouble for his sake, he smiled. He looked very handsome in his dark wine breeches and frock coat, his maroon-and-white-striped waistcoat and white silk neckcloth. He had never been so appealing, that wavy brown hair so dark and glossy, those serious blue eyes filled with pleasure. Some young woman was going to be lucky indeed, I thought.

The carriage was waiting in front of the gate, horses standing patiently in the moonlight. Bruce handed me into the seat, and I adjusted my skirts. There was hardly room for him to sit beside me, but I pulled the rustling material aside to make room. The seat made a groaning noise as he took his place and gathered up the reins. A moment later we were off. It was a lovely night, the sky an ashy gray-black alight with gleaming moonrays. The weather was warm, almost sultry, and the night air was laden with the perfumes of spring.

"I'm glad you decided to come," he said.

"I had no choice," I replied. "Remember?"

"I recall being rather masterful."

"You were," I agreed.

"I intend to be even more so in days to come."

"Oh?"

"I've decided to change my tactics," he informed me. "I've been altogether too polite, too considerate. From now on, I'm going to be insistent and very firm, and, incidentally, I'm going to make you very happy."

He was like a young knight, I thought, a strong, handsome Sir Galahad who wanted to make me his lady fair. After tonight he would probably hate me, but that would ultimately be for the best. It would leave him free to find the girl he deserved, as young, as inexperienced as he, with whom he could build a future.

"I told my parents I was bringing you," he said.

"Did you?"

"I told them Schnieder asked me to bring you. That put a whole new light on it as far as they were concerned, made it much more acceptable. Both are prepared to like you."

"How very encouraging," I remarked, not without irony.

Bruce realized that he had been tactless and concentrated on his driving. Lights burning in windows made warm yellow squares against the darkness, and as we left the town behind and rounded a bend we could see the Mississippi far below, a pale silver ribbon shimmering in the night, the steep banks dark blue-black. The horses moved along at a brisk pace, the wheels skimming over the road. Clouds drifted across the moon, causing a constant play of moonlight and shadow below. Fireflies swarmed among the dark shrubbery, tiny golden lights flickering on and off.

We reached Roseclay ten minutes later. It was ablaze with lights, and the sounds of laughter and music spilled out into the night. The drive was lined with carriages. As Bruce stopped the horses in front of the house, a black footman came down the steps to meet us. He wore black pumps, white stockings, and sky-blue satin knee breeches. His frock coat was blue satin, too, and he wore a wig powdered in the French style. After helping me alight, he told Bruce that he would tend to the carriage and drove it away as we went up the steps to the front door.

Another footman in identical attire met us at the door and led us through the enormous hall. I was thoroughly composed, but I saw that Bruce was both nervous and apprehensive. I took his hand and smiled as yet another footman, this one carrying a silver-headed cane, asked our names and led us toward the ballroom. The music had temporarily ceased, but we could hear voices and polite laughter. Bruce made a valiant effort to control his apprehension. I gave his hand a squeeze as we paused before the wide archway leading into the ballroom.

The footman rapped on the floor with his cane. The assembled guests immediately fell silent and turned to see who was arriving. When he had their full attention, the footman announced our names in a deep, resounding voice, then stepped aside. Bruce led me down the two narrow steps and into the room. I could see shocked expressions on most faces, and there were several gasps. Bruce held himself straight, his demeanor both haughty and disdainful. He had heard the gasps, too, and they made him furious. I had never admired him so much.

Several moments passed, and still no one spoke. It was exceedingly awkward, but Helmut Schnieder soon mended that. He sauntered toward us with a smile, greeted us both warmly, shook Bruce's hand. Bruce relaxed a bit, relieved that the worst was over.

"I was beginning to think you weren't coming," Schnieder told me. "I would have been extremely disappointed—and surprised."

"Sorry we're late," Bruce said.

"You're the last to arrive, but it's of no consequence."

"I'm afraid it's my fault," I remarked. "It took me longer to dress than I had anticipated."

Schnieder looked at me. Those hard blue eyes took in every detail with slow deliberation. He liked what he saw. His wide, sensual mouth grew taut at the corners, and I had the feeling that if we had been alone he would have crushed me to him in a brutal embrace. It gave me a feeling of power.

"The time was well spent," he said.

"Thank you, Mr. Schnieder."

"The orchestra has been playing, but we haven't yet started dancing. If Trevelyan has no objections, I'd like to open the ball with you as my partner."

Bruce was taken aback, but he could hardly object.

He gave his assent in a tight voice that caused Schnieder to smile.

"It's settled, then, but first you must let me introduce you to a few of my other guests, Miss Danver. I'm sure Trevelyan would like to say hello to some of his friends before the dancing starts."

The other guests had resumed talking by this time, but almost everyone in the room was observing us while trying to appear not to. Schnieder took my hand and led me toward a statuesque woman in a deep-purple gown. She had a large, pale face with pursed mouth and dark, hooded eyes that widened in horror as we approached. Her black hair was arranged in an elaborate coiffure, and as we drew nearer, I saw that the diamonds dangling from her ears and dripping over her bosom were a very good imitation of the real thing.

"I'd like you to meet Mrs. Charles Holburn, Miss Danver. Her husband is one of our leading citizens."

"How do you do," I said.

Mrs. Holburn nodded curtly, unable to bring herself to speak. I knew she was the grandest of grand dames, the self-appointed leader of Natchez society. Schnieder was enjoying himself, relishing the outrage she wasn't quite able to conceal.

"Miss Danver is an old friend of mine," he continued, "connected with one of England's best families. I believe you mentioned something about sending your daughter Arabella to school in England. Miss Danver might be able to give you some advice. She attended the academy at Bath, the finest of its kind, I hear."

Mrs. Holburn was clearly nonplussed, not certain how she should react. My reputation was unsavory, yet I had the manner and the accent of an aristocrat. Could she possibly have been mistaken about me? The fake gems told me quite a lot about the woman, primarily that she couldn't afford to offend her wealthy and powerful host. She forced herself to smile.

"We must discuss schools some day soon, Miss Danver," she said.

"We must," I agreed politely.

"Why did you say that about the academy at Bath?" I asked as Schnieder led me toward another group.

"It was important to get in the first word. I knew you must have attended one of those exclusive schools, so I selected the first that came to mind."

"I understand your sister will be returning from school in Germany a few weeks from now."

"In June," he replied, somewhat tersely I felt.

"How wonderful for her to come back to such a magnificent house. I believe you'd scarcely begun it when she left."

"It was a mere shell. Come, let me introduce you to a few more people."

I wondered about his motives as he introduced me to first one, then another distinguished citizen. Most were chilly, one or two actually friendly, but all were polite, however restrained their politeness might have been. I hadn't realized before the extent of Schnieder's power. How many of these people were indebted to him? Ordinarily they would have been as disdainful of a man like Schnieder as they had been of me. Was it fear of reprisal that kept them in line?

"I hear the plantation is coming along nicely," he remarked to one of the men whose wife had just been forced to chat with me. "There should be a rich yield. You must keep me informed, Ashton."

"I shall," Ashton replied. "If all goes well, I should be able to repay you in—"

"No need to discuss that now," Schnieder interrupted. "This is a party. Enjoy yourself."

His manner was brusque. Ashton smiled nervously, but his eyes were full of resentment. Schnieder chuckled to himself as we moved on. It gave him pleasure to be rude to people who were obviously his betters.

"They're getting restless," he remarked. "I think we should open the ball and let them dance."

"As you wish."

Schnieder stepped over to speak to the musicians, and

as he did so, I took the opportunity to examine the ball-room more closely. It was a wonder of grace and beauty. Four enormous crystal chandeliers hung from the elaborately molded ceiling of gold gilt patterns against a pale-yellow background. There were yellow silk panels on the tall white walls, framed in gilt, and the floor was a dark-golden parquet. High French windows opening onto the gardens were hung with luxuriant yellow silk draperies held back with golden cords. The elegant French sofas upholstered in pale blue were surrounded by gilt chairs and fragile tables holding porcelain vases abrim with pink roses. At least a dozen black footmen in blue satin livery and powdered wigs circulated among the guests with silver trays laden with drinks. It was hard to believe such splendor, impossible not to be impressed.

I noticed Bruce standing across the room with two other young men. He was drinking a glass of brandy and pretending to listen to his companions' merry talk, but he was keeping an eye on me. His expression told me that he was both hurt and resentful. Coming back to join me, Schnieder turned to see whom I was observing. Bruce scowled and turned his back on us. Schnieder chuckled.

"Your young man seems upset."

"With good reason. You took me away from him the moment we arrived."

"He's served his purpose," Schnieder said.

"Oh?"

"We both know that, Miss Danver."

Before I could reply, there was a roll of drums. Guests began to clear the floor, and as the musicians began to play a slow minuet, Schnieder took my hand. Everyone watched as he led me onto the floor. I had expected him to be rough and clumsy, but he executed the steps with a subdued energy that made the rather stilted movements seem both natural and virile. After we had danced for a few moments alone, other couples joined us on the floor. Schnieder never took his eyes off me. A half-smile played on his lips. It was as though this exceedingly formal dance were some kind of intimate mating ritual between the two of us, the other dancers merely background.

"You dance well, Miss Danver," he said.

"Thank you."

"It seems you have a number of accomplishments."

"I try to do my best, no matter what I undertake."

"You're doing very well at the moment."

The polite conversation was full of double meanings. We were already fully aware of each other's motives. His hard blue eyes held mine as we went through the paces of the dance, and his lips lifted slightly at one corner as though at some private amusement.

I suddenly had the feeling that I was out of my depth, that I should retreat before it was too late. Instinct told me that Helmut Schnieder was much too formidable an adversary, one I was ill equipped to handle. Even though I might achieve my goals, I would be at his mercy, and he would use me brutally for some secret purpose. I immediately dismissed the idea. Things were going exactly as I had planned, even better than I had hoped. It would be madness to turn back now when success was clearly within reach.

"You find Roseclay impressive?" he asked.

"Very."

"You must let me show you more of it later on."

"I'd be delighted."

"We have much to discuss, Miss Danver."

"Do we?"

He nodded slowly, looking at me with that half-smile that so resembled a leer. We continued to dance, the chandeliers shedding a dazzling light, the women's gowns making a constantly shifting kaleidoscope of color. When the music finally stopped, Schnieder bowed politely, thanking me for the dance.

"I must perform my duties as host," he informed me, "must dance with all the ladies and their daughters, but I'll get back to you before the evening is over."

"I'm quite sure of that."

"Till later, Miss Danver."

469

He sauntered away, and I was relieved to see Bruce moving purposefully toward me. There was a tenseness about him I had never seen before, and I sensed anger boiling up beneath the surface. He clasped my elbow tightly and led me off the floor as the music started again. I felt that in his present mood he might easily become unmanageable, and that wouldn't do at all. I made a concentrated effort to soothe his ruffled feelings, chatting lightly, letting him fetch us some champagne, flattering his vulnerable young ego.

Bruce finally relaxed, and after we finished our champagne he took me to meet his parents. Alicia Trevelyan was a plump, pretty woman in pink satin, her blond hair a bit wispy. There was a dreamy vagueness about her as if she weren't certain who I was. George Trevelyan was sternly handsome, his sharp blue eyes studying me as his son made the introductions. His manner made it quite clear that he considered me a predatory adventuress with a penchant for cradle-snatching. There were a few moments of forced conversation, Trevelyan barely civil, his wife vague, and then Bruce asked me to dance. He was a poor dancer, as clumsy as I had expected Schnieder to be, but I found that somehow touching.

If the women at the ball were less than enthusiastic about accepting me, most of the men were more than eager to make my acquaintance. When the dance with Bruce ended, Charles Holburn asked me to be his partner, and he was merely the first of a long line. I danced for well over an hour and a half without pause. When Bruce finally rescued me and took me into the drawing room for refreshments, I was most grateful. His neckcloth was beginning to wilt slightly. That errant wave had flopped over his forehead again, and his cheeks were flushed a faint pink.

"You've been very busy with the ladies," I teased.

"Cynthia made me promise to dance with all her friends. Tiresome lot, full of silly chatter."

"Who was that lovely brunette in blue velvet? I saw you dancing with her twice."

470

"You mean Denise? She's just a friend, not at all like the rest of 'em. She wants to argue about politics and doesn't give a hoot if her petticoat is showing. She reads a lot, just like I do. We exchange books now and then."

"I see."

"Her family lived next door to us back in Massachusetts. We grew up together, used to get into fierce wrestling matches when we were kids. I always beat her soundly. Denise wouldn't know how to flirt if her life depended on it. You've nothing to fear."

He spoke of her with considerable fondness, and I felt much better. I had seen the look in the girl's eyes when she was dancing with him, and I thought she would be a great consolation to him in days to come. Bruce led me over to one of the elaborately laden tables. Another liveried servant in powdered wig filled our plates, and Bruce carried them to a sofa upholstered in gold silk, passing me a plate when we were seated.

The drawing room was spacious and, in its way, as spectacular as the ballroom. It was done in white and gold, with French furniture and a ceiling painted with nymphs and figures from mythology against a pale-blue sky, golden-pink clouds surrounding them. The room was as beautiful as anything to be found in the stately homes of England. I was beginning to see why it had taken Schnieder so long to finish his mansion. The artist must have spent months on the ceiling alone.

As we ate, the girl named Denise came into the drawing room on the arm of one of the young men Bruce had been talking to earlier. She had intelligent brown eyes and strong, attractive features, and her dark hair gleamed in the candlelight. Bruce waved, grinning, and the girl waved back, then turned away with studied disinterest. She might not know how to flirt, but it was clear to me that she was in love with Bruce. If he didn't know it, it was because she didn't want him to, not yet. She and her escort carried their plates out into the gardens,

471

moving through one of the open French windows. Bruce frowned.

"Blake Gutherie has a very bad reputation as far as the ladies are concerned. I hope Denise knows what she's doing."

"I rather imagine she does," I replied.

When we had finished our food and had more champagne, Bruce took me back into the ballroom for another dance. His sister Cynthia claimed him then, and I danced with a rather tipsy young man who was positively fascinated by my low-cut dress. There was another round of dancing, and some of the guests were already beginning to leave when Helmut Schnieder took me by the hand and led me down the hallway that connected with the main entrance hall.

"Time for our tour," he said.

"I've been looking forward to it."

"I imagine you have."

He opened a door and led me into a beautifully appointed library with a white marble fireplace and floor-to-ceiling white shelves filled with exquisitely bound volumes, brown, tan, dark gold, red. Windows on either side of the fireplace looked out over the front lawn, and there was a lovely Sheraton desk. I studied book titles with great interest, finding half a dozen I longed to pull from the shelves and read. Schnieder watched me with heavy lids hooding his eyes.

"Your library is very impressive," I said. "Do you read?"

"I have neither the time nor the inclination. I assembled this library with my sister in mind. She reads a great deal."

He led me out of the room and into another, a smaller drawing room with a grand piano of gleaming mahogany, a blue sofa, a fireplace of light-gray marble. For all its luxury, the room was cozy and inviting. Purple flowers stood in tall white porcelain vases. The draperies were a soft lilac velvet. Schnieder showed me the elegant dining room, the masculine study, and eventually we ended up

472

in front of the majestic staircase with its polished mahogany banister and deep-blue carpet.

"The bedrooms are upstairs," he said.

"I think I'll forgo seeing them just now"

"Nervous, Miss Danver?"

"Not in the least."

"I don't frighten you?"

"Should I be frightened?"

Schnieder nodded, his eyes holding mine. "I'm a ruthless man, Miss Danver. I use people. Sometimes they get hurt. Is that a risk you're willing to take?"

"I think I can look after myself, Mr. Schnieder."

He smiled, and again I sensed some private amusement in his eyes. Now was the time to retreat. Now was the time to bid him farewell and get away as quickly as possible. He had just warned me that I was likely to get hurt. But I stood my ground, my eyes meeting his with a level gaze.

"You haven't seen the gardens," he remarked. "They're quite lovely by moonlight."

"I'd love to see them."

Moving ahead of me down the hall toward the back door, he held it open for me. I stepped outside, denying the apprehension that stirred inside me. Schnieder closed the door and led the way toward the gardens. The carriage house and servants' quarters were on our right. We could hear music streaming out into the night, the sound growing dimmer as we strolled under the elms toward the spacious gardens. I had expected to find guests strolling about, but there was no one else in sight.

The gardens had been laid out in levels by a master landscape artist, shallow marble steps leading from one level to the next. There were ponds and fountains with water splashing softly, and there were elegant flower beds and evergreen trees tall and dark in the moonlight. We paused behind a trellis of climbing roses. Everything was brushed with silver, white marble gleaming, shadows a deep blue. Leaves rustled with a scratchy noise. A lonely bird called out. The music from the ballroom was barely audible.

"You've changed in four years," he remarked.

"Then you remember?"

"Vividly. I very much wanted to buy you from Rawlins. I assume you're still for sale?"

"You might find the price a bit steep," I replied.

"I doubt that, Miss Danver."

"I want security."

"And luxury," he said.

"That, too."

"I can give you both."

"I'm talking about marriage."

Schnieder was silent. I studied his face in the moonlight. That fringe falling across his brow made him look like some crafty peasant monk from the middle ages, sensual and avaricious, capable of any crime. The eyes were hooded again. He was standing in front of me, so close I could feel his breath on my cheek.

"It just so happens I need a wife," he said.

"Oh?"

"That was the reason I planned this ball. I intended to select one of the nubile young women with mothers eager to make a grand match. Then I saw you, and I knew there was no need to look further."

Schnieder plucked one of the roses and idly crushed it in his hand.

"One of the others would have been . . . uh . . . extremely difficult to break in. You suit my purposes ideally. You're beautiful and intelligent, and there would be no emotional nonsense. It would be a very sensible arrangement."

"I—don't quite understand."

He chuckled quietly. "I've no doubt you're confused. You came here in your seductive gown prepared to use your wiles on me, prepared to tease and tantalize until you brought me round, had me under your spell. Then you discovered it wasn't at all necessary."

"What exactly do you want, Mr. Schnieder?"

"A wife," he said. "Oh, not in the usual sense of the word. I don't want love and devotion. That would be extremely tiresome. I want someone to act as hostess at Roseclay, someone to entertain my guests and be at my side at all the social functions where a wife is called for."

"Your sister could do that when she returns."

Schnieder scowled. "I want a *wife*," he said harshly.

"What—what else would it involve?"

"A good rousing tumble every now and then. I've no doubt you could handle that well enough. I've no doubt you'd enjoy it. In return you'd have the security you mentioned, and all the luxuries a very rich man's wife could expect."

This was too simple, and it was happening too quickly. It was all so cold-blooded. I felt that he despised me, that he had some ulterior motive he kept concealed. *But isn't this what you wanted?* I asked myself. *Isn't this why you came? You planned to ensnare him, and here he is offering the very thing you were after.* With Helmut Schnieder there would be no need for any pretense of emotional involvement.

"Well, Miss Danver?"

"I accept your offer."

"I imagined you would," he replied. "We'll be married tomorrow."

"Tomorrow? But—"

"I see no reason to wait. I can arrange it easily enough. Don't look so apprehensive. You're going to be the wife of the richest man in the territory, mistress of the grandest house in America."

Footsteps approached us. Over Helmut's shoulder I saw a dark figure moving through the shadows. Schnieder turned around, irritated, just as Bruce stepped into the moonlight. Bruce looked distraught. I felt my heart lurch. Oh, no, I thought, not this way, not so cruelly. Schnieder

475

and I were half-concealed by the trellis, and Bruce hadn't seen us yet. He peered into the shadows, came nearer, and then he spied us.

He stood very still in the moonlight, staring at us. I could see him striving to control his emotions, striving to conceal the shock. My heart went out to him. I wanted to rush to him, to try to explain, but I knew I couldn't. It was too late to soften the blow. Bruce took a deep breath, and when he spoke, his voice was amazingly calm.

"I've been looking for you, Marietta. Everyone's leaving. It's time for us to go."

"Run along, Trevelyan," Schnieder said.

"You go to hell," Bruce replied. "Are you coming, Marietta?"

"She's staying with me tonight."

Bruce clenched his fists, and his facial muscles tightened. For a moment I thought he was going to fly at the German with fists swinging. But Bruce controlled himself and took another deep breath.

"Is it true?" he asked.

"Yes, Bruce," I said quietly.

"You're going to stay with him?"

I nodded. Bruce stared at me, incredulous. I knew what he must be feeling. It could scarcely be worse than what I was feeling myself.

"I see," he said. "All those things they said about you are really true, aren't they?"

"Bruce—"

"I actually fell in love with you, and all the while you were laughing at me, using me. I guess I made a fool of myself. Goodbye, Marietta. I wish you well."

He turned then and walked quickly away into the shadows. I could hear his footsteps moving back toward the house. I felt my heart would break, and then I sighed, forcing the emotions aside. I wasn't supposed to feel. I was supposed to be hard and cool and calculating. I was going to have exactly what I wanted. I had tried to remind myself of that. As the sound of Bruce's footsteps died away, I turned to Helmut Schnieder. Roughly he caught hold of me and, pulling me to him, covered my mouth with his own.

XXV

My husband was in a foul mood as we returned from the plantation that Sunday afternoon two and a half months after our quick, business-like marriage in a dusty, cluttered office in town. I hadn't particularly wanted to go with him to inspect the plantation, but Helmut had insisted. Several other planters, each heavily indebted to him, were there to meet him to discuss various improvements on their land. He wanted me on hand to pass out cigars and serve cool drinks and add a touch of domesticity. He seemed determined to establish the fact that he was respectably married at every opportunity.

We had entertained at Roseclay several times. Curiously enough, those formal dinner parties had been quite successful. The very women who had refused to patronize my shop were eager to be my friends now. There had been an initial resistance, but my accent, my breeding, my gracious welcome had won them all over. Mrs. Charles Holburn herself had firmly announced to her circle that I must have been forced to work in that dreadful gambling house in order to survive. It was amazing what wealth could do, I mused. The ladies doing a complete turnabout in their attitude toward me, were eager to make excuses for me. That shockingly low-cut gown I had worn to the ball was the height of fashion in New Orleans, for example, and those rides I had taken with Bruce Trevelyan were, in retrospect, perfectly innocent.

Bruce had never mentioned that scene in the gardens to anyone. When Helmut and I married so suddenly, Bruce informed family and friends that he wasn't at all surprised. He told them that I had met Schnieder years ago while visiting Germany with my family. When Schnieder had returned from his trip to Europe and discovered I was in Natchez, orphaned, trying to run a dress shop, he had been aghast. Bruce's glib, gentlemanly lies had done much to reverse the town's opinion of me. He was indeed a gallant knight, defending his lady even after she had betrayed him.

Bruce had married Denise Brandon only a few days ago. The newlyweds were now on their way to Boston where they intended to live, despite the rebels who had driven both their families away in the first place. In fact, Bruce planned to take a commission in the army and do his part to put those rebels down. Both he and his wife were extremely loyal and actively interested in the conflict that most of Natchez preferred to forget. Denise Trevelyan had declared herself proud of her husband's decision and, for reasons of her own, had been eager to get him away from Natchez.

My leaving Bruce had actually been a blessing in disguise, I reasoned. I thought of Denise's strong features, her intelligent brown eyes, and I remembered the fond way Bruce had spoken of her the night of the ball. I was confident that the lovely young woman who shared so many of his interests would soon make him forget all about me.

As we drove along now, Helmut was scowling. His meeting with the other planters had not gone well at all. None of the six men who joined him in the cool, simply furnished plantation parlor was eager to accept loans for the improvements he suggested for their spreads. Each man was already deeply in debt to him and had no desire to increase the load. But the menace in his voice as he described the desirability of the improvements was hardly subtle. Finally, after he reminded them of the mortgages he held, all but one agreed to make the improvements with money he would put up. Only Robert Page rebelled, stubbornly refusing to give Helmut more power over him. I had no doubt he would soon find himself without a plantation. Helmut would take delight in crushing him.

I had married a thoroughly unscrupulous man, but I had known that from the beginning. Actually, I had found little personal reason to be dissatisfied with my lot. Helmut expected me to play my social role to perfection, but beyond that he made very few demands. For some reason he seemed to have lost interest in me sexually after the initial conquest. He had taken me roughly the night of the ball with the brutal, battering strength of a bull, but once we were married, he had made little attempt to exercise his legal rights. I was puzzled, but I was also greatly relieved. Of course, he did own a house in Natchez-under-the-hill, which was a strong source of revenue, and I knew that he made frequent visits to that establishment. The visits were made secretly and well after midnight. I didn't care to speculate about them. I was merely thankful that there had been no repetition of that furious assault that had so closely resembled rape.

He treated me with cool civility, and if there was a slight derision in his manner, an underlying sarcasm in his voice, that was no more than could be expected. I knew what he thought of me, and he knew what I thought of him. Each of us had precisely what we had bargained for. I lived in a sumptuous mansion, surrounded by luxury, and Helmut gave me a generous allowance. He had also given me an incredibly beautiful diamond and emerald necklace with earrings to match, for Schnieder's wife must have appropriate jewels. I enjoyed giving dinner parties and acting as hostess, and, even more, I enjoyed the long hours alone at Roseclay when I could read in the library, stroll in the gardens, and sketch in the sunshine with sketch pad on my knees, free from any emotional commitment.

I tried not to think about the past. That could only lead to pain. Jeff was dead. Derek was gone. There was no love in my heart, and I was glad. If sometimes I felt empty, if sometimes I experienced vague longings I was unable to control, well, that was to be expected. I knew that this cold-blooded arrangement was far better than the frustration, the anguish, the terrible grief that love's tender fury had brought into my life. Marrying Helmut Schnieder had been an extremely sensible move. I was convinced of that. Only on rare occasions was I prey to small, niggling doubts, and I was able to squelch them almost immediately.

I hoped to have a friend and confidante soon, for Helmut's sister Margaret was arriving tomorrow afternoon, the boat due to dock shortly before three. I found myself looking forward to her arrival with great anticipation. Although she might well resent me, at first, I felt sure I could win her over. After four years in a German school Meg would surely welcome the friendship of a woman only a few years her senior. What fun it would be to share things with someone. Perhaps we could plan our wardrobes together. As Helmut deemed it unsuitable for me to make my own clothes, I made sketches and sent them to Lucille in New Orleans with minute instructions, and she sent the dresses back to Natchez, each one perfect in every detail. I would do the same for Meg. Every young woman was interested in clothes, and there must be many other interests we had in common, as well.

Immersed in thought, I didn't hear the horseman approaching our carriage. I emitted a startled cry as Helmut gave a vicious jerk on the reins, causing the horses to rear and stop abruptly. Had he not thrown his arm around my shoulders I would have been hurled forward. Shaken, I clasped a hand to my heart and looked at him for an explanation. His expression was thunderous, mouth turned down at the corners, his hard blue eyes filled with a cold fury. He gripped my shoulders tightly, completely

481

unaware of the pressure he was applying. All his attention was focused on the man who rode slowly toward us on a sturdy bay stallion.

When the rider was almost upon us, the man brought his bay to a halt. I stared at him. Because of the dim afternoon light and my own alarm, I didn't recognize the man at first, but then I had only seen him once in my life.

"What are you doing here?" Helmut challenged.

The man on the bay was unperturbed by Helmut's menacing tone and murderous expression. He sat lightly in the saddle, hands on his knees, the reins draped across one thigh. When he spoke, his voice betrayed no emotion.

"That, Mr. Schnieder, is none of your business, but since you're interested, I'll tell you. I've just been hired to act as overseer at one of the plantations."

"You'll be out of work tomorrow, Norman."

The man allowed himself a faint smile. "My employer is Mr. John Kirkwood. He was a friend of my father's, you might recall. As he is one of the few independent planters who's never accepted a penny from you, you'll find it difficult to get me dismissed. Kirkwood has no great fondness for you, rest assured."

Helmut's arm squeezed my shoulders brutally. I gave a small cry in spite of myself and, scowling, he removed his arm. He looked as though he wanted to hurl me off the seat, but I knew his anger wasn't directed at me. I couldn't help but be frightened, nevertheless. I had never witnessed such fury. A tall bullwhip stood in its holder on his side of the carriage. I was afraid he would pull it out and slash the young man to ribbons.

"You've made a mistake coming back here, Norman."

"Have I, Mr. Schnieder?"

"If you know what's good for you, you'll leave Natchez immediately."

"You don't own the town yet, Schnieder."

The man who so calmly defied my husband had the lean, sturdy build of a young gladiator, hard and muscular. Four years ago James Norman had been a strikingly handsome youth charged with vitality and eager to elope with Meg Schnieder. His brown eyes had flashed with passionate urgency. Now, he was grave and confident, and there was a mature strength in his features that made him even more handsome. The impetuous youth had become a man.

"I broke you before, Norman. I'll break you again!"

"You caused me to lose my plantation, true, and yes, you were responsible for my leaving Natchez, but things are different now. You see, I'm no longer a boy."

"I'll crush you under my heel!"

"Don't count on it, Schnieder. I'll fight back this time."

"You've been corresponding with my sister!"

"Have I?"

"You know she's coming back tomorrow. That's why you've returned to Natchez."

"Is it?"

"If you come near her, I'll kill you! That's a promise."

"Meg is no longer sixteen years old. She's twenty now, capable of making her own decisions. If she wants to see me, I'll see her, and there's not a thing you can do about it."

The carriage rocked as Helmut leaped to his feet and jerked the whip out of its holder. I cried out as the thin black lash streaked through the air with a hissing crackle. The tip cut across Norman's right shoulder, tearing through his shirt. When Helmut swung his arm back to deliver another blow, I jumped up and threw myself in front of him, grabbing his arm.

"No, Helmut!"

"Get away, woman!"

"You mustn't!"

He tried to shake me off, but, as he did so, the carriage lurched and we both lost our balance, toppling back down onto the seat. Helmut dropped the whip. It fell to the floorboard like a coiling black snake. He thrust me away from him, his cheeks ashen, but he didn't reach for the whip. I could see him struggling to control himself, trying to overcome that blazing rage. Then, I looked up at the young man who sat so calmly on the bay. His shirt was torn, and there was a thin red streak on the exposed flesh. He hadn't so much as flinched.

"Please," I said urgently. "Please go now."

James Norman nodded. Taking up the reins, he tugged on them and nudged the bay gently with his knees. Horse and rider moved around the carriage and on down the road. Several moments passed. Helmut was breathing heavily, but his face had regained its normal ruddy color and his eyes no longer blazed with that insane fury. His pale blond hair was damp with sweat, the monkish fringe plastered against his brow. The carriage rocked slightly as the horses stirred in the shafts. Helmut finally reached down, picked up the whip, and stuck it upright in its holder. He was thoroughly composed now. That savage incident might never have happened.

"I was afraid you'd kill him," I said.

"I probably would have."

"I had to stop you."

"You needn't justify yourself, Marietta. You acted wisely. I lost control of myself. It doesn't happen often."

"Thank God for that," I retorted.

"You seem shaken, my dear."

I ignored the sarcasm in his voice, his mocking use of the term of endearment. Helmut would have enjoyed making me angry, but I was immune to his subtle derision. Turning away, I brushed a lock of hair from my temple and rearranged my skirts.

"Lucky for Norman you intervened," he said. "It would have given me great satisfaction to cut him to ribbons."

"I believe you actually mean that."

Helmut lifted a brow. "But of course I do."

"You hate him so much? Just because he wanted to marry your sister?"

"There are things you don't know. Things you don't

484

understand," Helmut said, grimly, as he gathered up the reins. "It's time we got back to Roseclay."

We started back down the river road at a brisk pace, the wheels skimming over the hard-packed earth. His last remark had been curiously enigmatic. What didn't I know? What had happened in the past that would cause even the sight of Norman to arouse such violent fury? Helmut usually acted with cool premeditation, every move carefully planned with Machiavellian thoroughness, but for a brief instant back there he had actually taken leave of his senses. I had known there was a deep vein of cruelty in him from the first, but I had never seen it take such a violent form.

The incident disturbed me far more than I cared to admit.

Monday was a gloriously beautiful day, the sky, a pale blue, and the sun, a round white ball half-obscured by puffy clouds. It wasn't nearly as warm as it had been. I stretched lazily. A fresh breeze caught the thin curtains in my bedroom causing them to billow inward like white silk sails. Dressed only in a petticoat with a snug bodice and half a dozen ruffled skirts, I turned as my maid tapped nervously on the opened door and stepped into the room. Lelia, a small, delicately boned creature with skin the color of ebony and dark, luminous eyes, was quite lovely in her blue cotton dress.

"Yes, Lelia?" I asked.

"Th' mastah, he wanna know effin you feel awright."

"I feel fine, Lelia. Oh, I suppose he was concerned because I didn't come down for lunch. Tell him I simply wasn't hungry. I'll be downstairs in plenty of time to go with him to meet the boat."

"Yes'um," the girl replied and left the room silently.

Though Lelia brought my breakfast tray each morning and was responsible for taking care of my room, she had nervously resisted all my efforts to be friendly. Like all the other slaves, she was silent, efficient, unobtrusive.

485

There was a large household staff, over twenty, and whenever I encountered any of them they seemed to withdraw behind an invisible shield, never speaking unless it was necessary. Helmut had made it clear from the beginning that I was to have no say in the running of Roseclay. He issued his orders to butler, cook, and chief footman every morning, and that seemed to be all that was necessary to keep things running with model efficiency.

How different they were from the slaves back in Carolina, I thought. There was no noise from their quarters out back at night, no music, no vitality. They all seemed cowed, even those who ran the household. But I had never heard Helmut raise his voice to any of them, and there had certainly been no whippings since I had arrived. I just assumed they had been strictly trained. Still, it would be nice to see an occasional smile, hear an occasional rumble of husky laughter.

I moved about the airy room, which was done in shades of white and pale blue, delicate gold gilt patterns on the elegant French furniture. Marie Antoinette herself would have felt at ease amidst all this tasteful splendor, I thought as I sat down at the mirror to brush my hair. However, like all the other rooms at Roseclay, it was undeniably cold. At first, overwhelmed by the beauty, I had hardly noticed the atmosphere of chill that pervaded the mansion, but lately it seemed to have grown worse.

Even if it was cold, I told myself, it was a far cry from a damp brown cell on Bow Street, or a filthy bunk in the hull of a prison ship. I had come a long way indeed, from indentured servant to wife of one of the richest men in America. Hair finally arranged to my satisfaction, I stepped over to the wardrobe to take out the dress I intended to wear. Meg's arrival might help dispel the chill. Perhaps she would bring the vitality and friendly warmth that would breathe life into the formal, sumptuously beautiful rooms.

I took my time getting ready, for I wanted to make a good first impression on my sister-in-law. My dress, newly

486

arrived from Lucille's shop, was dark blue with short, narrow sleeves and a high lacy neckline, very snug at the waist. The skirt was adorned with row upon row of black lace ruffles, and my elbow-length gloves were of matching black lace. There was a black lace parasol as well. I had just turned to fetch it when Helmut came into the room.

"It's time to go," he said.

"Oh. You—you startled me!"

"Did I?"

"I'm not accustomed to your coming into my bedroom."

"Is that supposed to be a complaint?" he inquired.

"Hardly that," I replied coldly.

Helmut smiled a humorless smile. He was handsomely attired in dark-gray breeches and frock coat, his white satin waistcoat heavily embroidered with black silk flowers. Adjusting his black silk neckcloth, he asked, "You haven't felt neglected?"

"Not in the least."

"I've the feeling you didn't enjoy our first little tussles. Perhaps we should have another go-round soon."

"Forgive me if I seem less than eager."

He liked that. He chuckled softly. "Truth to tell, Marietta, you're a magnificent creature, but a shade too patrician for my taste. I prefer an earthier type."

"I'm sure there's no shortage of them in Natchez-under-the hill."

"You know about that? But of course. You would. I'm pleased to know you haven't been pining away. You could always take a lover, you know. So long as you did it discreetly, I wouldn't have the least objection."

"I'm quite content with things as they are, Helmut. You needn't concern yourself about my welfare. We have a very nice arrangement." I picked up my parasol. "Shall we go now?"

He nodded, and we went downstairs and out to the drive where the carriage stood waiting. Larger than the one we had ridden in the day before, it had two richly upholstered seats facing each other. A liveried black driver sat on a high perch in front. A cart had been sent on ahead to accommodate the trunks and baggage.

Helmut handed me up into the carriage and, sitting down on the seat opposite, signaled for the driver to start. I opened the black lace parasol and rested the handle lightly against my shoulder. We were soon on the river road, the horses moving at a steady pace. Helmut sat leaning forward slightly, his palms spread over his knees. My cool demeanor seemed to irritate him.

"You still upset about that little incident with Norman?"

"I'm trying to forget it," I replied.

"Good. I wouldn't want Meg to hear about it. She's extremely sensitive. No need for her to be unnecessarily distressed."

"I've no intention of telling her."

"Norman's not likely to come around, not after the sample of the whip I gave him yesterday. He's not that big a fool."

"I hope Meg and I can be friends," I remarked.

Helmut did not reply. We were soon passing through Natchez proper. It was a busy Monday afternoon, people trading at the shops, holding lively conversations on the walks. Before we turned and started down the slope toward the docks, I caught a glimpse of my former shop at the end of the street. Helmut had taken care of all the arrangements, disposing of the goods, leasing the place to a hardware merchant. I had not known it before, but he owned the building, just as he owned so many others.

The docks were alive with activity. Two ships that had just come in this morning were still being unloaded. Meg's boat wasn't due for twenty minutes or so, but Helmut had been impatient to arrive. I could sense his tension as he climbed down from the carriage and helped me alight. He peered up the river, scowled, took out his pocket watch and examined it, and then turned to look in the direction of his three warehouses that stood some distance away.

"I might as well take care of some business while I'm waiting," he informed me. "I'll be back before the boat arrives. You stay here by the carriage."

"Very well."

Moving with all the authority of a lord, he strolled briskly toward the warehouses. People made way for him, stepping aside quickly. I had the feeling he would have shoved them out of his way had they not done so. He disappeared into one of the warehouses, and I turned my attention to the men unloading heavy wooden crates from one of the ships. They moved swiftly up and down the gangplank, stowing the crates in wagons, hurrying back for more.

Farther along, fisherman were mending nets, and a prostitute in a vivid red dress strolled past boxes and barrels, pausing to chat with sailors who loitered about. There was a cart filled with bunches of bananas, another with baskets of oranges and lemons. Over a dozen ships stood lined up on the water, masts towering, hulls rocking slightly. I could smell hemp and tar and mud. The noise was deafening. Boxes banged. Men shouted. A monkey chattered. Wood scraped against wood. It was all vivid and stimulating, a lively and absorbing scene.

"I'll be damned! Marietta?"

I turned to see one of the men who had been unloading crates moving toward me. Bronzed, muscular, he had sun-bleached hair and roughhewn features, his wide mouth spread in a merry grin. He wore tight, faded blue breeches and a red-and-black-striped jersey with the sleeves shoved up over his forearms. I didn't recognize him at first, and drew myself up imperiously, ready to send him on his way with a cutting comment. He stopped a few feet away, his blue eyes filled with delight.

"Don't ya recognize me?" he asked.

I hesitated. "Jack?"

"Big as life," he retorted. "I say, this's a surprise. What're you doin' in Natchez? Just passin' through?"

"I—I live here. I had a dress shop for a while, but I'm married now. I knew you had come to Natchez, but when I didn't run into you in all these months, I assumed you'd moved on."

"Never get up to th' bluff much," he told me. "Got me a job loadin' an' unloadin'. 'Ave me a lean-to behind th' warehouses I share with a couple uv other chaps. Any free time I 'ave I generally spend at th' gin shops an' fancy 'ouses under-th'-'ill. Reckon that explains why we ain't run into each other."

"It's good to see you, Jack. You're looking well."

"Oh, I ain't got nothin' to complain about. It's a good life. I work 'ard durin' th' day and play 'ard at night. Lotsa gin, lotsa wild women, a good rowdy brawl every now 'n' then."

"The life evidently agrees with you."

"Never been 'appier. Beats swabbin' decks an' fightin' 'urricanes."

Jack grinned again, folding his arms across his chest. Brawny, amiable, uncomplicated, he glowed with health and vitality. I remembered his kindness to me so many years ago, remembered his curious tenderness, and I was glad he had found his own brand of contentment.

"You're lovelier'n ever," he remarked.

"Thank you, Jack."

"So you left that gamblin' 'ouse to open a dress shop 'ere in Natchez?"

"That's right."

"An' found yourself a 'usband right away. Judgin' from them clothes you're wearin' and that fancy carriage with th' nigger in 'is fancy suit, I'd say you got yourself a rich one."

"I did."

"One of them wealthy chaps who came to get away from the rebels?"

"No, I married a German."

Jack looked surprised. "German? You—you don't mean—" He paused, his blue eyes alarmed. "You ain't

490

talkin' about 'elmut Schnieder, are you? I 'eard 'e got 'imself a wife. You ain't married to 'im?"

"We were married almost three months ago."

His manner changed abruptly. The breezy amiability vanished. He frowned and looked down at the ground, avoiding my eyes. When he finally looked up, his manner was guarded. He tried to be casual, but he wasn't able to carry it off.

"You know who he is," I said.

"Reckon I do. Reckon everyone does. I—I just 'ope you know what you got yourself into."

"What do you mean?"

"Some of th' things I've 'eard—they ain't pretty. Several of th' girls—" He cut himself short. "Does he treat you all right?"

"He's very generous."

His frown deepened. "I see. Well . . . uh . . . look, I gotta get back to work now."

"It was nice to see you, Jack."

He nodded and turned away, preparing to leave. Then he hesitated. He turned back around to face me, his mouth tight, his brows pressed together. He seemed to be debating something, and when he finally spoke, his voice was very sober.

"Look, if—if you ever have any kinda trouble, if you ever need help, you just call on Jack Reed. Okay? If you ever need me for anything, you know where to find me."

Jack hurried away before I could reply, and Helmut joined me almost immediately. He had seen the two of us talking together as he returned from the warehouse and asked me who Jack was. Instinct told me to keep his identity a secret, and I managed to be very casual, replying that he was only a workman I had been questioning about the cargo. Helmut seemed satisfied and asked no further questions. Meg's ship had come up the river as Jack and I were talking, and the gangplank was being

491

lowered. Helmut led me down the dock to where the passengers would disembark.

A crowd had gathered. There was much shouting and waving, an air of excitement prevailing. Helmut and I stood some distance from the gangplank beside a stack of wooden crates. I had never seen him so tense. His face was like granite, and I noticed that his fists were clenched. He looked as though he wanted to strangle all these shrill, merry people who greeted each other so effusively. He kept his eyes on the gangplank, growing more and more tense at his sister's failure to appear. Most of the passengers had already disembarked, and men were beginning to bring down trunks and boxes.

The girl finally came to the top of the gangplank, but stepped aside to let one of the men pass. Slowly, hesitantly, she moved down the wooden ramp, as though she were not certain there would be anyone to meet her. She wore a soft gray muslin frock sprigged with lilac and blue forget-me-nots, and her light-brown hair took on a silvery sheen in the sunlight. Even more slender than I remembered, she had a fragile, vulnerable quality that was immediately apparent. Her face was pale, saved from plainness only by those enormous violet-blue eyes that reflected her emotions so openly. She seemed much younger than her twenty years, but perhaps the demure, girlish frock was partly responsible for that. She paused at the foot of the gangplank, looking about nervously. Helmut left my side and strode through the crowd toward her.

They didn't embrace. Helmut wore a stern expression, and his manner was brusque. They spoke together for a moment, and then Meg turned to look in my direction. Helmut said something else. The girl nodded. He clasped her arm and led her toward me. As they approached, I could see that the girl was fighting to control some powerful emotion. I smiled as Helmut made the introductions. Meg smiled, too, a faint, timorous smile that

492

trembled on her lips and failed to reach her eyes. I saw what the emotion was then. It was fear. Meg Schnieder looked terrified.

XXVI

I was surprised to find Meg in the library. Ever since her arrival, she had kept to her room, having her meals brought up on a tray. The long sea voyage had worn her out, Helmut informed me, and she needed to rest. Not once had she dined with us. I had gone to her room to see if there was anything I could do for her. She had obviously been ill. But she made it quite clear that she didn't want to talk, nor did she want me to visit her. I had seen her only once since then. She had been standing at the hall window upstairs, looking out at the gardens, and when she heard me approaching she returned quickly to her room.

Meg was examining titles when I entered the library. She gave a start and looked at me with wide, nervous eyes, as though I had caught her in some petty misdemeanor. I smiled warmly, trying to put her at ease, but she didn't smile back. She stood stiffly, her manner anything but welcoming.

"I didn't mean to disturb you," I said quietly. "It's such a lovely day I thought I'd select a book and go out into the gardens to read for a while. It's—it's nice to see you up and around."

"Helmut decided it was time I left my room," she said coldly. "I'm to come down to meals, and I'm to

494

stop acting like a child. When my brother decides something, it's done."

"Are you feeling better?"

"I'm feeling better."

She was distinctly thorny, but somehow or other I felt that this was merely a kind of defense. There was no reason for her to dislike me—or to like me, either—but I sensed that her antagonism wasn't directed against me personally, and I was not put off by her manner. She had grown even thinner since her arrival, and her dress seemed to hang on her. Her cheeks were very pale and drawn. Her light-brown hair was pulled back severely and worn in a tight bun on the nape of her neck, a few wispy tendrils escaping to curl over her temples.

"Is my brother around?" she inquired.

"He's gone out to the plantation this afternoon. There's some kind of problem he has to attend to. He didn't tell me any of the details. You used to live at the plantation, didn't you?"

She nodded. "I hated it."

"Roseclay is much nicer."

"I suppose."

"I really am glad to see you're feeling better, Meg. I looked forward to your return."

She seemed surprised. "You did?"

"I was hoping we could be friends. It gets rather lonely without anyone to talk to."

"I imagine it does."

Standing directly in a shaft of light, Meg looked like a twelve-year-old child with those thin cheeks and enormous eyes, but there was nothing childish in her manner. I sensed bitter disillusionment and mature depth that she kept carefully hidden.

"You married him for his money, didn't you?" she asked abruptly.

"Of course I did," I replied.

The answer seemed to please her. "It couldn't have been for love. My brother isn't a very lovable man. At least you're honest about it. I admire that."

She turned away and began to study the books again.

"Would you like to come out into the gardens with me?" I asked.

"I think not," she replied, pulling a book from the shelf.

"I really would like to be your friend, Meg."

The girl took another book, pulled down the volume beside it, and tucked all three under her arm. When she turned around to face me, her eyes were cool.

"I don't think Helmut would like that," she said.

"That—that's absurd."

"You think so? You don't know him very well. He doesn't want me to have friends. He doesn't want me to have a lover. He likes to keep me to himself."

"I know he thinks a great deal of you and is deeply concerned about your welfare, but—"

"I don't care to discuss it," she said tartly.

"Meg—"

"I'm sure you have very good intentions," she interrupted, "but you really know nothing about it. You married him for your own reasons, and he married you for his. Let me give you a word of advice—don't meddle, don't probe. Leave things alone."

"But—"

"I really must get back up to my room now. As you can see, I'm not a very friendly person. I'm sorry to disappoint you, but it's really much better this way."

She left the room abruptly, the books clutched under her arm. I was sure that beneath that thorny façade Meg was a deeply sensitive and responsive person, but she hadn't given an inch. If it wasn't personal dislike that had caused that rigid defensiveness, I wondered what it could be. Somehow I felt certain that the cause went much deeper, and I suspected that the thwarted romance with James Norman was somehow involved.

Helmut always insisted that we dress for dinner and dine in the formal dining room, even when there were just the two of us. He enjoyed sitting at the head of the little table like some all-powerful monarch, being waited on by silent, apprehensive slaves fearful of displeasing him. It gave him a chance to savor his power and position. He was already waiting in the parlor adjoining the dining room when I came down that night. That surprised me, for he usually didn't come down until the last moment.

"Good evening, Helmut," I said.

"Good evening, my dear. You're looking splendid."

"Thank you."

"New dress?"

"It arrived last week. You approve?"

"You look quite ravishing. Pity there isn't an attractive young man to appreciate it. We must give another party soon, invite a few single men. I imagine you'd enjoy that."

"I might," I replied.

Helmut smiled. He seemed very pleased with himself, I thought. His sarcasm was delivered in an almost playful manner. Blond hair sleekly brushed, cheeks ruddy, he looked like an evil courtier who anticipated practicing a subtle form of devilment. Helmut loved to bully people, but my refusing to be cowed always took the edge off his pleasure.

"Did you get your problem at the plantation solved?" I inquired.

"Thoroughly. I rather imagine they'll toe the line after today."

"What happened?"

"One of the niggers was getting a bit surly, encouraging the others to follow his example. I took care of the situation. Personally. I doubt if you'd care to hear the details."

"I don't imagine I would."

His eyes gleamed with amusement. "You know, I suspect you have a very tender heart beneath that cool façade. I suspect you're not nearly as hard and mercenary as you pretend to be."

I ignored his remarks, and Helmut merely curled his lips in a sarcastic smile. A few moments later Meg stepped into the room. She wore a loose-fitting dress of crushed brown velvet, and two spots of pink rouge glowed

497

on her cheeks, enhancing her pallor. She hadn't bothered with her hair. It was still worn in the tight bun,
those wispy tendrils still brushing her temples.

"Ah," Helmut said. "We're honored. The invalid has
decided to join the living at last."

So Meg was to be his victim, I thought. The girl stared
at him coldly, refusing to rise to the bait, yet I could sense
a nervous tension in the way one hand clutched her skirt,
wadding the velvet beneath her fingers. Helmut studied
her with his head tilted slightly to one side.

"We must do something about you," he remarked.
"You look like a scarecrow in that dress, and that paint
you've smeared on your cheeks hardly helps matters."

"I don't give a damn how I look, Helmut."

He arched his brows, pretending to be shocked. "My
little sister has grown up, it seems. She even uses curse
words."

"I know a few others, as well."

"I'm certain you do, but you won't be using them,
will you?"

Meg didn't reply. Her fingers clutched at the velvet,
and I felt she was trembling inside. Helmut strolled toward her like a sleek cat toying with a mouse. Meg looked
at him defiantly. He crooked his arm, indicating that she
should take it, and after the slightest hesitation she did,
bowing her head submissively. They led the way into the
dining room.

"It's nice having you with us," Helmut said after the
soup was served. "You're quite over your illness?"

"I came down, Helmut. Just as you ordered."

"I shouldn't think it would be necessary to give orders.
I should think you'd be eager to take part in things."

Meg kept her eyes lowered. Helmut sighed wearily.

"I rather imagine you were indulging yourself—staying
in your room like that."

"Think what you will," she replied.

"I hope you're through with such nonsense now. We
must get you some new clothes. Marietta should be help-

498

ful there. She was a seamstress, you know. Among other things."

"I'd love to help you get a new wardrobe, Meg," I said, ignoring his sarcasm.

"I've no interest in clothes," she said coldly.

"We can't have you looking like a starved scarecrow," her brother continued. "Granted you're no great beauty, but you can at least look presentable."

Meg lifted her eyes, meeting his gaze for the first time. "Presentable?" she said. "For whom?"

"Why, for society. There'll be parties. People will be coming to Roseclay, and you'll be visiting them."

"Will I?"

"But of course."

"You intend to launch me, it seems. Does that mean you intend selecting a husband for me?"

She seemed to be challenging him in some way, and Helmut wasn't at all pleased. He glared at her.

"After all," Meg continued, "*you* saw fit to marry. Under the circumstances, an unmarried sister should only be in the way. Particularly one so drab and unattractive."

"That'll be enough," he said harshly.

"Oh dear, have I said something wrong?"

"I'd advise you to be careful what you say."

Meg glanced at me, then looked back at Helmut. I had the feeling that they were discussing something else altogether. A disturbing undercurrent charged the air with tension. Helmut's eyes fairly blazed, and Meg finally lowered her own, looking meek again, all the fight gone out of her. A footman took away the soup bowl. Another brought in the second course. Helmut's eyes never once left his sister.

"I don't like your attitude," he said.

"I'm sorry, Helmut."

"I should think you'd show a little gratitude."

"I'm . . . very grateful."

Thoroughly chastened, now, she looked on the verge of tears. That bright candle of defiance had flickered out, leaving her frail and defenseless. Helmut smiled a private smile, pleased with himself, and I detested him for what he had done. There were several minutes of silence, and when he spoke again his coarse, guttural voice was tempered with genuine compassion.

"Finish your meat, Margaret. You need to build up your strength."

She nodded meekly, like a child.

"Perhaps you'll play for us after dinner," he said, still speaking in that curiously softened voice. "I bought the piano especially for you, knowing how you love music and how beautifully you play. It would give me great pleasure."

"Very well," she replied.

"Only if you want to, Meg. Only if it will give you pleasure, too."

"I'll play for you, Helmut. Just as I used to."

"Fine," he said.

His manner was amazingly gentle. The bully had vanished completely, and his blue eyes gleamed with an emotion that was unmistakably love. How complex it all was, I thought. Meg was very dear to him, the one person on earth he cared about, yet he treated her mercilessly, deliberately tormenting her. Why? Once again I had the feeling that James Norman was involved. Did the girl know he was back in Natchez? Did she love him still?

After the meal was finished, we went into the parlor, and Meg sat down at the piano with humble obedience. She stared at the keys for a moment, her shoulders hunched, and then she began to play a soft, sad melody. She did indeed play beautifully, coloring each note with subtlety. She poured out her soul in the music, I thought, as though she were expressing through music emotions too fragile and dear to risk exposing in any other way. Helmut sat with his chin propped on his fist, legs stretched out in front of him, gazing at his sister with hooded eyes. The brutish quality was still in evidence in the set of his jaw, in the curl of his lip, but his usual harshness was temporarily subdued.

500

Meg finished the piece and turned to look at him, her fingers resting on the keys. Helmut nodded, and she began to play again, this piece as lovely and melancholy as the last. It was hard to believe that the girl who was playing was the same person who had been so bitter and thorny in the library earlier. I wondered what she was thinking as she played. Was she lamenting her lost love? Was that why the music was suffused with such poignant sadness? The melody rippled and flowed, gradually slowing, eventually ceasing. Meg sat back, folding her hands in her lap, her head bowed. She gazed at the keys as though in a trance.

"That was lovely," Helmut remarked.

"I'm glad you're pleased," she said in a hollow voice.

"You know how to please me, Meg. You always have."

Meg stood up. She looked depleted. Her whole body seemed to droop, and her eyes were incredibly weary, deep shadows underlining them.

"I'll go to my room now," she said.

"You look worn out," her brother replied, getting to his feet. "I'd better accompany you. Wouldn't want you stumbling on the stairs. Here, take my arm."

"Good night, Marietta," Meg said softly.

"Good night."

She took her brother's arm, and they left the room. Meg moved slowly, as though she might indeed stumble were it not for his assistance. I heard their footsteps in the hall, heard Helmut speaking to her in a husky voice, although I couldn't make out the words. The candles flickered, filling the room with a hazy gold light that reflected in the polished surfaces of wood. I sat there for a long time, thinking about the strange, complex young woman who somehow brought Greek tragedy to mind.

Several days later, while taking a stroll in the garden, I found myself again pondering the mystery of Meg. It had been a long day, taxing as well. Meg and I had been planning her new wardrobe, and her resigned, apathetic

501

manner hadn't made it easy. No matter how I tried, I couldn't seem to reach her. She was quiet and polite and acquiescent, never unfriendly, never really responsive.

I would almost have preferred a return of the defensive, bitter creature who had been so cool toward me, but that Meg seemed to have vanished entirely. She dined with us every night, and she no longer remained in her room all day. Instead, she wandered about the house like a wraith in her loose, unattractive clothes, avoiding me whenever possible, taking an interest in nothing. An aura of sadness hung over her, but Helmut didn't seem to notice. He appeared to be quite satisfied with her "improvement" and treated her with gentle consideration, insisting only that she take care of herself and let me help her plan a wardrobe.

Helmut's manner toward me had changed, too. He had made very few denigating remarks, rarely took the trouble to be sarcastic. He could never be friendly, of course, but his subtle antagonism had been replaced by a welcome indifference. He spent most of his time planning the downfall of Robert Page, the planter who had refused to accept a loan for improvements, and I knew the man was about to lose his plantation. At dinner each night Helmut gave us an account of the steps he was taking, describing his progress with gleaming eyes, a smile on his lips.

He seemed to have temporarily abandoned another of his favorite sports. During the past five days those nocturnal visits to Natchez-under-the-hill had ceased entirely. I hadn't heard his carriage leaving Roseclay after midnight even once. This rather surprised me, for Helmut was an extremely sensual man with strong animal appetites, but I assumed he could go a few days without suffering unduly. So long as he didn't come into my bedroom, I was quite content to let him work out his own sexual arrangements. How fortunate he found me too "patrician" to suit him. It was one time when being undesirable to a man was a distinct advantage.

502

I tried not to think about bedrooms too often. I had no desire to take a lover, for without deep feeling it would have meant nothing. I had been fond of Jack Reed, had loved Derek to the point of desperation, had felt a great tenderness for Jeff. Each had been superbly satisfying. There were times when I remembered sturdy limbs and warm skin and plunging sensations, times when I longed to fill the emptiness inside, but I always managed to reject both memory and need. Of late, I had allowed myself to think of Derek now and then, and I found that most of the bitterness was gone. I knew that I loved him still, but that love was locked tightly away inside, and it would remain there. I refused to allow the pain to take hold. Even if the love remained, its fury was under rigid control. Thinking of Derek was a luxury I allowed myself only in small doses.

Twilight settled heavily over the gardens now, filling the air with a soft haze, as the last golden-orange banners faded against the horizon. Standing at the foot of the gardens, I looked back at the house where lights already burned in the windows. I paused near the gazebo, touching a shrub, smelling damp soil and leaf mold and the perfumes of roses. Leaves rustled quietly. As I stood there, I had the feeling that someone was watching me, but I knew it must be my imagination. I was quite alone in the gardens.

The sensation of being watched persisted, but I refused to let it disturb me. Perhaps one of the slaves was hiding in the woods directly behind the gardens, waiting for me to leave so that he could slip back to his quarters. I strolled toward the gazebo. I had left a book on the cushion yesterday morning, and I decided to retrieve it and take it back to the library. I had been reading a great deal lately, mostly novels, romantic in nature, all of them unsatisfying. The gazebo was filled with shadows and, as I stepped inside and moved across to fetch the book, I heard a floorboard creak behind me. Before I could cry out, an arm grabbed me around my waist and a hand clamped over my mouth.

I was terrified. I struggled furiously. My captor tightened his grip around my waist, pressed his hand more firmly over my mouth, drawing my head back against his shoulders. He was very strong, and I realized that struggle was futile. My heart pounded violently. When I tried to break free, he tilted my head back even more, causing the muscles in my neck to strain painfully.

"I'm not going to hurt you," he said urgently. "I just want to talk. Do you understand?"

Shaken and unnerved though I was, I recognized the voice. Some of the panic receded.

"Promise you won't scream?"

I just managed to nod. He hesitated a few seconds, uncertain whether or not to trust me, and then he cautiously released me. Heart still pounding, I turned. James Norman looked at me with an expression that was half threatening, half beseeching. It was several moments before I could speak, and even then my voice trembled.

"You—frightened me out of my wits!"

"I'm sorry for that."

"Do you often do things like this?"

"Only when I'm desperate," he replied.

"I ought to call my husband—"

"Please . . . That day on the river road, you were sympathetic. I felt it immediately. Your husband's conduct appalled you. Surprised you, too. I had the feeling you'd never seen him act that way."

"You didn't seem surprised."

"I knew what to expect," Norman told me.

"You've come about Meg, haven't you?"

He nodded, his handsome face grave, his dark-brown eyes glowing with determination. He must have come directly from the fields, boots and breeches dusty, shirt damp with sweat. I could feel his urgency.

"I've been coming every evening for the past two weeks, hoping I'd see her, hoping she'd come out for a walk in the gardens."

504

"That was extremely risky."

"To hell with the risk!"

"You must love her very much."

Norman ignored the remark. "I've hidden here in this gazebo for hours every night, waiting, hoping, but I've never had so much as a glimpse of her. I must see her, must talk to her."

He paused, consumed with emotion. He looked as if he wanted to strike out at something with his fist, but he also looked as if he wanted to cry. I was touched. Norman took a deep breath and continued.

"I want you to take a letter to her. I've been carrying it around with me. I figured if Meg didn't appear, you might. At last, you did."

"What makes you think I won't take the letter straight to my husband?"

"I know very little about you, Mrs. Schnieder, but I fancy myself a pretty good judge of character. You'll help me because you've listened to me this far. You'll do it for Meg's sake, won't you? She's very unhappy."

"If you haven't seen her, how could you possibly know that?"

"She's with her brother. She must be unhappy."

He said it as though that were a perfectly rational explanation, and I suspected it was. I looked toward the house. The sky was growing darker by the minute, the gardens rapidly filling with shadows. I would have to get back immediately if I was to have time to change for dinner.

"Give me your letter," I said quietly.

He pulled it out of his pocket and handed it to me.

"I know I can depend on you," he said.

"I don't know *how* you know, but you can. I'll see that she gets it. I must get back to the house now."

Norman seized my hands and squeezed them tightly. Then he left the gazebo and disappeared into the woods. As I hurried back to the house to change for dinner, I was filled with admiration for this handsome young man who loved so fiercely, and I was eager to give Meg his letter.

The meal seemed interminable. Helmut talked about the papers that had been delivered to Page that afternoon. As he told us that the man would have to pay off the loan in two weeks' time or else lose his plantation, he chuckled softly, eyes dark with amusement.

"I'd like to go over one or two more sketches with you tonight, Meg," I remarked casually as the three of us left the dining room.

"I'm very tired," she replied.

"I wish you'd just let me show them to you. I'd like very much to get them off to Lucile on tomorrow afternoon's boat."

"Go ahead," Helmut told her. "I need to go over some papers in my office, anyway, and the sooner you get some decent clothes, the better."

Meg followed me upstairs to my sitting room. Closing the door firmly behind us, I was both nervous and excited. It must have shown, for Meg gave me a puzzled look.

"Is something wrong?"

"I saw James Norman tonight, Meg."

The girl looked stunned. For a moment I thought she was actually going to faint. I took hold of her arms, guided her over to the sofa, and eased her down onto it. She looked up at me in disbelief, and then her eyes grew wide with fear.

"It—it's a trick. Helmut—"

"Helmut knows nothing about it."

"James . . . is in Natchez?"

"You didn't know? I thought—I assumed you'd exchanged letters while you were in school."

She shook her head. "Helmut made arrangements to have all my letters read by the head of the school. I never received any that weren't from him. I—I wanted to write to James, but I didn't know where—"

506

She cut herself short. Her hands were trembling. She clasped them together in her lap.

"It's been four years," she said, and her voice was barely a whisper. "He promised he would wait. He said nothing would ever change the way he felt . . . You saw him?"

"He was in the gazebo, hoping you'd come out for a stroll. He's been there every night for the past two weeks." I took the letter out and handed it to her. "He asked me to give you this."

Meg stared at the envelope for a long time, and I could tell that she was trying to control her emotions. The fear was gone now, and the shock finally passed. She managed to compose herself, and when she stood up, her expression was calm, yet there was a dreadful resignation in her eyes. She slipped the letter into the pocket of her skirt.

"He shouldn't have come," she said. She might have been speaking to herself. "It's hopeless. He knows that."

"Hopeless? But . . . he loves you, and you love him."

Meg looked at me as though she'd been unaware of my presence.

"You don't understand," she said.

"Meg—"

"Don't ask questions, Marietta. Please don't. I—I must get back to my room. I must think." She paused, and the fear flickered in her eyes again. "You—you won't tell Helmut about this?"

"Of course not."

She left then, and I had a very restless night, thinking about her curious reactions, wondering what they meant, wondering what the letter said. She was no longer sixteen years old. Helmut couldn't keep them apart now, not if she really wanted to marry Norman. Or could he? What was it I didn't understand? It was tantalizing, and I was consumed with curiosity.

Meg was cool and reserved the next day, refusing to

mention the letter, silently defying me to bring it up. She spent most of the day in the library, and at dinner that night she was decidedly nervous, merely picking at her food. Frowning, Helmut asked her if something was bothering her. She didn't reply, and immediately after dinner she went upstairs to her room. Helmut was displeased, and he looked at me as though I were responsible, all his old antagonism returning.

"What's going on?" he snapped.

"I wouldn't know."

"She's got something on her mind."

Refusing to spar with him, I went upstairs myself. I sat down to finish the book I had started the day before. It was almost one o'clock in the morning when I finally turned the last page, but I knew I wouldn't be able to get to sleep for some time yet. Since I hadn't undressed, I decided to go down to the library and select another book. Placing a candle in a polished copper holder, I lighted it and stepped into the dark hallway.

It took me fifteen minutes to select the right book. As I started back up the staircase, I thought I heard stealthy footsteps moving down the hall above. The candle flickered out, intensifying the darkness beyond. Reaching the top of the stairs. I paused and peered down the hall just to reassure myself. My heart seemed to stop beating. and I almost dropped the candlestick. Faint rays of moonlight seeped through the window at the end of the hall. I saw a man standing in the shadows.

I was paralyzed with fright. I tried to call out, but my throat was constricted and no sound would come. The man stood very still, a dark form barely visible. I realized that he was standing directly in front of the door to Meg's bedroom. As I watched, he opened the door and slipped quickly inside. Fear gave way to amazement. I found it hard to believe that either of them would take such a risk. She must have left the back door unlocked for him; he must have slipped into the house while I was in the library. I stood there for several minutes, overwhelmed by

508

the boldness of it all, and then I returned to my room, still a bit shaken. I would keep their secret, but God only knew what would happen if Helmut found out.

XXVII

The letter arrived the following afternoon. Soiled, crumpled, the ink faded, it had come all the way from Wales. I found it miraculous that it had reached me at all, addressed as it was simply to "Marietta Danver, Natchez." It had been written months before, and I wondered how many hands it had passed through before it had finally reached mine. The ship's captain who had brought it to New Orleans had entrusted it to another captain who was departing for Natchez, and he had given it to a man who, fortunately, remembered that Marietta Danver had become the wife of Helmut Schnieder.

I was greatly relieved that Helmut wasn't in when the man brought the battered, water-stained missive to Rose-clay. There would have been far too many questions. I took the letter into the small drawing room downstairs and, sitting down on the sofa, opened it with trembling fingers. Written in a bold but childish hand and full of dreadful errors in grammar and spelling, it was charged with vitality and aglow with Angie's personality.

The village, she informed me, was bleak, bleak, bleak, all brown and gray and black. Kyle's relatives were bleak, too, so grim and taciturn they looked as though they spent most of their time staring into open graves. Nevertheless, she was determined to cope, and she had absolutely transformed the dank, depressing cottage they had moved into. She had had the place completely whitewashed, had put up red curtains, hung polished copper pots over the fireplace. She had waxed the dingy hardwood floors until they gleamed like dark gold. She had become *quite* domestic and was even learning to cook.

Instead of going into competition with the owner of the solitary pub in the village, Kyle had simply bought him out, and Angie had been aghast when she saw the place. It was so dark you could grow mushrooms, and the smell was not to be believed. It had taken a solid month to clean it up, paint it, make it sparkle. They had enlarged the fireplace and put in new windows and a long brass rail for the bar. She had outraged Kyle's relatives by insisting on working the taps herself, had outraged them further by wearing her fancy dresses. *Someone* had to make the place lively, she insisted, for Kyle was still silent and stern and rarely cracked a smile.

Be that as it may, he was ever so generous, amazingly considerate and, she confessed, absolutely incredible in bed. Wales might be a desolate place filled with windswept moors and driving rain, but she had never even dreamed she could be so happy. She hoped that I would find such happiness myself, if I hadn't already. She asked about the shop, begged me to write and, in closing, said she thought I might like to see the clipping she was enclosing. She had come across it in a London newspaper.

I retrieved the envelope and shook it. The yellow clipping fluttered into my lap. It contained an account of the case that had taken London by storm, involving as it did greed, deception, adultery, and one of the most distinguished families of the aristocracy. I read the piece shaking with emotions I thought I had buried. Derek had finally won his case. He was declared his father's legitimate heir and legal owner of both title and estates that his uncle had appropriated. He was now Lord Derek Hawke, and Hawkehouse belonged to him, along with all the annual revenues.

I put both letter and clipping back into the envelope

and slipped the envelope into the pocket of my skirt. Surely he was happy now. He had his title, had the majestic old Elizabethan mansion and countless tenant farms. I had no doubt he would soon have a wife, as well. A cool, refined woman of impeccable background, she would be everything I wasn't. Angie's letter had been written months ago. Perhaps he had already married. Conflicting emotions began to well up inside me, and I was amazed to find my lashes damp with tears. I brushed them away. I wasn't going to think about it. *I wasn't.*

After I went up to my room and put the letter away in my desk, I began to look for Meg. I had to talk to someone. I had to *be* with someone. All those feelings that had been locked away for so long were trying to break free, and I knew that if I allowed them to do so, I would be utterly demolished. That hard shell I had built around myself was threatening to collapse. I had to fight the flood of memories swelling up, gathering force, ready to crash over me and sweep away my defenses. I would talk to Meg, no matter what her mood. I didn't trust myself to remain alone. We would discuss books, clothes, talk about anything . . . anything to take my mind off tousled dark hair, cool gray eyes, perfectly chiseled features. . . .

I knocked on the door of her bedroom. When there was no answer, I opened the door to find the room was empty. Perhaps she was down in the library. I checked, but she wasn't. The library was empty, too. I moved briskly through the house in search of her, but she was nowhere to be found. Hurrying outside, I decided to check the grounds and walked quickly down the path toward the gardens. I saw her then. She was coming back toward the house. As I called out to her, Meg stopped and seemed to pull back. Drawing nearer, I saw her white face, her tear-stained cheeks, saw her shoulders trembling.

All thought of my own problems quickly vanished, for Meg looked as though she was going to collapse at any moment. Reaching her at last, I took hold of her hand.

512

She didn't try to pull away. Her eyes were filled with terrible anguish.

"Meg, what's wrong?"

She didn't answer. She seemed not to have heard.

"Something's happened. You look deathly pale. You're trembling. What is it?"

She shook her head and made a feeble effort to free her hand.

"You must let me help you," I said.

"No one can help me." Her voice was a bare whisper.

"Come. We—we'll go back inside."

"Leave me alone. Please—please leave me alone."

"Meg—"

She looked up at me with those pain-filled violet-blue eyes, her cheeks stained with salty trails, the corners of her soft pink mouth quivering. I realized that she was in a state of shock, incapable of coherent speech, and I had to get her back to the house. As I led her up the pathway, she moved as one in a trance might move. Once inside, I took her into the small parlor and sat her down on the sofa.

Pouring a small glass of brandy, I forced her to take it. She gazed at it as though she had no idea what it might be.

"Drink it, Meg," I said.

She obeyed. I took the empty glass from her and set it down. She held her hands clasped in her lap, staring down at them as though they belonged to someone else. The windows behind the sofa were open. The long draperies stirred in the breeze.

"Do you feel better?" I asked.

"I suppose so," she said.

The anguish in her eyes had been replaced by a grim resignation that, in some ways, was even worse. She looked up at me, and I saw that she had summoned at least a surface calm. Her cheeks were still deathly pale, her hands still clasped tightly in her lap, but when she spoke, her voice had only the faintest tremor.

"He's leaving," she said. "We—we had an argument.

513

He said we must marry immediately. I told him it was impossible. He wanted to know why, and I couldn't explain."

"You're talking about James?"

"He was waiting in the woods behind the gazebo, just as he said he would in his letter. I didn't want to see him, but I knew I had to. I knew I had to send him away before—before something terrible happened."

"I—Meg, I don't quite understand."

"You brought the letter. He asked me to meet him. I did."

"But—"

"He said he would be waiting at two o'clock in the afternoon, said he would be there every day until—until I came. I didn't—I couldn't bring myself to meet him yesterday, but today—I knew I had to get it over with. I knew I had to send him away."

"You haven't seen him before?"

"This afternoon was the first time I've seen him in four years."

I suddenly felt very, very weak. A cold wave of horror washed over me, and I tried to tell myself it couldn't be. I must be mistaken. Stepping over to the table, I took glass and decanter and poured myself a brandy. My hands were trembling. Meg continued to talk, speaking calmly, but her voice seemed to come from a long way off.

"He was there in the woods, waiting just as he'd said he would be. He pulled me into his arms. 'At last,' he said, and I thought he was going to burst into tears of happiness. I did not let him kiss me. He loves me—still. After four years he loves me as much as ever, perhaps more. He said we must be married immediately, must elope at once, and—"

I drank the brandy. All the pieces fitted together now, and I realized what I should have guessed from the first. I knew why he had married me. Helmut didn't give a damn what people thought, but there were certain taboos even he didn't dare break publicly. I moved over to the window and peered out, clutching the drapery with my hand, staring at the sunshine-washed lawn. He needed a wife as . . . as a smokescreen. If he had a wife, if he flaunted her in public, no one would ever suspect . . . I let the drapery fall back in place and closed my eyes, trying to fight back the horror that seemed to shriek inside.

"James asked me if I loved him," Meg continued. "I lied. I said I didn't. I said it had—had just been a youthful infatuation. I told him he was a fool to think I would still—feel anything after four years. He looked as though I'd struck him. His face turned white. He seized my arms and said I had to be lying. I just stared at him coldly, hurting so terribly inside, knowing I mustn't let him—"

"You still love him?" I asked. My voice was flat.

"I love him with all my heart."

I moved over to the table to pour another glass of brandy, but after I had poured it, I set the glass down. It wouldn't help. I turned to look at Meg again. She seemed composed, yet fresh tears were streaming down her cheeks. She didn't seem to be aware of them.

"He said there was no reason for him to stay in Natchez. He said he couldn't live in the same town with me, knowing how I felt. He's going back to New Orleans. He—he said he was going to pack immediately and take the first boat in the morning. I told him that was best. I wished him well. I—I felt as though I was dying inside."

"You must go with him."

"I'd give anything in the world if that were possible."

"Why isn't it?"

"I can't discuss it," she whispered.

"I know, Meg."

She raised her eyes, and when she saw the expression on my face, she drew back against the cushions. Her cheeks turned even paler.

"Last night I went down to the library to fetch a book. When I started back upstairs, I thought I heard someone moving down the hall." My voice was as calm as if I were discussing the weather. "When I reached the top of the stairs, I saw a man slip into your bedroom. I just

515

assumed it was James. I assumed you'd left the door unlocked for him, that he had slipped upstairs while I was looking for a book."

"You know," she whispered.

"It was Helmut, wasn't it?"

Meg bit her lower lip. She nodded. The tears still streamed in tiny, sparkling rivlets.

"How long, Meg?"

She was silent for a moment, staring across the room at the gray marble fireplace without seeing it. She was seeing something else, a terrible scene that must have been burned into her memory. When she spoke, her voice trembled.

"Since . . . I was fourteen years old."

"You didn't—it wasn't of your own free will—"

"He took me by force the first time, and—and I never had the strength to resist him. I . . . I've wanted to kill myself ever since it—ever since it began, but I . . . I could never bring myself to do it."

"How could he? How *could* he?"

"He loves me," she said. "You must understand that. I'm the only person in the world he cares about. There were just the two of us, you see. My mother died when I was born, and then when I was eight, my father's estates were taken away from him. He had a heart attack and he died. Helmut and I had to leave Germany. My father had offended someone very important, a member of the Royal Family—it was over some political issue. I don't know all the details. Helmut was twenty-four. He had said some dangerous things and they were going to arrest him. They had seized the house and everything in it, but he managed to slip inside and steal all my mother's jewels. We fled. We managed to get out of the country. He sold the jewels in France. That was the beginning of his fortune."

She paused, her violet-blue eyes begging me to understand.

"He—he took such good care of me. He gave me everything. We came to America and he started buying

516

land and making deals and—and he said he was doing it all for me. My father had been a baron and we had lived in splendor. Helmut promised me we would live like that again, and—and he kept that promise. Everything he did, he did because he loves me, and the—the other—that's because he loves me, too. I never wanted it that way, but I . . . I've never had the strength to—" She cut herself short, forcing back a sob.

"I understand, Meg," I said quietly.

"I thought—I hoped—when I got his letter saying that he'd married, I hoped it would mean he would no longer—that that part of it was over. I was wrong. He married you because he didn't want people to suspect the truth."

She was silent for a moment, looking down at her hands. The tears were beginning to dry on her cheeks. When she continued, her voice was calmer, but she didn't raise her eyes.

"When I first returned, I tried to fight him. I kept my bedroom door locked. I told him—I told him there would be no more, and then—then he began to work on me. I had to give in. I had to let him or—or else kill myself. I wish I had. I wish I had killed myself a long time ago."

"You must go with James, Meg."

"I can't."

"There's nothing Helmut can do, particularly if you leave Natchez."

"I can't," she repeated.

"You love him. He loves you."

"I—I'm soiled. I could never marry him, not after what—"

"He need never know."

"He'd know I wasn't pure. He'd know that, the first time we—"

"Not necessarily. You could tell him there'd been a —some sort of accident. A riding accident, at school, in Germany. That would explain the lack of blood. As for the other, all it would take would be a bit of skillful acting."

"Helmut would never let me go."

"Helmut needn't know anything about it until you'd already gone. You must, Meg."

I tried to sound calm, firm. I was shaken to the core, but I knew I had to hold on, hold back the horror that threatened to render me helpless. I couldn't stay at Rose-clay any longer, not now, not after what I'd learned, but I would think of my own situation later on. First I must help this poor girl who had been driven to the brink of insanity. I could almost see the hope springing to life in her as she looked at me, her eyes filled with fear and indecision.

"You'd help me?"

I nodded, glancing at the clock. "It's just after three. Helmut won't be back until six at the earliest. I'll have one of the grooms saddle a horse for me. I'll ride out to Kirkwood's plantation and see James."

"He won't want me. Not after I told him to go."

"Don't be absurd!" I snapped. "I'll tell him to be waiting in the gazebo at one o'clock in the morning. He'll be there. You'll leave together tonight."

"If Helmut were to——"

"Don't think about Helmut!" My voice was sharp. "Think about James. Think about your love for him and his for you. You'll go away together. You'll be married."

"But James has no money. I haven't any, either. We—how will we live? How can we?"

"I'll take care of that."

Meg stood up, frail, nervous, the corners of her mouth quivering. She was badly frightened, but hope glowed in her eyes. She looked at me for a moment, and then, giving a little sob, rushed over to me, flinging herself into my arms. I held her tightly as the sobs racked her body. Feeling an overwhelming pity for this defenseless girl who had been so terribly victimized, I stroked her hair and tried to comfort her. When her sobs began to subside, I eased her away from me.

"You must be strong, Meg. You must be very strong."

"Helmut will expect me to come down for dinner. I

518

couldn't possibly face him. He—he'd know immediately. I wouldn't be able to hide—"

"You need never lay eyes on him again," I said firmly. Go to your room and pack a few things, and you can wait there until I come for you. I'll tell Helmut you've developed a headache and have gone to bed early. He may want to go to your room to check on you, but—somehow I'll prevent that. You must'nt worry. You must just do as I say."

Meg nodded, on the verge of tears again. So, I took her up to her room and deposited her there with instructions to pack. Ten minutes later I was riding down the river road on the sleek gray mare, my skirts bunched up about my knees, my hair flying behind me. Anyone seeing me would have been scandalized, but that couldn't possibly concern me at this point, and there had been no time to hitch up a buggy. I dug my knees into the mare's flanks, urging her on, racing beneath oak trees and past fields of cotton, past slopes covered with orange and yellow wildflowers. Dust swirled up behind me in thin tan clouds. The wind stung my face. The speed, the movement was a glorious release, an outlet for emotions I was determined to hold off as long as possible.

Kirkwood's plantation was large. The house, a ramshackle two-story white frame badly in need of paint, was surrounded by giant oaks. Chickens wandered about the front yard pecking at the grass. They squawked angrily and flapped their wings as I rode past the house toward the quarters in back. A plump black woman in faded blue dress and red bandana was hanging wash on lines strung out beyond the slave quarters. Dismounting, I tied the reins to a post and asked the woman where I might find James Norman. Totally unruffled to find herself confronted with a disheveled, wind-blown white woman asking for the young overseer, she took another piece of wet wash from the large brown basket, draped it over the line, and pointed to a small, unpainted frame building on the edge of the fields.

A shaggy rust-colored dog, asleep on the front porch,

519

stirred lethargically as I knocked on the door. Norman opened it almost at once. His face was white, his dark eyes ablaze with emotion. Scowling, he asked me what I could possibly want and looked as though he wanted to throttle me.

"I must talk to you," I said.

"The woman I love has just called me a fool for loving her! I've just given up my job. I'm leaving Natchez first thing in the morning. I've no time to chat, Mrs. Schnieder."

"May I come in?"

"Come ahead!" he thundered.

He led me inside and then, ignoring me, began pulling clothes out of a chest of drawers, carrying them over to a large, battered suitcase opened out on the bed. Shards of a broken blue pitcher glittered in a pool of water on the hardwood floor, wilting pulple flowers scattered about them. I had the feeling he had hurled the pitcher against the wall only moments before. Cramming the clothes into the suitcase, he glared at me, brows lowered, jaw thrust out.

"She's going with you," I said.

"What are you talking about?"

"Meg is going to New Orleans with you."

"She detests me! She told me I—"

"Will you be quiet and *listen* to me!"

James stared at me with his lips parted, his eyes full of confusion, and then those blazing fires of emotion died out abruptly. He looked worn and incredibly weary. Moving back over to the chest, he slowly pulled out a pile of shirts.

"She sent me away," he said. "She made it quite clear that she never wanted to see me again. I'm leaving. It's the only thing left for me to do. I can't remain in Natchez. Four years I've waited, and now—"

"She had her own reasons for sending you away. She—she was afraid of her brother and what he might do. But she realizes she can't live without you. She cried and cried, and then—then she begged me to help, begged me to come to see you."

"Why didn't she—"

I interrupted before he could finish his sentence. "Helmut told her that if she tried to see you he would do you bodily harm. That's why she lied to you this afternoon, why she sent you away. She was afraid for you. She thought she was—protecting you."

His eyes began to smoulder again. "I'm not afraid of him! He can't dictate—"

"Meg *is* afraid of him. That's the important thing. I made her see reason. I told her the two of you could elope, leave for New Orleans the first thing in the morning."

"We should be able to marry freely and openly. We should be able to live right here in Natchez so that I could keep my job and—"

I was exasperated and James, noticing my expression, cut himself short.

"What do you want me to do?" he asked.

"I want you to be waiting in the gazebo at one o'clock tonight. I'll bring Meg out to you. It—it must all be done in secrecy. Helmut mustn't know until you're already safely on the boat."

He nodded curtly, and I told him that I had to get back immediately. He stepped outside with me. The dog thumped its tail on the wooden boards of the porch. I paused on the step, turning to look at him with serious eyes.

"One more thing," I said. "You mustn't question her about anything. This has all been a great strain on her and —and she hasn't been well. You must concentrate on making her happy. Make her forget the past. Your future together is all that matters. Don't—don't ever mention her brother."

"I understand," he replied grimly.

He didn't, of course, but I was convinced he would heed my advice. I bade him goodbye and rode back to Roseclay. Leaving the horse in the stable, I walked wearily up to my room. I had Lelia prepare a bath for me, and I soaked in the hot, scented water for a long time, hoping

521

it would help me to relax. It didn't. I was tense and edgy as I arranged my hair, for I knew that the most difficult part was yet to come. I must be cool and calm at dinner. I mustn't let Helmut suspect anything.

I dressed with great care, selecting a deep yellow brocade embroidered all over with floral patterns in gold thread. It was an elaborate garment, meant for a far more splendid occasion, but I wanted to dazzle and distract him tonight, and the gown gave me confidence. It was almost eight when I moved down the staircase, still tense, praying I would be able to hide it.

Helmut was waiting in the parlor, in a bad mood already because Meg and I hadn't appeared earlier. I smiled, apologizing for my tardiness and explaining that I had had trouble with my hair. Helmut made a grimace, refusing to be mollified. I added casually that there would just be the two of us tonight as Meg had already gone to bed with a headache.

"She doesn't intend to join us?"

"I'm afraid she overtired herself," I replied. "We spent all afternoon working on a dress. She knows the Holburns have invited the three of us to dinner next Tuesday. But none of her new clothes will have arrived by then, so she asked me to help her re-do one of her gowns."

That seemed to please him. "She mentioned the Holburns?"

"She said that you had insisted she go with us and, since she must go, she wanted to look nice. 'I don't want Helmut to be ashamed of me' were the words she used, I believe. The dress is going to be rather nice. It's pale-blue silk, and we've taken it up and trimmed it with—"

"Spare me the details," he said, leading me into the dining room. "I'm glad to see she's taking an interest. I suppose a night of rest will be good for her."

"She's most anxious to finish the dress. We'll probably be through with it tomorrow."

Helmut was in a tolerant, almost genial, mood through-

522

out dinner, listening to my chatter with lordly condescension, eschewing his usual sarcasm. My nerves were ajangle, and I kept up the chatter, hoping he would take my nervousness for vivacity. I couldn't allow silence to fall, and when my supply of small talk began to run low, I plied him with questions about his various enterprises, subtly flattering his ego by pretending to be very impressed. He arched an eyebrow in amusement.

"If I didn't know better, my dear, I'd think you were trying to seduce me. You come down wearing an elaborate gown, smelling of perfume, radiant and smiling. You chatter most engagingly, and you look at me with eyes that are suddenly full of admiration."

"I was merely trying to be friendly."

Helmut curled his lip. "I suspect you're beginning to feel a bit deprived."

"Deprived?"

"You want a man, my dear. It's obvious. It's been quite a long time, hasn't it? We must do something about that."

"I—if you want to—"

He chuckled, delighted. "I'm flattered, Marietta. My cool, haughty wife has finally decided to warm to me. You want me to come to your bedroom? You want me to give you a good, rousing session in bed?"

I stared down at my plate, trying not to tremble.

"I'm afraid I must disappoint you, my dear," he continued. "I appreciate your efforts, but, as I've mentioned before, you fail to appeal to me in that particular way. We really must find you a lover soon, though. I wouldn't want you to suffer unduly."

I tried my best to look disappointed. Helmut was extremely pleased with himself, feeling he had just scored a small triumph. He was still in that expansive, self-congratulatory mood as we left the dining room, and I managed to look slightly dejected.

"What are you going to do this evening?" I asked.

"Since Meg is ill and you've expended all your charm, I imagine I'll do a bit of paperwork. Several accounts

523

need my attention. After I've gone over them, I'll probably go to bed rather early myself."

I hoped he wasn't planning to go to Meg's room. My remarks seemed to have convinced him that she genuinely needed her rest and wasn't faking illness as she had done earlier. I felt a wave of relief. There was just one more thing I needed to take care of. James and Meg would need money. I had little of my own, but I did have the diamond and emerald necklace and earrings Helmut had given to me. Although they were a "gift," he kept them locked away in his office safe, taking them out only on those occasions when he deemed it fitting for me to wear them. I had to get them, and I knew it would be quite impossible to break into the safe.

"I suppose I'll go through my wardrobe and pick out something to wear to the Holburns' next week," I said casually. "I had thought the blue velvet, but as Meg will be wearing blue—" I hesitated. "I suppose you'll want me to wear the necklace and earrings?"

"But of course. Mrs. Holburn will be dripping with jewels—all paste, no doubt."

"Then I'll need to have them tonight," I remarked. "I'll want to make sure they won't clash with what I select to wear. If you'll get them out of your safe, I'll return them in the morning."

He seemed to find this reasonable enough and, nodding, sauntered out of the room, returning a few minutes later with the long black leather case containing both necklace and earrings. I took the case, amazed that it had all been so easy.

"Be careful with them," he said. "They represent quite an investment, you know."

"I will be, Helmut."

"I've been very pleased with you of late," he remarked. "I've found our arrangement extremely satisfactory. If you continue to please me, I might decide to purchase another little trifle. Your lovely neck would look fetching draped with several strands of pearls, or perhaps a web of rubies. Your good behavior shall not go unrewarded."

"I'm glad you're pleased."

"I must get to work now. See you in the morning, Marietta."

When I finally got back to my bedroom I was exhausted, and my nerves seemed to shriek from the strain I'd been through. It was after nine. There was almost four hours to wait. I prowled around restlessly, unable to relax. I tried to read. I couldn't. I kept remembering Helmut's insane rage on that afternoon we had first encountered James, kept remembering the way he had seized the whip, wielding it with murder in his eyes. When he discovered that Meg was gone . . . I fought back the fear beginning to well up inside.

There was no reason to be afraid, I told myself. He wouldn't dare do physical harm to me. My knowledge was a powerful weapon. He wouldn't risk my using it against him. There were laws against incest and, if I told the authorities what had been going on at Roseclay, Helmut could be imprisoned. I held all the cards, and I would play them ruthlessly. I would demand that our marriage be annulled—that would be easy enough to arrange if the right palms were filled with gold—and I would demand a very large settlement. It wouldn't be pleasant, but he wouldn't dare refuse to meet my demands. I would leave Natchez a free woman, and I would never set eyes on him again.

First, though, I must get Meg safely away. I looked at the clock again. Only ten-thirty. Two and a half more hours. I opened the leather case and took out the necklace and earrings. Emeralds flashed with deep green fires. Diamonds shimmered with silver and gold lights, alive, lovely, each gem exquisitely set. With the money they would realize from the sale of these gems Meg and James could go anywhere they pleased, start anew, together. How fortunate she was to have someone who loved her so recklessly, so intensely. I put the gems back into the case, and a few minutes later I head Helmut come upstairs and go to his room.

As I waited, nerves on edge, the hands of the clock

seemed to creep. If I was tense and edgy, Meg must be doubly so, but at least she would soon be united with the man she loved. She had something to look forward to. I had nothing. Nothing. No, I wasn't going to start feeling sorry for myself. Not at this point. I had made this marriage with my eyes wide open. I had brought this all upon myself, deliberately. It was almost . . . almost as though I had wanted to punish myself for causing Jeff's death. I had thought I was marrying Helmut for his money, but perhaps there had been another reason, one I hadn't been consciously aware of at the time.

At twelve-thirty I blew out all the candles and opened the hall door. I stood there listening. Roseclay was silent. It had never seemed so cold and formidable. I hated this house. I had hated it all along, even though I hadn't admitted it. Roseclay had been built for an evil purpose, and for all its beauty the place seemed cursed. No one would ever be happy within these icy walls. I shivered, forcing myself to wait a few minutes longer, and then I started down the hall. My eyes had already grown accustomed to the darkness, but even so I could barely see two feet ahead of me. Only a few rays of moonlight spilled through the windows at the very end of the hall.

Nearing the door to Helmut's bedroom, I held my breath, moving past on tip toes. My yellow brocade skirt rustled crisply, and the sound seemed like great noise in the tense silence. Finally, reaching the door to Meg's room, I tapped lightly. She opened it immediately. There was enough moonlight to reveal her slender form and her pale face. I saw that she was carrying a small bag. Meg stepped into the hall and closed the door behind her. She was trembling.

"Is everything all right?" she whispered.

"Helmut's asleep. We have only to go downstairs and go outside. James will be waiting in the gazebo."

"I'm so frightened."

"There's nothing to be afraid of. Come."

I took her free hand, and we started toward the staircase. We had gone only a few yards when Meg stumbled, dropping her bag. It landed with a loud bang that reverberated in my ears like an explosion. She gasped. I tugged her hand, motioning her to be still. My heart was pounding now, and Meg was trembling more than ever. Both of us expected Helmut's door to be flung open and him to come charging into the hall, but he didn't. A minute passed. Another. I sighed with relief and, still holding her hand, reached down to pick up the bag.

"I'd better carry it," I whispered.

"I'm sorry. I'm just so—"

"Come on. Let's go downstairs."

We started down the stairs, descending into darkness, and it was only after we had gone halfway down that I realized I had forgotten the jewels. I stopped and let go of Meg's hand. She stiffened, terrified.

"What's wrong?"

"You'll have to wait here for me. I have to go back to my room. Here, take the bag. I'll only be gone a minute."

"Marietta—"

"Take the bag!" I hissed.

I left her standing there on the dark staircase and moved back up to the hall, cursing myself for my stupidity. It seemed to take me an eternity to get back to my room, and then I couldn't remember where I had left the leather case. I didn't dare light a candle. Groping around in the darkness, I almost sent a vase crashing to the floor. I caught it only as it began to topple off the table. That completely unnerved me, and I wanted to scream. I stood very still, forcing myself to be calm, and then I remembered placing the case on the table beside the large chair. I found it immediately and hurried back to join Meg on the staircase.

"Is that you?" she whispered.

"Of course it is. Come. We'd better hurry."

We moved on down the staircase and along the lower hall, reaching the back door a few moments later. What a relief it was to step outside into moonlight that streamed down in mellow rays. I pulled the door shut behind us and led Meg toward the gardens. The elm trees traced lacy black patterns over the silvered lawn. The carriage house and slave quarters were quiet. Both of us moved rapidly now, hurrying along the path with skirts flying.

Hearing our approach, James stepped out of the gazebo and stood sculptured in moonlight like some beautiful Greek statue incongruously dressed in modern attire. Meg gave a little cry and dropped the bag, flying toward him. James clasped her to him in a passionate embrace, covering her lips with his own. Meg wrapped her arms around his back, clinging to him with a desperate urgency. I picked up the bag and waited for that tumultuous kiss to end. When James finally drew back, Meg began to babble in a breathless voice, and he placed his hand gently over her mouth. Her tears glistened in the moonlight.

"Hush," he said tenderly. "There's no need to talk. There's no need to cry, either. I've purchased two passages on the boat leaving for New Orleans at six o'clock in the morning. I've got a buggy waiting for us on the road beyond the woods. Kirkwood loaned it to me."

He removed his fingers from over her mouth and brushed away her tears. Looking down at her, eyes aglow with love, he folded her against him once more.

"We'll be married as soon as we get to New Orleans. I'll find some kind of work. It—the going may be a bit rough at first, but we'll survive. I can't give you luxury, Meg, but I can give you such love, such love—"

Meg sobbed, resting her head on his shoulder, and James held her fast, stroking her hair. Both of them seemed to have forgotten my presence, but I didn't mind. Seeing them together like that was deeply moving, and it was painful as well, for their closeness, their joy made the emptiness inside me seem all the more difficult to endure. I had deliberately dismissed love from my life, and now I realized that life without that vibrant, exultant emotion was hardly worth living. I thought of Derek again, and the sense of loss was like a sharp stab in my heart.

"We'd better go now," James said quietly.

"Yes. I never want to see this place again."

"You'd better take your bag," I said.

"Marietta!" Meg exclaimed. "I'm so sorry. I forgot—"

"I understand, dear."

James took the bag. "I don't know how to thank you," he said.

"No thanks are necessary," I replied. "Just remember what I told you this afternoon."

He nodded curtly, and I handed the case to Meg.

"What's this?" she asked, bewildered.

"When you get to New Orleans, I want you to sell these. There's a man named Dawson. He's a crook, but he'll give you as much as anyone if you're firm and don't let him bully you."

"I don't understand." She paused, her eyes widening. "Marietta—surely not your diamond and emerald—"

"I want you and James to have them," I said firmly. "It's—it's the least I can do."

"But they're worth—"

"I don't intend to argue, Meg. Consider them a dowry. With what you'll get for them the two of you can go anywhere you like. James can open some kind of business. I'll feel so much better knowing you're provided for."

"Marietta—"

She flew into my arms, hugging me ecstatically. The moonlight was radiant, and I could see her face clearly. She was smiling, and her eyes were filled with happiness. For the first time I realized that Meg was a beautiful girl. Love had made her beautiful. With James at her side, she would be able to forget all that had gone before. I kissed her cheek, and she hugged me one more time.

"Goodbye, dear," I whispered.

"You—you'll be all right?"

"I'll be all right," I promised.

James took her hand, drawing her away, and the two of them moved toward the woods. At the very edge, just before they disappeared into the shadows, Meg turned to wave. I waved back, and then they were swallowed up in darkness. I turned and walked slowly back toward the house, exhausted now, so exhausted I could hardly move. Meg and her stalwart young lover were on their way to a happy ending, and I thought about another couple I had sent away under similar circumstances. Where were Cassie and Adam now? I felt certain they were happy, for they had each other.

And I had no one. I was quite good at helping others find happiness, it seemed, yet I had been a dismal failure at finding it for myself. I felt weak and defenseless, filled with a sadness that was almost unbearable. Moving through moonlight and shadow, passing the marble fountain with its jets of water dancing in the night, I wondered what I had done wrong. I had loved so fully, so fervently, and it had led only to grief. Once I was free of Helmut, I would try to build a new life . . . Once more I would try. That was all I could do.

I entered the house and moved slowly down the hall and up the stairs, passing through darkness without apprehension now. Meg was safe, and that was all that mattered. Reaching my room, I closed the door behind me and leaned against it for a moment. I was far too exhausted to undress just yet. Moving across the room, I sat down in the large chair. After I rested for a little while perhaps I would feel like preparing for bed. I was going to need all my strength in the morning when Helmut discovered that Meg was gone, but I wouldn't think about that now. I closed my eyes. I was tired, so very tired . . .

When I opened my eyes, the room was filled with dazzling sunlight. I sat up, startled, not knowing where I was for a moment, and then I realized that I must have fallen asleep almost as soon as I sat down last night. I stood up. My brocade gown was rumpled, my hair falling loose. I glanced at the clock. It was after nine. A sudden movement behind me made me turn.

The door was open. Helmut stood just inside the room, his face chalk white, his eyes ablaze.

"She's gone," he said.

"I—"

"Her bed hasn't been slept in."

He moved further into the room and closed the door. "Where is she?"

I didn't answer. He moved slowly toward me, exuding a controlled menace that was far more terrifying than explosive rage. I had never seen him so tight, so steely. Every muscle in his body was taut. I stepped back, knocking against the chair.

"Where is she?" he repeated.

"She's with James Norman."

"You helped her."

I nodded, trying to fight back the panic. He stopped a few feet away, breathing heavily now, his hands balled into tight fists. His eyes were flashing with blue fire. My heart began to beat rapidly.

"Helmut, she told me everything. Meg told me what you were doing to her. Yes, I helped her. I planned everything myself. I even gave her the jewels so she and James could sell them."

"You're going to pay for this," he said.

"I think not," I replied. My voice was steady now. "I think you're the one who's going to pay. There are laws against what you did, and all I need do is go to the authorities."

He lifted one brow. The rage still burned in his eyes, but there was a perverse amusement as well, and something I could only identify as anticipation.

"My dear Marietta, do you really think I'd give you the opportunity?"

"Keep away from me, Helmut."

He smiled, sensing my terror, thriving on it.

"What you did to that poor girl is—unspeakable." I said, my voice rising in fear." If I reported it you would be ruined, imprisoned. I—I want my freedom, Helmut. Our marriage must be annulled, and you will settle a sum of money on me—a very large sum. I'll leave Natchez—"

"So brave," he said. "So defiant. It's going to be a pleasure to crush you."

He swung his arm back, then brought it forward in one quick movement. I saw the tight fist coming toward my jaw, and then there was a crushing impact and an explosion of shattering pain. I fell, crashing to the floor. I went spinning through a void of black and bright orange fires, screaming silently as the pain burned through my whole body, and then, crumpled on the floor, I opened my eyes, unable to focus properly. I saw Helmut through a filmy blur, saw him looming there with fists at his side, saw those blazing, murderous blue eyes.

"You're going to pay for this," he repeated. "Yes, indeed. You're going to pay. Before I'm through with you, my dear, you're going to wish you'd never been born!"

XXVIII

I was dimly aware of the pain and, as I struggled up through layers of darkness, it grew worse. My jaw seemed to be on fire, and there was a terrible ache in my side where Helmut had kicked me. I moaned, and the darkness finally parted. Opening my eyes, I found myself on top of the bed, still wearing the yellow brocade gown. A lamp was burning. It was dark outside. Had one whole day already gone by?

I felt disembodied, groggy, and nothing seemed real but the pain. I remembered Helmut seizing my hair and pulling me to my feet, and then he had slapped my face repeatedly, his eyes gleaming with pleasure, a smile twisting on his lips. When he finally let go of me, I crumpled to the floor again, and he kicked me viciously. He must have carried me to the bed afterwards, for I couldn't possibly have made it on my own. What time was it? I tried to see the clock, but it was impossible to focus. I tried to sit up. That was impossible, too. I fell back against the pillows, and darkness claimed me once more.

"You must drink," she said nervously, holding the glass to my lips.

"No," I murmured. "No, don't—please—"

Lelia stood beside the bed, her eyes wide with terror. She seemed to materialize out of fog. I took the glass and drank thirstily, vaguely aware that the room was filled with sunlight, aware that the pain in my jaw was not nearly so bad now, the pain in my side almost gone. I was ravenously hungry.

"Can—can you sit up?" she asked.

I nodded, but it took great effort to raise myself. Every bone in my body felt bruised. Lelia helped me struggle into a sitting position, and I leaned back against the headboard as she placed the tray over my knees. She had brought a bowl of hot soup, slices of buttered bread, some cheese. My hands trembled as I ate, and I sank back into unconsciousness almost as soon as she took the tray away.

When I awoke it was to find the lamp burning once again, darkness pressing against the windows. I was hungry again, terribly hungry. I managed to get off the bed. My legs trembled as I moved across the room to the elegant blue and white screen. Behind it stood a table holding a ewer, a chamber pot, a basin of water. After I had performed my ablutions I was so weak I could hardly make it to the door leading into the hall. The door was locked. The door leading into the sitting room was locked, too.

I was a prisoner.

Waves of dizziness swept over me. My head seemed to spin. Afraid I was going to faint, I moved quickly back to the bed, collapsing immediately, trying not to panic. He was deranged. Right and wrong simply failed to exist for him. What a fool I had been to believe I could hold him off by threatening to go to the authorities. I should have fled with James and Meg. It was too late now. He was holding me prisoner, and I knew the worst was yet to come. He had some diabolical revenge in mind, or else he would have killed me already. I must escape, I thought. I must . . . And then the swirling black clouds enveloped me and I went spinning into oblivion.

A bird was warbling throatily, and I awoke with a start. It was daylight again. My head was clear. Although I still felt bruised and sore, most of the pain was gone. I realized that two days must have passed. Meg and James would be in New Orleans now, already married, beginning

534

their life together. I had saved Meg, and now I must save myself.

I got off the bed and moved behind the screen once more, and a few minutes later I sat down in front of the mirror. I wanted to hurl myself against the door and bang on it with my fists and scream. Instead, I began to brush my hair, slowly, forcing back the hysteria that could only make things worse.

There was a bruise on my jaw, but it had already begun to fade. Thank God he hadn't broken it. My side still ached, not painfully. The beating had been brutal, but he had restrained himself. He could have killed me, but he hadn't. He had something else in mind. I was sure of that. I finished brushing my hair, and then I made up my face, applying coral to my lips, soft-blue-gray shadow to my eyes, covering the bruise with powder. It was a foolish thing to do, but it helped.

I removed the brocade gown and hung it up in the wardrobe. I was still in my petticoat when a key turned in the lock and Helmut stepped into the room with a small tray.

"Good morning," he said. "I've brought you some coffee and a sweet roll."

"Thoughtful of you," I replied.

"Oh, I've no intentions of letting you starve, my dear."

"Where is Lelia?"

"Lelia has gone to the plantation, as have all the other servants except my coachman. I won't be needing any of them for a while, and I don't want them around."

"You don't want witnesses," I said.

He ignored my comment, setting the tray on the bedside table. "You look remarkably fit this morning. Feeling better?"

"You're not going to get away with this, Helmut."

"You mustn't let your imagination run away with you, my dear. Here I am, kind and attentive, inquiring about your health. I've even brought you your breakfast. What more could a wife ask?"

"What do you plan to do?"

He lifted a brow. "Do? I have a number of things in mind, but I haven't decided yet. I want to arrange something very special for you."

I took a dressing robe from the wardrobe and slipped it on, tying the sash securely at the waist. Helmut watched me with gleaming blue eyes, the corners of his mouth turned up. I forced myself to remain calm. I knew he wanted me to cringe and plead, and that was a satisfaction I had no intention of providing him.

"You must eat your breakfast," he said. "You need to build up your strength. I've a feeling you're going to need it."

"Do you plan to beat me again?"

"That was really rather thoughtless of me. I'm afraid I lost control. Oh, by the way, I brought you a news sheet that arrived yesterday from New Orleans. Rather uninteresting as a whole, but there was an advertisement I thought you might like to see."

"Oh?"

"A request for any information concerning Miss Marietta Danver, late of Rawlins Place. The man who placed it offered a substantial reward to anyone who could help him locate said Miss Danver."

I was startled, only half believing him.

"It seems you moved in very exalted circles at one time," he continued, watching me closely. "The man who placed the advertisement is apparently an English aristocrat. Lord something-or-other, he signed himself. Oh, yes, now I remember. Lord Derek Hawke."

I could feel the color leaving my face. My body seemed to go limp. I caught hold of the wardrobe.

"Someone you know?" Helmut inquired.

I didn't reply. I couldn't. Helmut shook his head in mock sadness.

"I'm afraid the chap is out of luck," he told me. "Even if by some wild chance he manages to track you down, it's highly unlikely you'll be around to greet him with open arms."

He smiled, blue eyes alight with pleasure, and then he

536

sauntered out of the room, locking the door behind him. I stepped over to the bedside table and picked up the news sheet he had left folded on the tray. I sat down on the bed, trembling inside, my hands shaking as I turned the pages searching for the advertisement. There it was, just as he had said. Derek was in New Orleans. He was looking for me. That could only mean . . . The paper rattled as I gripped it tightly. I put it down, awash with emotions I could no longer control. I cried.

I cried for a long time, giving in to all of the feelings that overwhelmed me—panic and fear, wild elation that Derek had come, crushing despair that he had come too late, remorse and recrimination that I had ever married Helmut in the first place. Finally, when all the tumult was spent, when the last tear had slipped down my cheek, I felt better. I was glad that I had broken down, for now that I had given some release to my emotions I could concentrate on escape. I took several deep breaths and looked around.

There was no way I could get out of the room. The windows were unlocked, but it was a sheer drop to the ground far below. In my weakened state, I would probably break my neck if I tried to tie bedsheets together and climb down. Both doors were securely locked, impossible to open. I could not overcome Helmut physically, but if I used my head, if I remained calm, I was bound to find an opportunity to escape. Above all, I must put on a bold front. I must not let Helmut suspect my fear.

The hands crept slowly around the clock and the hours passed. Roseclay was silent, and even though it was warm outside, the walls seemed to emanate an icy chill. Twelve o'clock, one, two, and he did not come with food, and I began to grow weak with hunger. I drank water from the pitcher behind the screen, thankful I hadn't used it all. Three o'clock, four, five. I paced the room, fearing that if I stretched out on the bed lethargy and despair would claim me. Shadows began to lengthen across the floor at six, and the sky was a darker blue, the sunlight paling.

At six-thirty he unlocked the door and came inside. His

537

cheeks were slightly flushed, and I could smell the liquor on his breath. He brought no tray.

"Hungry, my dear?"

I refused to reply. He smiled.

"I'd like to oblige, but the cook left, too, with Lelia and the rest. I'm afraid you'll have to do without for a while longer."

"I can manage."

"So very heroic," he remarked. "Still haughty and proud, full of disdain. We'll soon mend that. We're going to take a little trip together tonight, my dear."

"Indeed?"

He stepped over to the wardrobe and began to examine my dresses. He had left the bedroom door unlocked. I looked at it and then looked at his back, but Helmut turned around.

"I shouldn't, my dear. I'd have to come after you, and I'd catch you, and I would be very, very angry. You know what I'm like when I'm angry. I might really hurt you the next time."

"And you'd enjoy it immensely."

"Mustn't get too cheeky, my dear. I'm in a very mellow mood, but I wouldn't go too far if I were you." He turned back to the wardrobe, going through the dresses, discarding first one, then another. "Ah, yes, this should do nicely. Tonight shall be very special, and I want you to look your best."

He pulled the dress down and flung it onto the bed. "Tart yourself up a bit, my dear. Use some more of your paint. I'll be back in an hour or so. I trust you'll be ready."

"Where are we going?"

"That needn't concern you now," he replied.

He left the room again, turning the key loudly in the lock. I was upset and apprehensive, just as he had planned, but I was optimistic as well. Once I was out of this room and away from Roseclay there was bound to be some opportunity to escape. I refused to speculate about our destination. That could only make things worse. Ob-

538

viously we would be with other people or else he wouldn't want me to wear such an elaborate dress.

Lighting the lamps, I sat down at the dressing table again and arranged my hair, forcing myself to concentrate. I cleaned my face and applied powder and lip rouge sparingly, and when I had finished there was no sign of the tears I had shed, no sign of the bruise. My blue eyes were dark with emotion, but my hand was steady as I applied a touch of coral rouge to each cheekbone, rubbing it in until there was only a suggestion of natural color.

I removed the robe and crumpled petticoat I had been wearing all day and dressed slowly. Twenty minutes later I was ready. The dress Helmut had chosen was a brown-and-orange-striped taffeta. It was a bold garment, and I was pleased with the total effect. I might be trembling inside, but on the surface I looked composed and attractive. That helped considerably.

It had already begun to grow dark before Helmut returned. I could see that he had been drinking even more; his cheeks were ruddy, his hair damp with perspiration.

"Ready, my dear?" he inquired.

"Quite," I retorted.

"You look ravishing. I'm sure they'll appreciate it."

"They?"

"I've arranged a little surprise for you. Come, the carriage is waiting. Oh, by the way, I think I should warn you not to try anything. If you do, if you try to break away and run or do anything foolish like that, then I'd be forced to act accordingly. I've no desire to damage the goods, but I wouldn't hesitate."

"I believe you," I said coldly.

"Just thought I'd warn you, my dear."

He took my arm and led me out of the room and down the hall. He seemed charged with energy, and his eyes were alight with perverse anticipation. I tried to maintain the surface calm, but it was growing more and more difficult. His hand gripped my arm tightly as we went downstairs and outside. A closed carriage was waiting. The black coachman sat on his high perch in front; four horses stamped restlessly between the shafts. Helmut opened the door and thrust me roughly inside. He said something harsh to the coachman and then climbed in himself, pulling the door shut with a loud bang. He settled beside me, his arm around my shoulders, and a moment later we were off.

"I suppose you're curious," he remarked.

"A little."

"I couldn't quite decide what to do with you," he said, speaking in a casual, chatty voice. "I wanted to kill you, of course. I could have done it the other morning—what pleasure it would have been to take your throat between my hands and squeeze the life out of you—but that would have been too quick, too final. I want you to suffer, my dear. I want you to suffer for a long, long time."

He was insane. He was as deranged as those gibbering madmen they kept in cells deep in the bowels of Newgate, even if his madness took another form. I shuddered in spite of myself. His arm tightened around my shoulders, drawing me closer.

"You've been wanting a lover," he continued in that same chatty tone. "I've arranged for you to have one—to have several, in fact. Madame Rosè recently lost one of her girls. Seems one of the sailors was a bit rough. The poor thing died of her injuries. Rose has been begging me to get a replacement. She's wretchedly understaffed."

I felt I was listening to something in a nightmare. The clopping of horse hooves, the shaking of the carriage, the man beside me in the dark interior, his voice so smooth . . . None of it was real. I began to tremble, all my strength and resolution melting away. Helmut drew me even closer, turning his head so that his lips almost brushed my ear. He seemed to croon.

"I've arranged a room for you. You'll begin tonight. I've no doubt you'll take to it with relish. You'll work in the house for three or four days, and then I've arranged for you to take a little trip. There's a ship leaving for Rio de Janeiro—a fine city, became the capital of Brazil only

540

twelve years ago. I have property there, including a house even more understaffed than Rose's establishment—"

"I'm your wife," I whispered. "You—you can't—people will—"

"People will ask questions, yes. I shall inform them that you've taken a trip to England to visit your people. A little later I shall inform them that, alas, you've died of the fever. I shall be the disconsolate widower. I shall go around with a very long face. I've no doubt they'll feel a great deal of sympathy."

The horse hooves pounded. The carriage shook. The man beside me chuckled quietly to himself. I could tell that we were moving downhill now. I could smell the river. A few moments later, I began to hear loud music and raucous laughter. Through the window of the carriage I could see brightly lighted buildings, the verandahs filled with drunken men and brassy, vividly dressed women. Two men were fighting on the steps of one of the houses. A group of shrieking women cheered them on. Helmut gave my shoulder another squeeze.

The carriage stopped. Helmut opened the door and climbed out, reaching in to help me get out. I drew back, shaking my head. He clamped his fingers around my wrist in a brutal grip and jerked me forward. I stumbled out of the carriage. I fought then. I slammed my free hand against the side of his face. I kicked. He swung my arm out, gave it a vicious twist, and wrenched it up between my shoulder blades, slinging his other arm around my throat. People on the verandah applauded and shouted encouragement, and he jerked my arm up even higher, forcing me ahead of him up the steps and into the hall of the building.

An enormously fat woman in a green velvet dress rushed from one of the side rooms to meet us. Her hair was the color of brass. Her lips were a bright pink. She wore dangling jet earrings. Her small black eyes were wide with alarm.

"Christ, Helmut! You said you were bringin' a new girl. but you didn't tell me she was a bleedin'—"

"Shut up!" he thundered.

I tried to break free. He tightened his hold, his forearm crushing my throat. I gasped, fighting for air, and the woman in green velvet began to quiver like jelly from fright. Several women in peignoirs crowded into the doorway of the side parlor, arching their necks to see what was happening. I could feel the blood rushing to my head. I could feel my throat begin to collapse beneath that brutal pressure.

"You're chokin' her!" Rose shrieked.

"Is the room ready?" he barked.

Rose nodded, her jet earrings shaking, and then I closed my eyes and saw black and orange shadows on the backs of my lids. I was swimming in darkness, but the nightmare went on and on. I was half conscious of being carried, half heard the loud, excited voices and the sound of doors slamming. As darkness claimed me, I prayed that it was over. I prayed that I was dead.

He was talking to me. His voice was loud. I opened my eyes. I was in a small room done all in shades of red, lying on a large brass bed with a scarlet covering. A gilt mirror ran along the wall opposite. I could see my pale face, my disheveled hair, my crumpled gown. The bodice had slipped down until my breasts were almost exposed. I wasn't dead. It wasn't over. He was talking to me, clamly now, and I turned to see him standing by the door, his blue eyes gleaming.

"—in just a few minutes," he was saying. "I'll be sure he's a strong, husky fellow, one of these rough chaps who work on the docks, perhaps. He'll be delighted to discover such an attractive whore awaiting his pleasure. You can fight him if you wish, my dear. He'll probably like that, though he might be less than gentle. Enjoy yourself, whore. I shall. I'll probably come up and watch after a while."

"You're insane," I whispered hoarsely.

Helmut curled his lips in that familiar sardonic smile, and then he stepped out of the room and closed the door and locked it. My head seemed to spin, and black wings

542

flapped viciously, threatening to close over me. I sat up, rubbing my arm. The pain still shot through it, but I could tell it wasn't broken. Every muscle in my throat ached. But after a few minutes I was able to get off the bed and stumble over to the table beneath the mirror. I poured a glass of water and drank it, my hand trembling violently. I set the glass down and closed my eyes, holding onto the edge of the table for support.

Several minutes passed before I was able to control the panic, though I was still far from calm. I began to look for some kind of weapon. Stumbling footsteps came down the hall. I heard a gruff voice calling merrily to someone downstairs, and then a key was inserted in the lock and the doorknob began to turn. I seized the water pitcher and backed against the red wall, as far away from the door as it was possible to be. The door opened. The man stepped inside. He gave a raucous whoop of delight and slammed the door shut.

"Tonight's my lucky night!" he roared.

He lifted his index finger to his lips, motioning me to be silent; his blue eyes urged me to play along. I felt every bone in my body dissolve, and I began to slip down the wall as the black wings closed in. He caught me before I reached the floor. Wrapping his arms around me, he held me close, and I seemed to be spinning in darkness. I heard hoarse, tormented sobs and wondered who could be sobbing like that. He drew my head against his shoulder and stroked my hair, and eventually the dizziness subsided. I gave one last sob and raised my head to look into his eyes.

"Oh, God," I whispered. "Oh, dear God——"

"Hush now. It's all right. I'm here."

"I'm not dreaming. Tell me I'm not."

"You're not dreamin'," he said in that rough, amiable voice. "I saw 'im bring you in 'ere. I 'ad an idea what was goin' on. I 'urried inside an' Rose was sayin' she 'ad a new girl and it'd cost th' lucky fellow twenty bleedin' pounds——"

"Jack——"

"I didn't 'ave that much. One o' my mates was gettin' ready to come upstairs with Tessie. I made 'im loan me enough to make up th' twenty, told 'im I'd kick 'is bleedin' teeth in if 'e didn't 'and it over. Your 'usband came down then. I wanted to fly at 'is throat, but I figured it'd be smarter to get you outta 'ere before I kill 'im."

"It—it's like a nightmare—"

"It's over now—almost over. There's a back stairs. I'll sneak you down 'em and take you to my place."

"I've got to—I can't stay in Natchez. He—he was going to—"

"There's a boat leavin' first thing in th' mornin'. I'll take you to New Orleans myself. Don't you worry about anything. I'm gonna get you outta 'ere, an' then I'm comin' back to kill him."

"He's insane. He's—"

"Hush," he said. "Stop your tremblin'. Jack Reed is 'ere, and there's no man gonna lay a finger on you while I'm around. Pull yourself together now. Ya 'ear me?"

I nodded, and Jack held me until the trembling finally stopped. He let go of me than and stepped to the door. Opening it cautiously, he peered up and down the hall. He closed the door quickly. There were footsteps; a man muttered something unintelligible; a woman laughed boisterously. After a few moments passed, Jack opened the door again, again surveyed the hall, and then motioned for me to join him.

"We gotta be quick," he said, "an' we gotta be fast. No tellin' when one of them doors might open. Think you're up to it?"

I nodded. Jack took my hand and we hurried down the hall, down a dark, narrow flight of enclosed stairs. As he opened a heavy wooden door the fresh night air rushed in, sweeping away the dreadful fumes of alcohol and cheap perfume and sweat. Jack peered out, and when he was satisfied that the coast was clear he gave my hand a tug and we stepped outside. The music was still blaring. The shrill voices and laughter spilled out into the night, but here in the back there was very little light. All the houses were built only a few yards from the steep bluff that rose directly behind them, forming a natural alley-way which was littered with garbage.

We moved quickly past house after a house. A dog barked. Jack scooped up a rock and hurled it at the animal. We hurried on. I stumbled and almost fell. My heart was beating rapidly. I was still in a state of shock, and this seemed as unreal, as dream-like as that hideous red room and all that had gone before. Clearing the last house, we turned and moved toward the river, and then on toward the docks, leaving Natchez-under-the-hill behind us. I was panting now, almost out of breath, and Jack deemed it safe to slow down a bit. I could see the warehouses ahead in the moonlight, see the dark silhouettes of ships and a moving yellow light as someone walked along the docks with a lantern.

"We're almost there," Jack told me. "You all right?"

"I—I think so—"

"The docks'll be alive with activity in a little while. The last boat from New Orleans is due to arrive in less than an hour. That's the one we'll be takin' in th' mornin'."

We were moving past the warehouses when we heard the carriage rumbling down the road behind us. Jack let go of my hand. I whirled around, instinct telling me who it was. I don't know what had happened to the coachman, for Helmut was driving himself, his pale blond hair gleaming in the moonlight. I screamed. The horses seemed to be charging directly toward us, and then they reared, hooves waving in air. The carriage almost toppled over.

Helmut leaped off the driver's seat. A horrifying roar emerged from his throat, an inhuman bellow of rage. He propelled himself toward us, his face distorted in the moonlight, the face of a madman. Jack shoved me back against the warehouse wall, and then Helmut was upon him. They began a bizarre, murderous dance, locked together, staggering, reeling, finally crashing to the ground to become a tangle of thrashing limbs. The horses stamped and neighed in terror, and I could hear the terrible grunts and groans and the sound of flesh pounding flesh as the two men rolled out of a patch of moonlight and into the shadows.

I could barely see them. Two dark silhouettes grappled in the darkness. I was unable to tell which was which. One was shoved aside and the other reached down and picked up a piece of lumber that looked like a club and slammed it against his adversary's skull. There was a hideous crunching noise, and the piece of lumber snapped in two. The man who had been hit sank slowly to his knees and then fell face forward on the ground. The other stood there for a long time, breathing heavily, chest heaving, and at last he turned, stepping out into the moonlight.

Panting, unable to speak, he stared at me with crazed blue eyes, and I shook my head, sobbing with fear. He strove to control his breathing, his chest lifting and falling, his hands balled into tight fists, knuckles bruised. He finally managed to speak. His voice was a hoarse growl.

"I came to watch. The room was empty. One of the whores said she'd seen the two of you heading toward the back stairs in a hurry. She told me where the bastard lived—"

"You've killed him," I whispered.

"I certainly hope so. Now it's your turn—"

He moved slowly toward me. I cried out, and the next moment I flew into the darkness, running as I had never run before. I could hear his footsteps thundering behind me, closer and closer. Then he made a flying leap and both his arms encircled my waist. I pitched forward, crashing to the ground. Bright lights exploded inside my head like shattering stars as the breath was knocked out of me and I went careening into unconsciousness.

I awoke to find myself on the sofa in the parlor at Roseclay. The blazing candles hurt my eyes. I groaned and tried to sit up. Instead I sank into darkness again. When I finally fought back to consciousness, I felt the pain of bruised flesh and aching bone. Bright golden flames flickered as I lifted my lids, wondering why I wasn't dead and wishing desperately that I were. I struggled up into a sitting position, shoving my tangled hair away from my face. My gown was torn in several places and covered with dirt.

Helmut stood in front of the gray marble fireplace, drinking. He must have been drinking for a long time, for the bottle on the table beside the fireplace was almost empty, and he was weaving just a little as he stood. He had removed coat and waistcoat, and his shirt, moist with sweat, was beginning to pull out of the waistband of his dirt-streaked gray trousers. His right cheekbone was badly skinned. His eyes were glazed, and they were full of anguish.

Finishing one glass of whiskey he poured another, staggering slightly as he did so. He emptied the bottle and, scowling, hurled it angrily into the fireplace. The sharp, splintering explosion caused me to jump. He must have seen the movement out of the corner of his eye, for he turned and stared at me, but he didn't speak. He drank the whiskey, watching me all the while with lowered brows. I caught hold of the arm of the sofa and, using it for support, got to my feet, surprised to find that I could stand.

"So you brought me back to Roseclay."

"Couldn't risk you getting away again. Men would help you. Men like that one I knocked out." His voice was thick, his words slurred. "Couldn't risk that. Brought you back. I'm going to kill you.'

I stared at him with a level gaze, feeling oddly detatched. He tilted back the glass and downed the rest of the whiskey.

"She's gone," he said. "I did it all for her. She was everything. I loved her. I *loved* her! Meg's gone. You helped her. You helped rob me of the one thing in life that mattered. Nothing means anything now. This house was for her. Everything I did was for her. Meg, my Meg—"

For a moment I thought he was going to cry. He stared down at the carpet with anguished eyes that beheld only the beloved face, but when he lifted his head the anguish

547

had vanished. Replacing it was a look of hatred so venomous that it seemed to crackle like blue fire in his eyes.

"I'm going to kill you!"

I stood very still.

"Drink—first I want another drink. Then—then it's going to be such pleasure—"

He burst into laughter. It came rumbling up from his chest, and it was horrendous, inhuman. He shook with it, and I realized that the last vestiges of sanity were slipping away from him. The laughter died down to a barely audible chuckle, and Helmut lurched across to the liquor cabinet that stood in front of the windows. I turned to watch him jerk out a bottle and try to open it. He couldn't get it open. He hurled the bottle to the floor, and whiskey splattered all over the draperies hanging behind the cabinet. He pulled out another bottle and smashed the neck across the edge of the table. Even more whiskey splattered, covering the draperies with dark stains. He seized a glass and, weaving back and forth, splashed whiskey into it.

"Going to make you beg," he said. "Going to make you plead. Going to crush you—crush you—"

He cut himself short, smiling that perverse smile, and I saw the bulge beneath the cloth of his breeches. The candlelight flickered, flames leaping in bright golden patterns. I reached over to the heavy silver candelabra on the table beside the sofa. Hardly aware of what I was doing, I closed my hand around the base, lifted it, my arm aching terribly from the weight as I raised it over my head and hurled it at him. It crashed against the drape only inches from his head, shattering the window behind him. Helmut cried out, startled, and suddenly the drape was ablaze, a solid sheath of raging orange fire.

He leaped aside, dropping the glass of whiskey. A flaming shred fell to the floor, landing on the spilled whiskey, and then the carpet was ablaze as well, flames crackling, smoke swirling in thick black clouds. He moved back, his lips parted, and then he turned to look at me and his eyes began to gleam. He laughed again, nodding his head, his hands resting heavily on his thighs. The flames were spreading, devouring one of the chairs, snakes of orange fire slithering across the floor, moving up the back of the sofa.

"Perfect!" he cried. "Perfect!"

He lurched toward me. I backed away, but I stumbled against a table and lost my balance. Helmut's fingers closed over my wrist and he dragged me out of the blazing room. I tried to pull back, pull free, but he didn't even notice. He just kept walking, pulling me behind him. Though my heart was pounding in my ears I thought I heard someone pounding on the front door as well. I thought I heard a frantic voice calling my name, and I screamed as Helmut started up the stairs, his fingers like iron bands about my wrist.

I grabbed hold of the banister with my free hand. He gave a mighty jerk. As my hand was torn loose from the railing, I was slammed against the wall. He dragged me up the rest of the steps and down the hall to my rooms. Flinging open the bedroom door, he thrust me violently inside. I fell to my knees. I looked up to see him looming there in the doorway, the mad smile still on his lips, and then he slammed the door and locked it. Getting to my feet, I threw myself at the door and banged on it with my fists. I heard him roaring with laughter as he started back down the hall.

Minutes passed, and I was out of my mind with fear. I could smell the smoke now, could hear the flames crackling and feel the heat. Roseclay was blazing. The fire had spread over the ground floor, and in just a few minutes the flames would come searing up the stairs. I pounded on the door, unable to think coherently, filled with panic. As smoke began to curl under the bottom of the door, I backed away, tears spilling down my cheeks. It was all going to end. I would never see him again. He had come back for me, and I would never see him, never know if he . . .

"Marietta!" he shouted.

I was imagining it, of course. I had to be. I was hearing his voice because I so desperately wanted to hear it.

"Marietta! Where are you!"

"Derek!" I cried. "Derek!"

The key turned in the lock. The door burst open. He flew toward me, scooped me up into his arms and raced down the hall. This must all be a dream, I thought, yet I saw the staircase with blazing banister, saw the clouds of smoke, and heard his heart thumping in his chest as his arms tightened around me. He started down the stairs, keeping against the wall, away from the crackling flames. I was coughing, and he coughed as well. As he raced toward the open door the blazing wall began to lean toward us. Tilting, crumbling, it crashed down just as Derek stumbled out the door and onto the verandah.

He moved down the steps and across the lawn, carrying me away from the smoke and flames. In the distance I could see a carriage on the drive, two men standing beside it, one of them with a white bandage wrapped around his head. Derek moved on and finally sat me down under the trees on the slope beyond the front lawn. Flames leaped out of the windows of the distant mansion. The roof was blazing. A savage orange glow that seemed to scorch the sky illuminated the dark night. I turned to look at Derek, who knelt at my side.

"It's—really you. You came back."

"I came back," he said.

His arms folded around me, and I leaned against him, closing my eyes, resting my head against his shoulder. Roseclay was burning to the ground and Derek was holding me in his arms, and if this was all a dream, my last dream before death, then I was going to die content.

XXIX

The inn had changed very little in all these years. It was still comfortable, mellow, spotlessly clean. The jovial proprietor had died two years before, leaving the inn to his plump, ebullient daughter. Lizzie and her husband ran the place with friendly efficiency. During the past week she had been wonderful to me, looking after me as though I were a queen, filling the room with hand-cut flowers and merry gossip. She had given me two of her dresses and a cotton petticoat, and had even altered them for me. Lizzie fancied me a glamorous creature, and it delighted her to take care of me as I recovered from the 'tragedy' that had all Natchez abuzz.

The citizens of Natchez had no inkling of what had really taken place that night. They knew merely that Roseclay had burned to the ground, that Helmut had died in the fire, and that I had been rescued by one of his 'business associates' from New Orleans who, providentially, had arrived on the scene in time to save me. Derek took charge of everything. He sent for Meg and James Norman, and they arrived two days later. I was too ill to attend Helmut's funeral, but the next day I was well enough to sign over all Helmut's estate to my sister-in-law, keeping not a pound for myself. Both Meg and James were stunned and, at first, refused to accept, but I finally convinced them that it was something I needed to do.

Roseclay was no more, but the rest of Helmut's vast holdings now belonged to the Normans. James immediately marked 'Paid in Full' on all the notes Helmut had been holding against those planters who were so deeply in debt to him. He and Meg were already talking about building a new church, a school, a library. The city of Natchez was going to profit greatly from my husband's death.

The Normans came to see me every day. They were beautiful young people blissfully in love. If Meg felt grief over her brother's death, she didn't show it. She was radiant, her cheeks a vivid pink, her violet-blue eyes shining with happiness. Her husband couldn't keep his hands off her. All the time they were in the room he was either squeezing her hand or holding her by the waist or around her shoulders. Toward the end of each visit he was always eager to leave so that the two of them could be alone. Meg clearly found all this ardent attention sheer rapture. It was difficult to believe she had ever known anything but joy.

Jack Reed had come to see me too. Jack and Derek had pieced together the story of that terrible evening for me as they visited. James Norman had seen the advertisement that Derek placed in the New Orleans news sheet and had contacted Derek, telling him where I could be found. Derek had taken the next boat to Natchez. When he disembarked from the boat, a man, bleeding profusely and babbling incoherently, had bumped into him and then collasped on the dock. Derek was able to find the doctor that had been on the boat with him, and the two of them carried Jack back onto the boat and tended his wounds. When Jack's head finally began to clear and he was able to speak coherently, he begged Derek to take him to Roseclay. That, of course, astonished Derek, who was planning to come there to find me in any case. When Jack impressed upon Derek and the doctor the desperate situation that I was in, they found a carriage and raced to the mansion.

The house had already begun to burn when they arrived. Derek, who rushed into the mansion, encountered Helmut just after Helmut had locked me in my room. They fought, but Derek easily knocked down the drunken man. Derek had carried me from the burning mansion just in time, and no one was able to go back into the mansion to bring Helmut out. No one mourned his loss.

Jack's head was still bandaged, but his grin was as wide as ever. When I asked him about his injury he just laughed.

"Just got a little lump is all," he informed me. "It'd take more'n a block o' lumber to hurt *this* thick skull, I can tell ya flat. Take a piece 'o lead pipe at least. Only reason I ain't taken the bandage off yet is the girls think it makes me romantic-lookin'."

"I'll never be able to thank you for what you did, Jack."

He looked uncomfortable. "Wusn't nothin'. I recommend you forget the whole incident. I reckon you'll be leavin' Natchez soon as you get better. This English lord 'ere, 'e acted 'alf outta 'is mind when I told 'im you were in trouble, needed 'elp. I reckon you'll be leaving with 'im."

"I imagine so, Jack."

"I wish you 'appiness," he said.

"And I wish you the same."

That was yesterday. Today, I had finally received permission from the doctor to get out of bed. Though fully recovered from the shock, I was still a bit bruised. I was also rather weak, but I felt better after a long hot bath. It was late afternoon, and as I dressed, I couldn't help but feel a faint nervous apprehension. Tonight would be my first evening to go downstairs to dine. Derek was to fetch me in less than an hour. He had looked in on me each day and we had talked, but we hadn't really discussed the future. I tried not to worry, but I still found it difficult to believe he was actually here.

I was wearing the more attractive of the dresses Lizzie and I had altered to fit me. It was vivid yellow cotton and a far cry from the silks and velvets I had grown accustomed to, but it was quite fetching just the same. Skirt and petticoats rustled as I stepped over to the mirror to make a final inspection. Faint shadows still tinted my lids, and I looked a bit drawn, but the pallor was gone.

Lizzie tapped on the door and stepped in to see if I needed anything. When she saw me in front of the mirror, she sighed heavily and shook her head.

"That dress never looked like that on *me*," she complained. "It's not fair for anyone to look so ravishing, and you just out of the sick bed, too! Are you sure you feel like goin' down tonight?"

"I feel wonderful, Lizzie."

"I suspect that handsome Lord Hawke has a lot to do with it," she remarked. "I suppose you're eager to spend some real time with him—and who could blame you? Both the maids are all a-titter over him, and if it wasn't for my Johnny, I guess I'd be titterin' right along with 'em."

Lizzie was as plump as she had been four years ago, her blonde curls as bouncy. She was even wearing the same dangling jet earrings. The giggling, effusive girl was gone, however, and had been replaced, after three years of marriage, by a warm, matronly woman. Seating herself on the edge of the bed, Lizzie watched me dab cologne behind my ears.

"I remember you comin' here with that dashing Jeff Rawlins," she said. "What a card he was—so full of life. Then you came back to Natchez and married Helmut Schnieder, the richest man in the territory—can't say that I cared for him myself, but he was certainly intriguing. Now you have that gorgeous English lord dyin' to take you away with him. Some women have *all* the luck."

I smiled, and Lizzie sighed again.

"When I first saw you, I so longed to be an adventuress too, I thought it would be ever so grand and excitin', but I guess it wouldn't of suited me after all. I've just had one man, my Johnny, and he's more than enough to last me a lifetime. I guess I've been pretty lucky at that."

"Far more than you realize, Lizzie."

Lizzie stood up, brushing aside an errant blonde curl.

"I'd better get back to my work. I've reserved a table for you and his lordship that's as private as I could make it, but people're still goin' to be able to stare. They're goin' to expect you to be wearin' black and lookin' all teary-eyed and mournful, though I don't imagine you care a fig about that."

"Not a fig," I agreed.

Lizzie grinned, delighted with my wicked glamor. Then she bustled out of the room, her blue cotton skirts crackling. It was still half an hour before Derek was due to come take me down to the dining room. I was weary of my room and knew I'd never be able to sit still that long, so I decided to walk in the gardens for a while. As I moved down the hall and the back stairs, I remembered the last time I had come this way. I had been wearing a red dress, had been intent on running away from Jeff. I remembered it all vividly as I stepped out the back door and into the fading sunlight.

It seemed so long ago, yet in another respect, it seemed only yesterday. I remembered climbing down the cliff, fleeing through Natchez-under-the-Hill, encountering Helmut on the docks. I remembered Jeff's weary, amiable expression as he strolled toward us in his buckskins, and I felt a dreadful sadness. We had come into these gardens that night, and he had torn my Article of Indenture into tiny pieces, tossing them to the wind. They had fluttered like tiny white moths in the darkness. He had given me my freedom, and I had been unable to give him the love he so desperately wanted.

Pensive now, filled with sadness, I strolled past the neatly arranged beds of flowers, moving toward the edge of the cliff. The sky was pale and stained with yellow on the horizon as the sun began its gradual descent. Below the river was a deep blue, spangled with shimmering silver reflections, and on the opposite shore the trees cast long black shadows. I remembered the way Jeff had wrapped his arms around me as we stood here together. Dear Jeff. How I wished I could have changed the course of events that followed.

As I stood there near the edge, the gardens behind me, the wind lifted my skirts and set the yellow ruffles aflutter. Strands of hair blew across my cheek. Brushing them aside, I thought about what Lizzie had said only a few minutes ago. She was indeed lucky. She saw me as a glamorous creature whose life had been filled with tempestuous excitement and romance, an exotic adventuress who lived life to the brim. She envied me, and she would find it hard to believe that I actually envied the happiness she had found so easily, and so early. True happiness was within reach for me at last, but it had come at such a cost, after so much grief.

I heard his footsteps on the path, but didn't turn. I knew instinctively that it was Derek.

"I saw you from my window," he said. "I was not sure you should be out here. The doctor said you needed a long rest, and it's only been a week. I don't want you to tire yourself—"

"I'm fine, Derek."

"I've been very worried about you."

"Have you?"

"Worried sick," he admitted. "That's why I've stayed away as much as possible, seeing you for just a short time each day. I didn't want to tire you. There are so many things we have to talk about, and I wanted to be sure you'd recovered completely."

I turned to face him. In his perfectly tailored black trousers and frock coat, his white satin waistcoat patterned with maroon silk flowers, and neckcloth of matching maroon silk, he looked very much the English aristocrat. Lean, handsome, stern, yet somehow a softer, more loving Derek than I had known before.

"You seem sad," he said.

"I was thinking about the past."

"You must think about the future now," he said.

"What kind of future is it going to be, Derek?"

"A splendid one. For both of us."

His voice was low, his gray eyes solemn.

"I love you, Marietta. I love you with all my heart and

soul. I always did, even from the first. It took me a long time to realize it, and still I fought it. Even after I returned to England and won my case to obtain my inheritance, I felt little triumph. Without you it meant nothing. I came back for you because I had to. Life without you is life without meaning."

"I never thought I'd hear you say that."

"I never thought I'd say it. I mean every word."

"Derek—"

He pulled me into his arms then and kissed me for a long time, conveying with that kiss an urgent passion that was incredibly tender as well. When he raised his head I saw the love glowing in eyes that would never again be cool or remote. I turned to face the river, and he wrapped his arms around me, drawing me back against him. I felt his strength, his warmth, and the joy that welled up inside me was so elating that I felt I might die of it. Derek leaned his head down and brushed his lips against my cheek.

"I'll never let you go," he murmured. "The past is over, Marietta. The future is ours—together."

"Together," I whispered.

"From this moment on," he said.

And so the future began.

BESTSELLERS FROM WARNER BOOKS

THE OFFICERS' WIVES
by Thomas Fleming   (A90-920, $3.95)
This is a book you will never forget. It is about the U.S. Army, the huge unwieldy organism on which much of the nation's survival depends. It is about Americans trying to live personal lives, to cling to touchstones of faith and hope in the grip of the blind, blunderous history of the last 25 years. It is about marriage, the illusions and hopes that people bring to it, the struggle to maintain and renew commitment.

(R90-920, $3.95

(A96-924, $3.75

BELLEFLEUR
by Joyce Carol Oates   (A96-924, $3.75)
A swirl of fantasy, history, family feuds, love affairs and dreams, this is the saga of the Bellefleurs who live like feudal barons in a mythical place that might perhaps be the Adirondacks. A strange curse, it is said, hovers over the family, causing magical and horrible events to occur. Past and present appear to live side-by-side, as the fantastic reality of the Bellefleurs unfolds.

F90-034, 3.50

RICH DREAMS
by Ben and Norma Barzman   (F90-034, $3.50)
He's the world's sex novel king with a personal life to match. He's rolling in royalties, champagne and mistresses. He's a Bel Air baron—the Boston slum kid who hustled his way through Hollywood orgies, poured out a bestseller at age 23, and operates with mob connections.